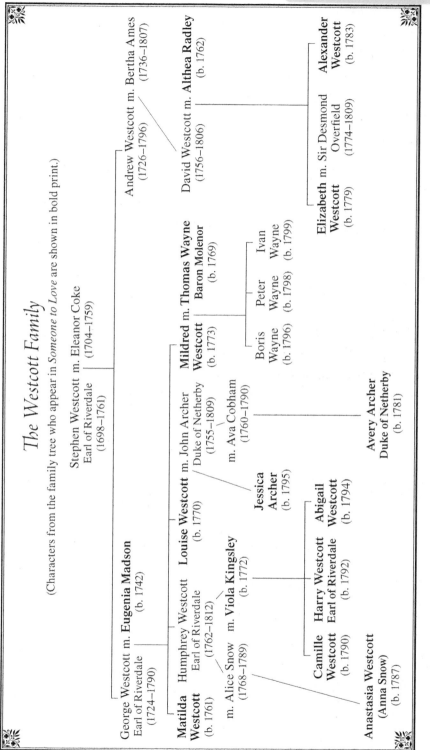

The Westcott Family

(Characters from the family tree who appear in *Someone to Love* are shown in bold print.)

Stephen Westcott m. Eleanor Coke
Earl of Riverdale
(1698–1761)
(1704–1759)

Andrew Westcott m. Bertha Ames
(1726–1796)
(1736–1807)

David Westcott m. Althea Radley
(1756–1806)
(b. 1762)

Elizabeth m. Sir Desmond   Alexander
Westcott   Overfield   Westcott
(b. 1779)   (1774–1809)   (b. 1783)

George Westcott m. Eugenia Madson
Earl of Riverdale
(1724–1790)
(b. 1742)

Matilda   Humphrey Westcott   Louise Westcott m. John Archer
Westcott   Earl of Riverdale   (b. 1770)   Duke of Netherby
(b. 1761)   (1762–1812)   (1755–1809)

m. Ava Cobham
(1760–1790)

Mildred m. Thomas Wayne
Westcott   Baron Molenor
(b. 1773)   (b. 1769)

Boris   Peter   Ivan
Wayne   Wayne   Wayne
(b. 1796)   (b. 1798)   (b. 1799)

Jessica
Archer
(b. 1795)

Avery Archer
Duke of Netherby
(b. 1781)

m. Alice Snow   m. Viola Kingsley
(1768–1789)   (b. 1772)

Abigail
Westcott
(b. 1794)

Camille   Harry Westcott
Westcott   Earl of Riverdale
(b. 1790)   (b. 1792)

Anastasia Westcott
(Anna Snow)
(b. 1787)

Someone to Love

Mary Balogh

W F HOWES LTD

This large print edition published in 2018 by
W F Howes Ltd
Unit 5, St George's House, Rearsby Business Park,
Gaddesby Lane, Rearsby, Leicester LE7 4YH

1 3 5 7 9 10 8 6 4 2

First published in the United Kingdom in 2016
by Piatkus

A CIP catalogue record for this book is available
from the British Library

ISBN 978 1 52884 314 0

Typeset by Palimpsest Book Production Limited,
Falkirk, Stirlingshire

Printed and bound by
T J International in the UK

CHAPTER 1

Despite the fact that the late Earl of Riverdale had died without having made a will, Josiah Brumford, his solicitor, had found enough business to discuss with his son and successor to be granted a face-to-face meeting at Westcott House, the earl's London residence on South Audley Street. Having arrived promptly and bowed his way through effusive and obsequious greetings, Brumford proceeded to find a great deal of nothing in particular to impart at tedious length and with pompous verbosity.

Which would have been all very well, Avery Archer, Duke of Netherby, thought a trifle peevishly as he stood before the library window and took snuff in an effort to ward off the urge to yawn, if he had not been compelled to be here too to endure the tedium. If Harry had only been a year older – he had turned twenty just before his father's death – then Avery need not be here at all and Brumford could prose on forever and a day as far as he was concerned. By some bizarre and thoroughly irritating twist of fate, however, His Grace had found himself

1

joint guardian of the new earl with the countess, the boy's mother.

It was all remarkably ridiculous in light of Avery's notoriety for indolence and the studied avoidance of anything that might be dubbed work or the performance of duty. He had a secretary and numerous other servants to deal with all the tedious business of life for him. And there was also the fact that he was a mere eleven years older than his ward. When one heard the word *guardian*, one conjured a mental image of a gravely dignified graybeard. However, it seemed he had inherited the guardianship to which his father had apparently agreed – in writing – at some time in the dim distant past when the late Riverdale had mistakenly thought himself to be at death's door. By the time he did die a few weeks ago, the old Duke of Netherby had been sleeping peacefully in his own grave for more than two years and was thus unable to be guardian to anyone. Avery might, he supposed, have repudiated the obligation since he was not the Netherby mentioned in that letter of agreement, which had never been made into a legal document anyway. He had not done so, however. He did not dislike Harry, and really it had seemed like too much bother to take a stand and refuse such a slight and temporary inconvenience.

It felt more than slight at the moment. Had he known Brumford was such a crashing bore, he might have made the effort.

'There really was no need for Father to make a will,' Harry was saying in the sort of rallying tone one used when repeating oneself in order to wrap up a lengthy discussion that had been moving in unending circles. 'I have no brothers. My father trusted that I would provide handsomely for my mother and sisters according to his known wishes, and of course I will not fail that trust. I will certainly see to it too that most of the servants and retainers on all my properties are kept on and that those who leave my employ for whatever reason – Father's valet, for example – are properly compensated. And you may rest assured that my mother and Netherby will see that I do not stray from these obligations before I arrive at my majority.'

He was standing by the fireplace beside his mother's chair, in a relaxed posture, one shoulder propped against the mantel, his arms crossed over his chest, one booted foot on the hearth. He was a tall lad and a bit gangly, though a few more years would take care of that deficiency. He was fair-haired and blue-eyed with a good-humored countenance that very young ladies no doubt found impossibly handsome. He was also almost indecently rich. He was amiable and charming and had been running wild during the past several months, first while his father was too ill to take much notice and again during the couple of weeks since the funeral. He had probably never lacked for friends, but now they abounded and would have filled a sizable city, perhaps even a small county, to overflowing. Though perhaps *friends* was too kind a word to use for most of them. *Sycophants* and *hangers-on* would be better.

Avery had not tried intervening, and he doubted he would. The boy seemed of sound enough character and would doubtless settle to a bland and blameless adulthood if left to his own devices. And if in the meanwhile he sowed a wide swath of wild oats and squandered a small fortune, well, there were probably oats to spare in the world and there would still be a vast fortune remaining for the bland adulthood. It would take just too much effort to intervene, anyway, and the Duke of Netherby rarely made the effort to do what was inessential or what was not conducive to his personal comfort.

'I do not doubt it for a moment, my lord.' Brumford bowed from his chair in a manner that suggested he might at last be conceding that everything he had come to say had been said and perhaps it was time to take his leave. 'I trust Brumford, Brumford & Sons may continue to represent your interests as we did your dear departed father's and his father's before him. I trust His Grace and Her Ladyship will so advise you.'

Avery wondered idly what the other Brumford was like and just how many young Brumfords were included in the '& Sons.' The mind boggled.

Harry pushed himself away from the mantel,

looking hopeful. 'I see no reason why I would not,' he said. 'But I will not keep you any longer. You are a very busy man, I daresay.'

'I will, however, beg for a few minutes more of your time, Mr Brumford,' the countess said unexpectedly. 'But it is a matter that does not concern you, Harry. You may go and join your sisters in the drawing room. They will be eager to hear details of this meeting. Perhaps you would be good enough to remain, Avery.'

Harry directed a quick grin Avery's way, and His Grace, opening his snuffbox again before changing his mind and snapping it shut, almost wished that he too were being sent off to report to the countess's two daughters. He must be very bored indeed. Lady Camille Westcott, age twenty-two, was the managing sort, a forthright female who did not suffer fools gladly, though she was handsome enough, it was true. Lady Abigail, at eighteen, was a sweet, smiling, pretty young thing who might or might not possess a personality. To do her justice, Avery had not spent enough time in her company to find out. She was his half sister's favorite cousin and dearest friend in the world, however – her words – and he occasionally heard them talking and giggling together behind closed doors that he was very careful never to open.

Harry, all eager to be gone, bowed to his mother, nodded politely to Brumford, came very close to winking at Avery, and made his escape from the library. Lucky devil. Avery strolled closer to the fireplace, where the countess and Brumford were still seated. What the deuce could be important enough that she had voluntarily prolonged this excruciatingly dreary meeting?

'And how may I be of service to you, my lady?' the solicitor asked.

The countess, Avery noticed, was sitting very upright, her spine arched slightly inward. Were ladies taught to sit that way, as though the backs of chairs had been created merely to be decorative? She was, he estimated, about forty years old. She was also quite perfectly beautiful in a mature, dignified sort of way. She surely could not have been happy with Riverdale – who could? – yet to Avery's knowledge she had never indulged herself with lovers. She was tall, shapely, and blond with no sign yet, as far as he could see, of any gray hairs. She was also one of those rare women who looked striking rather than dowdy in deep mourning.

'There is a girl,' she said, 'or, rather, a woman. In Bath, I believe. My late husband's . . . daughter.'

Avery guessed she had been about to say *bastard*, but had changed her mind for the sake of gentility. He raised both his eyebrows and his quizzing glass.

Brumford for once had been silenced.

'She was at an orphanage there,' the countess continued. 'I do not know where she is now. She is hardly still there since she must be in her middle twenties. But Riverdale supported her from a very young age and continued to do so until his death.

We never discussed the matter. It is altogether probable he did not know I was aware of her existence. I do not know any details, nor have I ever wanted to. I still do not. I assume it was not through you that the support payments were made?'

Brumford's already florid complexion took on a distinctly purplish hue. 'It was not, my lady,' he assured her. 'But might I suggest that since this . . . person is now an adult, you—'

'No,' she said, cutting him off. 'I am not in need of any suggestion. I have no wish whatsoever to know anything about this woman, even her name. I certainly have no wish for my son to know of her. However, it seems only just that if she has been supported all her life by her . . . father, she be informed of his death if that has not already happened, and be compensated with a final settlement. A handsome one, Mr Brumford. It would need to be made perfectly clear to her at the same time that there is to be no more – ever, under any circumstances. May I leave the matter in your hands?'

'My lady.' Brumford seemed almost to be squirming in his chair. He licked his lips and darted a glance at Avery, of whom – if His Grace was reading him correctly – he stood in considerable awe.

Avery raised his glass all the way to his eye. 'Well?' he said. '*May* her ladyship leave the matter in your hands, Brumford? Are you or the other

Brumford or one of the sons willing and able to hunt down the bastard daughter, name unknown, of the late earl in order to make her the happiest of orphans by settling a modest fortune upon her?'

'Your Grace.' Brumford's chest puffed out. 'My lady. It will be a difficult task, but not an insurmountable one, especially for the skilled investigators whose services we engage in the interests of our most valued clients. If the . . . person indeed grew up in Bath, we will identify her. If she is still there, we will find her. If she is no longer there—'

'I believe,' Avery said, sounding pained, 'her ladyship and I get your meaning. You will report to me when the woman has been found. Is that agreeable to you, Aunt?'

The Countess of Riverdale was not, strictly speaking, his aunt. His stepmother, the duchess, was the late Earl of Riverdale's sister, and thus the countess and all the others were his honorary relatives.

'That will be satisfactory,' she said. 'Thank you, Avery. When you report to His Grace that you have found her, Mr Brumford, he will discuss with you what sum is to be settled upon her and what legal papers she will need to sign to confirm that she is no longer a dependent of my late husband's estate.'

'That will be all,' Avery said as the solicitor drew breath to deliver himself of some doubtless unnecessary and unwanted monologue. 'The butler will see you out.'

He took snuff and made a mental note that the blend needed to be one half-note less floral in order to be perfect.

'That was remarkably generous of you,' he said when he was alone with the countess.

'Not really, Avery,' she said, getting to her feet. 'I am being generous, if you will, with Harry's money. But he will neither know of the matter nor miss the sum. And taking action now will ensure that he never discover the existence of his father's by-blow. It will ensure that Camille and Abigail not discover it either. I care not the snap of my fingers for the woman in Bath. I *do* care for my children. Will you stay for luncheon?'

'I will not impose upon you,' he said with a sigh. 'I have . . . things to attend to. I am quite sure I must have. Everyone has things to do, or so everyone is in the habit of claiming.'

The corners of her mouth lifted slightly. 'I really do not blame you, Avery, for being eager to escape,' she said. 'The man is a mighty bore, is he not? But his request for this meeting saved me from summoning him and you on this other matter. You are released. You may run off and busy yourself with . . . things.'

He possessed himself of her hand – white, long-fingered, perfectly manicured – and bowed gracefully over it as he raised it to his lips.

'You may safely leave the matter in my hands,'

he said – or in the hands of his secretary, anyway.

'Thank you,' she said. 'But you will inform me when it is accomplished?'

'I will,' he promised before sauntering from the room and taking his hat and cane from the butler's hands.

The revelation that the countess had a conscience had surprised him. How many ladies in similar circumstances would voluntarily seek out their husbands' bastards in order to shower riches upon them, even if they did convince themselves that they did so in the interests of their own, very legitimate children?

Anna Snow had been brought to the orphanage in Bath when she was not quite four years old. She had no real memory of her life before that beyond a few brief and disjointed flashes – of someone always coughing, for example, or of a lych-gate that was dark and a bit frightening inside whenever she was called upon to pass through it alone, and of kneeling on a window ledge and looking down upon a graveyard, and of crying inconsolably inside a carriage while someone with a gruff, impatient voice told her to hush and behave like a big girl.

She had been at the orphanage ever since, though she was now twenty-five. Most of the other chil-dren – there were usually about forty of them – left when they were fourteen or fifteen, after suitable employment had been found for them. But Anna had lingered on, first to help out as housemother to a dormitory of girls and a sort of secretary to Miss Ford, the matron, and then as the school-teacher when Miss Rutledge, the teacher who had taught her, married a clergyman, and moved away to Devonshire. She was even paid a modest salary. However, the expenses of her continued stay at the orphanage, now in a small room of her own, were still provided by the unknown benefactor who had paid them from the start. She had been told that they would continue to be paid as long as she remained.

Anna considered herself fortunate. She had grown up in an orphanage, it was true, with not even a full identity to call her own, since she did not know who her parents were, but in the main it was not a charity institution. Almost all her fellow orphans were supported through their growing years by someone – usually anonymous, though some knew who they were and why they were there. Usually it was because their parents had died and there was no other family member able or willing to take them in. Anna did not dwell upon the loneliness of not knowing her own story. Her material needs were taken care of. Miss Ford and her staff were generally kind. Most of the children were easy enough to get along with, and those who were not could be avoided. A few were close friends, or had been during her growing years. If there had been a lack of love in her life, or of that type of love one associated with a family, then she did not particularly miss it, having never consciously known it.

Or so she always told herself.

She was content with her life and was only occasionally restless with the feeling that surely there ought to be more, that perhaps she should be making a greater effort to *live* her life. She had been offered marriage by three different men – the shopkeeper where she went occasionally, when she could afford it, to buy a book; one of the governors of the orphanage, whose wife had recently died and left him with four young children; and Joel Cunningham, her lifelong best friend. She had rejected all three offers for varying reasons and wondered sometimes if it had been foolish to do so, as there were not likely to be many more offers, if any. The prospect of a continuing life of spinsterhood sometimes seemed dreary.

Joel was with her when the letter arrived.

She was tidying the schoolroom after dismissing the children for the day. The monitors for the week – John Davies and Ellen Payne – had collected the slates and chalk and the counting frames. But while John had stacked the slates neatly on the cupboard shelf allotted for them and put all the chalk away in the tin and replaced the lid, Ellen had shoved the counting frames haphazardly on top of paintbrushes and palettes on the bottom shelf instead of arranging them in their appointed place side by side on the shelf above so as not to bend the rods or damage the beads. The reason she had put them in the wrong place was obvious. The second shelf was occupied by the water pots used to swill paint brushes and an untidy heap of paint-stained cleaning rags.

'Joel,' Anna said, a note of long suffering in her voice, 'could you at least try to get your pupils to put things away where they belong after an art class? And to clean the water pots first? Look! One of them even still has water in it. Very *dirty* water.'

Joel was sitting on the corner of the battered teacher's desk, one booted foot braced on the floor, the other swinging free. His arms were crossed over his chest. He grinned at her.

'But the whole point of being an artist,' he said, 'is to be a free spirit, to cast aside restricting rules and draw inspiration from the universe. My job is to teach my pupils to be true artists.'

She straightened up from the cupboard and directed a speaking glance his way. 'What utter rot and nonsense,' she said.

He laughed outright. 'Anna, Anna,' he said. 'Here, let me take that pot from you before you burst with indignation or spill it down your dress. It looks like Cyrus North's. There is always more paint in his water jar than on the paper at the end of a lesson. His paintings are extraordinarily pale, as though he were trying to reproduce a heavy fog. Does he know the multiplication tables?'

'He does,' she said, depositing the offending jar on the desk and then wrinkling her nose as she arranged the still-damp rags on one side of the bottom shelf, from which she had already removed the counting frames. 'He recites them louder than anyone else and can even apply them. He has almost mastered long division too.'

'Then he can be a clerk in a counting house or perhaps a wealthy banker when he grows up,' he said. 'He will not need the soul of an artist. He probably does not possess one anyway. There – his future has been settled. I enjoyed your stories today.'

'You were listening,' she said in a mildly accusatory tone. 'You were supposed to be concentrating upon teaching your art lesson.'

'Your pupils,' he said, 'are going to realize when they grow up that they have been horribly tricked. They will have all these marvelous stories rolling around in their heads, only to discover that they are not fiction after all but that driest-of-all realities – *history*. And geography. And even arithmetic. You get your characters, both human and animal, into the most alarming predicaments from which you can extricate them only with a manipulation of numbers and the help of your pupils. They do not even realize they are learning. You are a sly, devious creature, Anna.'

'Have you noticed,' she asked, straightening the counting frames to her liking before closing the cupboard doors and turning toward him, 'that at church when the clergyman is giving his sermon everyone's eyes glaze over and many people even nod off to sleep? But if he suddenly decides to illustrate a point with a little story, everyone perks up and listens. We were made to tell and listen to stories, Joel. It is how knowledge was passed from person to person and generation to generation before there was the written word, and even afterward, when most people had no access to manuscripts or books and could not read them even if they did. Why do we now feel that story-telling should be confined to fiction and fantasy? Can we enjoy only what has no basis in fact?'

He smiled fondly at her as she stood looking at him, her hands clasped at her waist. 'One of my many secret dreams is to be a writer,' he said. 'Have I ever told you that? To write truth dressed up in fiction. It is said one ought to write about what one knows. I could invent endless stories about what I know.'

Secret dreams! It was a familiar, evocative phrase. They had often played the game as they grew up – *What is your most secret dream?* Usually it was that their parents would suddenly appear to claim them and whisk them off to the happily-ever-after of a family life. Often when they were very young they would add that they would then discover themselves to be a prince or princess and their home a castle.

'Stories about growing up as an orphan in an orphanage?' Anna said, smiling back at him. 'About not knowing who you are? About dreaming of your missing heritage? Of your unknown parents? Of what might have been? And of what still might be if only . . .? Well, if only.'

He shifted his position slightly and moved the paint jar so that he would not accidentally tip it.

'Yes, about all that,' he said. 'But it would not be all wistful sadness. For though we do not know who we were born as or who our parents or their families were or are, and though we do not know exactly why we were placed here and never after-ward claimed, we do know that we *are*. I am not my parents or my lost heritage. I am myself. I am an artist who ekes out a reasonably decent living painting portraits and volunteers his time and expertise as a teacher at the orphanage where he grew up. I am a hundred or a thousand other things too, either despite my background or because of it. I want to write stories about it all, Anna, about characters finding themselves without the hindrance of family lineage and expectations. Without the hindrance of . . . love.'

Anna gazed at him in silence for a few moments, the soreness of what felt very like tears in her throat. Joel was a solidly built man, somewhat above average in height, with dark hair cut short – because he did not want to fulfill the stereotypical image of the flamboyant artist with flowing locks, he always explained whenever he had it cut – and a round, pleasant face with a slightly cleft chin, sensitive mouth when it was relaxed, and dark eyes that could blaze with intensity and darken even further when he felt passionately about something.

He was good-looking and good-natured and talented and intelligent and extremely dear to her, and because she had known him most of her life, she knew too about his woundedness, though any casual acquaintance would not have suspected it.

It was a woundedness shared in one way or another by all orphans.

'There are institutions far worse than this one, Joel,' Anna said, 'and probably not many that are better. We have not grown up without love. Most of us love one another. I love you.'

His grin was back. 'Yet on a certain memorable occasion you refused to marry me,' he said. 'You broke my heart.'

She clucked her tongue. 'You were not really serious,' she said. 'And even if you were, you know we do not love each other *that* way. We grew up together as friends, almost as brother and sister.'

He smiled ruefully at her. 'Do you never dream of leaving here, Anna?'

'Yes and no,' she said. 'Yes, I dream of going out there into the world to find out what lies beyond these walls and the confines of Bath. And no, I do not want to leave what is familiar to me, the only home I have known since infancy and the only family I can remember. I feel safe here and needed, even loved. Besides, my . . . benefactor agreed to continue supporting me only as long as I remain here. I – Well, I suppose I am a coward, paralyzed by the terror of destitution and the unknown. It is as though, having been abandoned once, I really cannot bear the thought of now abandoning the one thing that has been left me, this orphanage and the people who live here.'

Joel got to his feet and strolled over to the other side of the room, where the easels were still set up so that today's paintings could dry properly. He touched a few at the edges to see if it was safe to remove them.

'We are both cowards, then,' he said. 'I did leave, but not entirely. I still have one foot in the door. And the other has not moved far away, has it? I am still in Bath. Do you suppose we are afraid to move away lest our parents come for us and not know where to find us?' He looked up and laughed. 'Tell me it is not that, Anna, please. I am *twenty-seven* years old.'

Anna felt rather as if he had punched her in the stomach. The old secret dream never quite died. But the most haunting question was never really *who* had brought them here and left them, but *why*.

'I believe most people live their lives within a radius of a few miles of their childhood homes,' she said. 'Not many people go adventuring. And even those who do have to take themselves with them. That must turn out to be a bit of a disappointment.'

Joel laughed again.

'I am useful here,' Anna continued, 'and I am happy here. You are useful – and successful. It is becoming quite fashionable when in Bath to have your portrait painted by Joel Cunningham. And wealthy people are always coming to Bath to take the waters.'

His head was tipped slightly to one side as he regarded her. But before he could say anything more, the classroom door was flung open without the courtesy of a knock to admit Bertha Reed, a thin, flaxen-haired fourteen-year-old who acted as Miss Ford's helper now that she was old enough. She was bursting with excitement and waving a folded paper in one raised hand.

'There is a letter for you, Miss Snow,' she half shrieked. 'It was delivered by special messenger from London and Miss Ford would have brought it herself but Tommy is bleeding all over her sitting room and no one can find Nurse Jones. Maddie punched him in the nose.'

'It is high time someone did,' Joel said, strolling closer to Anna. 'I suppose he was pulling one of her braids again.'

Anna scarcely heard. A letter? From London? By special messenger? For *her*?

'Whoever can it be from, Miss Snow?' Bertha screeched, apparently not particularly concerned about Tommy and his bleeding nose. 'Who do you know in London? No, don't tell me – that ought to have been whom. *Whom* do you know in London? I wonder what they are writing about. And it came by *special messenger,* all that way. It must have cost a *fortune.* Oh, do open it.'

Her blatant inquisitiveness might have seemed

impertinent, but really, it was so rare for any of them to receive a letter that word always spread very quickly and everyone wanted to know all about it. Occasionally someone who had left both the orphanage and Bath to work elsewhere would write, and the recipient would almost invariably share the contents with everyone else. Such missives were kept as prized possessions and read over and over until they were virtually threadbare.

Anna did not recognize the handwriting, which was both bold and precise. It was a masculine hand, she felt sure. The paper felt thick and expensive. It did not look like a personal letter.

'Oliver is in London,' Bertha said wistfully. 'But I don't suppose it can be from him, can it? His writing does not look anything like that, and why would he write to you anyway? The four times he has written since he left here, it was to me. And he is not going to send any letter by special messenger, is he?'

Oliver Jamieson had been apprenticed to a boot-maker in London two years ago at the age of fourteen and had promised to send for Bertha and marry her as soon as he got on his feet. Twice each year since then he had faithfully written a five- or six-line letter in large, careful handwriting. Bertha had shared his sparse news on each occasion and wept over the letters until it was a wonder they were still legible. There were three years left in his apprenticeship before he could hope to be on his feet and able to support a wife. They were both very young, but the separation did seem cruel. Anna always found herself hoping that Oliver would remain faithful to his childhood sweetheart.

'Are you going to turn it over and over in your hands and hope it will divulge its secrets without your having to break the seal?' Joel asked.

Stupidly, Anna's hands were trembling. 'Perhaps there is some mistake,' she said. 'Perhaps it is not for me.'

He came up behind her and looked over her shoulder. 'Miss Anna Snow,' he said. 'It certainly sounds like you. I do not know any other Anna Snows. Do you, Bertha?'

'I do not, Mr Cunningham,' she said after pausing to think. 'But whatever can it be about?'

Anna slid her thumb beneath the seal and broke it. And yes, indeed, the paper was a thick, costly vellum. It was not a long letter. It was from Somebody Brumford – she could not read the first name, though it began with a J. He was a solicitor. She read through the letter once, swallowed, and then read it again more slowly.

'The day after tomorrow,' she murmured.

'In a private chaise,' Joel added. He had been reading over her shoulder.

'*What* is the day after tomorrow?' Bertha demanded, her voice an agony of suspense. '*What* chaise?'

Anna looked at her blankly. 'I am being summoned

to London to discuss my future,' she said. There was a faint buzzing in her ears.

'Oh! By who?' Bertha asked, her eyes as wide as saucers. 'By *whom*, I mean.'

'Mr J. Brumford, a solicitor,' Anna said.

'Josiah, I think that says,' Joel said. 'Josiah Brumford. He is sending a private chaise to fetch you, and you are to pack a bag for at least a few days.'

'To *London*?' Bertha's voice was breathless with awe.

'Whatever am I to do?' Anna's mind seemed to have stopped working. Or, rather, it *was* working, but it was whirring out of control, like the innards of a broken clock.

'What you are to do, Anna,' Joel said, pushing a chair up behind her knees and setting his hands on her shoulders to press her gently down onto it, 'is pack a bag for a few days and then go to London to discuss your future.'

'But what future?' she asked.

'That is what is to be discussed,' he pointed out.

The buzzing in her ears grew louder.

CHAPTER 2

Anna could count on the fingers of one hand the number of times she had ridden inside a carriage. Perhaps that explained one of the few memories she had of her infancy. The conveyance that drew up outside the doors of the orphanage early in the morning two days after the letter came and set every child dashing to the windows of the long dining room in which they were eating breakfast was perhaps not the grandest of equipages, but some of the girls declared that it was just like Cinderella's coach. Even to Anna, who dreaded climbing into it, it looked far too impressive to be intended for her.

She was not to travel alone, it seemed. When she was summoned to Miss Ford's sitting room, she was introduced to Miss Knox, a solid, gray-haired, large-bosomed woman of severe mien, who had Anna thinking of Amazons. Miss Knox had been engaged by Mr Brumford to accompany Anna to London, since apparently it was not proper for a young lady to travel any great distance alone.

It was the first Anna had heard of being a lady. She was very thankful for the company, however.

A few minutes later, out in the hall, Miss Ford shook hands firmly with Anna while Roger, the elderly porter, lifted her bag into the carriage. It was neither a large nor a heavy bag, but what was there to pack, after all, but her spare day dress and her Sunday dress, her best shoes, and a few sundries? A number of the girls, released temporarily from the regular routine of their day, rushed about her to hug her and shed tears over her and generally behave as though she were going to the ends of the earth in order to face her own execution. Anna shed a few tears of her own, for she shared their feelings. A few of the boys stood at a safe distance, where they were in no danger of being accidentally hugged, and beamed at her. She suspected that they smiled, the rascals, because they hoped her going would mean no school today.

'I will be gone for a mere few days,' she assured them all, 'and will return with so many stories of my adventures that I will keep you up one whole night. Be good in the meanwhile.'

'I will pray for you, Miss Snow,' Winifred Hamlin promised piously through her tears.

As the carriage pulled away from the curb a couple of minutes later, children crowded the windows of the dining room again, smiling and waving and weeping. Anna waved back. This all felt alarmingly *final*, as though she would never return. And perhaps she would not. What was it about her future that needed to be discussed?

'Why has Mr Brumford summoned me?' she asked Miss Knox.

But the woman's face remained blank of all expression. 'I have no idea, miss,' she said. 'I was hired from the agency to come here and fetch you and see you safely delivered, and that is what I am doing.'

'Oh,' Anna said.

It was a long journey, with only a few brief stops along the way for refreshments and a change of horses and one night spent at an uncomfortable, noisy inn. Throughout it all Anna might as well have been alone, for Miss Knox did not utter more than a dozen words, and most of those were directed to other people. She had been hired to accompany Anna, it seemed, not to provide any sort of companionship.

Anna might have been intolerably bored if her heart had not been palpitating with a nervousness bordering on terror and if her mind had not still been spinning quite beyond her control. Everyone at the orphanage had learned of the letter, of course, and everyone had heard it read aloud. There had been no point in trying to keep its contents private even if Anna had felt so inclined. If she had done so, Bertha would have recounted what she recalled with heaven knew what embellishments, and the most hair-raising rumors would have been shooting about the home in no time at all.

Everyone had had an opinion. Everyone had had a theory.

The one most likely to be true was that Anna's benefactor, whoever he or she was, was ready to turn her loose upon the world and withdraw the monetary support she had relied upon for the past twenty-one years. He – or she – did not have to summon her all the way to London in order to inform her of that, though. But perhaps he had found her employment there. What could it be? Would she agree to take it and begin a new phase of her life, cut off from everyone she had ever known and the only home she could remember? Or would she refuse and return to Bath and try to subsist on her teacher's wages? She would have a choice, she assumed. The letter had, after all, stated that her future needed to be *discussed*. A discussion was a two-way communication.

She wondered if there were enough coins in her purse for a ticket home by stagecoach. She had no idea what the fare was, but she had a little money of her own – a very little – and Miss Ford had pressed a whole sovereign into her palm last night despite her protests. What if it was still not enough? What if she found herself stranded in London for the rest of her life? The very thought was enough to make her feel bilious, and the state of the road over which they were traveling did nothing to settle her stomach.

A few times she tried determinedly not to think. She tried instead to marvel at the unfamiliar sensation of being in a carriage, of actually leaving Bath, climbing the hill away from it until it was no longer in sight behind her when she peered back. She tried to marvel at the passing countryside. She tried to think of this experience as the adventure of a lifetime, one she would remember for the rest of her life. She imagined how she would tell the children at the orphanage about it – about the tollbooths and the villages through which they passed; about village greens and taverns with quaint names painted upon their swinging signs and small churches with pointed steeples; about the posting inns at which they stopped, the food they ate there, the lumpiness of the bed in which she tried to sleep, the bustle of hostlers and grooms in the innyards; the deep ruts in the road that rattled the very teeth in one's head and even occasionally made Miss Knox look less like a sphinx.

Soon enough, however, her mind would spin back to the great, frightening unknown that lay ahead of her. What if she was about to meet the person who had taken her to the orphanage all those years ago and paid to keep her there ever since? Would it be the man with the gruff voice? What if she really was a princess and a prince was waiting to marry her now that she was grown-up and out of danger from the wicked king – or witch! – from whom she had been carefully hidden all these years? The absurd thought made Anna smile despite herself and almost laugh aloud. That had been nine-year-old Olga Norton's theory after she had listened to Anna's letter the night before last.

It had been eagerly espoused by several of the other little girls and soundly ridiculed by most of the boys.

All she could do, Anna thought with great good sense for surely the two hundredth time in the last few days, was wait and see. But that was more easily said than done. Why had the summons come through a solicitor? And why was she traveling in a private carriage when stagecoach tickets must cost far less? And why had she been provided with a chaperone? What was to happen when she arrived in London?

What did happen was that the carriage kept driving and driving. London was endlessly large and endlessly dreary, even squalid, for what seemed like miles and miles. So much for the story of Dick Whittington and the gold-paved streets of London town, though admittedly it might all look more inviting in full daylight instead of the dusk that was falling upon the outside world.

But the carriage did stop eventually outside a large, imposing stone building that turned out to be a hotel. They stepped inside a reception hall, and Miss Knox spoke with a man in uniform behind a high oak desk, was handed a large brass key, and led the way up two broad, carpeted flights of stairs and along a corridor before setting the key in the lock of a door and opening it wide. There was a spacious, square, high-ceilinged sitting room beyond it with doors on either side, each standing open to show a bedchamber within.

There was a lamp alight in each of the three rooms, a great extravagance to Anna's weary mind. It was a huge improvement over last night's accommodations.

'I am to stay here?' she asked, moving sharply to one side when she realized that another man in uniform had come along behind them, her bag and Miss Knox's in his hands. He set them down, looked expectantly at Miss Knox, who ignored him, and withdrew with a scowl.

'The bigger room on the left is yours, miss,' the older woman said. 'The other one is mine. Dinner will be fetched up soon. I shall go and wash my hands.'

She disappeared into the bedchamber to the right, taking her bag with her. Anna carried hers into the other room. It was at least three times larger than her room at the orphanage. The bed looked wide enough to accommodate four or five sleepers lying comfortably abreast. There was water in the jug on the washstand. She poured some into the bowl and washed her hands and face and combed her hair. She ran her hands down her dress, which was sadly wrinkled after two days of sitting.

By the time she stepped back into the sitting room, two servants had come to set the table with a crisp white cloth and gleaming china, glass, and cutlery, and to deposit several covered tureens of something hot and steaming and delicious smelling. At least, Anna assumed it would smell delicious if only she were hungry and not so desperately tired.

She wished with all her heart that she was back at home.

Having a superlatively efficient secretary, Avery, Duke of Netherby, mused, was both a good thing and occasionally a bothersome one. On the one hand, one came to rely upon him to conduct all the troublesome and trivial business of one's life, leaving oneself free simply to live and enjoy it. On the other hand, there was the odd occasion when one found oneself forced into something tedious that might have been avoided if one had been left to one's own devices. It did not happen often, admittedly, for Edwin Goddard was well acquainted with what might be expected to bore his employer. This, however, was one of those infrequent occasions.

'Edwin,' Avery said with a pained sigh late one afternoon as he appeared in the doorway of the secretary's office. 'What is this, pray?'

He held aloft between a thumb and forefinger a card Goddard had left on the library desk with two other memos, one reminding His Grace of a ball he would wish to attend tonight because the Honorable Miss Edwards was to be there, and the other informing him that a pair of new boots for which he had been fitted last week was awaiting his pleasure at Hoby's whenever he chose to go and try them on to make sure they fit like the glove that was always said to be so comfortable upon one's foot. If it were really so, Avery mused, then it was strange that men persisted in wearing boots rather than gloves. But his thoughts had digressed.

'Mr Josiah Brumford has requested an hour of your time here tomorrow morning, Your Grace,' Goddard explained. 'Since he is the Earl of Riverdale's solicitor and his lordship is your ward, I assumed you would be happy to grant his request. I have given instructions that the rose salon be prepared for ten o'clock.'

'*Happy,*' His Grace repeated faintly. 'My dear Edwin, what a very peculiar choice of word. You have indeed mentioned here that this, ah, audience is to be granted in the rose salon at the time you stated. I can read. But you omitted a reason for the choice of room. The rose salon seems rather a large chamber for just one solicitor and my humble self to rattle about in. He is not bringing along with him any large sort of retinue, is he? The other Brumford, perhaps, or some of the "& Sons"? Or the whole lot of them? That would be too, too much, I am moved to inform you.'

'Mr Brumford mentioned in his letter, Your Grace,' Goddard said, 'that he has taken the liberty of requesting the attendance too of more persons, including the earl and the countess, his mother, and other members of his family.'

'Has he indeed?' Avery's fingers curled about the handle of his quizzing glass as he strolled toward his secretary's desk, dropped the memo upon it, and held out his hand. Goddard eyed it for a moment and then rummaged through a neat pile of papers on one corner of his desk in order to produce Brumford's letter. It was as pompous as the man who had penned it, but it did indeed request the honor of addressing His Grace of Netherby at Archer House at ten o'clock tomorrow morning upon a matter of grave importance. It also begged His Grace's pardon for having taken the liberty of inviting his ward and his lordship's mother and sisters as well as other close family members, including Mr Alexander Westcott, Mrs Westcott, his mother, and Lady Overfield, his sister.

Avery returned the letter to his secretary without comment. Three weeks had passed since Brumford had stridden from Westcott House like a crusader bent upon the mission of sending forth his most trusted investigator to run one bastard orphan to earth in order to press riches upon her in return for her written promise never to appeal to Harry for more. Had not the arrangement been that Brumford report privately to Avery when the woman was found in order to discuss the exact sum to be settled upon her?

Was this meeting about something else altogether?

It had better be, by thunder, if Brumford did not wish to find himself strung up from the nearest tree by his thumbs. It had been the countess's express wish that Harry and Camille and Abigail never know of the existence of their father's by-blow. And why the devil had Alex Westcott been invited? And his mother and his sister? They were cousins of Harry's – second cousins, to be exact, with maybe a remove or two. Westcott was also the heir to the earldom until such time as Harry settled down to marriage and the dutiful production of an heir of his own body and a couple of spares to be on the safe side. And who were the other *close family members*? What *was* this meeting? Had some secret will been unearthed after all?

Avery left the room and went in search of the duchess, his stepmother. She would be interested to know that they were to expect her sister-in-law and nephew and nieces tomorrow, as well as her cousins and other unidentified relatives. She had a mother and two sisters in town. Though perhaps she had received her own personal invitation and already knew. She would certainly wish to attend the meeting, as no doubt would Jess – Lady Jessica Archer, his half sister, who at the age of seventeen and three-quarters already had all ten toes lined up firmly at the threshold of the schoolroom doorway, ready to bolt free the very moment she turned eighteen. This time next year, perish the thought, he would probably be squiring her about to all the parties and balls and breakfasts and picnics and whatnots at which the great marriage mart conducted its business during the Season.

She might as well attend the meeting, he thought, since it was to be here in her own home. He looked into the drawing room and found her there with her mother, admiring a pile of brightly colored embroidery silks they must have just purchased. It would be hard to keep Jess away tomorrow anyway when she was informed that Abigail was coming. It would be well nigh impossible when she knew Harry was to be here too. She did not, Avery hoped, see him as future husband material since he was her first cousin, but she did worship and adore at the altar of his youthful good looks. However, her presence or absence would be for her mother to decide. Thank heaven for mothers.

A matter of grave importance, Brumford had written. The man ought to be on the stage. He really ought.

Both ladies looked up and smiled at him.

'Oh, Avery,' Jessica said, hurrying toward him, her face brightly eager, her hands clasped to her bosom, 'guess who is coming here tomorrow morning.' But she did not wait for him to participate in the game she had set up. 'Abby. And Harry. And Camille.'

In order of importance, it seemed.

'Brumford has a decided flair for the dramatic,' Alexander Westcott remarked to his mother and his sister as they dined together at home that same evening. 'This gathering cannot be for the reading of Riverdale's will. There apparently was no will. Besides, the solicitor would not have chosen Archer House for such a reading even if Netherby is Harry's guardian. Why our presence is necessary for whatever the business happens to be, heaven knows. I suppose we had better put in an appearance, however.'

'I have not seen either Louise or Viola since the funeral,' his mother said, naming the Duchess of Netherby and the Countess of Riverdale. 'I shall enjoy a chat with them. And if we are invited, perhaps Cousin Eugenia and Matilda and Mildred will be there too.' Cousin Eugenia was the Dowager Countess of Riverdale, the late earl's mother, the other two ladies her eldest and youngest daughters.

'And you must admit, Alex,' Elizabeth, Lady Overfield, said with a twinkle in her eye, 'that a mystery is always intriguing. You at least are Harry's heir. Mama and I are not closely related to Harry.'

'Your papa and Harry's papa were first cousins,' her mother reminded them, 'though they were never close. Your papa detested the man. So did everyone else, it seemed to me, and that probably included Viola, though she was ever the loyal wife.'

'Being Harry's heir is not something I covet,' Alexander said. 'Perhaps I am peculiar, but I am perfectly happy with who I am and what I have. He cannot be expected to marry soon, of course. He is not even of age yet. But I devoutly hope he marries young and fathers at least six sons in as many years to put the succession beyond doubt. In the meanwhile I hope he remains in perfect health.'

Elizabeth laughed and reached out to pat the back of his hand. 'It is not peculiar at all,' she said. 'You have worked hard to restore Riddings Park to prosperity after Papa ran it into the ground – pardon my bluntness, Mama – and you have succeeded and can be proud of yourself. You are much respected there, even loved, and I know you are contented. I know too that you are not over-fond of being dragged to London just because it is the Season and you knew Mama and I fancied sampling some of the frivolities it has to offer this year. You did not really need to come with us, but I appreciate the fact that you did, and that you have leased this very comfortable house for us.'

'It was not entirely for your sakes I came,' he admitted after sipping his wine. 'Mama is always urging me to live a little, as though being home on my own estate, which I love, were not living. But occasionally even I feel the urge to set aside my manure-encrusted boots and don dancing shoes instead.'

Elizabeth laughed again. 'You dance well,' she said. 'And you invariably cause a stir among the ladies whenever you set foot inside a ballroom, for you are always the most handsome gentleman in attendance.'

'Is there any hope,' their mother asked, looking at her son in some despair as though this were not the first or even the twenty-first time she had posed the question, 'that somewhere among all those ladies you will find a bride, Alex?'

He hesitated before answering, and she looked hopeful enough to set down her knife and fork across her plate and lean slightly toward him.

'Yes, actually,' he said. 'It is the next logical step for me to take, is it not? Riddings is prospering at last, everyone dependent upon me is well looked after, and the only thing lacking to make all secure is an heir. My next birthday is my thirtieth. I came here with you and Lizzie, Mama, because I cannot like either of you being here without a man to lend you countenance and offer escort wherever you wish to go, but I came too on my own account to . . . look about me, if you will. I am not in any hurry to make a choice. It may not even happen this year. But I do not need to marry money, and I am not so highly ranked that I am obliged to look high for a bride. I hope to find someone who will . . . suit me.'

'Someone with whom to fall in love?' Elizabeth suggested, leaning slightly to one side so that the footman could refill her water glass.

'I shall certainly expect to feel an affection for the lady,' he said, flushing slightly. 'But romantic love? Pardon me, Lizzie, but is that not for females?'

His mother tutted.

'Like me?' Elizabeth sat back in her chair and watched him eat.

'Ah.' His fork remained suspended halfway to his mouth. 'I did not mean it that way, Lizzie. I did not mean to offend.'

'And you did not,' she assured him. 'I fell head over heels in infatuation with Desmond the moment I set eyes upon him, silly girl that I was, and called it love. It was not love. But the experience of a bad marriage has not made a cynic of me. I still believe in romantic love, and I do so hope you discover it for yourself, Alex. You deserve all that is good in life, especially after all you have done for me.'

Sir Desmond Overfield, her late husband, had been a charming man but a heavy drinker, the sort who turned uglier the more he drank and became verbally and physically abusive. When Elizabeth had fled back to her childhood home on one occasion, her face scarcely recognizable beneath all the swelling and bruises, her father had sent her back, albeit reluctantly, when Desmond came for her, with the reminder that she was now a married lady and her husband's property. When she had fled there again two years later, after her father was dead, this time with a broken arm as well as bruises over most of her face and body, Alex had taken her in and summoned a physician. Desmond had come again to claim his property, sober and apologetic, as he had been the first time, but Alex had punched him in the face and broken his nose and dislodged a few of his teeth. When her husband had returned with the nearest magistrate, Alex had blackened both his eyes and invited the magistrate to stay for luncheon. Desmond had died less than a year after that, stabbed in a tavern brawl in which ironically he had been only a spectator.

'I will choose a bride with whom I can expect to be comfortable and even happy,' Alex promised now, 'but I shall ask your opinion, Lizzie, and Mama's too before making any offer.'

His mother gave a little shriek of horror. 'You will not marry just to please your mother,' she said. 'The very idea.'

'Oh, you will do no such thing,' Elizabeth protested simultaneously.

He grinned at them. 'But you will both have to share a house with my wife,' he said. 'All this is purely hypothetical, however, at least for now. I have talked and danced with a number of ladies in the couple of weeks since the Season began, but none have tempted me to courtship. I am in no great hurry to make a choice. In the meantime, we have a soiree to attend tonight and had better be on our way within the half hour. And tomorrow we will discover what earth-shattering disclosures Harry's solicitor has to make that necessitate our presence. I am sure neither of you is under any obligation to go with me, though.'

'But Mama and I have been invited too,'

Elizabeth reminded him. 'I would not miss it for worlds. Besides, I have not seen any of the cousins since the funeral either, and their enforced seclusion must be quite irksome to them, especially when the Season is tempting them with so many entertainments. Camille must be hugely disappointed at having been forced to postpone her wedding to Viscount Uxbury, and poor Abigail must feel even worse done by at having to wait until next year to make her come-out when she is already eighteen. Perhaps we will see young Jessica too, since this meeting is to be at Archer House. Oh, and I must confess, Alex, that I look forward to seeing the Duke of Netherby. He is so deliciously . . . grand.'

'Lizzie!' Alexander looked pained as he nodded to the footman to remove their plates. 'He is nothing but bored artificiality through to the very heart. If he has one.'

'But he does it all with such magnificent flair,' she said, the twinkle back in her eyes. 'And he is so very beautiful.'

'*Beautiful?*' He looked thunderstruck before relaxing and shaking his head and chuckling. 'But the word does fit, I must confess.'

'Oh, it does,' their mother agreed. 'If I were but twenty years younger.' She sighed and fluttered her eyelashes, and they all laughed.

'He is the very antithesis of you, Alex,' Elizabeth said, patting his hand once more while they all got to their feet. 'Which fact must be an enormous relief to you, since you really do not like him one little bit, do you?'

'The antithesis?' he said. 'I am not beautiful, then, Lizzie?'

'Absolutely not,' she said, linking her arm through his while he offered the other to his mother. 'You are handsome, Alex. Sometimes I think it is unfair that you got all the stunning good looks – from Mama's side of the family, of course – while I have never been anything but passably pretty. But it is not just your looks that disqualify you from being called beautiful. You never look bored or haughty, and you definitely have a heart. And a conscience. You are a solid citizen and a thoroughly worthy gentleman.'

'Good God,' he said, grimacing. 'Am I really such a dull dog?'

'Not at all,' she said, laughing. 'For you have the looks.'

He was, in fact, the quintessential tall, dark, handsome man – with an athletic, perfectly toned body and blue eyes to boot. He also had a smile that would melt frozen butter, not to mention female hearts. And, yes, he had a firm sense of duty to those dependent upon him. Elizabeth, four years his senior, was beginning to recover some of the bloom she had lost during her difficult marriage, though she was neither as dark nor as strikingly good-looking as her brother. She did, however, have an even temper, an amiable countenance, and a cheerful disposition that had

41

somehow survived six years of disappointment and anxiety and abuse.

'Lizzie!' her mother exclaimed. 'You have always been beautiful in my eyes.'

CHAPTER 3

'The devil!' Harry, the young Earl of Riverdale, frowned down the stairs at his sisters, who were frowning right back up at him. 'Is it *today* old Brumford wants to see us at Avery's house? Not tomorrow?'

'You know very well it is today,' Lady Camille Westcott said. 'You had better make haste. You look a fright.'

He looked as though he had been up all night carousing, which, in fact, was exactly what he had been doing. His fine evening clothes were creased and rumpled, his shirt cuffs soiled, his neckcloth limp and askew, his fair, wavy hair disheveled, his eyes bloodshot, and no one would particularly wish to come within smelling distance of him. He was in dire need of a shave.

'You did not even come home last night, Harry,' Lady Abigail remarked rather obviously, her eyes moving over him from head to toe with open disapproval.

'I would dashed well hope not,' he said. 'I would hardly be returning from a morning ride dressed like this, would I? Why the devil did

Brumford have to choose today? And in the morning, of all the ungodly times? And why Archer House and not here? What the devil does he have to say anyway that cannot be put in a letter or conveyed through Mama or Avery? He does a great deal too much posturing and prosing, if anyone were to ask me, not that anyone ever does. I am of half a mind to get rid of him as soon as I turn twenty-one and choose someone else who understands that a solicitor's absence is more appreciated than his presence and his silence more than his eloquence.'

'I must protest your language, Harry,' Camille said. 'It may be all very well for your male acquaintances, but it certainly will not do in the hearing of your sisters. You owe Abby and me an apology.'

'Do I?' He grinned and then winced and grasped his temples with the thumb and middle finger of one hand. 'You both look like avenging angels, I must say – just what a fellow needs when he has come home for a well-earned sleep.'

At least he had not said they looked like two crows, as he had when they first put on their blacks. Camille was darker haired than her brother, tall, very upright in bearing, rather severe of countenance, her features too strong to be described as pretty, though she could certainly be called handsome with some justification. Abigail had her brother's coloring and good looks and slender build, though she was small of stature.

'Mr Brumford will soon be awaiting us at Archer

House,' Abigail reminded him. 'So will Cousin Avery.'

'But what can be left to discuss?' he asked, releasing his temples. 'He droned on for hours when he came here a few weeks ago, though he had absolutely nothing new to say. And why do the two of you have to go this time as well to be bored silly? I shall have a few questions for him when I see him, you may rest assured.'

'Which will perhaps be *within the hour*,' Camille said, 'If you will but go and change, Harry, rather than continue to stand there clutching your temples and looking like a tragic hero. You would not wish Cousin Avery to see you like that.'

'Netherby?' Harry grinned – and winced again. 'He would not care. He is a good egg.'

'He would look at you through his quizzing glass, Harry,' Abigail said, 'and then he would lower it and look bored. I would hate above everything for him to look at me like that. *Go.*'

Their mother appeared behind him at the top of the stairs at that moment. He smiled shame-facedly at her and ducked out of sight. Their mother followed him.

'He is still half inebriated, Abby,' Camille said to her sister. 'I wish Cousin Avery would put his foot down, but one knows he will not. Uxbury had a word with Harry last week, but our brother told him to mind his own business. Uxbury implied that he used stronger language than that, but he would not quote him verbatim.'

'Lord Uxbury does have an unfortunate way of saying things that set Harry's back up, you must admit, Cam,' Abigail said gently.

'But he is *right* every time,' Camille protested. 'Yet it is Cousin Avery who is the *good egg*. Harry gets away with altogether too much. He is wearing a black armband – a *crumpled* black armband – while we are decked out in black from head to toe. Black is not your color, and it most definitely is not mine. You are supposed to be making your come-out this spring, and I am supposed to be marrying Uxbury. Neither event is going to happen, yet Harry is out every day and night, sowing wild oats. And neither Mama nor Avery utters one word of reproach.'

'Sometimes life does not seem fair, does it?' Abigail said.

Camille turned away from the stairs to return to the morning room, where they had been about to take their coffee when they heard their brother stumble his way into the house. Their mother came into the room behind them.

'What is this summons to Archer House all about, Mama?' Abigail asked.

'If I knew that,' the countess said, 'we would not need to go. But you girls have been starved for entertainment, and the outing will do you good. Your aunt Louise and Jessica will be happy to see you. It is too bad mourning precludes you from attending all but the most sober and dull of the Season's entertainments. But if you are about to complain to me, Cam, that your brother's social life is not as restricted as yours and Abby's, then you might as well save your breath. He is a man and you are not. You are old enough to understand that gentlemen live by a wholly different set of rules from the ones by which we must abide. Is it fair? No, of course it is not. Can we do anything about it? No, we cannot. Complaints are pointless.'

Abigail took her a cup of coffee. 'Are you worried about something, Mama?' she asked with a frown.

'No,' her mother said quickly. 'Why should I be? I just wish to have this morning over with. Goodness knows what it is all about. I must advise Harry to change his solicitor. Avery will not object. He finds Mr Brumford tedious beyond endurance. If the man has business to discuss, then he ought to come here and discuss it in private.'

The sisters sipped their coffee, exchanged glances, and regarded their mother in thoughtful silence. *Something* was worrying her.

Edwin Goddard, His Grace of Netherby's secretary, had seen to the setup of the rose salon. Chairs had been arranged in three neat rows to face a large oak table from behind which Brumford presumably intended to hold court at the appointed hour. Avery had viewed the room with distaste earlier – so many chairs? But now he stood out in the tiled hall, awaiting the arrival of the last of his guests. At least, all these people must be called guests, he supposed, though it was not he who had invited them. Standing out in the hall was preferable, however, to being in the salon, where his stepmother was playing the part of gracious hostess to an alarmingly and mysteriously large number of her relatives, and Jessica was in transports of delight at seeing Harry and his sisters and was talking to them at great speed and at a pitch high enough to have brought a frown of censure from her governess if that worthy woman had been present. She was not, however, Jess having been released from the schoolroom for the occasion.

Brumford was in the hall too, though he had taken up a position at some distance from the duke and was uncharacteristically silent – mentally practicing his speech, perhaps? – and easily ignored. Avery had asked him upon his arrival if this family gathering had anything to do with the delicate and very private matter the countess had entrusted to his skill and discretion a few weeks ago. But Brumford had merely bowed and assured His Grace that he had come on a matter of grave concern to the whole Westcott family. Beyond regarding the man in silence for a little longer than was strictly necessary through his quizzing glass, Avery had not pressed him further. Brumford was, after all, a man of the law and could therefore not be expected to give a direct answer to any question.

Avery tried not to think of any of the dozen or so more congenial ways in which he might be spending his morning. He raised his eyebrows at a burst of merry laughter from the rose salon.

There was a knock upon the outer doors, and the butler opened them to admit Alexander Westcott, Mrs Westcott, and Lady Overfield. Westcott was looking his usual immaculate, dignified self. Avery had known him since they were boys at school together, and if Westcott had ever had a hair out of place, even after the most rugged scrimmage out on the playing fields, or set one toenail out of line behavior-wise in all the years they had spent there, Avery had certainly never witnessed it. Alexander Westcott and gentlemanly reserve and respectability were synonymous terms. The two men had never been friends.

Westcott nodded briskly to him, and Mrs Westcott and her daughter smiled.

'Netherby?' he said.

'Cousin Avery,' both ladies said simultaneously.

'Cousin Althea.' He stepped forward, extended one languid, beringed hand for the elder lady's, and raised it to his lips. 'A pleasure indeed. Cousin Elizabeth.' He kissed her hand too. 'Looking ravishing as always.'

'As are you.' The younger woman's smile had acquired a twinkle.

He raised his eyebrows. 'One does one's utmost,' he said on a sigh, and released her hand. He had always liked her rather more than he did her brother. She had a sense of humor. She had a good figure too. She had inherited both from her mother, though not the mother's dark good looks. The son had got those.

'Westcott,' Avery said by way of greeting.

Brumford, bowing reverentially from the waist, was ignored.

The butler ushered the new arrivals into the salon, and there was a swell of greetings from within and even a squeal or two. It was time he went to join them, Avery thought with an inward sigh, taking his snuffbox from a pocket and flicking open the lid with a practiced thumb. Everyone was present and accounted for. But before he could move, the knocker rattled once more against the outer doors and the butler hurried to open them.

A woman stepped inside without awaiting an invitation. A governess – Avery would wager half his fortune on it. She was young and thin and uncompromisingly straight backed and clad from head to toe in a darkish blue, with the exception of her gloves and reticule and shoes, which were black. None of her garments was either costly or stylish, and that was a kind assessment. Her hair was scarcely visible beneath the small brim of her bonnet, though there appeared to be a large bun at the back of her neck.

She stopped just inside the door, clasped her hands at her waist, and looked about her as though expecting a pupil or three to materialize from the shadows with books and slates at the ready.

'I do believe,' Avery said, closing the snuffbox

with a snap, 'you have mistaken the front door for the servants' entrance and the house for one in which there are infants in anticipation of instruction. Horrocks will set your feet in the right direction.' He raised one eyebrow in the butler's direction.

She turned her eyes upon him – large, calm gray eyes, which did not falter when they encountered his. She stayed where she was and looked neither abashed nor terrified nor horrified nor frozen in place nor any of the things one might have expected of someone who had just stepped through the wrong door.

'I was brought from Bath yesterday,' she said in a soft, clear voice, 'and today I was set down outside the door of this house.'

'If you please, miss.' Horrocks was holding the door open.

But Avery was arrested by a sudden realization. By God, she was not a governess, or not *just* a governess anyway. She was a bastard.

Specifically, she was *the* bastard.

'Miss Snow?' Brumford had taken a step forward and was actually . . . bowing again.

She turned her attention upon him. 'Yes,' she said. 'Mr Brumford?'

'You are expected,' Brumford said while Avery replaced his snuffbox in his pocket and raised his glass to his eye as Horrocks shut the door. 'The butler will show you to a place in the rose salon.'

'Thank you,' she said.

51

Horrocks's back was almost visibly bristling with disapproval and indignation as he led the woman away. But Avery scarcely noticed. His glass was trained fully upon the solicitor, whose face was shining with perspiration, as well it might, by thunder. He turned unwilling eyes the glass's way.

'What the devil have you done?' Avery asked, his voice soft.

'All will be made clear shortly, Your Grace,' Brumford assured him as one bead of moisture trickled down his forehead, spread through his eyebrow, and dripped onto his cheek.

'Have a care,' Avery said. 'You would not enjoy my displeasure.'

He lowered his glass and strolled off to the rose salon, where an unnatural silence seemed to have fallen. Everyone was seated, the family members on the three rows of chairs before the table, the . . . *woman* behind and apart from them, just inside the door and to one side of it. But the fact that she was seated at all in company with a roomful of aristocrats, only two of whom lacked some sort of title – and even one of those was heir to an earldom – was astonishing enough to plunge the room into an uncomfortable and outraged silence. No one was looking back at her, and Avery doubted anyone had spoken to her, but that they were all aware of her to the exclusion of all else was patently obvious.

Who could she be *but* the bastard?

Every head turned toward him as he entered the room. All must be wondering why such a person was in his house at all, let alone in one of the salons, and why he was not doing something to rectify the situation. The Countess of Riverdale looked unnaturally pale, as though she had come to the same conclusion as Avery had. He ignored the remaining unoccupied chair and strolled to one side of the room, where he propped a shoulder against the rose-colored brocaded wall before taking his snuffbox from his pocket again and availing himself of a pinch of its contents. It was a newly adjusted blend and very nearly perfect.

Much as he always avoided exerting himself unnecessarily, he might well find it necessary to wring Brumford's neck after this morning was over.

The silence had become loud. Avery looked unhurriedly about him. Harry appeared irritable. He had had another late night, by the look of him, surrounded, no doubt, by the usual hangers-on, who laughed at his every attempt at wit and drank deep at his expense. Camille, on one side of him and clad in deep, hideous mourning, looked prunish. She would probably be even more so after she married Uxbury, who had probably been laid in a crib of prunes at his birth and absorbed them through his pores. Abigail, on Harry's other side, looked even worse in black, poor girl. It positively sapped her of all her youthful animation and prettiness. Harry, unlike his mother and sisters, was paying homage to his late parent with a mere armband. Sensible boy.

The duchess, Avery's stepmother, sat behind them. She looked distinguished in black, though she would not need to wear it much longer, since Riverdale had been only her brother, not her husband or father. What a ghastly invention mourning clothes were. Jessica sat beside his stepmother in a dress that was refreshingly white. Her grandmother, the dowager countess, was on her other side, so swaddled in black that her face looked like a ghost's. Lady Matilda Westcott, her eldest child, the one who had dutifully remained at home and unmarried to be a prop to her parent in old age, looked no better. Beside her was the youngest of her siblings, Mildred, Lady Molenor, with Thomas, Baron Molenor, her husband. Alexander Westcott sat in the third row, between his mother and Elizabeth, his sister.

What the devil was Brumford up to? Why was this business not being conducted privately as the countess had specifically directed? Avery was inclined even now to stride from the room to hurl the solicitor bodily out through the door, preferably without opening it first. But that woman would remain behind on her chair by the door and so would too many questions for the matter to be hushed up. Fate, it seemed, must be allowed to run its course.

He ought to have exerted himself yesterday, Avery thought, after reading Brumford's letter.

She continued to sit alone close to the door, looking perfectly in command of herself. She had removed her cloak. It was draped over the back of her chair. She had removed the bonnet and gloves too – they were beneath her chair. Her cheap blue high-waisted dress covered her from neck to wrists to ankles. She had a slender, neat figure, Avery noticed as his eyes rested upon her, not a thin one as he had thought at first. Nevertheless, it was a figure totally unremarkable to a connoisseur of feminine figures. He had noticed when she was standing that she was on the small side of average in height. Her hair was a midbrown and looked as if it must be perfectly straight. It was scraped back from her face and twisted into a heavy knot at the back of her neck. Her hands were clasped loosely in her lap. Her feet in their sensible, unattractive shoes were set neatly side by side on the floor. The woman looked about as alluring as a doorknob.

She was remarkably calm. There was nothing bold about her demeanor, but nor was there anything shrinking. She did not keep her eyes lowered, as one might have expected. She was looking about her with what seemed to be mild interest, her eyes resting for a few moments upon each person in turn.

Her attention turned last upon him. She did not look hastily away when her eyes met his and she realized she was the object of his scrutiny. Neither did she hold his gaze. Her eyes moved over him, and he found himself wondering what she saw.

What *he* saw surprised him just a little. For when he withdrew his attention from all that was unappealing in her appearance – and that was almost everything – and concentrated instead upon her face, he realized that it was quite startlingly beautiful, like the Madonna in a medieval painting his mind could not immediately identify. It was neither a smiling nor an animated face. It was not set off by enticing curls or beckoning fan or peeping dimples or come-hither eyes. It was a face that simply spoke for itself. It was an oval face with regular features and those wide, steady gray eyes. That was all. There was nothing specific to account for the impression of beauty it gave.

She had finished inspecting him and was looking into his eyes again. He pocketed his snuffbox and raised both his quizzing glass and his eyebrows, but by that time she had looked unhurriedly away to watch Brumford make his self-important entrance. One of his boots was squeaking.

There was a stirring of interest from the family gathered there. The countess, though, Avery saw, looked as though she had been carved of marble.

Throughout her life Anna had cultivated one quality of character above all others, and that was dignity. She always tried to instill the importance of it in her fellow orphans too whenever they were under her care.

As an orphan one had so very little. Almost nothing at all, in fact, except life itself. Often one did not even have identity. One might know the name by which one had been christened – if one had been christened – or one might not. For everything else except life itself one was dependent upon the charity of others. It might be said, of course, that the same held true of all children, but most had families who cared for them and whose love was unconditional. They had a defined identity within that family.

It would be so very easy as an orphan to become abject and cringing, a nothing and a nobody, or else bold, demanding, and angry, asserting rights that did not exist. Anna had seen both types and could understand and sympathize with both. But she had chosen a different path for herself. She had chosen to believe that she was no better than anyone – and there *were* orphans who occasionally lorded it over others when they were sent gifts or were taken out for the day, for example. She had also chosen to believe that she was no worse than anyone, that she was no one's inferior, that she belonged on this earth as surely as anyone else did.

It was an attitude and a quality of character that had never stood her in greater stead than it had today. For she had been in the clutches of terror from the moment the carriage stopped outside this grand house in its stately London square – she did not know its name – and Miss Knox, taking a firm stand on the pavement, had told her to climb the steps alone to the front door and rap the knocker. As soon as the door opened, Anna had been aware of the carriage moving off with Miss Knox inside it.

Anna had soon realized that the man who had opened the door was a servant, but it had not been apparent to her at the time. He had probably not expected her to step right inside past him without a word. It was probably not done in polite circles – and it certainly seemed she had stepped into polite circles. And then there had been the other two men in the large tiled hall in which she had found herself. One was stout and pompous looking and no more disconcerting than some of the governors of the orphanage who sometimes made an official visit and patted a few orphans on the head and laughed too heartily. The other one . . .

Well, Anna had still not been able to categorize the other man to her satisfaction. She guessed, though, that he was someone very grand indeed, perhaps even a lord. It was a distinct possibility if this house – this mansion – was his. He had filled her with a knee-weakening terror when he had spoken to her in a light, bored, cultured voice and suggested that she had come to the wrong door, even the wrong house. It would have been the easiest thing in the world to turn tail and scurry out through the still-open door.

She was very glad she had not done so. Where

would she have gone? What would she have done? She was glad she had stood her ground, remembering that she was everyone's equal and that she had been summoned here and brought in a carriage.

She sat now in the room to which the butler had brought her and wished she could melt into her chair and through the floor and reemerge in her classroom in Bath. Thirteen heads had turned at her entry – she had counted them since – and all thirteen persons had looked identically astonished, especially when the butler had indicated a chair just inside the door and instructed her to be seated. Only one of them had spoken, though – a plumpish lady seated at one end of the second row of chairs.

'Horrocks,' she had said in a commanding, haughty voice, 'you will oblige me by taking this . . . person elsewhere immediately.'

The butler had bowed to her. 'Mr Brumford directed me in the hearing of His Grace to escort her here, Your Grace,' he had said.

His Grace. Your Grace.

No one had said another word, either to Anna or to one another. They had sat instead in a stiff, disapproving silence that seemed louder than the conversation that had been in progress when Anna stepped into the room.

She had consciously practiced *dignity* and sat with an apparently calm, relaxed demeanor despite the fact that her stomach felt as though it had clenched itself into a tiny ball and was about to squeeze out what little breakfast she had eaten before leaving the hotel. She had even removed her cloak and arranged it neatly over the back of the chair without getting to her feet. She had set her bonnet and her gloves and reticule on the floor beneath the chair.

She had forced herself to look, not downward at her hands as she desperately wanted to do, but about her at the room and the people in it. If she looked down, she might never be able to bring herself to look up again. After a few minutes the man from the hall – His Grace? – who had tried to get her to leave, stepped into the room, and everyone turned to look at him in mute appeal, probably in the hope that he would get rid of her. He did not say anything. He did not sit down either. He went instead to stand on the other side of the room and propped one shoulder against the wall. He would have been reprimanded for that at the orphanage. Walls were not to be leaned against.

It was a large, square, high-ceilinged room. The walls were covered in deep pink brocade. Landscape paintings in heavy gilded frames were hung upon them. The ceiling was coved and framed by a gilded frieze. There was a scene painted directly onto the ceiling. It was something from the Bible or mythology, Anna guessed, though she did not gaze upward long enough to identify exactly what it was. There was a patterned carpet underfoot, its colors predominantly rose. The furnishings were solid and elegant.

But it was at the people she looked most closely. Sitting in the row closest to the table were three young people and a more mature lady. The ladies were dressed in deep mourning. The young man – he was actually a boy more than a man – was wearing a dark green coat over white linen, but there was a black band on his sleeve. A brother and his sisters and mother? There was something about them that suggested a familial connection.

The six people in the row behind them were also in black, except for one young girl who wore white. The lady who had told the butler to remove Anna sat with regal dignity, her spine not quite touching the straight back of her chair. What sort of lady was addressed as *Your Grace*? Anna did not know. The only one of their number who turned a head to look back toward Anna after that first shocked glance from all of them was the younger of the two ladies who sat in the back row. She was not wearing mourning. She had what looked like a good-natured face, though she did not smile. The man next to her was broad shouldered and looked tall and well formed and very handsome, though Anna had not seen him on his feet or full faced after that first brief glance he had given her.

And then there was the man from the hall – the one who was standing against the wall. Anna almost did not look directly at him, though she had been very aware of him from the moment he walked into the room. She looked at him at last simply because she would not give in to cowardice. As she had sensed, he was gazing steadily back, a jeweled snuffbox in one hand, a fine linen handkerchief in the other. Almost – oh, almost she looked away. But she did not do so. *Dignity,* she reminded herself. *He is no better than I.*

He was of barely average height and slight of build. She was surprised at that. He had seemed far larger when she first set eyes upon him. He was as elegant as the handsome gentleman in the back row, but while the other man was quietly immaculate, he was . . . not. There was something exquisite about the folds of his very white neck-cloth, about the close cut of his dark blue coat and the even closer fit of his gray pantaloons. There were silver tassels on his supple, shining boots, heavy rings on at least four of his fingers, which even from this distance she could see were perfectly manicured. There were chains and fobs at his waist, a silver stud in his neckcloth. His posture as he leaned against the wall was . . . graceful. His hair was fair – no, it was actually golden – and had been cut in such a way that it hugged his head neatly and yet seemed to wave softly about it at the same time, like a halo.

His face would have looked like that of an angel if it were not for his eyes. They were very blue, granted, but his eyelids drooped over them and gave him a slightly sleepy appearance. Except that he did not look sleepy at all but very keenly alert, and while Anna's eyes had roamed over him because she would not look away as she was sure he expected her to do, his had been roaming over her. Doubtless he was gaining a very different impression of her than she was of him.

He looked . . . beautiful. And graceful. And exquisite. And languid. They were all feminine qualities, yet he did not even for one moment give the impression of effeminacy. Quite the opposite, in fact. He looked a bit like an exotic wild animal, waiting to spring with perfectly timed grace and lethal intent upon its prey.

He looked dangerous.

All because he had regarded her as though she were a worm beneath his boot and had tried to get her cast out of the house?

No, she did not think it was just that.

But there was no time to ponder the matter further. Someone was coming through the door and passing her chair – Mr Brumford, the solicitor. She was about to discover why she was here.

So, she suspected, were all these people.

CHAPTER 4

Josiah Brumford spread his papers before him, laid his hands flat on top of them, and cleared his throat. If anyone had dropped a pin, Avery thought, everyone would have jumped a foot in the air even though there was carpet underfoot.

'Your Graces,' the solicitor began, inclining his head to Avery and the duchess. Fortunately, he did not then proceed to list all the other titles in the room. 'I thank you for your hospitality and for providing me with this opportunity to address those gathered here on a matter of considerable concern to all. My services were engaged a few weeks ago to search for a certain young lady with a view to making a monetary settlement upon her from the estate of the late Earl of Riverdale.'

'Mr Brumford!' the countess protested, her voice as cold as ice.

Avery raised his quizzing glass to observe the perspiration beaded upon the solicitor's brow.

'Bear with me for a few minutes, if you will, ma'am,' Brumford said. 'You requested that the matter be kept confidential, and wild horses would not have induced me to divulge this information

64

to anyone else but you and His Grace had not unexpected circumstances compelled me to call this meeting.'

Abigail had turned her head to look inquiringly at her mother beside her. Everyone else continued to face forward. Avery lowered his glass.

Brumford cleared his throat again. 'I sent my most experienced and trusted investigator to Bath,' he said, 'in order to find a young woman who had been left at an orphanage there more than twenty years ago and supported thereafter by the late Earl of Riverdale. Until his death, that is.'

The very woman who was now seated behind everyone else, beside the door, if Avery was not very much mistaken. He turned his head to look at her, but her eyes were fixed upon Brumford.

'It was not impossible to find her,' the solicitor continued, 'even though we did not know by what name she had been admitted to the institution or indeed which orphanage it was. Neither was it difficult to find the solicitor through whom the business of supporting her was conducted. Mr John Beresford is a lawyer of some distinction in Bath and has his offices close to the Abbey. He was not willing to talk to my man, for which I can only commend him, but knowing that his lordship was deceased and that Brumford, Brumford & Sons had represented him in all his other business dealings as well as his father and grandfather before him, he did agree to talk with me if I would go to Bath in person and show him ample proof of my identity. I went without hesitation or delay and was able to reassure Beresford that I had the young lady's best interests at heart in that his late lordship's widow, with the full concurrence of the Duke of Netherby, the present Riverdale's guardian, had commissioned me to find her and make a generous settlement upon her.'

If there was a long version of a story to be told, Brumford would invariably choose it, Avery thought. Camille had heard enough. Her back had stiffened and she spoke up.

'If you are about to disclose that this . . . *woman* for whom you searched was my father's—' But she could only inhale sharply rather than speak the word. 'You really ought to have followed your instructions and made this report privately to my mother and His Grace, Mr Brumford. Such sordid details are not for my sister's ears or mine or those of Lady Jessica Archer, who is not even out of the schoolroom yet. I wonder at your temerity, at your vulgarity. I wonder that His Grace—'

'Bear with me, ma'am, if you please,' Brumford said, holding up one hand, palm out. 'In a moment it will be clear why this must be said to all of those gathered here, painful as I am sure it is. Beresford informed me, with full documentation to put the truth of what he said beyond any doubt, that twenty-six years ago the recently deceased Earl of Riverdale, who bore the courtesy title of Viscount Yardley at the time, being his father's heir, but called himself merely Mr Humphrey

66

Westcott, married Miss Alice Snow in Bath by special license and settled her in rooms there. One year later, almost to the day, Lady Yardley, who appears to have known herself only as Mrs Westcott, was delivered of a daughter. When the child was a year or so old, however, she moved back to live with her parents, the Reverend Isaiah Snow and his wife, in a country vicarage several miles from Bristol, her health having broken down. She died there of consumption two years later. The Reverend Snow and his wife for undisclosed reasons found themselves unable to keep the child and raise her, and the girl's father, by then the Earl of Riverdale, removed her from the vicarage and delivered her to the orphanage in Bath, where she grew up and where she was still living, in the capacity of teacher at the orphanage school, until a few days ago.'

'Good God!' Harry had leapt to his feet and turned to stare behind him at the woman sitting close to the door. '*You?* You are our father's . . .? No, you are not his by-blow, are you? You are his legitimate daughter. Good God. You are my half sister. Good God.'

The dowager countess too had turned her head and raised a lorgnette to her eyes.

The woman herself looked back at Harry, apparently unmoved by what she had just heard. But Avery, observing her more closely through his quizzing glass, noted that her knuckles were whiter than they ought to be.

What she *was*, he thought, was Lady Anna Westcott, legitimate daughter of the late Earl of Riverdale. Interesting. Very interesting indeed. But Brumford had not finished.

'There is more, sir,' he said, addressing Harry and clearing his throat again, 'if you will be seated.'

Harry sat, turning his head slowly away from his newfound sibling. He was looking more pleased than outraged.

'I checked certain crucial facts and made a disturbing discovery,' Brumford continued. 'I had Beresford check them too, but I had not been mistaken. The dates on the relevant official documents showed to our shocked eyes – and you may believe me that we were very deeply shocked – that Humphrey Westcott, Viscount Yardley, married Miss Viola Kingsley at St George's Church here on Hanover Square four months and eleven days before the death of his first wife.'

Ah. All was suddenly clear.

Avery let his glass drop on its ribbon. A stunned silence fell upon the room. Brumford mopped his brow with a large handkerchief before continuing.

'The marriage of Lord Yardley to Miss Kingsley was bigamous and therefore invalid,' he said. 'It remained invalid after the death of his first wife. The children of that illicit union were – and are – illegitimate. The late Earl of Riverdale had only one legitimate child, Lady Anastasia Westcott.'

For a moment longer the silence resumed and held. Then someone wailed horribly – Jess

68

– and Avery pushed himself away from the wall. The dowager countess was on her feet, her lorgnette trained upon the woman by the door while Lady Matilda Westcott produced a vinaigrette from her reticule and tried to press it upon her mother while making bovine noises probably intended to be soothing. Elizabeth, Lady Overfield, spread both hands over her face and bowed her head forward until it almost touched her knees. Baron Molenor set an arm about Mildred's shoulders in an unprecedented display of public affection for his wife. The countess too was on her feet and turning to look back, her face drained of color. The duchess, also out of her chair, Jess clutched to her bosom, was promising to call down fire and brimstone upon Brumford's head and to have him disbarred for incompetence and other assorted crimes and cast into some deep, dark dungeon. Abigail had buried her face against her brother's shoulder and got to her feet when he did. Camille was loudly declaring that such vulgarity was *not* for the ears of delicately reared ladies and she would listen to no more of it. Alexander Westcott was sitting rigidly to attention and gazing at an ashen-faced Harry. His mother was clutching Alexander's arm.

Lady Anastasia Westcott, alias Anna Snow, sat straight-backed on her chair, her hands clasped in her lap – without his quizzing glass Avery could not see if they were still white-knuckled – and looked calmly back at them all. Perhaps, Avery thought, she was in shock.

He strolled forward and set a hand on his stepmother's shoulder. He squeezed slightly while smoothing the other hand over Jessica's head. 'A lawyer,' he said, 'cannot be disbarred or imprisoned or cast into hell merely for telling the truth.' Unfortunately.

He had not raised his voice. Yet it seemed everyone had heard him, including his stepmother, who stopped talking and closed her mouth with a clacking of teeth. Everyone looked at him – the dowager through her lorgnette while she batted away her daughter's hand and the vinaigrette. There was expectation on almost every face, just as there had been earlier when he walked into the room, as though they expected him to wave some magic wand – his quizzing glass, perhaps? – and set their world to rights again. But ducal powers were, alas, finite.

'I believe,' he said, 'Brumford has more to say.'

Miraculously everyone who was standing sat down again, Molenor removed his arm from about his wife, and there was silence once more. The solicitor looked as though he wished he had been disbarred years ago, or had never been barred, if that was indeed the opposite of *disbarred*. He must ask Edwin Goddard, Avery thought. He would know.

'The late Earl of Riverdale's nearest legitimate paternal male relative and therefore the rightful successor to his title and entailed properties is Mr Alexander Westcott,' Brumford said. 'Congratulations, my lord. All his unentailed properties and all of his fortune, according to the will he made at Beresford's office in Bath twenty-five years ago, now belong to his only daughter, Lady Anastasia Westcott, who is here present, having been fetched from Bath.'

The countess rose again and turned, a look of strangely mingled blankness and resentment on her face. 'And this is all my doing,' she said, addressing the woman who was Lady Anastasia Westcott, sole legitimate daughter of the late earl. 'I thought to do you a kindness. Instead, I have disinherited my own son and shamed and beggared my daughters.' She laughed, but there was no amusement in the sound.

'Harry is no longer the earl?' Abigail asked of no one in particular, her hands creeping up to cover her mouth, her eyes huge with shock.

'But I have no wish to be the Earl of Riverdale,' Alexander Westcott protested, getting to his feet and frowning ferociously at Brumford. 'I have never coveted the title. I certainly have no wish to benefit from Harry's misfortune.'

'Alex.' His mother rested a hand on his arm again.

'*You,*' Camille said, rising to her feet and pointing an accusing finger at Lady Anastasia. 'You conniving, scheming . . . *creature.* How dare you sit here with your betters. How dare you come here at all. The Duke of Netherby ought to have had you tossed out. You are nothing but a vulgar, ruthless, fortune-hunting *b-b-bastard.*'

'Camille.' Lady Molenor rose and reached across the chair in front of her to try to draw her niece into her arms. But Camille pushed them away and took a step back.

'But it is we, Cam, who are the bastards,' said Abigail, as ashen faced as her mother.

There was a beat of shocked silence before Avery's sister Jessica wailed again over the horrible blow that had just been dealt her favorite cousins and launched herself once more at her mother's bosom.

Harry laughed. 'By Jove,' he said, 'and so we are, Abby. We have been disinherited. Just like that.' He snapped a finger and thumb together. 'What a lark.'

'Humphrey was always trouble,' the dowager countess said. 'No, Matilda, I do not need smelling salts. I have always maintained that he worried his father into an early grave.'

Another voice spoke, soft and low pitched, and silenced them all, even Jess. It was the voice of a schoolteacher accustomed to drawing attention to herself.

'I am Anna Snow,' the voice said. 'I do not recognize the other person you say I am, sir. If I am indeed the legitimate daughter of a father and mother I now know by name for the first time, then I thank you for disclosing those facts. And if I have indeed inherited something from my father, I am pleased. But I have no desire to take more than my fair share, however much or little the whole might be. If I have understood you correctly, the young man in front of you and the young ladies on either side of him are also the children of my father. They are my brother and sisters.'

'How dare you! Oh, how dare you!' Camille looked as if she were about to burst with outrage.

Harry laughed again, a little wildly, and Abigail clutched his arm.

'Miss Westcott,' Brumford said. 'Perhaps—'

But Camille, realizing suddenly that he was addressing her, whipped about and turned her outrage on him. 'I am Lady Camille Westcott to you,' she said. 'How dare you!'

'But you are not, Cam, are you?' Harry said. He was still laughing. 'I am not even sure we are entitled to the name Westcott. Mama certainly is not, is she? What an absolute lark.'

'Harold!' his aunt Matilda said. 'Remember that you are in the presence of your grandmother.'

'Brothers! Oh, I could murder Humphrey,' the duchess said. 'I am only sorry he is already dead.'

'You would have to stand in line behind me, Louise,' Lady Molenor said. 'He was always a toad. I was never fond of him even if he was my own brother. I would not have said that in your hearing before today, Viola, or in yours, Mama, but now I will not hold back.'

'My love.' Molenor patted her hand.

Avery sighed. 'Let us retire to the drawing room to imbibe tea or whatever other beverage takes anyone's fancy,' he said. 'I find myself having had a surfeit of rose pink for one morning, and I daresay I am not the only one. It is too much like seeing red. Brumford doubtless has an office and other clients awaiting him and may be excused for the present. Her Grace will lead the way. I shall follow with Lady Anastasia.'

But Lady Anastasia Westcott had risen to her feet at last and was buttoning her cloak at the neck. Her bonnet and gloves and reticule were upon the seat of her chair. 'I shall return to Bath, sir,' she said as Brumford drew level with her on his way out. 'I have duties awaiting me there. Perhaps you would direct me to the stagecoach stop and lend me the money for a ticket if what I have with me is not enough. Or perhaps there is enough in my portion of the inheritance from my father to make a loan unnecessary.'

She drew on her bonnet and tied the ribbons beneath her chin while addressing the rest of the room. 'No one need worry that I will impose myself further upon a family that clearly does not want me. My father did none of us a good turn, but I cannot apologize for the devastating effects this morning's disclosures are having upon his other family any more than any of you can apologize to me for a near lifetime spent in an orphanage, not even knowing that Snow was not my legal name or Anna my full first name.'

They all watched her as they would a riveting performance onstage. She was just a little slip of a thing, Avery thought, and quite unappealing in her cheap, dreary garments and severe hairstyle, which had all but disappeared beneath her bonnet. Yet there was something rather magnificent about her, by Jove. She did not appear either upset or discomposed, though she had described them all as a family that clearly did not want her. She was like an alien creature to the world in which she had found herself this morning, and the world to which she belonged by right. She had just wondered if there was enough money in the fortune she had inherited to pay for a stagecoach ticket to Bath. She clearly had no idea she could probably buy every stagecoach in the country and all the horses that went with them without putting so much as a dent in her inheritance.

She followed Brumford from the room, and no one made any move to stop her. Everyone filed upstairs in an unnatural silence. Avery found the solicitor and the heiress still in the hall when he emerged last from the room.

'There is a great deal of business to be discussed, my lady,' Brumford was saying, rubbing his hands together. 'It would be altogether more convenient if you were to remain in London. I took the liberty of reserving you a suite of rooms at the Pulteney for an indefinite period as well as the services of Miss Knox as chaperone. The carriage is at the door. I will be happy to send you back there if you do not wish to go up to the drawing room with the Duke of Netherby.'

She looked consideringly at Avery. 'No,' she said.

'I need to be alone, and I believe the other people who were here this morning need to be able to talk freely without the encumbrance of my presence. I can walk back to the hotel, though, sir. I am far more accustomed to walking than to riding in a carriage.'

An alien creature, indeed.

Brumford made a suitably horrified response, and Avery strolled past them and outside, to where a carriage did indeed wait, complete with a large, hatchet-faced woman inside, who looked more like a prison guard than a chaperone. Brumford stood back with much bowing and scraping as Avery offered his hand to help Lady Anastasia in. She ignored it and entered unassisted. Perhaps she had not seen it – or him. She sat beside the chaperone and gazed forward.

Avery reentered the house and proceeded upstairs to the drawing room and the Westcott family, minus its newfound member – its wealthiest member.

Even he could not complain that this morning had been a crashing bore.

CHAPTER 5

Dear Joel,

Do you remember how Miss Rutledge's too-oft-uttered repertoire of wise sayings used to make us groan and cross our eyes at each other? One we always particularly hated was 'Beware what you wish for – your wish may be granted.' It seemed so cruel, did it not, when our dreams were so very precious to us? But she was right!

I have wished and wished all my life, just as you have and almost all the other children with whom we grew up and whom we teach now, that I knew who I was, that I could discover that I came of distinguished parents, and that I would be taken at last to the bosom of my rightful family and be showered with riches, not necessarily all of them monetary. Oh, Joel, my dream came true today, except that it seems more like a nightmare at this precise moment.

I am writing to you from my private sitting room at the Pulteney Hotel – I do believe it is one of the grandest London has to offer. It seems like a palace to me.

Were you told about Miss Knox, the chaperone appointed me for my journey? I daresay you were, and by more than one person. She is still with me. She has withdrawn to her own bedchamber, though she has left the door ajar between the two rooms, presumably so that she may feel she is keeping proper guard over me and is doing the job for which she was hired. She is a very silent person. Today, though, I am thankful for that fact.

This morning I was taken to a vast mansion on a regal square with a park at the center of it in surely the most exclusive part of London. As soon as I set foot inside the door, I was promptly ordered by the most frightening man I have ever seen to leave again – he turned out to be the owner of the house and A DUKE!

But after it was established that I really was in the right place, I was shown into a room where thirteen other people waited. One of them – she turned out to be A DUCHESS – instructed the very superior butler to remove me, but again it was confirmed that I was supposed to be there.

No one actually spoke to me or to one another after I had arrived, though it was quite clear they were all outraged. So much for my best Sunday dress and my best shoes! In addition to the duke (who came into the room after I did) and the duchess, who must be his mother rather than his wife, I believe, the young Earl of Riverdell or Riverdale – I am not sure which – was there with his mother and his two sisters. There was also a very young lady all in white and five other ladies and two gentlemen, of whose identities I am not perfectly sure.

Joel, oh, Joel, I must rush ahead with my narrative here. The young earl and his sisters are MY BROTHER AND SISTERS. Oh, I know, Miss Rutledge would have frowned her disapproval of those capital letters and the ones I used earlier. She would have said they are the written equivalent of a rudely raised voice. But, Joel, they are my half siblings! (Miss R was not overfond of exclamation marks either, was she?) Their father, the Earl of Riverwhatever, was also MY father. You see? I cannot help but rudely raise my voice again. Moreover – oh, moreover, Joel – my father was married to my mother, who was Alice Snow before she married him. My real name, though I am not at all sure I shall ever be able to bring myself to use it since it does not sound at all like me, is Anastasia Westcott, or more accurately LADY Anastasia Westcott. My mother, who had left my father and taken me to live with her at a vicarage somewhere near Bristol – the vicar was her father, my grandfather – died when I was still an infant, and my father died just recently. I narrowly missed knowing him, though I suppose that was by his choice. After my mother's death he took me to the orphanage in Bath and left me there.

Why, you may well ask, when I was his legitimate daughter and a lady? Well, partly, perhaps, it was because he had been estranged from my mother for a few years while her health declined. And partly – no, MAINLY, Joel – it was because a few months before her death he married the lady who was in the room there today as his widow, the countess – I believe an earl's wife is a countess, is she not, though I am not absolutely certain. And he proceeded to have three children with her – the son and two daughters I mentioned above.

Can you guess what is coming? I daresay you can since you certainly do not lack for wits and it would not take much intelligence anyway to understand. That second marriage was bigamous. It was not a legal, valid marriage, and all children of the union are therefore illegitimate. The countess, who has recently lost the man she thought to be her husband – my father! – is not the countess after all and never was. And the very young man, her son, is not the earl. Her daughters

80

are not Lady So-and-So. I must have heard their names but foolishly cannot remember them – my own sisters! I believe the young man is Harry. I am, in fact, my father's only legitimate child.

Today I found the family for which I have always longed – my half brother and half sisters – and today I lost them again in the most cruel fashion. Can you just imagine the bewilderment and anguish in that room, Joel, when the truth was revealed? And since every sufferer needs a scapegoat, someone to blame, and my father, the real culprit, was no longer available, then of course all their hostility was turned upon me. The man who has now become the earl since my half brother does not qualify might have been their choice as scapegoat, but he was wise enough to declare himself quite averse to his change in status, though to do him justice I believe he meant it.

It did not occur to me to declare that I would really rather not be my father's only legal child, though I did protest having been left the whole of his fortune while my brother and sisters have been totally disinherited. Oh yes, there is that too. Some parts of my father's property were entailed and go to the new earl. Other parts are not entailed and come to me because my father's only will was made just after my birth and left everything to me – and presumably to my mother if she had lived.

How could my father have behaved as he did, Joel? I do not suppose I will ever know the answer, though one lady there today said that he had always been a toad. I think she may have been his sister and therefore my aunt. Oh, how very dizzying this all is. I have not fully comprehended it yet. Can you tell? And can you blame me?

This is turning into a very long missive, but I had to write to someone or burst. And you were my obvious choice. What are best friends for, after all, but to burden with all one's woes? Some people would not call them woes, would they? I have no idea how much I am now worth, but it must be something, do you not think, or the word fortune would not have been used. I hope it will be enough, anyway, to allow me to send this very long letter. It will cost the earth.

I hope you do not become horribly bored and fall asleep in the middle of it. And surely there will be enough to get me back to Bath in a little more comfort than the stagecoach is said to provide. Perhaps there will be enough to enable me to take some modest rooms outside the orphanage and thus acquire more independence. How lovely that would be!

But oh dear, I do feel bruised and battered.

For I have found my parents and they are dead, and I have found a family that is mine – I do believe most of the people there in that room, if not all, must be related to me in some way – but they hate me with a passion. The elder sister – my half sister – in particular yelled the most horrible things at me. The boy – my half brother – could only seem to laugh and look dazed and talk about it all being a lark, poor thing. Oh, poor thing, Joel, and he is my BROTHER! The younger sister looked dazed and bewildered. And the dispossessed wife wrapped herself in dignity and looked like a stone monument about to crumble. I fear she will indeed crumble when the reality of it all hits full force.

My fingers are sore, my wrist is aching, and my arm is about to fall off. Mr Brumford sent me back here even though I wanted to return to Bath without further delay. He convinced me to stay until he has had a chance to come and talk business with me. I expect him any moment.

I will come home soon, though. Oh, how I long for my schoolroom and my children, even the naughty ones. How I long for you and Miss Ford and Roger and – oh, and my little room in which I would not be able to swing a cat even if I had one – another of Miss Rutledge's sayings. Maybe I will come tomorrow. Almost certainly I will come no later than the day after.

Meanwhile, you have my permission to share the contents of this letter if you wish – everyone will be longing to know why I was summoned here and will be vastly entertained by my story. You will be the most popular man in Bath.

Thank you for reading so patiently, my dearest friend – I trust you have read this far! What would I do without you?

Your ever grateful and affectionate
Anna Snow (for that is who I am!)

Anna blotted the final sheet of the letter, folded it neatly – it was indeed fat – and sank back in her chair, exhausted. She had had luncheon with Miss Knox soon after her return from that mansion, though she could not remember either what had been served or how much she had eaten. All she wanted to do now was crawl into the large bed in the bedchamber that was hers, pull the bedcovers over her head, curl up into a ball, and sleep for a week.

But there was a knock upon the door, and she sighed and got to her feet while Miss Knox strode past her to open it.

When Avery entered the drawing room, he found it much as he had expected. It was full of variously

84

distraught Westcotts – with the apparent exception of the Countess of Riverdale, who was no longer the countess and actually never had been, and Camille and Abigail, who were sitting in a row on the sofa, silent and motionless.

The dowager countess was seated on an adjacent love seat, her eldest daughter beside her.

'Do not *fuss*, Matilda,' she was saying in obvious exasperation. 'I am not about to swoon.'

'But, Mama,' Lady Matilda protested with an inelegant hiccup of a sob. 'You have had a severe shock. We all have. And you know what the physician said about your heart.'

'The man is a quack,' her mother said. 'I do not have heart palpitations; I have a heart*beat*, which I have always thought a good thing, though today I am not so sure of it.'

'Swallow this down, Mother-in-Law,' Molenor said as he approached from the sideboard with a glass of brandy.

Mildred, Lady Molenor, looked as though she needed it more. She was seated beside her sister, the duchess, her head thrown back, her handkerchief spread over her face and held there with both hands, while she informed anyone who cared to listen that the late Humphrey had been every nasty beast and insect the world has ever produced, and that was actually an insult to the bestial and insect kingdoms. The duchess was patting her knee but showing no inclination to contradict her. She was looking like thunder.

Mrs Westcott – Cousin Althea – was hovering behind the sofa, gazing down in obvious concern at the backs of the heads of the three seated there and assuring them that all would be well, that everything always turned out for the best in the end. For a sensible woman – and Avery had always considered her sensible – she was talking a pile of rubbish. But what else was there to say?

Alexander Westcott – the new Earl of Riverdale – was standing with his back to the fireplace, his hands clasped behind him, looking elegant and commanding, though his face was a bit waxy. His sister, standing a few feet away from him, was telling him that it was impossible, he could not refuse the title, and even if he could, it would not revert to Harry.

Of Harry himself there was no sign.

'Harry would not stay,' Jessica announced in tragic accents just as Avery was noticing his absence. She was standing in front of the sofa, literally wringing her hands and the thin handkerchief clutched in them and looking like a youthful Lady Macbeth. 'He laughed and then ran away down the servants' stairs. Why would he laugh? Avery, it cannot be true. Tell everyone it is not. Harry cannot have been stripped of his title.'

'Jessica,' her mother said firmly but not unkindly, 'come and sit quietly here beside me. Otherwise you must return to the schoolroom.'

Jessica sat, but she did not stop twisting her hands and pulling at the handkerchief.

'I certainly wish it were not true, Jessica,' the new earl said. 'I would give a great deal to find that it was not. But it is. I would return the title to Harry in a heartbeat if it were possible, but it is not.'

And the devil of it was, Avery thought as he strolled farther into the room, that he meant it. He was genuinely upset for Harry's sake and just as genuinely without ambition for himself. It was actually difficult to find a good reason to dislike and despise the man – an irritating realization. Perhaps perfection was inevitably irritating to those who were themselves imperfect.

The three on the sofa looked rather as if they had been bashed hard on the head but not quite hard enough to render them unconscious. Cousin Althea had stopped talking in order to listen to her son.

'Has that dreadful woman gone back to Bath where she belongs?' Camille asked Avery. 'I wonder she did not come up here with you to gloat over us.'

'Cam.' Her mother laid a hand over hers.

'Oh, how she must be rubbing her hands in glee,' Camille said bitterly.

'I thought her the most vulgar of creatures,' Lady Matilda said. 'I wonder that Avery allowed her inside the house.'

'She is my granddaughter,' the dowager said, handing the empty brandy glass back to Molenor. 'If she is a vulgar creature, it is Humphrey's fault.'

'Whatever are we going to do, Mama?' Abigail asked. 'Everything is going to change, is it not? For us as well as for Harry.'

That was probably the understatement of the decade.

'Yes,' her mother said, laying her free hand over Abigail's. 'Everything is going to change, Abby. But pardon me, my mind is rather numb at the moment.'

'You will all come to live with Matilda and me, Viola,' the dowager announced. 'The only good thing Humphrey did in his life was to marry you, and he could not even get that right. You are more my daughter than he was ever my son.'

'You can come here to live, if you would prefer,' the duchess said. 'Avery will not mind.'

'Abby is coming *here* to live?' Jessica brightened noticeably. 'And Harry? And Camille and Aunt Viola?'

Would he mind? Avery wondered.

'Uxbury is to call at Westcott House this afternoon,' Camille said. 'We must not be late returning home, Mama. I shall put off my mourning before receiving him, and I shall inform him that we no longer need wait until next year to celebrate our nuptials. He will be delighted to hear it. I shall suggest a quiet wedding, perhaps by special license so that we will not have to wait a full month for the banns to be read. Once I am married, it will not matter that I am no longer Lady Camille Westcott. I shall be Lady Uxbury instead, and

Abby and Mama may come and live with us. Abby may be presented next year, even perhaps this year, under my sponsorship. She will be the sister of the Viscountess Uxbury. You are quite right, Cousin Althea. All will turn out well in the end.'

'But what about Harry?' Abigail asked.

Camille's forthright, almost cheerful manner visibly crumbled, and she bit her upper lip in an obvious effort to fight back tears. Her mother clasped both sisters' hands more tightly.

'I could kill my brother,' the duchess said. 'Oh, how dare he die when he did and escape retribution. How dare he not be alive now at this very moment to face my wrath. Whatever was he *thinking*? I had never even heard of this Alice Snow woman before today. Had any of you? Mildred? Matilda? Mama?'

None of them confessed to any knowledge of the late Humphrey's first wife – his only wife, actually. Lady Molenor, Cousin Mildred, wailed briefly into her handkerchief.

'But he was *married* to her and had a *daughter* with her,' the duchess continued, sawing the air with the hand that was not patting her sister's knee and almost elbowing Jess in the eye. 'And then he abandoned her and married Viola as though that first marriage could just be ignored when it was no longer convenient to him. Of course, it was common knowledge that he never had a feather to fly with while Papa still lived, but was as wild and expensive as sin. We all knew that the last time Papa paid off his mountain of debts, he also told Humphrey never again to expect one penny more than his quarterly allowance, which was a great deal more than the pin money we girls had to be content with, let me tell you. I suppose he was in desperate straits by the time Mama and Papa chose a bride for him and married her in order to get the funds flowing again. I suppose he assumed no one would ever find out about his dying wife and their daughter – and no one ever did during his lifetime. I could kill him.'

'That daughter is my granddaughter,' the dowager said as though to herself, spreading her hands on her lap and examining the rings on her fingers.

Lady Matilda still hovered with the vinaigrette.

Jess was sobbing into the thin confection of a handkerchief she had twisted almost beyond recognition, and Avery toyed with the idea of sending her off to the care of her governess. But a chapter in her family history was being written here today – no doubt it would be a starred chapter – and he supposed it was wiser to allow her to experience it for herself in all its raw emotion. Besides, he rarely imposed his authority upon her, partly because he assiduously avoided exerting himself unnecessarily, but mainly because she had a mother who was reasonably sensible most of the time. And who could blame her today for wanting to murder a dead man? He was not feeling kindly disposed toward the late Earl of Riverdale himself and was selfishly glad he was not related by any tie of blood.

Bigamy was not, after all, a mild offense that could be attributed to wild oats.

'I had never heard of that woman either until today, Louise,' the former countess said, 'though I did know of the girl Riverdale was keeping at an orphanage in Bath. I assumed, quite wrongly, that she was his natural daughter by a former mistress. I even felt a grudging sort of respect for him for taking financial responsibility for her. I wonder if the truth would ever have come out if I had not commissioned Mr Brumford to find her and make a settlement upon her. It was not out of the goodness of my heart that I did it, I must add, but because I did not want her making any future claim upon Harry. I had hoped he and Cam and Abby need never know of their father's indiscretion.'

She laughed without humor and patted her daughters' hands briskly before continuing.

'Your idea is a good one, Cam,' she said. 'We will all cast off our mourning today. What an enormous relief that will be. We will wait and see what you arrange with Lord Uxbury this afternoon and move to a hotel if the wedding is to be within the next few days. Thank you all for the offers of hospitality, but it really would not be appropriate for us to stay with any of you. If the wait for the wedding is to be longer than a few days – Uxbury may well insist upon having banns called – then we will remove to the country and supervise the packing up of all our personal belongings while we wait. Either way we have a busy time ahead of us and must waste no more of it sitting here.'

'Pack our belongings?' Abigail looked bewildered.

'But of course,' her mother said. 'Neither Westcott House in town here nor Hinsford Manor in Hampshire belongs to Harry any longer. They belong to . . . her.'

'But where will you and I go after the wedding?' Abigail asked. 'I do not believe Lord Uxbury would like it if we imposed ourselves upon him permanently no matter what Cam says.'

'I do not *know* where we will go, Abby,' her mother said irritably, showing the first crack in her composure. 'I shall take you to your grand-mother – my mama – in Bath, I suppose. She will surely be happy to give you a home despite the disgrace, for which you are not even the slightest bit at fault. She adores you and Cam.'

'And you, Viola?' the duchess asked sharply.

'I do not know, Louise.' The countess flashed her a ghastly smile. 'I am Miss Kingsley again, you know. It would not do for me as a single lady to remain in Bath *with my daughter*. It would not be fair to my mother, and it would be potentially disastrous for any hope Abby may have of making some sort of eligible connection. I shall probably go to my brother. Michael is a clergyman in more than just name, and he has been lonely, I believe, since the death of my sister-in-law last year.

We have always been fond of each other. I shall stay with him, at least for a while, until I decide upon something more permanent.'

No, Avery decided, this was definitely not a morning of boredom. His stepmother, he noticed, had not even remembered to send for the tea tray.

'But what about Harry?' Abigail asked again.

'I do not *know*, Abby,' her mother said. 'He must find some suitable employment, I suppose. Perhaps Avery will help him, though he is no longer bound by the guardianship his father agreed to.'

All eyes turned Avery's way as though he had the answer to every question at the tip of his tongue. He raised his eyebrows. He was not in the habit of helping impecunious young men to find employment, especially wild young men who had been in possession of a seemingly bottomless coffer of funds until an hour or so ago and had been making profligate use of it. He fingered the handle of his quizzing glass, abandoned it, and sighed.

'Harry must be granted a day or two to stop laughing and telling everyone who will listen what a lark all this is,' he said.

'Oh, *Avery!*' Jessica blurted. 'How *can* you make light of such a tragedy?'

He leveled a look upon her that closed her mouth and set her to huddling against her mother's side, though she continued to glower at him.

'I am granting him a day or two,' he repeated softly. 'For his laughter does not derive from amusement, and when he describes the morning's disclosures as a *lark* he does not mean something that is fun.'

'Avery will look after him, Jess,' Abigail said, her eyes fixed upon him.

'Lady Anastasia seemed perfectly willing to share her fortune,' Cousin Elizabeth reminded them all. 'Perhaps Harry will not need to take employment. Perhaps he—'

'I will not touch one penny of what that woman offers out of condescending charity, Elizabeth,' Camille said, cutting her off. 'Neither, I trust, will Abby. Or Harry. How dare she even suggest it – as though she were doing us some grand favor.'

Which, in Avery's estimation, was precisely what she would be doing if more sober consideration did not cause her to retract her offer.

'She is my granddaughter,' the dowager said.

'*Is* she returning to Bath, Avery?' Abigail asked.

'Brumford persuaded her to remain at least for the present at the Pulteney, where she apparently stayed last night,' he said. 'He is to spend the afternoon there with her and her chaperone, doubtless boring her into a coma.'

'Poor lady,' Cousin Elizabeth said. 'Her life has just changed drastically too.'

'I would not describe her as *poor* in any way, Elizabeth,' Thomas, Lord Molenor, said dryly.

'Her education as Lady Anastasia Westcott must begin without delay,' the dowager said, and everyone looked at her.

'After today,' Camille said, a world of bitterness in her voice as she got to her feet, 'she will be able to move out of the Pulteney and into Westcott House, Grandmama. She will be thrilled about that.'

'Cam,' her mother said after heaving a sigh, 'none of this is her fault. We need to remember that. Just think of the fact that she has spent all but the first few years of her life in an orphanage.'

'I cannot think of anything else but that,' the dowager said. 'It is not going to be easy to—'

'I do not *care* where she has lived or how difficult it will be to bring her up to snuff,' Camille cried, rudely interrupting. 'I hate her. With a passion. Do not ever ask me to pity her.'

'I am sorry, Grandmama,' Abigail said, getting up to stand by her sister. 'Cam is upset. She will feel better after she has had a talk with Lord Uxbury.'

'Abby and Cam are not going to be staying here with us after all?' Jessica asked, teary eyed.

'Harry will stay here, I daresay,' the duchess said, 'after Avery has found him. You must not worry about him, Viola.'

'My mind is too numb to feel worry,' the former countess said. 'I suppose he is out getting drunk. I wish I were with him, doing the same thing.'

'Mama,' Jessica blurted, 'promise me that woman will never, ever be allowed inside this house again. Promise me I will never see her again. I may well scratch her eyes out if I do. She is *ugly* and *stupid* and she looks worse than a *servant* and I *hate* her. I want everything to be back as it was. I want H-Harry back as the earl and laughing because he is h-happy, not because he is s-sad and can never be h-h-happy again. I want Abby to be my proper cousin again and still living close by. I want – I hate this. I *hate* it. And why is Avery not out looking for Harry and fetching him home?'

Avery dropped his glass on its ribbon, sighing inwardly, and opened his arms. She glared at him for one moment, then scrambled to her feet and dashed into his arms and buried herself against him. She would have climbed right inside if she could, he thought. She wept noisily and inelegantly against his shoulder, and he closed one arm about her and spread the other hand over the back of her head.

'Do s-s-something,' she cried. '*Do* something.'

'Hush,' he murmured against her ear. 'Hush, love. Life is full of clouds. But clouds are lined with gold. You just have to wait for the sun to come out again. It will. It always does.'

Asinine words. He sounded worse than Cousin Althea had a few minutes ago. Where the devil did such drivel come from?

'Promise?' she said. 'P-promise?'

'Yes, I promise,' he said, removing his hand from her head in order to fish out a large handker-chief from his pocket. Since women were always the ones who wept buckets of tears, it seemed illogical that they were also the ones who carried handkerchiefs so thin and dainty they were invariably sodden within moments of a cloudburst. 'A cool glass of lemonade in the schoolroom will be just the thing for you, Jess. No, don't protest. It was not a question.'

Her mother thanked him with her eyes as he led his half sister from the room, one arm about her waist.

He wondered what Lady Anastasia Westcott was doing at this precise moment and whether she had any idea at all of what was facing her – apart from a life of ease as a very wealthy woman, that is.

And he wondered where exactly Harry was. It would not be difficult, though, to find him later and keep an eye on him. He would be in one of his usual haunts, no doubt. And in one of those haunts he must be allowed to remain until he had stopped laughing.

Poor devil.

CHAPTER 6

Mr Brumford handed Anna down from the carriage outside Westcott House early in the afternoon of the following day, and Miss Knox climbed down behind her, unassisted. Anna, looking both ways along South Audley Street and up at the house before her, saw that it was not quite as imposing as the mansion she had been taken to yesterday. Even so, everything here had been built on a lavish scale, and she felt dwarfed.

She owned the house.

She also owned a manor and park and farmland in Hampshire and a fortune so vast that her mind could not grasp the full extent of it. Her father had inherited part of the fortune from his father, but he had become unexpectedly shrewd in his later years and had doubled and then tripled it with investments in commerce and industry. The investments were still working to her advantage.

The knowledge of her wealth had actually made Anna feel quite bilious and even more desirous of going home to Bath and pretending none of this had happened. But it *had* happened, and she had reluctantly agreed to stay at least a few more days to consult at more length with her solicitor, for that was what Mr Brumford had called himself – not just her father's solicitor, but *hers*. Her mind was all bewilderment. She had to stay at least until everything was clear in her head and she under-stood better what it was all going to mean to her. Her life, she suspected, was going to change whether she wished it or not.

This morning Mr Brumford had sent a message that he would accompany her when she arrived at Westcott House and again encountered her family. If they were to meet her at the house, did it mean her half brother and half sisters had recovered somewhat from their shock, and were prepared to welcome her, or at least to converse with her in a more amiable manner? But what about their mother, poor lady? Oh, this was not going to be easy.

The door opened even as she set her foot on the bottom step, and a manservant dressed all in black bowed and stood aside to allow her to enter. The hall was rich wood and high ceiling and marble floor with a wide, elegant wooden staircase – was it oak? – rising at the back of it to fan out to either side halfway up and double back upon itself.

A lady was descending the stairs – the one who had sat at one end of the second row yesterday, the duchess. Anna recalled that she had declared she would kill her brother if only he were still alive. *Her brother* – Anna's father. This lady, then, was her aunt? Behind her, descending at a more leisurely pace, came the man who had stood throughout the proceedings yesterday, the one she had thought both beautiful and dangerous.

He still looked both today.

The duchess swept toward her, looking regal and intimidating. 'Anastasia,' she said, sweeping Anna from head to foot with a glance as she came closer. 'Welcome to your home. I am your aunt Louise, your late father's middle sister and the Duchess of Netherby. Netherby, my stepson, is no direct relative of yours.' She indicated the man behind her. She completely ignored Mr Brumford and Miss Knox.

'How do you do, ma'am,' Anna said. 'How do you do, sir.'

The Duke of Netherby was dressed in a combination of browns and creams today. He was holding a gold-handled quizzing glass in one hand, upon the fingers of which there were two rings, one of plain gold, the other of gold inlaid with a large topaz stone. He was regarding her, as he had yesterday, from beneath slightly drooped eyelids with eyes that really were as blue as she remembered them. He had a lithe-looking figure and was no more than two or three inches taller than she.

'That ought to be *Your Grace* and *Your Grace*,' he said. He spoke with a light voice on what sounded like a sigh. 'We aristocrats can be very touchy about the way we are addressed. However, since we have a sort of step-relationship with each other, you may call me Avery.' He turned his languid gaze upon Mr Brumford and Miss Knox. 'You may both leave. You will be sent for if you are needed.'

Anna turned. 'Thank you, Mr Brumford,' she said. 'Thank you, Miss Knox.'

The lazy blue eyes held perhaps a gleam of mocking amusement when she turned back.

'We will go up to the drawing room, where your family is waiting to meet you,' the duchess, her aunt, said. 'There is so much to be discussed that one scarcely knows where to begin, but begin we must. Lifford, take Lady Anastasia's cloak and bonnet.'

A few moments later Anna walked beside her up the stairs while the duke came behind. They turned up the left branch from the half landing and at the top entered a large chamber that must overlook the street and was bright with afternoon sunlight. The fact that all this was hers would perhaps have taken Anna's breath away if the people gathered in the room had not done it first. All of them had been present yesterday, and all of them were now silent – again – and turned to watch her.

The duchess undertook to make the introductions. 'Anastasia,' she said, indicating first the elderly lady who was seated beside the fireplace, 'this is the Dowager Countess of Riverdale, your grandmother. She is your father's mother, as I am your father's sister. Beside her is Lady Matilda

Westcott, my elder sister, your aunt.' She indicated another couple farther back in the room, the woman seated, the man standing behind her chair. 'Lord and Lady Molenor – your uncle Thomas and aunt Mildred, my younger sister. They have three boys, your cousins, but they are all at school. And standing over by the window are the Earl of Riverdale, Alexander, your second cousin, with his mother, Mrs Westcott, Cousin Althea, and his sister, Lady Overfield, Cousin Elizabeth.'

It was all too dizzying and too much to be comprehended. All these people, all these aristocrats, were her *relatives*. But the only thing her mind could grasp clearly was that the people she most wished to see were not there.

'But where are my sisters and brother,' she asked, 'and their mother?'

Everyone within her line of vision looked identically shocked.

'Oh, you will not be embarrassed by their presence, Anastasia,' the duchess assured her. 'Viola left for the country this morning with Camille and Abigail – for Hinsford Manor, your home in Hampshire, that is. They will not remain there longer than a few days, however. Viola will take her daughters to Bath to live with her mother, their grandmother, and she herself will take up residence with her brother in Dorset. He is a clergyman and a widower. He and Viola have always been dearly fond of each other.'

'They have *gone*?' Anna felt suddenly cold despite

the sunshine. 'But I had hoped to meet them here. I had hoped to get to know them. I had hoped they would get to know me. I had hoped . . . they would . . . wish it.'

She felt very foolish in the brief silence that followed. How could she have expected any such thing? Her very existence had ended the world as they knew it yesterday.

'And the young man, my half brother?' she asked.

'Harry has disappeared,' the duchess told her, 'and Avery refuses to search for him until tomorrow, assuming he has not returned of his own volition by then. You need not worry about him, however. Avery will see to his future. He was Harry's appointed guardian when he was still the Earl of Riverdale.'

'It is my understanding,' the duke said, 'that I inherited the guardianship of Harry himself from my late esteemed father, not just that of the Earl of Riverdale. I would rather dislike finding myself with Cousin Alexander as a ward. I daresay he would like it even less.'

'Oh, yes, he would indeed, Avery,' the new earl's mother said. The Duke of Netherby was by now sprawled with casual elegance in a chair in a far corner of the room, Anna saw, his elbows on the arms, his fingers steepled. Miss Rutledge would have told him to sit up straight with his feet together and flat on the floor.

'Come and stand here, Anastasia,' the dowager

countess, her grandmother, said, indicating the floor in front of her chair, 'and let me have a good look at you.'

Anna came and stood while everyone, it seemed, had a good look at her. The silence seemed several minutes long, though it probably lasted no longer than half a minute at most.

'You have good deportment, at least,' the dowager said at last, 'and you speak without any discernible regional accent. You look, however, like a particularly lowly governess.'

'I am lower even than that, ma'am,' Anna said. 'Or higher, depending upon one's perspective. I have the great privilege of being teacher to a school of orphans, whose minds are inferior to no one's.'

The aunt who was beside the dowager's chair gasped and actually recoiled.

'Oh, you may sheathe your claws,' the dowager said. 'I was merely stating fact. It is not *your* fault you are as you are. It is entirely my son's. You may call me Grandmama, for that is what I am to you. But if you did not call me that, *ma'am* would be incorrect. What would be correct?' She waited for an answer.

'I am afraid, Grandmama,' Anna said, 'that any answer I gave would be a guess. I do not know. *My lady*, perhaps?'

'What are the ranks directly above and below earl?' the aunt – Aunt Matilda? – asked. 'And what is the difference between a knight and a baronet, both of whom are Sir So-and-So? You do not know, do you, Anastasia? You ought to know. You *must* know.'

'I believe, Cousin Matilda,' the young lady by the window – the earl's sister, Elizabeth? – said, 'you are bewildering poor Anastasia.'

'And there are far more important matters to be dealt with,' the dowager countess agreed. 'Do sit down, Matilda, and stop hovering. I am not about to fall out of my chair. Anastasia, those clothes are fit only for the dustbin. Even the servants would scorn to wear them.'

If it was possible to feel more humiliated, Anna thought, she could not imagine it. Her Sunday best!

'And your hair, Anastasia,' the duchess's younger sister – Aunt Mildred – said. 'It must be very long, is it?'

'It reaches below my waist, ma'am – Aunt,' Anna said.

'It looks thick and heavy and quite unbecoming,' Aunt Mildred told her. 'It must be cut and properly styled without delay.'

'I will have a modiste come here with her assistants tomorrow,' the duchess said. 'They will remain here until they have produced the bare essentials of a new wardrobe. Anastasia absolutely must not leave the house until she is fit to be seen. I daresay word has already spread among the *ton*. It would be strange indeed if it had not.'

'It was being spoken of in the clubs this morning,

105

Louise,' the older man – Aunt Mildred's husband – said. 'Both the blow to Harry and his mother and sisters and the sudden discovery of a legitimate daughter of Riverdale's. And Alexander's good fortune, of course.'

'I have yet to discover what is good about it, Thomas,' the new earl said.

Looking at him, Anna concluded that her first impression of him yesterday had been quite correct. He was the most perfectly handsome man she had ever seen. He looked like the prince of fairy tales. She pictured herself describing him to the children in Bath while all the girls sank into a happy dream, imagining themselves as his princess.

'Do you know what the *ton* is, Anastasia?' Aunt Matilda asked sharply. She was seated now on a stool beside her mother's chair.

'I believe it is a French term for the upper classes, Aunt,' Anna said.

'The very crème de la crème of the upper classes,' Lady Matilda told her. 'We in this room are all of it, and so, heaven help us, are you. However are you to be whipped into shape when you are already twenty-five years old?'

It was hard not to strike back with equal sharpness and declare that she had no intention to being whipped into any sort of shape that was not of her own choosing. It was hard not to turn tail and stalk from the room and the house and find her way back home. Except that she had the feeling there was no real home at the moment. She was

106

between two worlds, no longer belonging to the old and certainly not yet belonging to the new. All she could do was explore this new world a little more deeply and then decide what to do with the knowledge. She called upon all the resources of an inner calm and held her tongue.

'Matilda,' the earl's mother said reproachfully, 'be fair. Anastasia cannot help either her age or her upbringing. She must feel that she is facing the enemy here from every side when in reality we are her family. Have you ever known any other family, Anastasia? On your mother's side, perhaps?'

'No, ma'am,' Anna said. 'I am sorry. You are Cousin—?'

'Althea,' she said, smiling.

'No, Cousin Althea,' Anna said. 'I knew nothing of my identity until yesterday. I have always been Anna Snow.'

'Then this must be overwhelming,' the lady said. 'Perhaps you would like to return home with Alex and Lizzie and me for a few days since this is a large house and you cannot remain here alone.'

'You would be very welcome, Cousin Anastasia,' the earl told her.

'No,' the duchess said. 'She must absolutely remain here, Althea. I will be arranging for a modiste and a hairdresser to be here early tomorrow. And her belongings, for what they are worth, are being fetched here from the Pulteney. You are quite right, though, that she cannot stay here alone without a companion or chaperone. Perhaps Matilda—'

'Oh, I would be delighted to remain here for a few days with Cousin Anastasia, if she will permit it,' the earl's sister said, her smile as warm as her mother's. 'May I, Anastasia? I promise not to overwhelm you with a litany of all that must be changed in you before you are indistinguishable from all the rest of us. Rather, I would like to find out about your life as it was before yesterday. I would like to find out about you. What do you say?'

Anna closed her eyes for a moment. 'Oh yes, please,' she said, 'if you will, Cousin Elizabeth. If it is no great trouble to you. But will not my half brother return here?'

'If he does,' the duchess said, 'he will be redirected to Archer House.'

'I am surprised,' the earl said, 'that you are not out searching for him, Netherby. I would do it myself, but under the circumstances I would expect to be the very last person he would wish to see. Perhaps the obligation you feel toward him is more irksome now that he is no longer Riverdale.'

Elizabeth turned her head to regard her brother reproachfully. The Duke of Netherby appeared quite unruffled, Anna saw, but she was not surprised to see that he had his quizzing glass to his eye. What an affectation that was. She would be very surprised to learn that he suffered from poor vision. Yet the glass somehow made him appear doubly dangerous.

'Had you been paying greater attention, Riverdale, though really, why should you?' he said softly, 'you might have noticed that I never run about searching for lost puppies when it is altogether probable I will end up chasing my own tail instead and looking foolish. Nor do I interfere with very young blades sowing wild oats. I am no one's maiden aunt. As for seeking out a young man who thinks it a rollicking good lark to have lost everything he ever believed to be his, including the legitimacy of his birth, no, it will not happen. It will be time enough to find him when he has stopped laughing, as he will.'

Anna felt chilled by the bored hauteur of his voice, and by his words. The Earl of Riverdale did not reply, but it occurred to Anna, even from this brief exchange, that there was no love lost between the two men.

'Please do not distress yourself, Cousin,' the earl said, regarding Anna steadily. 'You must put young Harry, and Camille and Abigail too, from your mind, at least for a while. They are all deeply upset and not inclined to look kindly upon you, even though they are well aware that you are quite blameless and indeed more sinned against than sinning. It will be some time before they can be induced to recognize any relationship to you. Give them that time if you will.'

Both his words and the look on his face were kind, but the words hurt anyway.

'Alexander is quite right,' the dowager said.

'Turn right around, Anastasia.' Anna turned. 'You do not have much of a figure, but at least you are slender. And stays will do wonders for your bosom. I do not suppose you have ever worn stays?'

Anna could feel heat in her cheeks. Goodness, there were men present. 'No, Grandmama,' she said.

'It will all be taken care of, starting tomorrow,' the duchess said briskly. 'We must decide too what tutors will be necessary – a dancing master, certainly, and a teacher of etiquette, and perhaps others too. In the meantime, you must not even think of venturing from the house, Anastasia. Elizabeth will keep you company indoors. Now, have a seat – you have been standing long enough. Matilda, pull on the bell rope for the tea tray, if you will.'

Anna sat at almost the same moment as the Duke of Netherby got to his feet and strolled across the room to stand before her chair. Everyone fell silent, as everyone always seemed to do whenever he as much as raised a finger or an eyebrow. He regarded her in silence for a few moments with those keen, sleepy eyes.

'Anna,' he said, startling her with the use of the name by which she knew herself, 'the sun is shining and the fresh air and Hyde Park beckon. If you accompany me there, there is a risk that the *ton* may catch a glimpse of an apparent governess with me and draw its own conclusions as to your identity. The *ton* may then proceed to fall into a collective swoon of shock, or it may scurry off to report the sighting to those less fortunate, or it may simply go on its way and about its own business. Knowing all this, would you care to come with me?'

Anna bit her lip to stop herself from laughing nervously, so unexpectedly bizarre were his words.

'Is this wise, Netherby?' Uncle Thomas asked. 'Louise has just been pointing out—'

The Duke of Netherby neither turned his head nor replied. 'Anna?' he said softly.

He was like some alien creature. She was not frightened of him. Never that. In fact, she had just been amused by him. But . . . well, far more than any of the other people in the room, he seemed to epitomize a universe so different from her own that there could be no possibility of any meaningful communication. Why would he wish to walk with her, to risk being seen with her – an apparent governess?

But . . . fresh air? And a temporary escape from this room and all the other people in it?

'Thank you,' she said. 'That would be pleasant.'

'Mother,' Aunt Matilda said. 'Anastasia must not be allowed to do this. Louise is quite right. Oh, this is not welldone of you, Avery.'

'If you must go, someone ought to go with you as a chaperone, Anastasia,' the earl suggested. 'Lizzie, perhaps you would be willing?'

'Ah, but you see, Cousin Elizabeth,' the duke

111

said softly, his eyes still upon Anna's, 'you are not invited.'

The lady in question smiled at the back of his head, merriment in her eyes, Anna noticed.

'My granddaughter does not need a chaperone when she steps out with the Duke of Netherby,' the dowager countess said. 'His father married my daughter, did he not? And Avery is quite right. We cannot keep Anastasia indoors here until she is ready. She may never be ready.'

CHAPTER 7

Five minutes later, having donned her cloak, bonnet, and gloves – the same ones as yesterday – Lady Anastasia Westcott stood on the pavement outside Westcott House. No doubt this was her best outfit, Avery thought, her only best one. It would be interesting to see her everyday clothes – or perhaps not.

She had looked in need of rescuing. Not that he would have rushed into the breach if there were not something about her that piqued his interest. Perhaps it was the way she had not taken fright yesterday when she set foot inside Archer House and encountered . . . him. He knew he intimidated most people. Or perhaps it was the quiet, dignified little speech she had delivered in the rose salon after Brumford had finished with all his disclosures. Or perhaps it was the answer she had given a short while ago when the dowager countess described her as looking like a lowly governess.

He offered his arm and was left with it cocked in midair when she did not take it. He raised his eyebrows.

'I do not need any assistance, thank you,' she said.

Well.

'I suppose,' he said, lowering his arm, 'orphan boys are not taught to offer an arm to orphan girls when they walk together on the street, and orphan girls are not taught to accept male gallantries when they are offered. It is not part of your school curriculum?'

'Of course not,' she said in all seriousness. 'How absurd.'

'I suspect you are about to encounter a whole world of absurdity,' he said, 'unless after the first or second time you lose heart or nerve or temper and scurry back to your schoolroom.'

'If I return to Bath,' she said, 'it will be because I have chosen to do so after careful, rational consideration.'

'In the meanwhile,' he said, 'your grandmother and aunts and uncles – uncle, singular – and cousins will work ceaselessly, day and night, to wipe clean the slate that has been your life for the past twenty-five years and transform you into their image of what Lady Anastasia Westcott ought to be. They will do it because of course it is more desirable for you to be a lady than an orphan and rich rather than destitute and elegant rather than dowdy – and because you are a Westcott and one of them.'

'I was not destitute,' she said.

'I will not take much of a hand in the education

114

of Lady Anastasia Westcott,' he told her, 'partly because my connection to the Westcott family is purely an honorary one and mainly because it would be a crashing bore and I avoid boredom as I would the plague.'

'I am surprised, then,' she said, 'that you came to Westcott House today. I am even more surprised that you invited me to walk with you instead of escaping alone.'

'Ah,' he said softly, 'but I suspect you are not boring, Anna. And yes, I did invite you to walk, did I not? I did not invite you to stand thus with me on the pavement outside your house, snapping at me and calling me absurd and very probably being peered down upon by a number of your relatives. Allow me to contribute my mite to your education, then, even against all my better instincts. When a gentleman walks with a lady, Anna, he offers his arm for her support and expects her to take it. If she does not, he is first humiliated beyond bearing – he might even consider going home and shooting himself – and then shocked by the realization that perhaps she is not a lady after all. Either way, actually, he may end up shooting himself.'

'Are you always so absurd?' she asked him.

He regarded her for a few silent moments while he curled one hand about the handle of his quizzing glass. If he raised it, she would probably laugh with incredulous scorn. He cocked his elbow again instead.

'This is really quite an easy lesson,' he said. 'It will not stretch your intellect to the breaking point. Give me your hand. No, the right.'

He took it in his right hand, drew it through his arm, and set her hand, palm down, on the cuff of his coat. If it were possible for her arm to stretch out of its socket, she would have remained standing where she was, he was sure, a safe distance away. But it was not, and she was compelled to come a few steps closer. Every muscle in her arm and hand stiffened.

Something was absurd, but he kept the observation to himself.

'We now proceed to walk,' he said. 'It is the gentleman's job to match his pace and his step to the lady's. Men do not have all the power in this world, you see, despite what women often believe.'

Her muscles remained stiff for a while and she looked more than ever like someone's governess or even someone's maid dressed in her Sunday best. She would not be mistaken for either today, however. Not when she was seen on his arm. News in London traveled faster than wildfire or the wind. It traveled by the servant underground and the gossip circuit aboveground, and the Westcott story was sensational indeed.

Avery was an admirer of women and a connoisseur of all things feminine. He admired beauty and elegance and charm in ladies and flirted with them and even bedded a few of them when appropriate.

He admired beauty and voluptuous curves and sensuality and sexual skills in women of a different class and flirted with them and entertained and bedded them as he desired – though with some discrimination. He liked women enormously. Becoming acquainted with them, escorting them about, flattering them, bedding them were among life's more enjoyable experiences. He could not recall, however, admiring many women for qualities of character. It amused him to discover that there were such qualities about Lady Anastasia Westcott.

I am lower even than that, ma'am, she had said in answer to her grandmother's remark about resembling a lowly governess. *Or higher, depending upon one's perspective. I have the great privilege of being teacher to a school of orphans, whose minds are inferior to no one's.*

He had had to turn to the window to hide his amusement, for she had not spoken in either anger or defiance. She had spoken what to her was the simple truth. She and her fellow orphans were every bit as good as the *ton*, she had been saying – the whole lot of it, himself included. He admired such poise and conviction. It would be a vast shame if her relatives had their way and she were made to change beyond recognition. He doubted, though, that she would allow it to happen except upon her own terms. It would be interesting to see what sort of person would emerge from the education of Lady Anastasia Westcott. He hoped she would remain interesting.

They passed two people on South Audley Street, a maid carrying a heavy bag and a gentleman Avery vaguely recognized. The maid kept her eyes lowered as she hurried past. The gentleman looked startled, recovered himself, touched the brim of his hat, and did not even wait to be fully past them before his head swiveled for a longer, closer look. He would have a tale to tell when he got wherever he was going.

'I am concerned about my half brother,' Anna said as they turned toward Hyde Park Corner, speaking for the first time since they had started walking. 'Are you concerned? He could be anywhere by now. He could be in grave danger or just very, very unhappy. I know he is no blood relative of yours, but he is your ward. Is it not irresponsible to say you will leave him be until he stops laughing?'

'I always know where Harry is likely to be found,' he told her. 'This occasion is no exception.' It had not taken him long last night to locate the boy, deep in his cups and sprawled in a low armchair in the scarlet visitors' parlor of a rather seedy brothel, surrounded by cronies as inebriated as he and painted whores with improbably colored hair. Avery had not shown himself. One glance had assured him that Harry was in no condition to avail himself of the main services the whores were there to provide and thus was safe from the pox.

'Are you so all-seeing, then?' she asked him. 'And

so all-powerful that you can rescue him from whatever depths he may have sunk to?'

Avery thought about it. 'I am,' he said.

He had made himself all-powerful. It had not been easy. He had had an exceedingly unpromising start to life when he had been born resembling his mother rather than his father. His father had been a robust, imposing, manly figure, who had stalked and frowned and barked his way through life, commanding terror in inferiors and respect in his peers. His mother had been a tiny, blue-eyed, dainty, sweet-natured, golden-haired beauty. Avery did not remember that she feared his father, or that his father had ever barked at her or been displeased with her. Indeed, it was altogether probable that theirs had been a love match. She had died when Avery was nine of some feminine complaint that had never been explained to him, though it was not pregnancy. By that time it was obvious that he had inherited most of his mother's traits and virtually none of his father's. His father had always treated him with casual affection, but Avery had once overheard him remarking that he would have been well enough if he had been a girl but was not what any red-blooded man would desire of his heir.

Avery had been sent away to school at the age of eleven and might as well have been consigned to purgatory. He had been horribly bullied. He had been small, puny, golden haired, blue eyed, meek, gentle, cringing, and terrified. And he had known nothing would change, for his nurse had once explained feet to him – the sort of feet that were attached to the ends of one's legs and had five toes apiece. The size of a boy's feet, she had said, was a sure predictor of the size of his person when one grew up. Avery's feet had been small, dainty, and slender.

He had been beaten up quite badly by a boy a year younger than himself on the playing fields one day when he had tried to catch a ball but had slapped his hands together instead while the ball bounced off one of his small feet and made him hop in pain. He had escaped sexual assault from the prefect to whose service he had been assigned only after he had burst into tears and the older boy had looked at him in disgust and complained that he was ugly when he cried, not to mention ungrateful and cowardly and girly. Both incidents had happened during his first week at school.

By the end of the second week he had learned very little from his books and his masters and tutors, but he had learned a number of other things, most notably that if he could do nothing to change his prospective height and body type and hair and eye color, he could change everything else, including his attitude. He joined the boxing club and the fencing club and the archery club and the rowing club and the athletics club and every other club that offered the chance of building his body and honing it and making of it something less pathetic.

It did not work well at the beginning, of course. In his very first bout in the boxing ring he pranced about on his little feet, his small fists at the ready, and was put down and out by the only punch thrown by his opponent. That opponent had, of course, been chosen deliberately to provide maximum enjoyment to the spectators who had gathered around in larger-than-usual numbers. The fencing instructor told him after his first lesson that if his foil was too heavy for him to hold aloft for longer than a minute at a stretch, he was wasting everyone's time by continuing – perhaps he ought to join a knitting club instead. The rowing instructor told him he would be a champion if only a race required rowing in a circle because he needed both hands to wield one oar. At his first footrace, every other runner, even the one dubbed Fat Frank, had crossed the finish line almost before he had left the starting line.

He had persisted with a dogged determination and endless additional practice time until he turned some invisible corner early in his second year by winning another of what he had privately dubbed *the amusement rounds* in boxing by knocking down an opponent two years older and a foot taller and several stone heavier than he in the second round. Admittedly it had happened when the boy was striking a pose for his friends and grinning like an idiot, but it had happened nevertheless.

121

The boy had even had to be carried off to the infirmary, where he had watched stars from dazed eyes for the next few hours.

The great change, though, had come when Avery was in his next-to-senior year. He was walking back to school from some unremembered errand and had taken an unfamiliar route for some variety. He had found himself walking past an open plot of waste ground between two old, shabby buildings and witnessing the strange sight of an old man in loose white trousers and tunic moving about barefoot in the middle of the lot with exaggerated steps and arm gestures, all of which were strangely graceful and slow, rather as if time itself were moving at less than half its usual speed. The man was about Avery's own height and build. He was also Chinese, a relatively unusual sight.

After many minutes the movements had ended and the old man had stood looking at Avery, seemingly quite aware that he had been there for a while but unembarrassed at having been observed behaving in such a peculiar manner. Avery had stared back. He was the one who had broken the silence. He doubted the old man ever would have.

'What were you doing?' he had asked.

'Why do you wish to know, young man?' the Chinese gentleman had asked in return – and he had waited for an answer.

Just curious, Avery had been about to say with a

shrug. But there had been something about the man's stillness, about his eyes, about the very air surrounding him that had impelled Avery to search his mind for a truthful answer. Two, even three minutes might have passed, during which neither of them moved or looked away from each other's eyes.

The answer when it came was a simple one – and a life-changing one.

'I want to do it too,' Avery had said.

'Then you will,' the man had said.

By the time he finished school two years later, Avery had learned a great deal about the wisdom of the Orient from his master, both philosophical and spiritual. He had learned too, not just *about* certain martial arts, but also how to perform them. The most wonderful discovery of all had been that his small stature and whip-thin body were actually the perfect instruments for such arts. He practiced diligently and endlessly until even his unrelentingly stern and demanding master was almost satisfied with him. He had made of himself a deadly human weapon. His hands could chop through piled boards; his feet could fell a not-so-very-young tree, though he proved that to himself only once before falling prey to remorse at having killed a living thing unnecessarily.

He had never practiced the deadliest of the arts on any human, but he knew how if he should ever need to use his skills. He hoped that time would never come, for he had also learned the corresponding art of self-control. He rarely used the weapon that was himself and never to its full potential, but the fact that he *was* a weapon, that he was virtually invincible, had given him all the confidence he would ever need to live his life in a world that admired height and breadth of chest and shoulder and manly good looks and a commanding presence. He had never told anyone about his meeting with the Chinese gentleman and its consequences, not even his family and closest friends. He had never felt the need.

His master had had only one criticism that had never wavered.

'You will discover love one day,' he had told Avery. 'When you do, it will explain all and it will be all. Not self-defense, but love.'

He had not explained, however, what he meant by that word, which had more meanings than perhaps any other word in the English language.

'When you find it,' he had said, 'you will know.'

What Avery did know was that men feared him even while they believed they despised him. He knew they did not understand their fear or even openly admit it. He knew women found him attractive. He had learned to surround himself with the weapon that was himself like an invisible aura, while inside he observed his world with a certain cool detachment that was not quite cynical and not quite wistful.

Lady Anastasia Westcott, he suspected, did not

find him either fearful or irresistibly attractive, and for that he admired her too. She had even called him absurd. No one ever called the Duke of Netherby absurd, even though he frequently was.

'When a gentleman walks with a lady,' he said as they approached the park, 'they make conversation. Shall we proceed to do so?'

'About anything at all?' she asked. 'Even when there is nothing to say?'

'There is always something to say,' he said, 'as your education will soon teach you, Anna. There is always the weather, for example. Have you noticed how there is always weather? It never lets us down. Have you ever known a day without weather?'

She did not reply, but around the hideous brim of her hideous bonnet he could see that she was almost smiling.

Carriages and riders were making their way in and out of the gates. Their occupants glanced Avery's way and then returned for a harder look. He turned off the main carriageway to cross a wide expanse of green lawn in the direction of a line of trees that hid the streets beyond from view. He did not intend exposing her to the curiosity of large numbers of the fashionable world today. There was a path through the trees where one could expect a measure of solitude.

She did not choose the weather, even though there *was* weather happening all around them in the form of sunshine and warmth and very little breeze. Those three subtopics could have kept them chatting for five minutes or longer.

'You must have known my father,' she said.

'He was the duchess, my stepmother's elder brother,' he said. 'And yes, I had an acquaintance with him.' As little as he possibly could.

'What was he like?' she asked.

'Do you wish for the polite answer?' he asked in return.

She turned her head sharply in his direction. 'I would prefer the truthful answer,' she said.

'I suppose in your world you can conceive of no other, can you, Anna?' he asked her.

She was small with a minimum of curves. She was small breasted. Her hair, even without the bonnet, was severely styled and heavy. Yet something came into her eyes for a moment, a certain awareness that he did not believe was fear, and somehow it flashed from her eyes into his body, and for a brief moment it did not seem to matter that the only physically appealing thing about her was her Madonna's face. It was an extraordinary moment. It was almost sexual.

'Why ask a question,' she said, 'if one does not want a truthful answer?'

Ah. Now he understood. He *liked* her. That was extraordinary enough, but it was easier to understand than sexual awareness.

'Anna,' he said by way of reply to her question, 'have you never asked a man if you look beautiful? No, foolish question. I do not suppose you have.

It would not occur to you to go on a fishing trip for a compliment, would it? Women who ask that question certainly do not want the truth.'

She was still looking directly as him. 'How very absurd,' she said.

He suspected that was going to become one of her favorite words in the days and weeks to come.

'Quite so,' he said. 'I believe the late Riverdale to have been the most selfish man of my acquaintance, though admittedly I did not know him well. He was, or so I have heard, wild and expensive as a young man. He married the lady his parents had chosen for him when his debts were such that he had no choice but to do whatever it took to restore the flow of funds from which he had been cut off. Apparently that included bigamy and the hiding away of his legitimate daughter. When his father died not long after his marriage and he became the earl, he continued his profligate ways for a while, and then suddenly saw the light, so to speak, and changed completely. It was not a religious epiphany that had assailed him, however. No divine light struck him down and made a penitent of him. According to my father, who knew him well, though reluctantly so as a brother-in-law, he had some extraordinary luck at the gaming tables, invested his winnings in a wild and improbable scheme, made a fortune from it, and turned suddenly and eternally wise. He found himself a brilliant financial adviser and became obsessed with making and hoarding money. He was extremely successful at both, as I discovered when I became Harry's guardian, and as you will have discovered from your consultations with Brumford.'

'I suppose, then,' Anna said, 'it was his dire need for funds that drove him to marry someone else when my mother was still alive. I wonder why she allowed it. Though she seems to have been living with her parents and apart from him at the time. And she was dying.'

'If someone you had met in Bath disappeared from your life and came to London and married and had children,' he said, 'would you know about it? Ever?'

'Probably not,' she said after giving the matter some thought.

'Your mother and her parents lived in a rural vicarage,' he said. 'It is unlikely they would know of the bigamy unless they had acquaintances who frequented London and were familiar with the aristocracy and knew of the connection between your mother and the man who soon became the Earl of Riverdale. It is even possible he did not ever use his courtesy title in Bath.'

'No,' she said. 'They probably did not even know, did they?'

'I would say,' he said, 'that your father felt quite safe in contracting an illegal marriage.'

'Why did he never revoke the old will?' she asked. 'Why did he never make another? Is that unusual?'

'It is,' he said, 'to answer your last question first. My father had a will that must have been twelve pages long, all written in such convoluted legalese that I daresay even his lawyer did not fully understand it. The will was unnecessary, of course, since I was the only son and the settlements upon my stepmother and half sister had been well taken care of in the marriage contract. One is left with the intriguing possibility in your father's case that the continued existence of the old will and the absence of a new one was deliberate on his part.'

She thought about it. 'His joke upon posterity when he could no longer be called to account?' she said. 'If that is so, he was being extraordinarily cruel to the countess and her children.'

'Or kind at last to you,' he said.

'There is no kindness in money,' she said.

They had reached the line of trees and turned to walk along the rough path among them. There was a nice sense of seclusion here. The harsher sounds of horses' hooves, vehicle wheels, children's shrieks, hawkers' cries, and adult chatter and laughter from the park on one side and the street on the other seemed muted, though it might be only imagination. Here one could hear birds singing and leaves rustling overhead. Here one could smell wood and sap, the fragrances of the earth and various trees. Here one could ignore the artificiality of town life.

He looked at her while her words rang in his

head. She was not delighted by her incredible good fortune, was she? He wondered if she had dreamed of it all her life and now found the reality a bit empty, because along with the fortune came the knowledge that her father had been a bounder of the first order and her half sisters had fled with their mother rather than meet her again or accept her offer to share her fortune. That Harry was off somewhere drinking deep until he touched bottom and some sort of rescue could be effected. That her family considered her impossible. *She may never be ready* were the last words her grandmother had spoken before they left the house. He wondered if she had friends back in Bath. A suitor, perhaps? Someone the family would not consider eligible for her.

'Now, there is a memorable saying,' he said. 'It ought to be a quotation from some famous sage – *there is no kindness in money*. I suspect, though, it is an original Anna-ism. To most people the motive would not matter. It would be enough that your father wanted you to be wealthy at last.'

'I hope it was not deliberate,' she said. 'I hope he merely forgot that will and was too lazy to make another. I hope he was not deliberately malicious to us all – to his wife and children and to me. I found my family yesterday. Do you understand, Avery, what that means to someone who has grown up in an orphanage not knowing who she is, not even certain that the name by which she is known is her real name? It means more than all the gold

130

and jewels in the world. And yesterday I lost my family, the part of it that means most to me, anyway. Today they are gone. They have fled rather than see me again. Oh, I am grateful for what remains. I have a grandmother, aunts and an uncle, cousins away at school – and your half sister is my cousin too, is she not? – and second cousins. They are all a treasure that was beyond my dreams just a few days ago, but perversely my heart is too sore to appreciate them fully just yet. Yesterday I learned that my mother is long dead and my father, a selfish, cruel man, is recently deceased. Yesterday I saw his second wife and his other children – my half siblings – crushed and their world destroyed. I am wealthy, probably beyond belief, but in some ways I am more impoverished than I was before – because now I know what I had and have lost.'

The one word that had registered most upon Avery's mind was his own name – Avery. Almost no one outside his family called him that. Even his mistresses called him Netherby.

But the rest of what she said did register too, and he stopped walking and steered her off the path and set her back against a tree trunk so that she could recover herself before they moved on. She was very upset. She had recently discovered that she was one of the wealthiest women in England, and she was upset – because family meant more to her than riches. She had never known either – family or money – and family meant more. One never really considered the matter when one had always had both. Which *was* the more important?

He braced one hand against the trunk beside her head and gazed into her face.

'No,' she said, 'there is no kindness in money, Avery, and there was absolutely none in the late Earl of Riverdale, my father.'

His name again – Avery. It was something else that had been against him from the start – his name, which suggested flowers and pretty birds and femininity. He could not have been Edward or Charles or Richard, could he? But somehow this woman, this Anna, made a caress of his name, though he had no doubt it was entirely unintentional.

'I wrote yesterday to my dearest friend in Bath,' she said. 'I reminded him of something our former teacher was fond of saying – that one ought to beware what one wishes for lest the wish be granted. All orphans have the grand dream of discovering just what I discovered yesterday. I told him Miss Rutledge had been quite right.'

Him. Avery only just stopped himself from asking the man's name.

There were other people coming along the path toward them. He drew her arm through his again and turned toward them. There were two couples. The men inclined their heads and touched the brims of their hats. The ladies half curtsied.

'Netherby,' Lord Safford said. 'This is a fine day for May.'

'Your Grace,' both ladies murmured.

But all eyes, Avery was fully aware, were upon his companion, avid and curious.

'Yes, is it not?' Avery agreed with a sigh, his quizzing glass in his free hand.

'It is warm but not overhot,' one of the ladies said. 'It is perfect for a stroll in the park.'

'And there is no wind,' the other lady added, 'which is most unusual and very welcome.'

'Quite so,' Avery agreed. 'Cousin, may I present Lord and Lady Safford and Mr Marley and Miss James? Lady Anastasia Westcott is the daughter of the late Earl of Riverdale.'

'How do you do?' Anna said, looking directly at each of them in turn.

The gentlemen bowed and the ladies curtsied – to her, not to Avery this time.

'This is a great pleasure, Lady Anastasia,' Mr Marley said as Miss James's eyes moved over her from head to toe. 'I hope we will see more of you during the Season.'

'Thank you,' she said. 'I have no firm plans yet.'

Avery raised his glass partway to his eye, and the two couples took the hint and moved off after some murmured farewells.

'You do realize, Anna, I hope,' Avery said as they resumed their own walk along the path in the opposite direction, 'that you have just made their day.'

'Have I?' she said. 'Because I am so dowdy? Because I am impossible?'

'For precisely those reasons,' he said, turning his head and regarding her lazily. 'You can continue being dowdy if you wish or allow yourself to be decked out in all the latest fashions and finery. And you can remain impossible or prove that to a lady of character all things are possible. You may even, the next time you are bowed and scraped to, choose to acknowledge the homage with a gracious inclination of the head and a cool glance along the length of your nose.'

'How absurd,' she said.

'Quite so,' he agreed. 'But behaving thus helps keep pretension and impertinence at bay.'

'Is that why you do it, then?' she asked.

Ah.

'I do it,' he said, 'because I am Netherby and am expected to be toplofty. Your relatives, Anna, will urge you to become Lady Anastasia Westcott to the exclusion of all else. The *ton* will certainly expect it of you. The four persons who just passed us have probably broken into a trot by now in their haste to spread the word about their first encounter with you. Their listeners will be fascinated and envious and scandalized and desperate to see you for themselves. The choice of whether you change and how much you change will be yours to make.'

'And what would you advise, Avery?' she asked, and he was encouraged to hear the slight edge in her voice.

He shuddered with deliberate theatricality. 'My

dear Anna,' he said, 'if there is something I never, *ever* do, it is offer advice. The tedium of it! Why would it matter to me whether you turn yourself into a diamond of the first water – that ghastly cliché – or remain a happy, dowdy teacher of orphans?'

'Perhaps,' she suggested, 'a dowdy teacher of orphans would offend your sense of consequence, since you have a connection to me through your stepmother.' She turned her head to look at him, and yes, she was angry. She had a bit of a stubborn jaw too.

'Ah,' he said faintly, 'but I never allow anything or anyone to reduce my sense of consequence.'

'And neither,' she said, 'do I.'

Their eyes met. 'A knockout line,' he said. 'My compliments, Anna.'

'I will change,' she told him. They had come to a stop again at a break in the trees that afforded a view across a grassy expanse to the Serpentine in the distance. 'One cannot live from one day into the next without changing. It is the nature of life. Small choices are always necessary even when large ones do not loom. I will change what I choose to change and retain what I choose to retain. I will even listen to advice since it is foolish not to, provided the adviser has something of value to say. But I will not choose between Anna and Lady Anastasia, for I am both. I merely have to decide, one choice at a time, how I will somehow reconcile the two without rejecting either. '

He smiled slowly at her, and she bit her lower lip.

'I do believe, Anna,' he said, 'that I may well fall in love with you. It would be a novel experience, but then, *you* are a novel experience. So earnest and so . . . principled. What do you choose, then, for the next moment? Shall we walk on? Or shall I kiss you?'

He said it to shock her, but he shocked himself at least equally. There were women with whom he flirted, and there were women with whom he most definitely did not. Anna fit quite firmly into the second category.

He watched shock wash over her and kept a wary eye on her right hand, assuming she was right-handed. Her nostrils flared.

'We will walk on,' she said. 'If this is how a gentleman and an aristocrat speaks to a lady, Avery, then I do not think much of a gentleman's education.'

'There are not many ladies,' he said, his expression and his voice restored to their habitual ennui, 'who would be outraged by the offer of a kiss from the Duke of Netherby. How humbling your rejection would be, Anna, if I were capable of humility. We will, as you say, continue on our way, then. We must return to Westcott House soon if we do not want Lady Matilda Westcott and the new Earl of Riverdale to send out in search of you.'

Glancing around the brim of her bonnet, he could not decide if she was amused or still angry and shocked. He could usually read women like a book. She was a closed and locked volume, and perhaps that was why he liked her and found her interesting. Who could resist the lure of a lock when the key was hidden somewhere?

They walked on.

CHAPTER 8

Dear Miss Ford,

By the time you receive this, I daresay you will know why I was summoned to London. I am sure Joel Cunningham will have shared my letter with you and everyone else. However, one thing has changed in just the day since I wrote that letter, and I must inform you that I will not after all be returning to Bath within the next day or two.

I wish I were. Indeed, I long to go home. Perversely, now that I have discovered that I am a lady of fortune, I want to go back to being who I was. I want my familiar life back. I want to be there with you and all my friends. I want to be teaching my dear children.

However, I have been persuaded – by others and by my own good sense – of the wisdom of remaining here, at least for a while. It would be foolish to take flight just when I have discovered what I have longed all my life to know. I must remain, I have decided, and learn just exactly who Lady Anastasia Westcott is and what her life would be if she had not been turned into Anna Snow at the age of four and left there at the orphanage. I must decide how much of her I can become without losing Anna Snow in the process. It may be conceited of me, but I am rather fond of Anna Snow.

Before I venture upon this strange voyage of discovery, however, I must resign from my teaching position. I do so with the deepest regret and something like panic in my heart, but I cannot expect you to inconvenience yourself and all the children while you wait for me to decide when I will return, if ever.

I shall be writing another letter after this one, but it seems only fair to give you advance notice that I will be trying to lure one of your girls away from you, and the one who has become your helper. It appears that Lady Anastasia Westcott, that pampered, helpless creature, cannot possibly dress herself or style her own hair or fetch hot water to her room or clean and iron her own clothes. She must have a personal maid to do those things for her.

I have been offered the temporary services of the maid of my second cousin, who is staying with me at Westcott House – which I own – but I have been warned that a maid of superior talents and experience will be chosen for me by my grandmother and my aunts. I tremble at the very thought – and I am only half joking. I picture someone stiff and humorless, who would look contemptuously along the length of her nose at poor me in my Sunday best, and me shaking with terror in my best and very sensible shoes. I would rather choose my own maid and have someone I know, someone with whom I can talk and laugh, even if she should find herself with as much to learn about her new life as I.

I am going to offer the position to Bertha Reed, since I believe the position might suit her and – more to the point – it would bring her closer to her Oliver. Oh, dear, does that make me a matchmaker? But the match has already been made, has it not? Those two have been devoted to each other since infancy.

I may deprive you of more of the older boys and girls too. This house of mine is vast. Indeed, I am inclined to call it a mansion. I have not yet been subjected to the terror of a meeting with my housekeeper – that is set for tomorrow morning – but I have learned that we are short staffed, as several of the servants went with my half sisters and their mother into the country this morning before I arrived here. My guess is that they will not be returning – or remaining there for long. They do not like the new order of things, and I cannot say I blame them. I am going to find out from the house-keeper what servants are needed and inform her that I will fill any suitable positions with candidates of my own choosing. I am thinking in particular of John Davies, who is a tall, strapping boy even though he is not quite fifteen, and he is always very neat and tidy, in both appearance and habits. I know you have tried to find an apprenticeship for him, but I know too that his dream is to be a doorman or a porter at one of the smarter hotels in Bath, someone who wears a uniform and looks strikingly handsome (John has never said that last, of course – he is far too modest). I shall see what Lady Anastasia Westcott can do for him. She must surely have some power.

This was intended to be a very brief note, but instead I have run on. Do please forgive me. And please give my love to all the children and assure them that I will always, always think of them. Wish me joy of my new iden-tity, which is not new, of course, as I have always been Lady Anastasia Westcott without knowing it. I do intend, though, always to remain

Your grateful friend,
Anna Snow

Anna and Elizabeth finished their letter writing at almost the same moment a short time later and smiled at each other.

'I do apologize,' Anna said, 'for writing letters during the first evening you are here to keep me company, but I did want to write to the matron of the orphanage without delay and to two of my friends.' She had written a letter to Joel too and a brief note to Bertha.

'No apology is necessary,' Elizabeth assured her. 'I had some of my own to write. You must miss your friends.'

She was not to go back to the Pulteney Hotel, Anna had learned on her return from the walk with the Duke of Netherby. Everyone had left the house except the duchess, Aunt Louise, and Lady Overfield, Cousin Elizabeth. Her belongings had already been fetched from the hotel, and Elizabeth's had been on the way. Tomorrow Anna would meet Mrs Eddy, her housekeeper, before the arrival of the hairdresser and the modiste. Her aunt was to arrange those appointments.

'You must not fear that it will be impossible to be brought up to snuff, Anastasia,' she had assured Anna. 'You have a face and figure that can be made presentable enough with a little work. It was decided while you were gone that it will be best if you do not wear mourning for your father. It would not be to your advantage to be wearing black when you are introduced to the *ton*. With the help of some tutors you will learn enough of the essentials of polite behavior not to disgrace either yourself or your family. And all except the highest sticklers will make allowances for any minor slips. Indeed, there will be some who will be charmed by them.'

At that point, Anna had glanced at the duke, who had stayed to escort his stepmother home, but he had merely looked bored. Just as though he had not tried to shock her earlier by telling her he might well fall in love with her. Just as though he had not then gone on to give her a choice – *Shall we walk on? Or shall I kiss you?*

The man gave her the shudders. No, to be honest it would be more accurate to say he gave her the *shivers,* for despite all his affectations, all the strange things he said, all the glittering splendor of his person, she had been well nigh suffocated all the time they had been in the park by the aura of power and sheer masculinity he seemed to exude. Having to take his arm – she had never taken anyone's arm before, not even Joel's – and walk close to his side had been one of the severest trials of her life.

And the worst – oh, the very worst – moment of that walk had come when he had given her the choice of being kissed or walking on, and her body had reacted quite independently of her mind. She had never come so close to losing control over the feminine needs she had been aware of since she was fourteen or fifteen but firmly quelled. She had wondered during that glance at him when they were back at the house what would have happened if she had chosen the kiss. Would he not have been shocked! She was quite, quite sure, though, that he would have kissed her – and her knees had felt wobbly at the very thought.

'We will all return here tomorrow,' her aunt had gone on to say. 'In the meantime, you will have Elizabeth for company and conversation. Listen to her, Anastasia. You can learn much from her.'

But instead of spending the evening in conversation, Anna had excused herself to write letters, and Elizabeth had written some of her own.

You must miss your friends, Elizabeth had just said.

'I hope,' Anna said, 'I will have a new friend in you.' Elizabeth had explained that she was a widow and lived with her mother and brother, Cousin Alexander, the new Earl of Riverdale.

'Oh, you will,' Elizabeth assured her. 'Poor Anastasia. How very bewildering all this must be for you. Even your name has changed. Would you prefer that I call you Anna?'

'If you please,' Anna said. 'I know I am Anastasia, but I do not feel like her. You see? I even think of her and talk of her in the third person.'

They both laughed. It was surely the first time she had laughed since before she left Bath, Anna thought.

'Then perhaps,' Elizabeth said, 'you will call me Lizzie, as my close family members and friends do.'

'I will.' Anna smiled at her.

'My cousins – your grandmother and your aunts

– can be a trifle overbearing,' Elizabeth said. 'I do not believe you will allow yourself to be overborne – I sense that you are of firm character – but they will try very hard to change everything about you until they have fashioned you into the person they believe Lady Anastasia Westcott ought to be. Bear with them if you can, Anna. They mean well, and you must remember that you are as new to them as they are to you. Until yesterday they had no inkling that you even existed. I believe your grandmama in particular is determined to love you.'

Anna watched Elizabeth cross the drawing room. 'Oh, Lizzie,' she said, 'you can have no idea what it feels like to have a grandmother and other relatives.'

'Forgive me for taking liberties in your house,' Elizabeth said, pulling on the bell rope beside the hearth, 'but I think we are both ready for a cup of tea and some light supper.'

'This is your house too,' Anna said. 'You have left your mother and brother to come and stay here with me for a while. I am very grateful. I would hate to be alone.'

'Alex really feels for you,' Elizabeth told her. 'He too has been thrust into an unfamiliar role he did not expect and has never coveted. But he has always had a strong sense of duty. He will shoulder all the responsibilities of the earldom along with the title. Poor Alex. The burden will be a heavy one.'

Anna wondered in what way it would be heavy.

145

'Are you hinting that I too should shoulder the burden of my duty?' she asked.

But Elizabeth merely laughed. 'Oh, goodness me, no,' she said. 'I have come here to offer you companionship and even cousinly affection, Anna. I will help you all I can to feel more comfortable in your new identity. I will even offer opinions when you solicit them. But I will not preach at you. That is not what friends do.'

'Thank you,' Anna said.

But the tea tray arrived at that moment together with plates of thinly sliced bread and butter and cheese and currant cakes.

'I wonder,' Anna said as they ate, 'if the Duke of Netherby has found my brother yet.'

'If he has not,' Elizabeth said, 'he surely will, and he will take care of him. I know Avery likes to give the impression that he is the ultimate in affected, indolent dandyism. Alex takes the outer appearance for reality and considers him irresponsible and heartily disapproves of him. But there is something about Avery – I believe it is in his eyes – that would make me turn to him with the utmost confidence if I ever found myself in difficulties and Alex was not at hand. He has kept Harry on the loosest of reins, I have heard, but nevertheless the reins have been there.'

'I do hope you are right,' Anna said. 'I cannot forget that when that young man first knew I was his sister, he looked pleased and eager to know me.'

'Have you been told what happened between Camille and her fiancé yesterday afternoon?' Elizabeth asked.

'No.' Anna set down her cup in its saucer.

'They were betrothed at Christmastime,' Elizabeth told her, 'but the death of the old earl forced them to postpone their wedding from this spring until next year. He was to call upon her here yesterday afternoon, and she very much expected that with her decision to leave off her mourning he would be happy to set the wedding for this year after all. But when he came and learned what had happened at Archer House during the morning, he left with what must have seemed indecent haste before any plans could be made. An hour later, poor Camille received a letter from him, suggesting that she be the one to send a notice to the papers announcing the ending of their betrothal, since it might be considered ungentlemanly if he did it himself.'

'Oh, Lizzie.' Anna set down her cup and saucer and gazed at Elizabeth in horror.

'Camille sent the notice,' Elizabeth said. 'I daresay it will appear in tomorrow morning's papers.'

'But why?' Anna's eyes widened.

'Perhaps,' Elizabeth said, 'because it will seem less humiliating to have the *ton* believe she was the one to sever the connection.'

'And *that* is how gentlemen behave?' Anna said. 'This is the world in which I am expected to learn to live?'

'At least give the man credit for not publicly shaming his betrothed,' Elizabeth said, but before Anna could express her outrage, she held up one hand. 'But I still think he ought to be boiled in oil – at the very least.'

Anna leaned back in her chair. 'Poor, poor Camille,' she said. 'She is my sister, Lizzie. I offered to share everything, but my brother ran away and my sisters fled to the country with their mother.'

'Give them time,' Elizabeth said. 'And give yourself time, Anna. I could have chosen a better moment to tell you than bedtime, could I not? I am sorry. But it is too late now for me to decide that it would have made better breakfast conversation.'

Anna sighed as they both got to their feet. Five minutes later she was alone in her vast bedchamber, having refused the offer of the services of Elizabeth's maid. She and her little bag had this room as well as a dressing room larger than her room in Bath and a private sitting room in which to move about. And, unlike the rooms at the hotel, these belonged to her, as did the entire house.

But there was an emptiness inside that was vaster than her whole body. She longed suddenly for the dear solidity of Joel. If he were here now and offered her marriage again, she would accept before the proposal was fully out of his mouth. Perhaps it was as well he was not here. Poor Joel. He deserved better.

I do believe, Anna, that I may well fall in love with you.

What would it be like to fall in love?

What would it be like to be kissed?

And, oh dear, what was it going to be like to be Lady Anastasia Westcott?

Was it too late to go back, simply to forget the events of the past few days? Her letters had not yet been sent. But yes, it was too late. Her leaving now would not solve anything for her brother and sisters and their mother. *They* could not simply forget the last few days and return to their lives the way they had been.

She fell asleep a long while later wondering what had happened to the Reverend and Mrs Snow, her maternal grandparents.

Avery found that he had rather badly miscalculated. It did not happen often. But then, he was not often called upon to deal with young earls who had just lost title and fortune and discovered themselves to be penniless bastards.

He did not discover Harry at any of the expected places during the evening or the night, though he spent weary hours wandering and looking and asking numerous questions of the boy's erstwhile cronies and hangers-on. Dispossessed ex-earls soon lost their appeal, it seemed. It was all enough to make one lose one's faith in humanity – if one had ever harbored any.

He did encounter Uxbury, however – Viscount

Uxbury, Camille's esteemed former betrothed – when he took a break from his search to call in at White's Club. Uxbury waylaid him as he was passing through the reading room, which was virtually deserted at that hour of the evening.

The viscount was someone to be avoided at the best of times. It had always seemed to Avery that if one were to pick him up and shake him vigorously, one would soon find oneself engulfed in dust, blinded and choked by it. What Camille saw in him, though she was admittedly rather starchy and high in the instep herself, Avery had never understood, though since he did not need to understand, he had been content with ignorance. By this evening, however, he resented even more than usual being hauled aside by this particular gentleman. The engagement was off, he had heard from his stepmother, hence Camille's having left London with Abigail and their mother. Avery did not know who had ended the engagement or exactly why. He really did not need or particularly want to know.

'Ah, Netherby, old chap,' Uxbury said. 'Come to celebrate your freedom from an irksome responsibility, have you?'

Old chap? Avery raised his eyebrows. 'Responsibility?'

'Young Harold,' Uxbury explained. 'The bastard.' He said the word not as an insult, but as a descriptor.

'A word of warning,' Avery said, possessing

150

himself of his quizzing glass. 'My ward does not like to be so called and will not scruple to tell you so. He claims that it makes him feel like a balding Saxon king awaiting an arrow through the eye. He prefers Harry.'

'What he is,' Uxbury said, 'is a bastard. I have had a very near escape, Netherby. You will wish to congratulate me upon it, I daresay. If the late Riverdale had died six months later than he did, I would have found myself riveted to his by-blow before discovering the truth. One can only shudder at the thought. Though you would have escaped altogether having to deal with a wild and petulant youth.'

'And so I would,' Avery said, dropping his glass on its ribbon. He was tired of this conversation.

He clipped Uxbury behind the knees with one foot and prodded the stiffened fingertips of one hand against a point just below the man's ribs that would rob him of breath for a minute or ten and probably turn him blue in the face into the bargain. He watched Uxbury topple, taking down a table and a heavy crystal decanter with him, and causing a spectacular enough crash to bring gentlemen and waiters and other assorted male persons running or at least hurrying from every direction. He watched Uxbury reach for a shout and not find it – or his next breath.

'Dear me,' he said to no one in particular. 'The man must have been drinking too deep. Someone ought to loosen his cravat.'

He strolled away after a few moments, when it seemed there was enough help to revive a swooning regiment. It was, he decided as he left the club to resume his search, Camille who had had the near escape yesterday, not her erstwhile betrothed.

Even the youngsters who might still be counted as Harry's friends were unable to point Avery in the right direction. He was told variously that Harry had gone off to a gaming hell, a brothel, a tavern, a postperformance theater party, another fellow's rooms, and home. He was to be discovered at none of those places. The boy was usually quite predictable. Finding him was generally no more arduous than following a blazing trail would be. But this time he appeared to have fallen off the map, and Avery was beginning to wonder if perhaps he had slipped off to join his family in Hampshire.

It was Edwin Goddard, his secretary, who finally discovered the lad the following morning, no more than an hour after Avery had enlisted his assistance. God bless the man, he was worth his weight in gold.

Harry – drunk and bleary eyed, disheveled, clothes stained and even torn, stinking after two days without any encounter with water or soap, razor or tooth powder or a change of linen – had encountered, or been encountered by, a recruiting sergeant and had taken the king's shilling in exchange for his spindly signature and a spot in some unprestigious regiment as a private soldier.

By the time Avery came up with the group – it consisted of a few other ragamuffin recruits as well as Harry and the sergeant – his ward was looking pale and glum and mulish and the obvious possessor of a gigantic headache.

The Duke of Netherby, who had bathed and changed his clothes since last night, regarded the disgusting huddle of military would-be heroes through his quizzing glass – he had chosen a jeweled one deliberately so that it would wink in the sun – while the disgusting huddle gawked back and Harry looked green and defiant.

'Harry,' His Grace said with a sigh. 'It is time to come home, my lad.'

''Ere, 'ere.' The sergeant stepped forward to within one foot of His Grace. 'The lad 'as been recruited, pretty boy, and belongs to the king, and there ain't a bleeding thing you can do about it.'

Pretty boy? This felt a little like that first year at school all over again.

The man was at least eight inches taller than Avery and at the very least twice his weight – more probably three times. His head had been shaved, and every inch of his body that was visible was pitted and scarred to show him for the great bruiser of a soldier he was.

Avery regarded him through his glass. It was not an attractive sight, especially when magnified, but it was an impressive one, and might well put the wind up a whole battalion of French soldiers, not to mention one pretty boy. The sergeant looked

153

uneasy under the leisurely scrutiny, but, to his credit, he did not retreat by even a fraction of one inch.

'Quite so,' Avery said with a long-suffering sigh. 'I will see my ward's signature, my man.'

'I ain't yur man, and I don't 'ave to—' the sergeant began.

'Ah, but you will,' the Duke of Netherby informed him, sounding bored.

The recruiting paper was produced.

'As I thought,' Avery said after taking his time perusing it through his glass. 'This is indeed my ward's signature, but it is shaky, for all the world as though he had been coerced into writing it.'

''Ere,' the sergeant said, frowning ferociously. 'I don't like your tone, guv, and I don't like wot you are hinsinuating.'

'I assume,' Avery said, 'one of the king's shillings is at this moment nestled in one of my ward's pockets?'

'Unless 'e 'as ate it,' the sergeant said.

The disgusting huddle snickered.

'Harry.' His Grace of Netherby stepped up to the boy, one hand outstretched. The other recruits were gawking again. A small but ever-growing crowd was gathering in a circle about them. 'If you please.'

'Give it to 'im, 'arry,' someone in the crowd yelled, 'and let the serge take 'im instead of you. The Frogs would eat 'im for tea, they would.'

There was a wag in every crowd.

Harry produced the battered shilling and handed it over. 'I've signed, Avery,' he said. 'I'm going to be a soldier. It's all I'm good for. It's what I want to do.'

Avery handed the shilling to the sergeant. 'You may take this back,' he said, 'and you may tear up that paper. It is worthless. It would not stand up in court.'

One element of the crowd cheered while another booed.

''e don't want it torn up,' the sergeant pointed out. 'You 'eard wot 'e said. Take yourself off, guv. 'e belongs to the king now, and I am the king's hagent. Take yourself off before I pop you a good one and make you cry and wet yourself.'

Wild cheering from the ever-growing crowd. It was a challenge almost worth accepting, but one really must not indulge in the temptation to show off. Avery sighed and lowered his glass.

'But you see,' he said, 'the boy is my ward. His signature, and what he believes to be his wishes, mean nothing without my permission. My permission is not granted.'

'And 'oo might I be haddressing?' the sergeant asked.

'He is the Duke of Netherby,' Harry said sullenly.

Instead of instantly groveling, the sergeant glowered, and Avery regarded him with approval. 'And I s'pose you 'ave the ear of the king whenever you want it,' the man said bitterly, 'and all the other nobs' ears 'oo don't 'ave to live by the laws of the land like all the rest of us salt of the earth 'umans.'

'It does seem rather unfair,' Avery agreed.

''e would be useless, anyway,' the sergeant said, turning his head to spit in the dirt, only narrowly missing the left boot of the nearest of the spectators. 'Just look at 'im. The best soldiers are the scum of the earth, like the rest of 'em there. I'll whip 'em into shape in no time flat, Lord love 'em.'

The scum of the earth gawked back at him. One of them then leered at Avery, favoring him with a view of a mouthful of rotten teeth.

'Take 'im,' the sergeant said, tearing the recruitment paper in two lengthwise and then again crosswise before dropping the pieces and setting a giant boot over them. 'And good riddance. Let 'im drink 'imself to death. 'e is well on 'is way already.'

'I don't want to leave,' Harry said mulishly.

'Of course you do not,' Avery said agreeably, glancing once at the boy through his glass before turning away. 'But there is nothing left for you here, Harry.' Except a good dose of lice and fleas and other vermin from the company in which he found himself.

Avery strolled away without looking back, and after a minute or two Harry fell into step beside him.

'Damn you, Avery,' he said, 'I *want* to be a soldier.'

'Then a soldier you shall be,' Avery said. 'If you are still of the same mind after a good bath and a good sleep and a good breakfast. But perhaps as an officer, Harry? You are an earl's son, after all, even if through no fault of your own or your mother's you were born on the wrong side of the blanket.'

'I cannot afford a commission,' Harry growled.

'Probably not,' Avery said – it was not the time to remind the boy that his newfound half sister had offered to divide her fortune with her siblings. 'But I can, you see. And I will, since you are my stepmother's nephew and Jessica's cousin and my ward. If you still wish it after you wake up sober, that is.'

Life had grown remarkably tiresome, he thought as he tried not to smell Harry. And decidedly odd. Had he really told Lady Anastasia Westcott, alias Anna Snow, yesterday afternoon that he might well fall in love with her? If he were to list the top one hundred types of women most likely to attract him, in descending order, she would be number one hundred and one.

And had he offered her the choice of walking on or being kissed?

He was not in the habit of kissing unmarried maidens, and he was in absolutely no doubt that she was both.

CHAPTER 9

Anna awoke the following morning feeling exhausted. The past few days had been so far outside any of her past experiences that she could find no place in which to rest her soul. Even her bed – wide and comfortable, with deep, downy pillows and soft, warm covers – felt too vast and too luxurious.

She threw back the covers, swung her legs over the side of the bed, got to her feet, and stretched. And there was no end in sight to all the strangeness. Yesterday she had made the decision to stay, at least for a while. She had written to Miss Ford to resign from her teaching position and to Bertha Reed inviting her to come and be her maid – she had even enclosed money for the stagecoach from what Mr Brumford had given her until some more regular arrangement could be made.

She stepped into her dressing room and selected one of her two day dresses – she could not wear her Sunday dress for a third day in a row. Someone had been in her dressing room recently. There was water in the jug on the washstand, and it was still warm. She poured some into the bowl, stripped off her nightgown, and washed herself all over before dressing and brushing her hair and twisting it into its usual knot at the back of her neck. She drew a few deep breaths and let herself out of the room. She would come back later to make her bed.

A manservant who was standing in the hall looked a little startled to see her, but bowed and led her to what he described as the breakfast parlor, which was smaller than the dining room where she and Elizabeth had eaten last evening. He drew a chair out from the table and pushed it back in as she seated herself. He would go and inform Mr Lifford, he told her, that my lady was ready for her breakfast.

Her breakfast arrived ten minutes later to an accompaniment of apologies from the butler for having kept my lady waiting. Anna had finished eating and drunk two cups of coffee – a rare luxury – before Elizabeth joined her.

'My maid came to inform me that you were up and at breakfast already,' she said, setting a light hand upon Anna's shoulder and bending to kiss her on the cheek. 'And goodness, she was right. I am the one who is usually accused of being an early riser.'

'But I was alarmed at how late I was,' Anna said, feeling warmed to the toes by the casual gesture of affection.

'Gracious!' Elizabeth said, and they both laughed.

But the time to relax soon came to an end. There

was the dreaded meeting with the housekeeper to face soon after breakfast, though it turned out to be not as intimidating as Anna had expected, perhaps because Elizabeth remained with her. Mrs Eddy gave them a tour of the house, and Anna was awed almost speechless by the vastness and splendor of it all. She did speak, though, when she saw the large portrait over the mantel in the library and the housekeeper casually named the subject of it as the late Earl of Riverdale.

Her father? Anna stepped closer.

'Is it a good likeness?' she asked. Her heart was beating rather heavily.

'It is, my lady,' Mrs Eddy said.

Anna gazed at it for a long time. High, starched shirt points and an elaborately tied neckcloth framed a fleshy, handsome, arrogant face from below and short, dark, artfully disheveled hair from above. He had been painted only from the waist up, but he looked portly. Anna could see nothing of herself in him, nor could she feel any of herself. A stranger gazed back at her from the canvas, and she found herself shivering and wishing she had brought her shawl down with her.

The tour ended in the kitchens belowstairs, where the cook signaled two maids and a manservant to come to attention while she presented them to my lady. Anna smiled and had a few words with them all. Then she remembered how some of the governors of the orphanage used to pay a visit to the home and nod with benevolent condescension upon orphans and staff alike but never spoke a word to anyone but Miss Ford. Perhaps, she thought, she was already committing a grievous error. But . . . perhaps she would continue committing it. She could not imagine herself, even in the persona of Lady Anastasia Westcott, ignoring servants as though they did not exist.

She would show my lady the linen closets and the silver and china and crystal cabinets another time, Mrs Eddy suggested as they climbed the stairs from the kitchens – and the account books, of course. My lady would have noticed a slight scarcity of staff, though it would not affect the running of the house until the servants who had left could be replaced by the agency from which they always drew new staff as needed.

'If you will provide me with a list of the servants required, Mrs Eddy,' Anna told her, 'I will see if I can replace some of them myself. I have friends who are fast approaching adulthood and would be delighted to be offered training and employment at a grand home in London.'

'Friends, my lady?' Mrs Eddy asked faintly.

Oh dear, another error. 'Yes.' Anna smiled at her. 'Friends.'

And that was when her day got really busy. The duchess, Aunt Louise, had arrived, and on her heels came Monsieur Henri, a hairdresser with waving hands and a French accent that was as fake as his name, if Anna's guess was correct. But her aunt described him as the most fashionable stylist in London, and Anna could only trust in her judgment. Soon she found herself seated in the middle of what had been described as the sewing room during her tour of the house, a square chamber at the back of the same floor as the drawing room, overlooking the long back garden. A large, heavy sheet had been draped about her, and her hair had been taken down out of its pins and brushed out. Elizabeth sat by the window. Aunt Louise was standing in front of Anna, though far enough away not to interfere with Monsieur Henri, who was wafting about her, a comb in one hand while the other made artistic figures in the air as his head tipped first to one side and then to the other.

'A short style to suit my lady's exquisite features, *n'est-ce pas?*' he said. 'With curls and ringlets to give 'eight and beauty.'

'Short hair is all the crack,' Aunt Louise agreed. 'And that hair is heavy and quite lifeless as it is.'

'My hair is straight,' Anna pointed out. 'It would take a great deal of time and effort to coax a curl into it.'

'And that is precisely what hot tongs and maids are for,' her aunt said. 'And a lady always has time to spend upon her appearance.'

Bertha loved fussing over the younger girls at the orphanage, braiding their hair and arranging the braids in different ways to give the girls some individuality. But . . . creating curls out of short, straight hair? Morning, afternoon, and evening?

Surely the curls would not hold all day. And how long would it take each time? Anna would be spending half her life sitting in a chair in her dressing room.

'No,' she said. 'Not short. I would like some of the length cut off, monsieur, if you will, and some of the thickness taken from it if that is possible. But it must remain long enough to be worn as I am accustomed to wear it.'

'Anastasia,' her aunt said, 'you really must allow yourself to be advised. I believe Monsieur Henri and I know far better than you what is fashionable and what is most likely to make you appear to advantage before the *ton*.'

'I have absolutely no doubt that you are correct, Aunt,' Anna said. 'I certainly appreciate advice and will always give consideration to it. But I would prefer to have long hair. Lizzie's is long. Surely she is a fashionable lady.'

'Elizabeth is a widow of mature years,' her aunt said. 'You, Anastasia, will be making a very late debut into society. We must emphasize your youth as best we can.'

'I am twenty-five,' Anna said with a smile. 'It is not so very old or so very young. It is what it is and what I am.'

The duchess looked at her in exasperation and the stylist with sad resignation, but he set about cutting several inches off her hair and thinning it until she could feel the lightness of it and watch it swing about her face in a manner that gave life and even some extra shine to it. When it had been coiled again at the back of her head, a little higher than usual, up off her neck, it looked altogether prettier than Anna remembered its ever being.

'Oh, Anna,' Elizabeth said, offering an opinion for the first time, 'it is perfect. It looks chic and elegant for daytime wear, yet leaves room to be teased and styled for more formal evening occasions.'

'Thank you, monsieur,' Anna said. 'You are very skilled.'

'It will do,' her aunt said.

It was not the end of Anna's ordeals, however. Her grandmother and other aunts arrived soon after luncheon and only just before Madame Lavalle and two assistants took up residence in the sewing room with enough bolts of fabric and accessories to set up a shop and piles of fashion plates for every type of garment under the sun. The modiste had been commissioned to clothe Lady Anastasia Westcott in a manner that would befit her station and permit her to mingle with the *ton* as the equal of all and the superior of most.

Anna was exhausted at the end of it. Not only had she had to be measured and pinned and prodded and poked; she had also been forced to look through endless piles of sketches of morning dresses and afternoon dresses, walking dresses and carriage dresses, theater gowns and dinner gowns and ball gowns, and numerous other garments – all of them plural, for one or even two of each would not do at all. She was going to end up with more clothes than all the ones she had ever owned put together, Anna concluded.

Even more overwhelming, perhaps, was the fact that apparently she could afford it all without putting even a slight dent in her fortune. Her aunts had all given her identically incredulous odd looks when she had asked the question.

She had fought several battles before they all withdrew to the drawing room for tea. Some she had lost – the number and type of dresses that were the bare essentials, for example. Some she had won simply by being stubborn, according to Aunt Mildred, and mulish, according to Aunt Matilda. Frills and flounces and trains and fancy lace trims and bows had all been firmly vetoed despite vigorous opposition from the aunts. So had low necklines and little puffed sleeves. She would be Lady Anastasia, Anna had decided, but she must also remain Anna Snow. She would *not* lose herself no matter how ferociously the *ton* might frown. And frown it would, Aunt Matilda had warned her.

Oh, and there was her court dress, over which she had almost no control whatsoever, since it was the queen herself who dictated how ladies were to dress when being presented to her – and Lady Anastasia Westcott must be presented, it seemed. Her Majesty expected ladies to dress in the fashion of a bygone age. Anna's mind had not even begun to grapple with that particular future event yet.

The Earl of Riverdale arrived with his mother soon after they had settled in the drawing room. The earl – Cousin Alexander – actually commented upon how pretty Anna's hair looked after bowing to all the ladies and before seating himself beside his sister and bending his head to talk with her. Anna found herself wondering if she was blushing and hoped she was not. She was unaccustomed to being complimented on any aspect of her appearance – especially by a handsome, elegant gentleman. He was looking at Elizabeth with a softened expression, almost a smile, and Anna felt a twinge of envy at the obvious closeness of brother and sister. Where was her own brother?

Their mother, Cousin Althea, sat beside Anna, patted her hand, agreed that her hair now looked prettier than it had, and asked how she did. But there was not much chance of conversation.

Aunt Matilda knew a lady of superior breeding and straitened means who would be only too happy to be offered genteel employment for a week or so, coaching Anastasia upon the subject of titles and precedence and court manners and points of fact and etiquette in which her education appeared to be sadly if not totally deficient.

Anna's grandmother expressed doubt over whether Elizabeth was chaperone enough for Anastasia in such a large house and suggested again that Aunt Matilda take up residence with them.

But before Anna could feel too much dismay, Cousin Althea spoke up.

'I would move here myself, Eugenia,' she said, addressing the dowager while patting Anna's hand, 'if I felt my daughter's presence did not lend sufficient countenance to Anastasia. However, I am quite convinced it does.'

'Lizzie is the well-respected widow of a baronet and sister of an earl,' Cousin Alexander said.

No more was said on the subject. Anna suspected that her grandmother would have been happy to rid herself of Aunt Matilda's oversolicitous attentions for a while.

Aunt Mildred knew of a dancing master employed by dear friends of hers to help their eldest daughter brush up on her dancing skills before her come-out ball. 'Do you waltz, Anastasia?' she asked.

'No, Aunt,' Anna told her. She assumed it was a dance. She had never heard of it.

Aunt Louise clucked her tongue. 'Engage him, Mildred,' she said. 'Oh, there is a great deal to do.'

It was almost a relief when the Duke of Netherby strolled into the room following the butler's announcement.

There were a dozen congenial ways – at the very least – in which he could be spending an afternoon, Avery thought. Prowling about his own home waiting for a drunken ward to awaken was not among them, though it was what he had been doing. And trotting around to South Audley Street to escort his stepmother home was not one either. Casually fond of the duchess he might be, but he did not involve himself a great deal in her life. Nor did she in his. Very rarely did he escort her anywhere. Nor, to be fair, did she expect it. And if he did go there to fetch her home, he would doubtless find himself knee deep in Westcotts and seamstresses and French hairdressers – were they not all French? – and Lord knew what else. Probably the very proper and very properly elegant Riverdale, with whom he had no sound reason to be irritated, would be there, for he was very definitely the sort who would escort his mother. Avery had every possible reason to pursue one of those dozen congenial activities and give South Audley Street a wide berth.

But that was where he found his feet leading him, and he did nothing to correct their course. He would see how well she was bearing up under the combined influence of a formidable grandmother and three aunts, not to mention one very proper earl and his mother and sister and some fake French persons. And she would wish to know that he had found and rescued Harry. For some reason it seemed she cared.

He was admitted to the drawing room to discover without surprise that they were all present except Molenor, who was probably ensconced in the reading room at White's or somewhere similarly civilized, wise man. Avery made his bow.

Something had been done to her hair, something that probably did not fully satisfy the aunts since there was nothing fussily pretty about it. For the same reason, perhaps, it ought to repel him too. But the knot on the back of her head no longer resembled the head itself in either size or shape and looked altogether daintier.

'Well, Avery?' his stepmother asked.

The whole room had gone silent as though the fate of the world rested upon his opinion. Anna was not wearing the Sunday dress today. She was wearing something lighter and cheaper and older. It was cream in color and might once upon a time have had some pattern on the fabric. But frequent washings and scrubbings in the orphanage laundry tub had worn it to near invisibility. Even so, the dress was a vast improvement upon the gloomy Sunday blue.

'Harry has been found,' he said, his eyes still upon her.

Her face lit up with what looked remarkably like joy. The aunts would doubtless work upon that until she learned never to display any emotion stronger than a fashionable ennui.

'I tucked him into a bed at Archer House late this morning,' he said, 'after every inch of his person had been scrubbed and scoured and he had been forcibly fed by my valet, who also poured some concoction into him to counter the effects of an overindulgence in liquor. He will doubtless stir with the beginnings of a return to consciousness sometime soon, but he will be as cross as a bear and not willingly to be endured. I shall leave him to my valet's care until later.'

'Oh.' She closed her eyes. 'He is safe.'

There was a general murmur of relief from Harry's relatives.

'Where did you find him, Avery?' Elizabeth asked.

'In company with an interesting collection of ragamuffins,' he said, 'and a fierce, bald giant of a recruiting sergeant.'

'He has enlisted?' Riverdale asked with a frown. 'As a private soldier?'

'Had enlisted,' Avery said. 'I unenlisted him.'

'After the fact?' Riverdale said. 'Impossible.'

'Ah,' Avery said with a sigh, 'but I happened to have my quizzing glass about my person, you see, and I looked at the sergeant through it.'

'My poor boy,' the dowager countess said. 'Why did he not simply come to me?'

'If the French but knew it,' Elizabeth said, 'they would arm themselves with quizzing glasses instead of cannons and muskets and drive the British out of Spain and Portugal in no time at all with not a single drop of blood shed.'

'Ah,' Avery said, looking appreciatively at her, 'but they would not have me behind all those glasses, would they?'

She laughed. So did her mother and Lady Molenor.

'Avery,' Anna said, bringing his attention back to her, 'take me to him.'

'To Harry?' He raised his eyebrows. 'He was not in the most jovial of moods before he went to sleep and will be worse after he has woken up.'

'I would not expect him to be,' she said. 'Take me to him. Please?'

'Ah, but I will not force him to see you,' he told her.

'That is fair,' she said.

Nobody protested. How could they? She wished to see her brother, and the people gathered here were equally related to both.

Though he had come with the express purpose of escorting his stepmother home, Avery abandoned her to her own devices and stepped out for the second day in a row with Anna on his arm. Today, he thought idly, she looked more like a milkmaid than a teacher. One almost expected to look down and see a three-legged milking stool clutched in her free hand.

'What would you have done,' she asked him, 'if the sergeant had refused to be cowed by your quizzing glass and your ducal hauteur?'

'Dear me.' He considered. 'I should have been forced to render him unconscious – with the greatest reluctance. I am not a violent man. Besides, it might have hurt his feelings to be downed by a fellow Englishman no more than half his size.'

She gave a gurgle of laughter that did unexpectedly

strange things to a part of his anatomy somewhere south of his stomach.

That was the entirety of their conversation. When they arrived at Archer House, he left her in the drawing room and went to see if Harry was still comatose. He was in the dressing room of the guest chamber that had been assigned to him, freshly shaved. He did not look any more cheerful, however, than he had earlier.

'You ought to have left me where I was, Avery,' he said. 'Maybe they would have sent me off to the Peninsula and stuck me in the front line at some battle and I would have been mown down by a cannonball in my very first action. You ought not to have interfered. Do not expect that I am going to thank you for it.'

'Very well,' Avery said with a sigh, 'I shall not expect it. I have your half sister in the drawing room. She wishes to see you.'

'Oh, does she?' Harry said bitterly. 'Well, I do not wish to see her. I suppose you are going to try to drag me down there?'

'You suppose quite wrongly,' Avery informed him. 'If I intended to drag you there, Harry, I would not *try*. I would do it. But I have no such intention. Why, pray, would it matter to me whether or not you go down to talk to your half sister?'

'I always knew you did not care,' Harry said with brutal self-pity. 'Well, I'll go. You cannot stop me.'

'I daresay not,' Avery said agreeably.

She was standing before the fireplace, warming her hands over the blaze – except that the fire had not been lit. Perhaps she was merely examining the backs of her hands. She turned at the sound of the door opening and gazed at Harry with wide eyes and ashen face.

'Oh, thank you,' she said, taking a few steps toward him. 'I did not expect that you would see me. I am so glad you are safe. And I am so sorry, so *very* sorry for . . . Well, I am dreadfully sorry.'

'I do not know what for,' Harry said sullenly. 'None of it is your fault. All of it is firmly on my father's head. *Your* father's head. *Our* father's head.'

'On the whole,' she said, 'I do not believe I was hugely deprived in never having known him.'

'You were not,' he said.

'Though I do have one memory,' she said, 'of riding in a strange carriage and crying and being told by someone with a gruff voice to hush and behave like a big girl. I think the voice must have been his. I think he must have been taking me to the orphanage in Bath after my mother died.'

'He must have sweated that one out,' Harry said with a crack of bitter laughter. 'He was already married to my mother by then.'

'Yes,' she said. 'Harry – may I call you that? – your mother and sisters have gone into the country, though they do not intend to stay even there longer than it takes to have all their personal possessions packed up and moved out. They do not wish to know me. I hope you do, or at least that you are willing to acknowledge me and will agree to allow me to share with you what ought to be ours – all four of ours – and not mine alone.'

'It seems you are my half sister, whether I want you to be or not,' Harry said grudgingly. 'I do not hate you, if that is what is bothering you. I have nothing against you. But I cannot . . . *feel* you are my sister. I am sorry. And I would not now accept even a ha'penny from that man who pretended to be my mother's husband and my legitimate father. I would rather starve. It is not from you I will not take anything. It is from *him*.'

Avery raised his eyebrows and strolled to the window. He stood there, looking out.

'Ah.' The single soft syllable seemed to hold infinite sadness. 'I understand. *Now* I understand. Perhaps in the future you will think differently and understand how it hurts me to be forced to keep it all. What will you do?'

'Avery is going to purchase a commission for me,' he said. 'I don't want him to, but he has made it impossible for me to enlist as a private soldier. It will be with a foot regiment, though. I am not going to have him kitting me out with all I would need as a cavalry officer. Besides, the officers of a foot regiment probably care less than cavalry officers do about having a nobleman's by-blow among their number. I will not have Avery buying me promotions either. I will move up in the officer ranks on my own merit or not at all.'

'Oh,' she said, and Avery would wager she was smiling, 'I *do* so honor you, Harry. I hope you end up as a general.'

'Hmph,' he said.

'Then I will be able to boast of my half brother, General Harry Westcott,' she said, and Avery *knew* she was smiling.

'I will excuse myself,' Harry said. 'I have the devil of a headache. Ah. Pardon my language if you will, Lady Anastasia.'

Avery heard the drawing room door open and close. When he turned from the window, Anna was back at the fireplace warming her hands over the nonexistent blaze. And he realized – devil take it! – that she was weeping silently. He hesitated for a few moments until she raised a hand and swiped at one cheek with the heel of it. She had turned her head slightly so that he could no longer see her full profile.

'He will look quite splendid in the green coat of the 95th Light Regiment,' he said. 'The Rifles. He will probably cause stampedes among the Spanish women.'

'Yes,' she said.

But dash it all. Damn it to hell. He closed the distance between them, drew her into his arms, and held her face against his shoulder just as though she were Jess. Whom she was not. She stiffened like a board before sagging against him. Unlike most women under similar circumstances, though, she did not then proceed to melt into floods of tears. She fought them and swallowed repeatedly. She was virtually dry-eyed when she drew back her head.

'Yes,' she agreed, smiling an only slightly watery smile, 'he will look splendid.'

His mind reached for something to say in reply and found . . . nothing.

He kissed her instead.

Devil take it and a thousand and ten damnations, but he kissed her. He did not know which of them was the more startled. It was not even just a fatherly or brotherly or cousinly peck on the lips either. It was a full-on, lips-parted, head-slightly-angled, arms-closing-about-the-woman-to-draw-her-even-closer kind of kiss. It was a man-to-woman kiss. And what the devil was he doing trying to analyze it rather than lifting his head and pretending that after all it was just a kindly, cousinly embrace designed to comfort her?

Pretending? What else *was* it, then? That was exactly it, was it not?

While he pondered the matter, his lips continued to move over hers, feeling their softness, their moistness. It was surely the most chaste kiss he had indulged in since he was fifteen or thereabouts. Yet it somehow felt like the most lascivious.

This, he thought, his mind verbalizing the biggest understatement of its thirty-one-year existence, was a mistake.

'I will return you to the bosom of your family if you are ready to leave,' he suggested as he raised his head and released his hold on her. He was happy to hear his voice sounding thoroughly bored.

'Oh yes, thank you,' she said – the brisk, sensible schoolteacher. 'I am ready.'

CHAPTER 10

Anna prattled her way through dinner, telling Elizabeth everything there was to tell about growing up in Bath. She dared not stop.

'Is Joel your beau?' Elizabeth asked as they ate their dessert.

'Oh, not really,' Anna said, awash in nostalgia and regret. 'We grew up together as the closest of friends. We could always talk upon any subject under the sun or about nothing at all. He was too close to become a beau. Does that make sense? He was more like a brother. And why am I using the past tense?' She felt a bit like weeping.

'Did he ever want to be your beau?' Elizabeth asked.

'A few years ago he fancied himself in love with me,' Anna admitted. 'He even asked me to marry him. But he was just lonely. It happens when people leave the orphanage and have no family or even friends beyond its walls. I am sure now he is thankful I said no.'

'He is very handsome?' Elizabeth asked.

Anna held her spoon suspended over her dish and considered. 'He is good-looking,' she said, 'and very attractive, I believe. It is hard, though, when you have known a man all your life, to see him dispassionately. But oh, goodness, Lizzie, I have done all the talking even though the meal is almost at an end, and even I know that that is bad-mannered. What about you? Do you have any beaux? Do you hope or even plan to remarry?'

'No, probably not, and no,' her cousin said, and laughed. 'Though the very fact that I am in London this year for the Season may mean that the *probably not* might be *perhaps not*. You are looking thoroughly confused. I did not have a happy marriage, Anna. In fact, it was worse than unhappy and it has made me skittish. It could be said, of course, that at the age of thirty-three I would make a far wiser choice than I did at the age of seventeen, when I fell head over ears in love with good looks and charm. But to be fair, I saw more in Desmond than just those things. He was a man of property and fortune. He was amiable and mild-mannered and kind. He loved his family and friends. Perhaps strongest in my defense is the fact that my mother and father liked him and approved his suit. I could not have known what actually being married to him would be like, and it is that fact that frightens me whenever I meet a personable and eligible gentleman and am tempted to encourage a courtship.'

'He drank?' Anna guessed.

'He drank,' Elizabeth said with a sigh. 'Everyone drinks, of course, and almost everyone drinks to excess once in a while. It is rarely a greater problem than the embarrassment of the fool one can make of oneself when in one's cups. He did not even drink very often. He would go weeks without. And often when he did drink, he would just grow merry and funny and be the life of the party, if there was a party. But sometimes there was a moment – it was always when we were alone together – when I would know he had crossed some line into becoming something or someone else altogether more ugly. There was something about his eyes – I cannot even describe it, but I would recognize it in a moment. It was as though he had been sucked into a dark hole, and then he would become viciously abusive. I could not always escape in time before he became violent.'

'I am so sorry,' Anna said.

'He was the loveliest man when he was sober,' her cousin said. 'Everyone loved him. Almost no one ever saw the dark side of him. Except me.' She closed her eyes for several moments, drew an audible breath, and pressed clasped hands prayer fashion against her lips. But she did not continue. She shook her head, opened her eyes, and attempted a smile. 'But let us not be gloomy. I cannot bear those memories or the thought of inflicting more of them upon you. Shall we go to the drawing room?'

'It is such a vast, uncozy room for just two people,' Anna said. 'Come up to my sitting room instead. It is very pretty and the chairs and sofa look comfortable, though I have not had any time to spend there yet.'

They settled there a few minutes later, each in a soft, upholstered chair. A servant came and lit the fire.

'I could grow accustomed to luxury,' Anna said after the servant had withdrawn. 'Oh, I suppose that is what I will be expected to do.'

They both laughed.

'Why did you say,' Anna asked, curling her legs to one side of her on her chair and hugging a cushion to her bosom before realizing that this was probably not the way a lady ought to sit, 'that the responsibilities of being the Earl of Riverdale would be burdensome to your brother? It must be very grand to be an earl.'

'I love Alex dearly,' Elizabeth said, taking her embroidery out of the bag she had brought up with her. 'He deserves every good thing that could happen to him, and I had high hopes for him just a few days ago. But now all this has happened and I am not sure he will be happy after all – and not just because he feels terrible for Harry.'

Anna watched as she threaded a length of silk through her needle and bent her head over her embroidery frame.

'As the Earl of Riverdale, for example,' she continued, 'Alex will be expected to take his seat in the House of Lords, and because he can never take responsibility lightly, he will feel obliged to be here each spring when Parliament is in session.

181

He does not enjoy London. He came this year just to please Mama and me, though he did admit too a few days ago that he intended to take the opportunity of being here to look about him for a bride at last, for someone to complete his life.'

'Can he not still do that?' Anna asked. 'Is he not even more eligible now than he was? Surely there must be any number of ladies who would be only too happy to marry an earl.'

'But would they also be happy to marry Alex?' Elizabeth said. 'I want someone to marry the man, not the title. Someone who will love him. Someone he will love.'

How wonderful it must be, Anna thought, to have grown up with a real brother and such obvious affection. But she had Joel. And really she wanted the same things for him as Elizabeth wanted for Cousin Alexander.

'Alex has always lived more for other people than for himself,' Elizabeth said. 'He has always had what Mama sometimes calls an overdeveloped sense of duty. And now, just when he seemed to have his head above water, along has come this deluge.'

Anna settled back in her chair to listen, as Elizabeth clearly wanted to talk.

She talked of her father, a cheerful, hearty, irresponsible man who had been mad for hunting and lavished most of his fortune on horses, dogs, guns, and other hunting gear, followed the hunt about the country, and hosted lavish hunting parties on his own property. By the time he died, his farms and all the buildings on it had been long neglected and there was very little ready money left with which to bring all back from the brink of financial disaster. But Cousin Alexander had done it through sheer hard work, determination, and the sacrifice of his own comforts. At the same time he had looked after their mother, who had sunk into the depths of a devastating grief for a year or so after the death of her husband. And he had taken on the care of his sister too not long after their father's death when she had fled from one of her husband's drunken rages. He had even defended her, with questionable legality, when the husband had come to take her back. Her brother had refused to give her up.

'Oh, Anna,' Elizabeth said, 'I had never before seen Alex resort to violence, and I have not seen it since. He was perfectly . . . splendid.'

His property in Kent having been restored to prosperity, Cousin Alexander had looked forward to securing some personal contentment by marrying and settling down to raise a family. He really had not wanted the earldom. He was not an ambitious man.

'And the worst of it is,' Elizabeth said, 'that Cousin Humphrey – your father – did not like Brambledean Court, his main seat in Wiltshire, and rarely spent time there. I have never been there myself, but we have always been under the impression that he neglected it shamefully. Alex is very much afraid it is in a similarly bad way as Riddings Park was when our father died, but on a far larger scale, of course. He could continue to neglect it, but that is not Alex's way, I fear. He will be very conscious of all the people who live and work on the estate or are otherwise dependent upon it for a livelihood, and he will consider it his duty to set matters right there. I do not know, though, how he will do it. His income had at last become sufficient for his needs until this happened, but now it will be woefully inadequate. And he will doubtless abandon his plans to marry until he feels he has something of substance and security to offer his bride. He may be forty by that time, or older. It may never happen.'

In the silence that followed it occurred to Anna that if she had not existed everything would have gone to Cousin Alexander and he would have had quite sufficient money to restore Brambledean Court and still look for a bride to complete his happiness. But she did exist, and the money was all hers.

'If I pull on that bell rope,' she said, 'will someone come?'

Elizabeth laughed. 'Doubtless bearing the tea tray,' she said.

Anna got to her feet and pulled gingerly upon it.

'Mrs Eddy wants to show you the account books and the house treasures tomorrow morning,' Elizabeth said. 'Mr Brumford wants to call upon you tomorrow at your convenience, preferably in the morning as well. Madame Lavalle will want your opinion and approval of a hundred and one little details in the sewing room. Cousin Matilda's genteel acquaintance will possibly arrive and wish to begin explaining to you to which persons you should curtsy, to which you should merely incline your head, and upon which you should look with gracious condescension as they bow or curtsy to you. And I daresay Cousin Mildred's dancing master will make haste to claim you as a pupil. Some or all of your aunts may call here before luncheon with further plans for your education.'

'Oh dear,' Anna said as the tray was carried in and set on a low table before her and Elizabeth put her work away in her bag. 'Will there be enough hours in the morning?'

'Absolutely not,' Elizabeth said, taking her cup and saucer from Anna's hand. 'Let us go shopping.'

Anna looked at her, the teapot suspended above her cup.

'I promised not to give you either instruction or unsolicited advice,' Elizabeth said, mischief in her smile. 'But I will break my own rule this once. Whenever a lady is overwhelmed by obligation, Anna, she goes shopping.'

'I am not supposed to venture out of the house for at least the next ten years,' Anna said, smiling back. 'Let us go shopping.'

An hour later Anna was curled up on one side of the huge, comfortable bed, no longer smiling. What she ought to do, she thought, and what she wanted to do more than anything else in life, was get up very early in the morning, or even now, and flee home to Bath before Miss Ford and the board of governors could appoint another teacher in her place. She would renounce her fortune – was it possible? – and go back to being Anna Snow.

But Bertha would be horribly disappointed. Besides, one could never really go back, could one? If she did return to Bath, she would take with her the knowledge of who she was and what she perhaps ought to have done about it if only she had the courage to face the unknown. For it was only cowardice that urged her to run away.

He had kissed her.

There – she could block the memory no longer.

He had held her against him while she fought back tears after that dreadfully sad meeting with Harry, and instead of accepting the gesture as the simple offer of comfort it had been, she had felt the shock of the contact with every last corner of her body and mind and spirit – especially with her body. And then she had tipped back her head without drawing firmly away from him at the same time, and she had said something – she could not for the life of her remember what. And he had kissed her.

She could feel it all again now. His body, his lips – no, it had been more than his lips. They had been parted. It was his mouth she had felt, soft, hot with moisture. There was an unfamiliar ache and throbbing between her thighs and up inside her at the memory, and she hid her face in the pillow and moaned with distress. It had been horrible, horrible. Or had it? She had nothing with which to compare it.

She would do her best to forget it. It had clearly not been intended to mean anything. He had lifted his head after a while and suggested bringing her home if she was ready. He had both looked and sounded his usual bored self. He had offered comfort but enough was enough, that look and that tone of voice had suggested, and thank heaven for her habitual sense of dignity.

He had not said a word on the way back to Westcott House. He had taken his leave of her with a careless bow in the hall and stepped back out onto the street without a backward glance.

She could not even begin to explain what it was about him that was so devastatingly attractive – or repellent. She truly did not know if she was attracted or repelled. She was both. He did not have the solid manliness of Joel – or the elegant presence of the Earl of Riverdale. He was all affectation and boredom. But there was . . . that aura.

Oh, she would give anything in the world to have seen him deal with that sergeant who had recruited Harry!

But the thought sent her head beneath the pillow, which she held over her ears as though to shut out the sound of her thoughts.

★   ★   ★

Avery stayed far away from Westcott House for the next several days. He spent long hours in his own very private space in the attic of Archer House, meditating, working his way through long series of stylized moves, holding some of the more impossible positions for minutes at a time, his eyes closed or unfocused, emptying his mind, emptying himself. He practiced more vigorous moves until the sweat poured down his face and body. He busied himself purchasing an ensign's commission in the 95th Rifles foot regiment for Harry while the boy took himself off to Hampshire to bid farewell to his mother and sisters. He took Jessica to a few galleries and museums for some culture and to the Tower of London because on a previous visit her governess had refused to let her see the more gruesome exhibits. And of course he then ended up taking her to Gunter's for an ice because that also had been forbidden on the former excursion. Jess's governess, Avery concluded, was invaluable in many ways. She had taught his sister a great deal, both academic and social. She was also a joyless mortal.

He spent two nights reacquainting himself with the sort of woman who would make the top five of his top one hundred list of favorite types if there were such a thing – he amused himself with the mental image of Edwin Goddard drawing up such a document. On both occasions he found himself disinclined to return for a repeat performance. Could one have too much of beauty and sensuality and sex? What an alarming possibility. Good God, he was only thirty-one. It was far too soon for senility and gout and eccentricity.

He stayed away from Westcott House, but he could not escape hearing about everything that was happening there, for his stepmother, who had complained only a week or so ago of so many social obligations that she needed at least forty-eight hours in every day, had happily forgotten about most of them in her crusade to bring her newfound niece up to snuff. It was an impossible task, of course, she proclaimed every evening when she returned home for dinner, but it simply must be accomplished if the whole family was not to be shamed. But whatever was the queen going to think?

Madame Lavalle and her assistants were working night and day in the sewing room at Westcott House, it seemed, but her hands were severely tied, poor woman, by the fact that Anastasia flatly refused to have anything added to her new garments that would make them pretty and feminine and fashionable. When Madame had sneaked a very modest flounce onto the hem of an otherwise starkly plain ball gown, she had been made to remove it. Anastasia's new maid had arrived – one of the orphans from Bath whom she treated more as a friend than as a lowly servant. The girl showed no inclination to take a firm line with her new mistress. Mrs Gray, the genteel lady suggested by the duchess's sister, had arrived as well to teach

Anastasia about the *ton* and the rules of precedence and correct etiquette and how not to freeze with terror when faced with the queen and other related topics. But more often than not one found the woman in a huddle with Anastasia and Cousin Elizabeth, laughing about something or other all of them found amusing.

'But is Anna learning as well as enjoying herself?' Avery asked.

'I do believe she is,' his stepmother said with obvious reluctance after stopping to consider. 'But that is hardly the point, is it, Avery? One would think she would take her education seriously. I could weep when I think of how my brother kept her incarcerated in that institution for so many years when she was the daughter of his lawful wife. And one cannot help having one's doubts about the wisdom of allowing Cousin Elizabeth to be her companion. On the morning after we had all specifically instructed Anastasia to remain at home until she could look presentable and behave like a lady, Elizabeth took her shopping on Bond Street and Oxford Street. They attracted a great deal of notice as they emerged from numerous shops loaded with packages and looking as though they were enjoying themselves immensely.'

'I daresay they were,' Avery said, wondering idly if Anna had embarked upon the shopping expedition looking like the prim governess or the country milkmaid. He might have taken a saunter along Bond Street himself if he had known . . . No, he would not. There was a certain kiss that needed to be forgotten. It certainly would not do to encounter his fellow kisser anytime soon.

The dancing master had also arrived at Westcott House with his own accompanist, Avery's step-mother reported one evening. Anastasia knew the steps of several country dances, but, oh dear, Mr Robertson had discovered that she danced them with vigor and no idea at all of what she should do with her hands and her head as she danced. She did not know how to waltz and apparently had never even heard of the dance until a few days ago.

'She certainly must not attend any balls for a while,' the duchess added. 'Perhaps not even this year. But by next year she will be twenty-six. I only wonder what sort of a husband we will be able to find for someone of such advanced years.'

'Probably the sort who fancies acquiring a vast fortune with his bride,' Avery said.

'I daresay you are right,' she agreed, brightening.

'And when are the waltz lessons to begin?' he asked.

'Tomorrow afternoon,' she said. 'Avery, you should just see the straw bonnet she purchased on Bond Street of all places. It is enough to make me weep, and the milliner ought to be ashamed of herself for stocking it. It is the plainest thing you could possibly imagine. Elizabeth bought a very pretty and fashionable hat at the same shop.

One wonders if she even tried to exert some influence . . .'

But Avery had stopped listening. He really was, he thought, going to have to start dining at his club more often. He drew the limit at ladies' bonnets as a topic of conversation. There was a ball this evening that Edwin Goddard had reminded him he wished to attend. The Honorable and delectable Miss Edwards had amassed a large court of admirers. A space on her very full dancing card could always mysteriously be found, however, whenever the Duke of Netherby hove into sight and sauntered by to ask for one, usually a waltz.

He dressed with meticulous care – but when did he not? – and made his appearance at the ball. He conversed amiably with his hostess for a few minutes, ambled along to join the crowd about Miss Edwards, conversed amiably with her for a minute or two while she flirted with her eyes and her fan, and the rest of her admirers fell back in almost open resentment, and then nodded amiably and moved on and out of the ballroom and right out of the house less than half an hour after he had entered it.

Nothing but bland amiability.

Tonight Miss Edwards had looked even more fetching than usual. But sometimes one was just not in the mood for a ball or even for an acclaimed beauty. He stood on the street taking snuff and considering his options before turning homeward in all his evening finery. It was not even midnight.

He wandered along to Westcott House the following afternoon to find a dancing lesson in progress in the music room. A severe-looking young woman with a very straight back and a sharp red nose upon which were perched wire-framed spectacles sat at the pianoforte, while a tall, thin man, clearly her father and presumably the dancing master, stood before it. The dowager countess was seated to one side of the room, the inevitable Lady Matilda beside her. Mrs Westcott, Cousin Althea, stood near them, smiling with pleasure at the scene before her. Riverdale was standing in the middle of the floor in waltz position with Cousin Elizabeth.

And beside the pianoforte stood Anna, her hair styled a little more severely than it had been after it was cut, with not one strand out of place, and wearing a white muslin day dress as plain as any dress could be that had clearly been expertly styled and made of expensive fabric. Her hands, her neck, and her face were the only parts of her body that were visible. The dress had a high round neckline and long, fitted sleeves. The skirt fell in soft folds from a high waistline to her ankles. Not for her, obviously, the newest fashion of showing the ankles. She was wearing stays, which emphasized her slimness and gave her a bit of a bosom, though not much of one in the eyes of a connoisseur. On her feet she wore white dancing slippers, which looked at least two sizes smaller than her black shoes and a ton lighter.

Avery looked her over through his quizzing glass while everyone turned his way. He lowered the glass and made his bow.

'Do carry on,' he said, gesturing to the dancing master with the hand that held the glass.

'Alexander and Elizabeth are demonstrating the correct positioning for the waltz,' Lady Matilda explained to Avery rather unnecessarily. 'I still maintain that it is an improper dance, especially for an unmarried lady or for a lady not dancing with her husband or brother, but my protests always fall upon deaf ears. It has become fashionable, and those of us who speak up for propriety are called old-fashioned.'

'I would have danced every single set of waltzes at every single ball I attended if someone had only invented the dance when I was still a girl,' the dowager said. 'It is impossibly romantic.'

'Oh, it is, Eugenia,' Cousin Althea agreed, 'and Alex and Lizzie dance it so well. Mr Robertson is fortunate to have them to demonstrate for Anastasia.'

Avery stayed where he was, just inside the door, while the dancing master pointed out to Anna just exactly where and how Elizabeth's hands were positioned and the exact angle of her spine and head and the expression upon her face – which Elizabeth immediately ruined by grinning at Anna and waggling her eyebrows. The dancing master bowed to Anna and invited her to stand with him as though they were about to waltz. She allowed her right hand to be taken in his left, rested the fingertips of the other hand gingerly upon his shoulder, and stood as far from him as the length of her arms would allow, her spine arched outward rather than in, a look of grim determination upon her face.

'A little more attention needs to be paid toward your posture, my lady,' Robertson said, and she shot upward to stand ramrod straight. 'And rest your palm upon my shoulder and spread your fingers elegantly just as Lady Overfield has hers. Allow your features to relax almost but not quite into a smile.'

She grimaced and clutched his shoulder, and Avery saw what his stepmother meant. At this rate she might be ready to attend her first ball five years from now, by which time she would be so firmly upon the shelf that she would be gathering dust there. Had she been taught the steps yet? Who the devil was this dancing master?

He sighed and wandered out onto the open floor. 'Allow me,' he said, waving the man back and taking his place. He took Anna's left hand in his right. It was cold and stiff, as he had rather expected. He stroked the fingernail of his thumb over her palm before placing the hand on his shoulder just where it needed to be. He drew his thumb along the length of her fingers before withdrawing his hand and spreading it behind her waist and taking her other hand in his. She looked into his eyes in clear dismay as he took a step closer to her, and he held her gaze while, without moving his hand in any way that would be visible to the onlookers, he coaxed her to arch inward slightly from the waist.

'If Robertson has his tape measure with him,' he said without looking away from her, 'he may inform you if you have allowed the requisite number of inches of space between us. One must not err by even half an inch if one does not wish to cause the banning of the waltz from every ball-room in the realm for all eternity. You are permitted to smile provided you do not bounce up and down with hilarity.'

Her lips twitched for a moment with what might have been amusement.

'Perfect, my lady,' the dancing master said, examining the space between them with the naked eye rather than with a tape measure.

'Now all that remains, Anna,' Elizabeth said with a note of quite improper levity in her voice, 'is to learn to waltz.'

'It is necessary, Lady Overfield,' Robertson said, a suggestion of reproach in his voice as he bowed gracefully in her direction, 'to perfect the positioning of the body first so that the steps may be performed with grace from the start. The steps themselves are simple, but what the accomplished waltzer does with the steps is not. Allow me to explain.'

Avery wondered if the man's accompanist ever got actually to play the pianoforte. It was possible that Riverdale had the same thought, which was a somewhat alarming possibility.

'Lizzie and I will be pleased to demonstrate the basic steps, Anastasia,' he said, 'while you watch and Robertson explains.'

'We will keep fancy twirls to a bare minimum,' Elizabeth added, 'though they are what are most fun, are they not, Alex?'

Avery released Anna, who proceeded to give her full attention to the demonstration that ensued, and the dancing master talked without stopping despite the fact that it had always seemed to Avery that any infant who could count to three could learn to waltz in one minute or less. Riverdale, of course, waltzed faultlessly – did he ever do anything that was not perfect? – as did his sister, though she did commit the cardinal sin of smiling up at her partner and even laughing at one point as though she were actually enjoying herself. It was enough to make one wince with horror.

'Perhaps, my lady, you would care to try the steps with me,' Robertson said after a few minutes, having held up one hand to stop the music. 'We will take them slowly without music while I count aloud.'

'Or,' Avery said with a sigh, 'you can waltz with me, Anna, at the proper pace, with music. I shall not count aloud, however, having discovered that it is possible to do so silently within the confines of one's own mind.'

For one moment she hesitated and he thought she was going to choose the dancing master.

'Thank you,' she said, and stepped up to him and set her hand on his shoulder without help.

She felt incredibly slender, he thought, and incredibly dainty, accustomed as he was to holding women of an altogether different physical type. His nostrils were teased by the smell of . . . soap?

His attempt to waltz with her met with little success for the first minute or so and he was aware of murmurings from the sidelines. Perhaps, he thought, beneath the simple folds of her white dress she had two wooden legs. That would explain the length of the skirt. Or perhaps she could not count silently after all. Or perhaps she was just terrified. He held her gaze, spread his fingers just a little more widely above and below her waist, circled the tip of his thumb once lightly over her right palm, and took her into a sweeping twirl. She stayed with him every step of the way, and he saw that slight lift at the corners of her mouth again. Her eyes gazed back into his with less desperation.

And she waltzed. After another minute or so he was aware that Riverdale and his sister waltzed too while their mother clapped her hands on the sidelines. But he kept his eyes upon Anna, who had surely been born to dance – strange thought. Stranger was the thought that he had never until this moment realized what a very – What was the phrase the dowager had used? He had never realized what an *impossibly romantic* dance it could be. He had only ever noticed the intimacy and the suggested sexuality of it.

'Very good, my lady,' Robertson said when the music came to an end and the dowager countess too clapped her hands. 'We will polish the steps and refine the positioning of your body at your next lesson. I thank you for your kind assistance, Your Grace.'

Avery ignored him. 'No frills or flounces, Anna?' he said. 'No curls or ringlets?'

'No,' she said. 'And I do not care that you disapprove. I will dress as I see fit.'

'Dear me,' he murmured, 'whatever gave you the notion that I disapprove?'

And he strolled away to converse with the older ladies for a few minutes before taking his leave.

CHAPTER 11

Dear Joel,

You would not recognize me if you were to see me now. My hair has been cut. It is not short, but it is definitely shorter, and Bertha Reed is learning from my cousin Elizabeth's maid how to dress it more becomingly than its usual style. I am even to have a few curls and ringlets when I venture out to an evening event – which I will be doing soon when I attend the theater as the Duchess of Netherby's (my aunt's) guest. She thinks it is time the ton had a chance to look at me now that I have been at least partially transformed. As though I were a prize bull – though that does not sound like a particularly appropriate analogy, does it? But I shall feel like a prize something. An idiot, perhaps?

And my clothes! I have refused to bow to that society idol, FASHION – what is it, after all, but a ploy to keep people buying and buying so that they will not become UNfashionable? – but even so I have been made to understand that I simply must change my dress at least three times every day, and often more than that. What one wears in the morning will not do for the afternoon, and what one wears in the afternoon will certainly not do for the evening. What one wears at home will not do for walking out or riding in a carriage or going visiting. And one cannot be seen to be wearing the same old thing – even if it is only two weeks old – or even the same old little collection of things wherever one goes. The goal of any lady, it seems, is to give the impression that she never wears the same garment twice. I resisted as far as I was able, but you cannot imagine the strain of pitting my will against those of a duchess (aunt), a dowager countess (grandmother), other titled ladies (aunts), and a French modiste, who is all French phrases and waving hands, though she slips occasionally into what I believe is a Cockney accent. I have so many clothes that Bertha declares she could open a shop and make her fortune. I went shopping with Lady Overfield (Cousin Elizabeth) one morning on fashionable – one cannot quite escape from that word – Bond Street and Oxford Street, and we came home with so many packages, most of which were mine, that it is amazing there was room left in the carriage for us or indeed that there were any goods left in the shops.

But, having already written so much, I realize that you probably have no interest whatsoever in all the details of my changed appearance, do you? I now know everything there is to know about the English upper classes. They – we, I suppose I should say – cannot all be lumped together as rich and privileged with nothing to distinguish them from one another except perhaps size of fortune. Did you know, for example, that if there are four dukes in a room – which heaven forbid there ever would be – all waiting to be seated at the dining table, they cannot be seated in any random order. Oh dear me, no. For no duke – or any other title or rank for that matter – is quite equal to any other. One will always be more important than the other three, and then one of those remaining will be more important than the other two, and so on. It is dizzying and ridiculous, but so it is. I have had to learn not only all the various titles and ranks, but also exactly who fits where into each and who must take precedence over whom. Anyone who makes a mistake has committed social suicide and will be consigned to aristocratic purgatory with only a faint hope of being sent back for a second chance.

I am learning to dance. Oh, you may well protest that I already knew how since you have danced with me on a number of occasions. It is not so, Joel. Our dancing education was woefully inadequate, for it taught us only what to do with our feet and not what do to with our hands and fingers and heads and facial expressions. I shall pass along just one hint for your own future use. Never, ever smile while you are dancing, at least not to the extent of showing your teeth. It is just not done.

But the waltz, Joel – oh, the waltz, the waltz, the waltz. Have you ever heard of it? I had not. It is – well, it is heaven upon earth. At least, I think it must be, even though I have tried it only once. Aunt Matilda, the eldest of my father's sisters, thinks it quite improper because one dances the whole set with just one partner, face-to-face and touching the whole time, but my grandmama describes it as impossibly romantic – her very words – and I have to agree with her. I believe I like my grandmother, though that is another subject altogether.

There is one other thing I will be able to tell you about only in retrospect, for I hardly dare think of it in advance. I am going to be presented to THE QUEEN, Joel!!!! (Miss Rutledge would have an apoplexy.) I am going to have to walk up to her chair (her throne?) and make my curtsy. I am in very intensive training, for there is a way to walk up and a way to retreat and a way to curtsy that applies only to the queen – and to the king, I suppose, but he is said to be mad, poor gentleman. I shall report after the ordeal is over – if I survive it, that is.

I must come to the point of this letter, which is already very long and will probably bore you to tears. Though we have never been boring to each other, have we? Anyway . . . I heard this morning from the Earl of Riverdale, Cousin Alexander, that my half sisters have indeed gone to Bath to live with their grandmother, Mrs Kingsley. Their mother has gone with them, though I do not believe she intends to stay. The letter I sent to Hinsford Manor in Hampshire, inviting them, even pleading with them, to stay and consider it their home for the rest of their lives if they wished, was not answered. Young Harry, my half brother, went to see them but only very briefly. He has a commission in a foot regiment and is to join it shortly. He refused my offer to share my fortune but did explain that it was our father's money he was rejecting, not me. I can understand that, though it breaks my heart that my attempts to share have been spurned.

Anyway, to come at last to the real purpose of this letter (will this woman never get to the point, you must be muttering between your teeth). Can you discover where Mrs Kingsley lives and somehow keep an eye upon my sisters? I really do not know quite what I am asking, but you see, they are no longer Lady Camille and Lady Abigail Westcott. They are merely the Misses Westcott, natural daughters of the late Earl of Riverdale. I am not sure how Bath society will take to them. Will it shun them? Much, I suppose, depends upon the influence wielded by their grand-mother – or upon their own attitude. My heart is heavy for them. I do not know them at all. Camille, the elder of the two, was very unpleasant during that horrid first meeting with Mr Brumford. She was haughty and rude and overbearing. But I hardly saw her under the most auspicious circumstances, did I? And oh dear, the very next day her betrothed jilted her because of her illegitimacy. I wish violence upon his person. Shocking, indeed, but I think I really do. How dare he break my sister's heart!

I still wish I could come home. I believe I would too if I had not put temptation out of the question when I brought Bertha here. She is exuberantly happy. She asked me yesterday if she could possibly have her half day off on Saturday instead of Tuesday as assigned by the housekeeper, because Oliver's half day is on Saturday. I said yes, of course, and she is in transports of delight at being able to report that they are officially walking out together.

And there – I changed the subject and never

did get around to saying exactly what I am asking of you. I do not know! But oh dear, Joel, can you possibly, possibly keep an eye upon my sisters? I do not know them and I probably never will, but I love them. How ridiculous is that? At least keep me informed if you possibly can. Are they social outcasts, or are they making some sort of new life for themselves? The end of another page is coming up fast, and I must not start another. Know yourself

the dearest friend in
the whole world of Anna Snow

P.S. Forgot to thank you for your lovely news-filled letter. Consider yourself profusely thanked. Out of space. A.S.

It had indeed been decided among the powers that be, namely Anna's aunts and grandmother, that her first official appearance in society would be at the theater, in the duke's private box, where she would be seen by a large number of the people who were now avidly eager to meet her but would not be called upon to mingle with them to any great degree. She still had much to learn, apparently, about polite behavior and who was who among the *ton*.

Anna had never watched a live dramatic performance, though there were theaters in Bath. She looked forward to doing so now, especially as she had read and enjoyed the play in question, Sheridan's *The School for Scandal.* It would not have occurred to her to be nervous if everyone else had not told her that she must be – even Elizabeth.

'You will probably find it a bit of an ordeal, Anna,' she said during an early dinner on the evening of the performance. 'Watching the play onstage is the least important reason for attending the theater, you know.'

Anna looked at her and laughed. 'No, I do not know,' she said. 'What else is there?'

'There are tiers of boxes,' Elizabeth explained, her eyes bright with merriment, 'filled with the crème de la crème of society, and the floor or pit, which is occupied mostly by gentlemen. And everyone is out to ogle everyone else, to observe and comment upon gowns and cravats and jewels and hairstyles and the newest pairings and flirtations and court-ships. The gentlemen in the pit gaze up upon the ladies, and the ladies, highly offended, gaze down upon the gentlemen from behind their fluttering fans. Half of society marriages are probably conceived at the theater.'

'Oh dear,' Anna said. 'And the other half?'

'In the ballroom, of course,' her cousin said. 'London during the Season is known as the great marriage mart.'

'Oh dear,' Anna said again.

Bertha had helped Anna into her turquoise

evening dress, which seemed very grand to both of them as it shimmered in the light and flattered Anna's figure with its expertly fitted bodice and softly flowing skirt, despite the modest simplicity of its design and lack of ornament. Bertha had set to work on her hair, brushing it until it shone and then twisting it into a knot high on the back of her head before curling the long tendrils she had left free to trail along her neck and over her ears and temples. She had been learning diligently from Elizabeth's maid.

'Ooh, it looks ever so nice, Miss Snow,' she had said immodestly as she stood back to assess her handiwork. 'All you need now is a prince.'

She giggled and Anna laughed.

'But I really would not know what to do with one, Bertha,' she said. 'I would be quite tongue-tied.'

Though a duke was not of much lesser rank than a prince, was he? She had not seen the Duke of Netherby since that afternoon when he had taught her to waltz – though it was her dancing master who took the credit. She had still not decided whether he attracted or repelled her, and that was strange. Surely the two were polar opposites. But she did know that the waltz was the most divine dance ever created.

'You must be ever so frightened, Miss Snow,' Bertha had told her as she gathered up the brush and comb and curling iron. 'You are going to be seen by all the nobs. But you are one of them now, aren't you? Well, hold your head up high and remember what you used to tell us in school – that you are as good as anyone.'

'It is gratifying,' Anna had said, 'to know that at least one of my pupils was listening.'

Cousin Alexander arrived with his mother soon after dinner to convey them to the theater in his carriage. He could very well be the prince of any fairy tale, Anna thought, especially in his black-and-white evening finery. And he was the perfect gentleman. He complimented both her and his sister upon their appearance and handed them all into his carriage with solicitous care before taking his place beside Elizabeth with their backs to the horses.

'You must be nervous,' he told Anna, smiling kindly at her. 'But you have no need to be. You look elegant, and you will be surrounded by family.'

'Of course you are nervous, Anastasia,' Cousin Althea said, patting her hand. 'It would be strange if you were not. I daresay some people will be at the theater tonight specifically because they have got wind of the fact that you will be there. Your story has caused a great sensation.'

'And if she was not nervous before climbing into the carriage, Mama,' Elizabeth said, 'she is doubt-less shaking in her slippers by now. Ignore us, Anna. I am very glad the play is to be a comedy. There is enough tragedy and turbulence in real life.'

Was she nervous? Anna asked herself. It was

all very well to tell herself that she was as good as anyone. It was another to step into a theater filled with people who were apparently anticipating a sight of her as much as they were looking forward to watching the play. How silly, really.

There was a huge throng of people and carriages about the theater, but precedence was important in London, Anna remembered as a lane opened to allow the carriage of the Earl of Riverdale through, and miraculously a space cleared for it before the doors. The Duke of Netherby was waiting there with Aunt Louise, but it was Cousin Alexander who handed his mother and Anna down onto the pavement before taking Anna's hand firmly through his arm and patting it reassuringly. He offered his other arm to his mother. The duke helped Elizabeth alight and escorted her and Aunt Louise inside to the crowded foyer and upstairs to his box.

He was dressed in a dark green tailed evening coat with gray knee breeches and embroidered silver waistcoat with very white linen and stockings and an elaborately tied neckcloth. His jewelry was all silver and diamonds, and his hair waved golden about his head. He was all grace and elegance and hauteur, and a path opened before him just as one had outside before the earl's carriage.

He had once kissed her. No, he had not. He had comforted her. And he had once waltzed with her, and she had felt as though they were dancing upon the floor of heaven.

Stepping into his private box was breathtaking, to say the least. It was like an intimately enclosed space that was missing one wall. Or perhaps it was like walking onstage, for it was close to the stage and almost on a level with it, as Anna was almost instantly aware, and visible from every part of the theater, from the boxes arranged in a horseshoe on their own level to the tiers above it to the floor below.

There were crowds of people already in attendance. The noise of conversation was almost deafening, but surely she did not imagine the extra buzz followed by a marked decrease in sound and then a renewed surge of conversation. And all heads appeared to be turned their way. Anna knew because she was looking. She might have looked down and pretended there was nothing beyond the safety of the box, but if she did not look out from the start, she might never find the courage to do so, and that would be mildly absurd when she had come to watch a play. But of course there were a duke and duchess in this box too, as well as an earl and a baron and baroness – Lord and Lady Molenor, Uncle Thomas and Aunt Mildred, were awaiting them there. All these people were not necessarily looking at her.

There were two other gentlemen in the box. Aunt Louise introduced them to Anna as Colonel Morgan, a particular friend of her late husband,

and Mr Abelard, a neighbor and friend of Cousin Alexander. They both bowed to Anna while she inclined her head and told them she was pleased to make their acquaintance.

'Everyone, it would appear, is looking at you, Lady Anastasia,' the colonel told her, his eyes twinkling from beneath bushy gray eyebrows. 'And may I be permitted to tell you how elegant you look?'

'Thank you,' she said.

Cousin Alexander seated her close to the outer edge of the box next to the velvet balcony rail and took the chair beside hers. He engaged her in conversation while everyone else took their places. He was obviously doing his best to set her at her ease. And what about him? This must be an ordeal for him too since he had just been elevated to the ranks of the aristocracy and did not spend much time in London. Anna smiled back at him and returned his conversational overtures.

The duke was amusing Elizabeth. She was laughing at something he had said. Mr Abelard, seated beside Cousin Althea, had his head bent toward hers as she talked.

And then, finally, the play began and the noise of conversation and laughter died to near silence. Anna gave her whole attention to the stage and within minutes was both engrossed and enchanted. She laughed and clapped her hands and lost all awareness of her surroundings. She was with the characters upon the stage, living the comedy with them.

'Oh,' she said when the intermission brought her back to herself with a jolt, 'how absolutely wonderful it all is. Have you ever seen anything so exciting in all your life?' She turned to smile at Cousin Alexander, who was smiling back at her.

'Probably not,' he said. 'It is particularly well-done. We may wait here for the second half to begin. There is no need to leave the box.'

All about the theater, Anna could see, people were getting to their feet and disappearing into the corridor behind their boxes. The noise level had become almost deafening again. Elizabeth was leaving with her mother and Mr Abelard.

'We will remain here, Anastasia,' Aunt Louise said, raising her voice. 'Your appearance here tonight is sufficient exposure for a start. If anyone should call here to pay his respects, all you need do is murmur the barest of civilities.'

'You really need not feel intimidated, Anastasia,' Uncle Thomas added. 'Only the very highest sticklers will venture to knock upon the door of Avery's box, and we will engage them in conversation. All you need do is smile.'

The duke himself was on his feet, though he had not followed Elizabeth into the corridor. He was taking snuff from a diamond-encrusted silver case and gazing about at the other boxes, a look of boredom on his face. The snuff dispensed with, he returned the case to a pocket and strolled closer to Anna.

'Anna,' he said, 'after sitting for so long I feel

the urge to stretch my legs. Accompany me, if you will.'

'Avery,' the duchess said reproachfully, 'we decided in advance that it would be altogether wiser on this first occasion—'

'Anna?' He raised his eyebrows.

'Oh, thank you,' she said, realizing suddenly how long she had been sitting. She got to her feet and he escorted her out into the corridor, where crowds milled about, hailing one another, conversing with one another, sipping drinks, and – turning to look at Anna and the Duke of Netherby. He nodded languidly at a few people, raised his jeweled quizzing glass almost but not quite to his eye, and that magic path opened again so that they could stroll unimpeded.

'It must have taken you a lifetime to perfect the art of being a duke,' she said.

'Anna.' He sounded almost pained. 'If there is an art I have perfected, it is the art of being me.'

She laughed, and he turned his head to look at her.

'You do realize, I suppose,' he said, 'that you are learning a similar art? By tomorrow half the female portion of the *ton* will be expressing shock at the simplicity of your appearance, and the other half will be suddenly dissatisfied with the fussiness of their own appearance and begin shedding frills and flounces and ribbons and bows and ringlets until London is wading knee-deep in them.'

'How—'

'—absurd, yes, indeed,' he said. 'And your behavior, Anna. Laughter and applause in the middle of a scene? And no private conversation with those sharing your box when the action onstage grew tedious? Laughing again now, out here?'

'The play did not grow tedious,' she protested. 'Besides, it would be impolite to the actors and to one's fellow audience members to talk aloud during the performance.'

'You have much to learn,' he said with a sigh.

But she knew he did not mean what he said. *He* had not talked during the performance. She would have noticed.

'I daresay,' she said, 'I am a hopeless case.'

'Ah,' he said, raising one finger to bring a waiter hurrying toward them with a tray of glasses. 'I would rather say the opposite.'

'I am a *hopeful* case?' She laughed.

He took two glasses of wine and handed her one as a tall, handsome gentleman with shirt points of such a stiffness and height that he could barely turn his head stepped up to them.

'Ah, Netherby,' he said. 'Well met, old chap. I have not set eyes upon you since that evening at White's when I had some sort of seizure. I must thank you for summoning help so promptly. My physician informed me that you probably saved my life. I was confined to my bed for a week as a precaution, but I have made a full recovery, you will be pleased to know.'

The duke's quizzing glass was in his free hand, and he was holding it to his eye.

'Ecstatic,' he said, his voice so cold that it almost dripped ice.

Anna looked at him in surprise.

'Perhaps,' the gentleman said, turning his attention to Anna, 'you would do me the honor of presenting me to your companion, Netherby?'

'And perhaps,' the Duke of Netherby replied, 'I would not.'

The gentleman looked as astonished as Anna felt. He quickly recovered himself, however.

'Ah, I understand, old chap,' he said. 'The lady is not quite ready for a full public unveiling, is she? Perhaps another time.' He swept Anna a deep bow and moved away.

'But how very . . . rude,' Anna said.

'Yes,' the duke agreed. 'He was.'

'*You*,' she cried. Sometimes his affectations were too much to be borne. '*You* were very rude.'

He thought about it as he sipped from his glass. 'But the thing is, Anna,' he said, 'that he did say *perhaps*. That implies a choice, does it not? I chose not to present him to you.'

'Why?' She frowned at him.

'Because,' he said, 'I would have found it tedious.'

'And I find your company tedious,' she retorted, handing him her glass – he dropped his quizzing glass on its ribbon in order to take it – and turning back toward the box.

Too late she realized that she had attracted

attention. A lane opened in front of her but for different reasons, she suspected, than when it had opened for the duke. She entered the box alone, but the duke was close enough behind her that no one remarked upon the fact. Cousin Alexander was standing talking with the colonel and Uncle Thomas while Aunt Louise and Aunt Mildred were conversing with each other, their heads almost touching.

'You are looking flushed, Anastasia,' Aunt Mildred remarked. 'I daresay it was hotter out in the corridor than it is in here.'

'I am flushed with enjoyment, Aunt,' Anna said as she took her seat again. Her eyes met the duke's, and she would not look away because *he* did not. He raised his eyebrows and had the gall to look almost amused.

He would have found it *tedious* to present that gentleman to her, indeed. How humiliating to the man himself, and how . . . rude to her, giving the impression as he had that she was not yet ready to be presented to polite society. What did he expect? That her mouth would pour forth obscenities and blasphemies, all learned at the orphanage?

And then, before looking away and resuming his own seat, he smiled at her. A full-on, dazzling smile that made him look like a golden angel and made her feel several degrees warmer than just flushed.

She disliked him, she decided. She despised him.

And it was definitely repulsion she felt for him rather than attraction.

She smiled as Cousin Alexander seated himself beside her again and engaged her in intelligent conversation about the play.

CHAPTER 12

'You know, Avery,' Harry said cheerfully as he surveyed himself in the long pier glass in his dressing room. 'I think maybe this was the best thing that could have happened to me. While I was my father's only son and heir, I could not even think of joining the military. I certainly could not do so after his death. But I have always envied those fellows who could, and now I can be one of them with a clear conscience. It is all going to be a great lark. And I am going to like wearing a green rather than a scarlet coat. Every officer and his dog wear scarlet. This will turn heads. Female heads, that is. Do you not think?' He turned to grin at his guardian.

The boy did indeed look dashing in the uniform of the 95th Rifles. And Avery did not doubt his enthusiasm, though there was definitely a slight edge of hysteria to it. Harry would do well – if he remained alive. And perhaps indeed what had happened would be the making of him. He was speaking with a forced bravado now, but he would make it reality. There was something admirable about Harry, after all.

'I do believe you will always turn female heads,' Avery said, looking his ward over without the aid of his quizzing glass, 'the color of your coat notwithstanding. You are ready?'

Harry was leaving today to join his regiment, or the small part of it that was in England, replenishing its numbers after losses in battle. Within a day or two they would be embarking for the Peninsula and the war against Napoleon Bonaparte. There would be no time for the boy to ease his way gently into his new role. He might find himself in a pitched battle within days of his arrival.

'Aunt Louise will not shed buckets of tears over me, will she?' Harry asked uneasily. 'Leaving my mother and the girls a week ago was one of the hardest things I have had to do in my entire life. Worse than watching my father die.'

'Her Grace will keep a stiff upper lip,' Avery assured him. 'Jessica will be another matter.'

Harry winced.

'Her mother has allowed her out of the schoolroom,' Avery told him. 'If she were not allowed to say farewell to you, she would probably run away to sea as a deckhand or some such thing and I would have to exert myself to go and fetch her home.'

'As you did with me when I enlisted with that sergeant,' Harry said. 'Did I tell you how much you made me think of David confronting Goliath, but with a quizzing glass rather than a slingshot? Devil take it, Avery, but I wish I could simply click my fingers and find myself with my regiment. Not that I do not love my relatives. Just the opposite, in fact. Love is the damnedest thing.'

Was it? But it was indeed hard to be sending Harry off, possibly to his death. 'I shall try my utmost to contain my own tears,' he said.

Harry gave a bark of laughter.

The duchess and Jessica were awaiting them in the drawing room. So was Anna.

Avery eyed her with displeasure. She had actually quarreled with him two evenings ago. She had found his company tedious and had stalked away from him, regardless of the curiosity she was stirring among those gathered in their vicinity. He would wager half his fortune that fashionable drawing rooms had been buzzing with the story yesterday and probably would again today unless someone had been obliging enough to wear a yellow waistcoat with a purple coat or elope with a handsome, brawny footman or otherwise arouse some new scandal. And now here she was to sob all over Harry when he least needed it.

'You look very smart, Harry,' the duchess said with hearty good cheer, getting to her feet as she looked him over. 'Goodbye, my boy. I will not ask you to make us all proud of you. I know you will.'

'Thank you, Aunt Louise,' he said, shaking hands with her. 'I will. I promise.'

Predictably, Jessica dashed into his arms, wailing horribly.

'You will be ruining Harry's new uniform, Jessica,'

her mother said after a few moments, and Jess hopped back and rubbed her hand over the slightly damp patch below one of his shoulders.

'I will *n-never* accept that you are no longer the Earl of Riverdale,' she told him, 'and I will n-never forgive Uncle Humphrey, though one is not s-supposed to speak ill of the d-dead. Nor will I forgive the f-family he hid away while he was alive. They were n-never his *real* family. You were and A-Abby and Camille and Aunt Viola. But I promised Mama that I would not m-make a scene, and I will not even though *she* is here and Mama would not send her away. Harry, it hurts my heart to see you g-go and to know you are g-going into such d-danger.'

'I'll come through safely,' he said, grinning at her. 'I am not easily got rid of, Jess. And you will be all grown-up when I return. You almost are now. You will have so many beaux I won't be able to forge a way through them, and you will have lost interest in a mere cousin anyway.'

'I will never lose interest in you, Harry,' she declared passionately. 'I only wish we were not related. But then I suppose I would not even know you, would I? How perplexing a thing life is. Oh, I *w-wish* you were not g-going. I *wish*—'

She shook her head and spread her hands over her face, and Harry turned his attention toward Anna, who was standing quietly some distance away.

'Anastasia,' he said.

'Harry.' She smiled at him. 'I had to come. You are my brother. But I did not come to burden you with more emotion when I am sure you are already oppressed with it. I came merely to say that I honor and admire you and look forward to the day when I can say it again.'

'Thank you,' he said. Nothing more, though he did not look either angry or resentful that she had come – or happy for that matter.

And then he turned to stride out of the room. Avery went with him as far as the outer doors, but Harry had already made it clear that he wished to leave the house alone. They shook hands, and he was gone. Avery raised his eyebrows when he realized that he felt something suspiciously like a lump in his throat.

He would have walked past the drawing room on his way back upstairs and gone about his own business if he had not heard raised voices from within – or, rather, one raised voice. He hesitated, sighed, and opened the door.

'. . . will always hate you,' Jessica was yelling. 'And I don't *care* that I am being unfair. I don't *care* – do you hear me? I care about Abby and Camille. I care about Harry. I want everything to be back—'

'*Jessica.*' The duchess, who almost never raised her voice, raised it slightly now. 'You will return to the schoolroom immediately. I will deal with you there later. When we have a guest in the house, we *always* exercise good manners.'

'I don't *care*—'

'I shall take my leave, Aunt,' Anna said in that soft voice of hers that was nevertheless clearly audible. 'Please do not be angry with Jessica. The fault is mine for coming here this morning.'

'And you will *not* take the blame for me,' Jessica cried, wheeling on her, fury in her eyes.

'Jess.' Avery spoke even more quietly than Anna, but his sister turned toward him and fell silent. 'To the schoolroom. I daresay you are missing a lesson in geography or mathematics or something equally fascinating.'

She left without a word.

'I do apologize, Anastasia,' the duchess said.

'Please do not.' Anna held up one hand. 'And please do not scold Jessica too harshly. All of . . . this has been a terrible shock to her. I understand that her cousins are very dear to her.'

'She adores them,' the duchess admitted. 'Are you missing a dancing lesson or an etiquette lesson or a fitting?'

'Merely my weekly meeting with the house-keeper,' Anna said. 'It can wait. But I will not take any more of your time, Aunt Louise. I will collect Bertha from the kitchen and be on my way.'

'Elizabeth—?' the duchess asked.

'She went to the lending library with her mother,' Anna explained. 'They wanted me to go too, but I chose to come here instead to see Harry one last time – at least I hope, oh, I *do* hope it was not really the last time. But it was a self-indulgence

I ought to have resisted, I fear. Good day to you, Aunt, and to you, Avery.'

She moved purposefully toward the door and looked ready to mow him down, Avery thought, if he did not step out of her way.

'Anastasia!' His stepmother's voice sounded pained. 'You are not by chance intending to descend to the kitchens in person to retrieve your maid, are you?'

'I daresay the girl is awash in tea and bread and butter and gossip,' Avery said. 'Allow her to finish and find her own way home when she learns that she has been abandoned. I will escort you, Anna.'

She was still finding him tedious, it seemed. She raised her eyebrows. 'Was that a question?' she asked.

He thought over exactly what he had said. 'No,' he said. 'If memory serves me correctly, it was a statement.'

'I thought so,' she said. But she did not argue further, and a couple of minutes later they were outside the house and she was taking his offered arm, also without argument.

'Are you still . . . bored with me?' he asked after they had walked in silence out of Hanover Square.

She evaded the question. 'Did you really save that man's life?' she asked him.

Ah, she was referring to Uxbury.

'It is really quite extraordinary that he remembers the incident that way,' he said. 'As I recall it, I almost *took* his life.'

Her head whipped about so that she could gaze into his face. She was wearing a pale green walking dress that was totally unadorned, though it had clearly been made by an expert hand. It emphasized her slender curves, and it struck him in surprise that she was just as sexually appealing as any of the more bountifully endowed females he had always favored. Her straw bonnet, tied beneath her chin with a ribbon of the same color, was surely the plainest hat he had ever seen, but there was something about the shape of it that made it unexpectedly alluring. The curls and wispy ringlets that had adorned her head at the theater two evenings ago had disappeared today, and every last strand of hair had been ruthlessly confined within the knot at her neck. He had not been quite serious when he had suggested that half the ladies of the *ton* would soon be imitating the simplicity of her style, but really he would not be at all surprised if it happened. Of course, they would need her figure and beauty of face to carry it off.

'I suppose you will not explain,' she said, 'unless I ask.'

'Are you sure,' he asked her, 'that you wish to hear about the violence I visited upon the person of another gentleman?'

She tutted. 'Yes,' she said. 'I have the feeling, however, that you are about to say something absurd.'

'I clipped him behind the knees with one foot and set three fingertips against a spot just below his ribs,' he told her, 'and down he went, gasping for air. Or *not* gasping, in fact. There has to be some air moving into the body if one is to gasp, does there not? He turned quite purple in the face, as well he might when he had shattered a costly crystal decanter and probably a table too on his way down. But he had plenty of help surrounding him before I took my leave.'

'Oh,' she said, exasperated, 'you have outdone yourself in absurdity. *Three fingertips*, indeed. He is twice your size.'

'Ah,' he said after nodding to a couple who passed them on the street, 'but everyone is twice my size, Anna. Though my fingers are probably as long as most men's.'

'Three fingertips,' she said again with the utmost scorn. She frowned at him, clearly not sure if he was teasing her or telling the truth.

'One's fingertips can be powerful weapons, Anna,' he said, 'if one knows just how and where to use them.'

'Oh, goodness,' she said. 'I do believe you are serious. But why did you do it – if indeed you did? Why did you almost kill him?'

'I was tired of his conversation,' he said, and smiled at her.

She stiffened and moved a few inches farther from him, then turned her head to face forward again. 'It was tedious?'

'Excruciatingly.'

He became aware then of footsteps pitter-pattering

up behind them at great speed and stopped and turned to see a young girl approaching. She was wearing a stiff new dress, which she was holding above her ankles, and a new bonnet and new shoes, and it took no genius to guess who she was.

'Bertha, I assume?' he asked as she came to an abrupt and breathless halt in the middle of the pavement a short distance behind them.

'Yes, sir, my lordship, your worship,' she said. 'Oh, which is it, Miss Snow? I have forgotten if I ever knew.'

'Your Grace,' Anna said. 'There was no need to hasten out after me, Bertha. You ought to have stayed a little longer to enjoy yourself.'

'I had already eaten two scones and didn't need the third,' the girl said. 'I'll be getting fat. You ought to have come and got me, Miss Snow. I am not supposed to let you out without me, am I? Not when you are alone, anyway.'

'But I am not alone,' Anna pointed out. 'The Duke of Netherby is escorting me home, and he is a cousin by marriage.'

'However,' Avery said with a sigh, 'dukes have been known to devour ladies on the streets of London when they do not have their maids with them to defend them. You did well to follow, Bertha.'

She astonished him by laughing with abandoned glee. 'Oh, *you*!' she exclaimed. 'He's a funny one, Miss Snow.'

'You may follow from that distance,' Avery told

her. 'Close enough to attack me should I take it into my head to pounce upon your mistress, but far enough not to overhear or – heaven forbid! – participate in our conversation.'

'Yes, Your Grace.' She grinned cheerfully at him as though they were involved in some mutual conspiracy.

'Thank you, Bertha,' Anna said.

'I suppose,' he said as they resumed walking, 'you walked arm in arm together on your way to Archer House, talking incessantly and laughing a good deal.'

'Not arm in arm,' she said. 'The first time I did that was with you on the way to Hyde Park. There is not much physical touching at the orphanage. Perhaps because we are all crowded together there, we respect what space there is to set us apart.'

But she had not denied chatting and laughing with her maid. What a strange creature she was. And he had to admit he was altogether too fascinated by her.

'My sisters are in Bath,' she said, 'living in a house on the Crescent with their grandmother, Mrs Kingsley. She must be wealthy – the Crescent is the most prestigious address in Bath. Do you know anything about her?'

'Her husband was born into money and did not squander any as far as I know,' he said. 'I believe she too is of a moneyed background. Hence the marriage between your father and their daughter. Their son chose the church as a career and has remained with his flock, though I very much doubt he has needed to since the death of his father. Camille and Abigail will be well looked after, Anna. They will not starve. Neither will their mother.'

'If only it were a matter of just money, I would be reassured,' she said. 'Abigail has been to the Pump Room with her grandmother for the morning promenade, but Camille has not been seen.'

'And who, pray,' he asked, 'is your spy?'

'That is a horrid word,' she said. 'I begged my friend Joel to keep an eye upon them if at all possible, to find out if they have been able to make a new life for themselves. I suppose I pictured them in near destitution. He discovered who their grandmother is and where she lives, and he saw Abigail entering the Pump Room one morning, though he did not go in himself. He found out it was she.'

'An admirable friend,' he said.

'He called upon Mr Beresford for me too,' she said, 'though I then had to write for myself. He would not reveal anything to Joel.'

'Beresford?' He raised his eyebrows.

'The solicitor through whom my father supported me at the orphanage,' she reminded him. 'I have not had a reply yet. I hope he can tell me who my mother's parents are or were, and where they live or lived – the Reverend and Mrs Snow, that is.'

'Anna,' he said, 'did they not turn you out after your mother's death and abandon you to your father's dubious care?'

'That is what Mr Brumford was told,' she said. 'But I need to discover for myself. '

They were on South Audley Street, moving in the direction of Westcott House.

'You enjoy causing yourself pain?' he asked her. 'Is it not to be avoided at all costs?'

She turned her head to look into his face, and their steps slowed. 'But life and pain go hand in hand,' she said. 'One cannot live fully unless one faces pain at least occasionally. You must surely agree.'

He raised his eyebrows. 'No pain, no joy?' he said. And actually he did agree. Life, he had learned, was a constant pull of opposites, which one needed to bring into balance if one was to live a sane and meaningful life. He knew it with his head, his heart, and his soul. Was there a part of him that did *not* know it, though, or that at least resisted putting it into practice? Had he erected a barricade against pain and thus denied himself joy? But did not everyone avoid pain at all costs?

What had his master meant by *love*? He had been unwilling to explain, and Avery had been teased by the question for more than a decade.

'Oh,' she said, 'I am not sure life can be defined with such simplistic phrases.'

He knew a moment of hilarity as he imagined having such a conversation with any other lady of his acquaintance – or with one of his mistresses. Or with any of his male acquaintances, for that matter. He took his leave of her after seeing her inside the house, having refused her invitation to go up to the drawing room for refreshments. He found himself taking his leave of her maid too.

'Goodbye, Your Grace,' she said, grinning cheekily at him. 'You did not pounce on Miss Snow and devour her after all, did you? But was it because I was there to rush to her rescue, or would you not have done it anyway? I will never know, will I?' And she laughed merrily at her own joke.

So did the very young footman, who was clearly new. Another orphan from Bath?

Avery was too astonished even to use his quizzing glass. But he did shake his head when he was outside the house again and startled two ladies on the other side of the street by chuckling aloud.

CHAPTER 13

A very kept his distance from South Audley Street during the following week. He also dined each evening at one of his clubs with acquaintances who made not a single mention of either bonnets or the education of Lady Anastasia Westcott. It was very refreshing. On the afternoon of the eighth day, however, having just returned from taking Jessica to Gunter's for an ice in an effort to raise her still-drooping spirits, he stepped into the drawing room to pay his respects to her mother.

'Anastasia is ready to meet the *ton*,' she told him without preamble, 'or as ready as she will ever be. We had quite an argument about how it is to be done, but I will not bore you with the details.'

'Thank you,' Avery murmured.

'We decided upon a full ball,' she said. 'Nothing less will do, though one hesitates to call it a come-out ball at her age. She will make her curtsy to the queen at the next Drawing Room, and the ball will be held on the evening of the following day. We had a spirited discussion upon where it would be held.'

And having promised not to bore him with details, she proceeded to do just that as she poured him a cup of tea he did not want any more than he wanted the details. It seemed that the dowager countess could not host the ball because she was too elderly, and Cousin Matilda was hopeless. The Molenors lived so far to the north of England that if they were to trip and fall they would land in Scotland. They came to town only once in a long while and really knew hardly anyone. So *they* would be a poor choice as hosts of such a grand event. The house the new Earl of Riverdale had leased for the Season did not even have a ballroom, a fact that more or less excluded him and Cousin Althea from the running, and it would be entirely inappropriate to use Westcott House for the occasion.

Avery could see where she was headed from a mile away.

'So you see, Avery—'

Must he? He interrupted her. 'The ball will be held here, of course,' he said with a sigh, and sipped his tea – it was just a little better than lukewarm. 'Was there ever any doubt?'

'Well, there was,' she said. 'Everyone knows you are finding this whole business with Anastasia tedious, Avery. You have not shown your face at Westcott House for a week or more, and you have not expressed one iota of interest in the progress we are making with her. She is not a relative of yours, of course, and you cannot be expected to care. I am delighted that you agree the ball must be held here. I shall borrow your Mr Goddard, if I may, and start planning.'

'Ah, but I do not lend out Edwin's services,' Avery said, setting his cup and saucer back on the tray and preparing to make his escape before he found himself being treated to a description of ball gowns. 'He might be offended. I shall have a word with him, and you may provide him with a list of prospective guests in the unlikely event he should forget anyone, and with any special request that may occur to you.'

'That,' she said, 'is what I meant by borrowing him, Avery.'

'Quite so,' he said, and strolled in the direction of the door. He had better warn his secretary of his impending doom.

He had been resigned to the fact that next year would be filled with tedious frivolity when Jessica made her come-out. But a ball at Archer House this year? It was enough to make one flee to a hermitage somewhere far away. There was no point, of course, in hoping that the guest list would be confined to a select few. His stepmother had distinctly referred to the occasion as a ball, and no ball in London could be deemed a success if it could not also be judged after the fact as having been a sad squeeze. The duchess and her mother and sisters would invite everyone with any pretension to gentility, and everyone with any pretension to gentility would accept, for Lady Anastasia

Westcott was still the sensation of the hour, probably of the whole Season, the more so as her unveiling, so to speak, had been a tantalizingly slow process so far. Even at the theater no one outside their own party had secured an introduction to her.

'You will, of course,' the duchess said before he could effect his escape, 'lead Anastasia into the opening set, Avery.'

'Will I?' he said, turning his head back toward her.

'It would certainly be remarked upon if you did not,' she told him. 'And Alexander will lead her into the second.'

'And then a succession of possible suitors for her hand?' he asked.

'Well, she *is* twenty-five years old,' she reminded him. 'There is no time to be lost.'

'But her fortune will knock several years off her age,' he said.

'Certainly,' she agreed, not having noticed any irony in his remark. 'But I do wish she would take more advice about her clothes, especially her ball gowns. They are all so very plain, Avery. And she does not have much of a figure to compensate.'

Ah. He had not escaped the ball gowns after all.

'But,' he said, 'it is always better to set the fashion than to follow it.'

'To set a fashion for plainness?' she said, her eyebrows shooting upward. 'How absurd you are sometimes, Avery. And it was very unwise of her to insist upon employing that girl from Bath as her personal maid. An experienced maid could do much for her appearance. And that new young footman of hers – have you encountered him yet? He is quite extraordinary. But do not set me off.'

'I shall not,' he promised, recalling the scene in which said footman had laughed aloud with said maid at something he, Avery, had remarked, just as though they were all chums of long standing.

Finally he made his escape. Though not unscathed, by Jove. He was doomed to host a grand ball at Archer House within the next few weeks. What a crashing bore.

Though perhaps not. It would be Anna's first real exposure to society, and it might be interesting to behold. *She* might be interesting to behold.

Ah, and he must ask Edwin Goddard after he was warned of what was looming if he had made any progress yet in his inquiries about the Reverend and Mrs Snow, possibly still alive, possibly deceased, of somewhere in the vicinity of Bristol – somewhere with a church. But everywhere had a church. That was not much of a clue.

If they were to be discovered at all, however, his secretary would find them. Avery had recently raised his salary. He must do so again in the not-too-distant future. If Edwin were to leave his employ, he would feel rather as if a limb had been lopped off.

Anna's debut into society had been the subject of much animated discussion with her grandmother and aunts. Her wishes had not been consulted. In Elizabeth's opinion, delivered with a twinkling eye when they were alone together, the dowager and the aunts would come to some sort of agreement, and an opinion from the rest of them would be so much wasted breath. Lady Anastasia Westcott must be presented to Queen Charlotte at an upcoming Drawing Room. That had been unanimously agreed upon early. All else was open to argument.

At one end of the spectrum was the notion that Anna ought to be eased into society gradually by appearances at various select soirees and dinner parties and concerts. At the other end was the suggestion that her debut appearance ought to be at a grand ball hosted by one of their number. One was more likely to learn to swim, Aunt Mildred had said by way of analogy, if one was hurled into the middle of a deep lake than if one merely waded into the shallow edge of it.

One was also more likely to drown, in Anna's opinion.

But she held her peace. It was a matter upon which she really had no firm preference. She had made the decision to remain in London, to learn the role of Lady Anastasia Westcott and take her place in society. Beyond that, she was at the mercy of her relatives, who knew better than she how the transition was to be accomplished. Balls, soirees, concerts – they were all beyond her experience and equally impossible to imagine.

The proponents of the grand ball idea won the day. And Aunt Louise won the less vigorous argument about where the ball would be held. It was to be at Archer House with the Duke and Duchess of Netherby as host and hostess. The date was set for the day following Anna's presentation at court. It would be preceded by a dinner, and then she would stand in a receiving line with the duke and duchess. Everyone who was anyone was to be invited, and Grandmama would be astonished indeed if anyone declined. The *ton* was agog to meet the earl's daughter who had grown up in an orphanage in provincial Bath. Anastasia would have a partner for each set of dances – no one had any doubt of that, though she would open the ball with the Duke of Netherby and dance the second set with the Earl of Riverdale.

Anna had not seen the duke since the day Harry left to join his regiment.

She would apparently be allowed to dance even the waltz because of her mature age, though there was a strange prohibition against younger girls waltzing until they had been granted permission by one of the patronesses of Almack's, whoever they were.

It was all enough to interfere with Anna's appetite for several days ahead of time. She had never attended so much as an assembly in Bath before coming to London, and the queen had been someone who sat upon a throne somewhere in the clouds, only a little lower than God's. It was easier, she found as the days went by, to keep her mind blank and live from hour to hour. Though that was more easily said than done, of course. The appetite loss did not reverse itself.

Dear Joel,

I am too exhausted to sleep. That is what utter, mind-numbing terror does to a person after it is over.

I HAVE MET THE QUEEN. AND I HAVE TALKED WITH HER. Forgive me for yelling again, but it is not every day a poor orphan gets to meet royalty. It is the most daunting thing one could possibly imagine, though the queen herself is the most ordinary-looking mortal and smiles vaguely about her and looks as though she wishes herself elsewhere, as I daresay she does, poor lady. But the liveried . . . persons who get one organized and properly lined up with one's sponsor (the duchess, my Aunt Louise) are far grander and altogether more intimidating than a mere queen. And the whole thing is set up to make the process as uncomfortable as it could possibly be for the participants. When one's turn comes and one has been properly announced, one has to approach the chair (throne?) and execute the curtsy one has rehearsed for weeks – a very deep and graceful one reserved purely for royalty. Then one has to subject oneself to the vague but kindly smile of Her Majesty and anything she may care to say. And THEN comes the hard part, for one must back out of The Presence without tripping over one's train. And the train IS OBLIGATORY but may not be looped over one's arm.

I hoped and hoped when my turn came that she would have nothing beyond a few murmured pleasantries to say to me, as with the two very young ladies who preceded me. But alas, she knew of me, Joel – me, Anna Snow! She looked at me with what seemed like a spark of real interest and asked if it was true that I had grown up in an orphanage on one bowl of thin gruel and a dry crust of bread each day. But I disappointed her. I told her that we had been served three wholesome meals every day as well as a light supper at bedtime. I believe – I cannot be sure – I even added that the soups had always been thick with vegetables and often some meat too and that the bread was freshly baked every day except Sundays. But by that time she was looking vague again and I was given the very firm signal from one of the frightening minions to start backing out.

I did not trip over my train. But did I PRATTLE? I shall have nightmares tonight, though Aunt Louise assured me I did not.

There are a thousand and one details of your last letter I want to comment upon, not least your all-too-brief mention of Miss Nunce, the new teacher. But I am too weary to hold my pen much longer. I shall write again tomorrow. My mind will need distracting, for tomorrow evening is THE BALL. Oh, sometimes I wish, wish, wish, that letter from Mr Brumford had never found me. I ought to have hidden beneath the desk. I am getting silly with tiredness. I am going. But know that you remain

The dearest friend and confidant
(however abused!) of Anna Snow

Late the following afternoon Anna was still wishing she could wake up as from a lengthy, bizarre dream and find herself in her narrow bed in her tiny room in Bath. But she was not dreaming, of course.

'And,' she said aloud, 'one can never go back.'

'Oh, I hope not, Miss Snow,' Bertha said as she twisted Anna's hair into a rather intricate knot high on her head and teased free some tendrils that she would proceed to curl and arrange becomingly about her face and along her neck. 'I would hate to have to go back. I hope you keep me on even if I did iron that crease into the back of your brown carriage dress yesterday without noticing. It came out when I ironed it again, though I really had to press hard. It's funny, isn't it, how creases go in so easily but are an absolute pest to get out? I love being here and being treated almost like a nob myself because I am your personal maid. And I love being able to see Oliver every week instead of having to wait for a letter twice a year. He has to be the world's worst letter writer. He has just had a very good report on his apprenticeship, though, and is almost certain to be kept on when he is finished, though his dream is to have his own shop. Oh no, I never want to go back. I only want the next three years to pass quickly until we can get married, though I ought not to think that way, ought I? It is wishing my life away, and my life is very sweet now just as it is. I can't believe how sweet it is. John Davies says the same thing, and Ellen Payne in the kitchen. Oh, look how these curls are turning out. Don't they make all the difference to your appearance? I always thought you were fine looking, Miss Snow, but I didn't realize how pretty you are.'

'Am I?' Anna asked with a laugh. 'Is not prettiness for girls, Bertha? I am twenty-five.'

'Well, you don't *look* old,' Bertha assured her. 'You don't look a day over twenty. You are going to be the most gorgeous lady at the ball.'

'Well, thank you.' Anna got to her feet, her coiffure complete, and looked at her image in the long mirror. She would very probably be the least gorgeous. She had seen the way everyone dressed for the theater, and presumably they would dress even more grandly for a ball. But she was satisfied with her appearance. Her gown would shimmer in the candlelight, and she liked the color, though she had hesitated over the bolt of fabric when she first saw it. It was a vibrant pink, and a color she had never associated with herself. But Madame Lavalle had unrolled some of it and draped it loosely across her body and directed Anna's attention to a mirror – and Anna had fallen in love. Perhaps she did look younger than her years, or at least no older. And the pink seemed to add a glow to her cheeks when she had feared that it might do just the opposite.

Madame Lavalle, she thought, had earned her fake French name and accent. She really was both talented and skilled. The neckline was a little lower than Anna would have liked, though not nearly low enough to please all her critics. But she liked it and the close-fitting bodice and short, straight sleeves. The gown flattered what little bosom she had – as did the stays she was wearing. The skirt fell straight from below her bosom and yet gave the illusion of wafting about her as she moved. The modiste had wanted to add a train, which would look very becoming, she had said, carried over my lady's arm as she danced, but Anna had declined. After yesterday, she was extremely glad she had. Her satin dancing slippers, embroidered with silver thread, matched the color of her dress almost exactly. Her elbow-length gloves were silver.

Oh, in the privacy of her dressing room she

would believe that she looked gorgeous. Why not? She thought ruefully of her Sunday best dress and the two day dresses she had brought from Bath, all of which had disappeared from her room. Her best shoes too and, of course, the old ones. She smiled at Bertha's image in the glass.

'No, we must never wish to go back, must we?' she said. 'Only forward. My first ball, Bertha. Spend the evening on your knees, if you will, praying that I will not trip over my partner's feet in the very first set – or, worse, over my own.'

Bertha shrieked and then laughed. 'Never tempt fate like that,' she said.

But the first set was to be with the Duke of Netherby, whom Anna had still not seen since the morning of Harry's departure more than two weeks ago. He would not let her trip over anyone's feet. It would be too much of a blow to his own consequence. Oh goodness, she would be dining at his table within the next couple of hours. After that she would be standing in a receiving line with him and Aunt Louise, and then she would be dancing a quadrille with him. She felt suddenly breathless and reminded herself that he would probably wish himself anywhere else this evening except where he actually would be. He would look bored and doubtless would be feeling bored too. How very lowering!

She was smiling as she turned from the mirror. 'Oh, I am nervous, Bertha,' she admitted.

'What? You?' Her maid looked incredulous. 'We

always used to marvel over how nothing could ruffle your feathers, Miss Snow. You have nothing to be nervous about, especially after yesterday. You look gorgeous, and you are Lady Anastasia Westcott.'

'So I am. Bless you.' Anna took up her plain silver fan, which had been her one extravagance when she had gone to the shops to help Elizabeth find new dancing slippers. She squared her shoulders and left the room. Cousin Alexander and his mother would be arriving soon with a carriage to escort Elizabeth and her to dinner at Archer House.

They were the last to arrive. All the other guests were gathered in the drawing room and turned as one to greet the new arrivals. There were hugs and handshakes. There were several voices speaking at once. And then Anna found herself the focus of critical attention.

'I suppose you look as fine as you can ever expect to look, Anastasia, if you remain stubborn and refuse to take advice from those who know better than you,' Aunt Matilda said – the first to offer an opinion. From her, it sounded almost like praise, and Anna smiled. 'Come and kiss my cheek – after you have kissed your grandmama's.'

Anna kissed both.

'It is a pity,' Aunt Mildred said, 'that your gown is too plentiful in the bodice and not plentiful enough in the skirt. Anastasia. A lower décolletage and a train or at least some flounces at the hem would have improved it nicely. But you look well enough.'

'Does not the color suit her wonderfully well, Mildred?' Cousin Althea said, beaming kindly at Anna.

'Your hair really ought to have been cut short, Anastasia,' Aunt Louise said, 'though it does admittedly look less severe than it usually does. You are right, Mildred. She does look well enough, even if she could have looked so much more fashionable.'

'No jewelry and no hair plumes or anything else in your hair, Anastasia?' Anna's grandmother asked. 'I ought to have expected it and taken you to my own jeweler. I shall do so before your next ball.'

'Sometimes, Mother-in-Law,' Uncle Thomas said with a kindly smile for Anna, 'a lady is a jewel in herself.' He raised the glass of sherry he was holding.

'I think you look perfectly lovely just as you are, Anna,' Elizabeth said. 'Would you not agree, Alex?'

Thus appealed to, Cousin Alexander regarded Anna gravely and inclined his head. 'I do indeed,' he said – but what else could he have said?

The Duke of Netherby's fingers were curled about the handle of his quizzing glass, but he had not yet raised it to his eye. He had also refrained from comment. Unlike Alexander and the other gentlemen present, all of whom were clad in what Anna understood to be fashionable and elegant black evening clothes, he was dressed in a dull gold tailed evening coat with paler gold knee breeches, very white stockings and linen, and a white waistcoat heavily embroidered with gold thread. His neckcloth frothed beneath his chin in snowy, intricate folds and lace foamed at his wrists. His jewelry was gold, inlaid with amethysts. There were gold buckles on his dancing shoes. He looked, Anna guessed, somewhat old-fashioned and quite startlingly gorgeous. The fact that he was smaller and slighter than any of the other gentlemen was of no matter. He reduced them all to insignificance.

The judgment of her family having been passed upon her appearance, he stepped forward at last and took it upon himself to introduce Anna to the only two people she did not know – Colonel Morgan and Mr Abelard she had met at the theater. The other two gentlemen, who made numbers even so that there would be an equal number of ladies and gentlemen at dinner, were Sir Hedley Thompson, the dowager countess's cousin, and Mr Rodney Thompson, his son. More relatives, Anna thought as they bowed to her.

The butler announced dinner soon after, and the duke offered Anna his arm. Now she was confused. This was not the strict order of precedence Mrs Gray had explained to her so painstakingly and she had memorized. It seemed that he read her thoughts.

'Sometimes,' he said, for her ears only,

'precedence gives place to occasion, Anna. This is the evening of your come-out, so to speak. You are the guest of honor.' His eyes regarded her from beneath lazy lids. 'You have been very clever, though I doubt you realize it. You will undershine every other lady tonight.'

She was amused rather than offended. 'And that is clever?' she asked.

'Indeed,' he said. 'It is rather like pitching one's voice low in a din and thus making oneself more clearly heard than everyone who is shrieking. It is a skill you know as a teacher.'

So the remark that she would *undershine* everyone was in a sense a compliment, was it?

'And you,' she said, 'will certainly outshine every other gentleman.'

'Ah,' he said as he seated her to the right of his place at the head of the table, 'one can but try.'

Oh, Anna realized in sudden surprise, she had missed him.

CHAPTER 14

Good God, he had missed her, Avery thought. It was not a comfortable realization, the more so as he could not for the life of him understand it. Her grandmother and aunts were quite right about her appearance. Her gown was too prim and plain, her hair too sleek despite the curling tendrils, her person too bare of jewels. He had spoken the brutal truth when he had told her she would undershine everyone else at the ball. He had also meant it when he said she had been clever, though he was perfectly well aware that it had been unintentional on her part.

She looked nothing short of gorgeous.

And he was nothing short of . . . puzzled.

He could not recall when he had last hosted an evening event. Arranging dinner parties, soirees, concerts, and the like required just too much exertion, though admittedly Edwin Goddard would have done all the real work as he had for this. Avery looked along the length of the dining table to where his stepmother was seated at the foot, and was half surprised that it was large enough to seat this many. He did a quick count – fourteen persons in all, himself included. And perfectly balanced numbers, seven ladies and seven gentlemen. How very punctilious of Edwin and the duchess. Such attention to detail would have been enough to give him a headache.

But he had Anna to his right as the guest of honor for this evening and the Dowager Countess of Riverdale to his left as the lady of highest rank after his stepmother. He set about entertaining them, dividing his attention roughly equally between each. Anna had Molenor on her other side, he noted, again a clever move on his stepmother's part, since Thomas was mild-mannered and kindly disposed and not likely to frighten Anna or tie her tongue in knots when she would need it to eat her food.

Not that he could imagine Anna frightened. She ought to have melted into a greasy pool of agony when she stepped inside this house on that very first day, but she had been as cool as her name. He would guess that had been the most frightening moment of her life so far. He must ask her. He was conversing with the dowager when the thought popped into his head. Or perhaps it was yesterday's presentation to the queen, at which she had acquitted herself well, according to his stepmother.

'It is to be hoped,' he said a few minutes later when the dowager turned toward Alex Westcott on her other side and Molenor turned toward Lady Matilda on his, 'that you have exhausted all there is to say about the weather we have been having and may hope to have in the near future, Anna. I may be able to make a few more observations on the subject if I must, but I doubt any of them would be original, and I hate not to be original.'

'The subject is exhausted,' she said.

'I am delighted to hear it,' he said. 'Tell me, Anna. What has been the most frightening moment of your entire life so far?'

She stared at him for a short while, her fork suspended above her plate. 'Where did that question come from?' she asked him.

'From my brain,' he said, 'via my mouth.'

The corners of her mouth quirked into a near smile, and her brow furrowed in thought. Her fork remained suspended. 'I think,' she said, 'it must be something I do not remember with my conscious mind, though my whole body recoils with a nameless dread when I try to recall what it was like.'

Ah. It was too bad of him to have assumed she would choose one of the two moments he had imagined. Now what had he stirred up?

'I think it must be the day I was left at the orphanage,' she said. 'The man who took me there was gruff and impatient with me, I believe, but at least I must have known who he was and what connection he had with me. But then – the sheer terror of abandonment and the unknown when I had experienced security and happiness up to that point. Perhaps it was not so at all. Perhaps I was quite happy to arrive at a place where there were other children to play with. Certainly I have no really bad memories of my life there. Perhaps that almost-memory is not a memory at all.'

And perhaps it was. Well, this was wonderful conversation for a festive evening.

'Eat your dinner, Anna,' he said, and the fork finally found its way to her mouth.

'And what was yours?' she asked him. 'The most frightening moment of your life, that is.'

He considered a flippant answer and decided upon honesty. 'Similar to yours in a way,' he said. 'When I was taken up to the dormitory I was to share with seven other boys on my first day of school when I was eleven, it was to find that I was last to arrive and the only boy who had not been there before. The hush that fell on the room was deafening. And then one of the boys said, *Oh, look, Paddy. Your father has sent your baby sister to join you.* And they all cackled like hens – or like budding cockerels, I suppose. That night they kept me awake as I cowered beneath the bedcovers with unexpected bangs and ghost noises and muffled laughter. But it was not ghosts I feared. It was them.'

She was gazing intently at him. 'Oh, poor little boy,' she said. 'When did you change?'

'Avery,' the dowager said from his left, 'I have been told that you are a severe disappointment to the ladies at every ball you attend. Apparently you dance two or three times with the prettiest girls and then disappear to the card room or off the

253

premises entirely. I hope the card room does not see more of you tonight than the ballroom does.'

He turned his attention back to her, and Anna resumed her meal and was soon conversing with Molenor again. He never, Avery mused, talked about his childhood and boyhood with anyone. But he had just done so.

'I have new dancing shoes,' he said. 'And though my valet has worked tirelessly upon them, they need to be properly broken in. I shall dance every set even if have to go to bed with ten blistered toes and two blistered heels.'

The ball that followed was so far beyond anything Anna had experienced before that she only wished she could sit on the sidelines as some mothers and chaperones did, simply observing it all. But it was all for her, and she was very much the focus of attention.

The ballroom itself took her breath away. It seemed enormous, though it was probably not much larger than the ballroom at Westcott House. It was decked with banks and pots and hanging baskets of pink, peach, and white blossoms and green ferns and was fragrant with their scents. Gilded chairs upholstered with dark green velvet were arranged side by side around the perimeter. The wooden floor had been polished to a high gloss. The coved, painted ceiling was hung with three large crystal chandeliers, all of them fully fitted with lit candles. A pianoforte and other instruments on the dais at one end of the room awaited the orchestra. Double doors at the other end were thrown back to reveal a square chamber set with white-clothed tables, silver urns, crystal decanters, and empty space that would soon hold trays of dainties for the refreshment of the guests. Floor-to-ceiling mirrors lined one long wall, doubling the light and effect of the floral displays. Along the wall opposite, French windows had been opened onto a wide, lantern-lit stone balcony.

'And it is all in your honor, Anastasia,' Aunt Louise said. 'How do you feel?'

'It is beautiful, Aunt,' she said, evading the question.

Guests started to arrive soon after and continued to stream in for longer than an hour as Anna stood inside the doors with Aunt Louise on one side and the duke on the other. She listened carefully to the majordomo as he announced each guest and tried for a while to memorize names and faces and to remember how perfect etiquette dictated she greet each one. But it was impossible. And how were so many people going to fit into the ballroom, let alone dance?

It did not take long for Anna to realize – as she had expected – that she did not look very gorgeous at all in comparison with every other lady who came through the doors. All of them glittered with jewels, their gowns marvels of frills and flounces, lace and ribbons and marvels too of the law of gravity. How could they possibly feel comfortable with bodices so low that disaster was a mere fraction of an inch away? Heads abounded with curls and ringlets and coronets and turbans and tall, waving plumes. Perfumes were almost overpowering.

And then it was time for the dancing to begin, and the duke led her onto the floor for the quadrille. She had learned the steps at school and brushed up on them with Mr Robertson, but it had been too formal a dance to be much favored at orphanage parties. Anna danced it now with her heart in her throat, for she knew everyone was looking at her – and it was not conceit that made her believe so. The Duke of Netherby really did outshine every other gentleman present, of course, and he danced with elegance and with his sleepy eyes directed fully at her, with the result that she soon forgot to fear she would miss a step or a whole sequence of steps. She looked back at him and forgot too that she was a curiosity to all these people – the crème de la crème of polite society – and that she would be spoken of and judged tomorrow in fashionable drawing rooms and club rooms throughout London. She simply enjoyed the dance.

She enjoyed dancing the second set with Cousin Alexander too. He was a complete contrast to the duke – tall and well built, darkly handsome, immaculately and fashionably elegant, and kindly.

'I hope you do not think, Anastasia,' he said before the music began, 'that Lizzie forced me into complimenting you on your appearance before dinner. I spoke the truth. Simplicity suits you. It speaks of your upbringing and yet is suited to the change in your station.'

'Thank you, Alexander.' She smiled at him.

'My family and close friends call me Alex,' he told her.

'And I am family,' she said. 'Oh, how I dreamed for years and years of being able to say that to someone, Alex. And now I can say it to several people.'

He danced the steps of the country dance with careful precision when it would have suited her better to dance with more exuberance. She followed his lead.

If she had half expected that after the first two sets she would have time to relax and enjoy watching for a while, she was soon to be disabused. She found herself and Aunt Louise surrounded by gentlemen, all eager to solicit her hand for the next set. And so it continued all evening. She had partners for every set but still was not able to dance with half of those who asked. It all would have been quite dizzying had she not understood that none of them had any real interest in the Anna Snow who was herself, but only in Lady Anastasia Westcott, who was newly unleashed upon the *ton* as an unknown curiosity.

She danced the supper dance with Lord Egglington, a tall, gangly young man with buck teeth and eyeglasses, who seemed terrified of her until she discovered that he was mad for horses and asked a few questions that got him talking with boyish enthusiasm. He led her into supper afterward and continued talking while Anna relaxed and listened with interest. He must be several years younger than she, she guessed. He had been at school with Harry, he explained, but he flushed rosily after saying so and quickly got back to the topic of horses as though he expected she would not appreciate any mention of her brother.

She excused herself when guests were beginning to return to the ballroom and hurried off to the ladies' withdrawing room. She was on the broad landing outside the ballroom a few minutes later, making her way back, when a gentleman stepped into her path and bowed to her.

'We have not been formally introduced, alas, Lady Anastasia,' he said. 'I was late arriving this evening. Though I did once ask to be presented to you before you were ready to be exposed to the *ton*. I apologize for my forwardness on that occasion and beg to introduce myself now.'

'Oh,' she said, recognizing him as the gentleman the duke had snubbed so rudely at the theater. 'Yes, I remember, and I would quite happily have made your acquaintance, sir. I made my displeasure known to the Duke of Netherby.'

'But I do not blame your family for being protective of you, Lady Anastasia,' he said. 'They must fear that such a rare and innocent bloom will take a misstep and be scorned by the very people with whom her birth intended her to mingle.'

Perhaps, Anna thought, the duke had had some reason – though no excuse – for avoiding introducing her to this man.

'Viscount Uxbury, at your service, Lady Anastasia,' he said with another deferential bow.

'I am pleased to make your acquaintance, Lord Uxbury,' she said, extending her right hand. He took it and raised it to his lips.

He was a tall, good-looking man, but also, she suspected, a bit pompous. And even she knew – it was one of the points of etiquette Mrs Gray had mentioned – that if he wished for an introduction to her he ought to have asked someone close to her, Aunt Louise, perhaps, to present him.

'Dare I hope, Lady Anastasia,' he said, 'that you are free to dance the next set with me?'

She opened her mouth to reply.

'Lady Anastasia Westcott is engaged to dance the next set with someone else,' a languid voice said from behind her left shoulder, 'as soon as that someone else has had an opportunity to ask. And the same applies to every other set this evening, Uxbury.'

Anna turned toward the Duke of Netherby, her eyes widening with incredulity. Inevitably, he had his gold quizzing glass raised almost to his eye.

'Someone has already asked,' she said icily, ignoring the fact that she did not really want to dance with Viscount Uxbury. 'And I was about to say yes, Your Grace.'

He ignored her. 'Pardon me if my memory has failed me,' he said, addressing himself to the viscount, 'but were you invited, Uxbury?'

'I was,' the viscount said stiffly. 'I would not have come uninvited. And pardon me, Netherby, but are you Lady Anastasia's guardian? I was under the impression that she is not related to you and that she is anyway of age.'

Oh dear. The landing on which they stood was a very public place. It was rather crowded with guests moving in and out of the ballroom or gathered in conversational groups until the dancing resumed. The atmosphere in this little group was growing hostile. They were going to be attracting attention in a moment.

'Ah,' the duke said, 'then let that be a lesson to me to scrutinize guest lists with greater care in the future and trust less to the good taste of Her Grace and my secretary. I would be obliged, Uxbury, if you would remove your person from my home.'

'I see that you are offended,' Lord Uxbury said. 'Yet in my place, Netherby, you cannot deny that you would have done exactly the same thing. No one wishes to find himself married to a bas – Ah, pardon me, there is a lady present. Lady Anastasia, will you bow to a ducal whim at your own come-out ball without protest, or will you rather honor me by partnering me in the coming set?'

The duke was no longer ignoring her. Nor did he continue to press his inexplicable quarrel upon the viscount. Instead, he dropped his quizzing glass on its ribbon and turned sleepy eyes upon her, awaiting her answer.

Other eyes were turned upon them too in some curiosity, and guests who had been returning to the ballroom paused before doing so.

'I would ask, Your Grace,' she said, keeping her voice low, 'what your quarrel is with Viscount Uxbury. Except that, whatever it is, it does not concern me, and I must beg leave to inform you that I resent being caught in the middle of it and somehow being made a party to your bad manners – again.'

His eyes gleamed for a moment with what looked like appreciation. 'Perhaps Lord Uxbury did not introduce himself fully, Anna,' he said softly. 'Perhaps he did not mention that he was recently betrothed to Lady Camille Westcott until he made the shocking discovery that she is merely Miss Westcott, illegitimate daughter of the late Earl of Riverdale.'

Her eyes widened and she stared at him a moment before turning toward the viscount.

'*You* are the man who jilted my sister?' she said.

'You have been misinformed,' he said stiffly. 'It was Miss Westcott who ended our engagement with a public notice to the morning papers. And her relationship to you is surely not something of which you can be proud, Lady Anastasia. The less said about her and her unfortunate sister, the better, I am sure you will agree.'

'Lord Uxbury.' Unconsciously she spoke with

261

her teacher voice, the one she used when her class was particularly inattentive. 'I informed you a few minutes ago that it was a pleasure to make your acquaintance. It is no longer a pleasure. I have no wish to be acquainted with you now or at any time in the future. I have no wish to speak with you again. I hope never to *see* you again. You are a man I despise, and I am only glad *my sister* was fortunate enough to avoid a marriage that would surely have brought her nothing but misery even if the truth of her birth had never been discovered. Archer House is not my home, but this ball is in my honor. I would ask you to leave.'

Too late she heard the silence around them. And a glance about the hallway confirmed her fear that no one had moved off into the ballroom since she last looked. Indeed, more people seemed to have spilled out, including Alexander, who stood a few feet away, his hands clasped at his back.

And then a group of five young ladies, in a huddle together outside the ladies' withdrawing room, clapped their hands. They did not make a great deal of noise, since every one of them wore gloves, but a couple of gentlemen joined them before a murmur of conversation rose again and everyone turned away as though nothing unusual had happened.

'Quite so,' the duke said agreeably. He raised his eyebrows in the direction of Alexander. 'I shall see you safely on your way, Uxbury. One would not wish you to have another of your seizures on the stairs, would one?'

'Anastasia,' Alexander said, 'allow me to escort you inside. There is already a crowd gathered about your aunt, hoping to solicit your hand for the next set.'

Anna set a hand on his sleeve and allowed him to lead her into the ballroom.

'How much of that did you hear?' she asked him.

'Netherby's explanation of who Uxbury is,' he said, 'and the whole of your magnificent setdown.'

'Was I speaking very loudly?' she asked.

'Not at all loudly,' he said, 'but quite distinctly.'

'Oh dear.' She grimaced. 'I have been a colossal failure at my very first *ton* appearance.'

'But are you sorry,' he asked her, 'for having given Uxbury such a public scolding?'

She thought about it for a moment, biting her lower lip. Then she smiled at him. 'No,' she said.

'I believe, Anastasia,' he said, and he surprised her by grinning at her, 'my cousins – your grandmother and aunts – are going to have to learn to present you as an original rather than as a perfect and perfectly docile lady.'

'I am an imperfect lady?' She grimaced.

'I do believe you are,' he said. 'And I like you.'

They had come up to Aunt Louise, who was indeed in the midst of a group of gentlemen, mostly young, who turned as a body to smile at her and welcome her into their midst and vie with one another over who would lead her into the next set. Word of what had just happened had not reached any of them yet.

But really, Anna thought, opening her fan for the first time and waving it before her face, how dared he. How *dared* he!

And her relationship to you is surely not something of which you can be proud, Lady Anastasia. The less said about her and her unfortunate sister, the better, I am sure you would agree.

Had he really expected that she would welcome his acquaintance? That she would be pleased to dance with him? She hoped Avery really had felled him that one night with three fingertips, though she was still not sure she believed him. She wished he would do it again on the stairs, preferably close to the top. And she was not at all ashamed at the viciousness of the thought. If Camille's heart had been broken, it would be little comfort to her to know that she had had a narrow escape from a bounder.

The next set, the first after supper, was a waltz, and she danced it with the portly Sir Darnell Washburn, who wheezed his way through the first few minutes and made no conversation because it was clear he was counting steps in his head – his lips were moving slightly. His lips stopped and so did their waltz, however, when a ringed, well-manicured, lace-trimmed hand closed upon his shoulder.

'The footman standing in the doorway to the refreshment room has a cool glass of ale just for you, Washburn,' the Duke of Netherby said. 'Go and drink it before it grows too warm. I shall waltz with Lady Anastasia in your place.'

'Oh, I say.' Sir Darnell's initial look of annoyance turned to something else when he saw who had interrupted him and was attempting to take his partner away. 'Decent of you, Netherby. Dancing is warm work. If you will excuse me, Lady Anastasia?'

'I will, sir,' she said, but she looked very pointedly at the duke as he drew her into his arms. 'That was rude.'

'To perspire all over you and count steps instead of murmuring flatteries into your ear?' he said. 'Forgive him, Anna. He can resist most temptations, but not a glass of ale.'

He moved her flawlessly into the waltz, twirling her about the perimeter of the dance floor with the other dancers.

'By tomorrow,' she said, 'I shall be notorious.'

'Ah, Anna,' he said, 'do the *ton* some justice. You are already notorious, and your aunts are just beginning to realize it.'

'If you had not been so secretive,' she said, 'and had explained at the theater who he is, then tonight's very public scene might have been avoided.'

'Remind me,' he said, 'never to be secretive with you again. And remind me never to offend you. One shudders at the prospect of being at the receiving end of your displeasure, especially in a public place.'

'Have I ruined the ball?' she asked. *Have I ruined my life?* she wondered silently.

'That,' he said, 'will depend upon whom you speak with in the coming days.'

'I am speaking with you now,' she said.

'And so you are.' He swept her around one corner of the room, twirling her twice about as he did so. 'I am not bored, Anna. And I am invariably bored at grand *ton* affairs, especially balls.'

And he did again what he had done only once before, though she was as little prepared for it now as she had been then. He smiled fully at her and twirled her again. And she smiled back, as caught up in the magic of the waltz as she had been during that first lesson in the music room at Westcott House.

She had probably disgraced herself beyond redemption. But she would think of that later.

She would think of it tomorrow.

CHAPTER 15

Nothing had been planned for the day following the ball. It would be a quiet time for rest and reflection, the aunts had decided, before they all gathered again to assess Anna's debut and plan the rest of her Season.

The day following the ball did not turn out to be a quiet one.

It started with exactly thirty bouquets being delivered to Westcott House before noon.

'I am almost tempted just to leave the front door open so that the knocker does not end up making a hole in it, Miss Snow,' John Davies said from behind a particularly extravagant bouquet of two dozen red roses as he brought it into the drawing room. 'But Mr Lifford says it would not be the thing. This one must have cost a fortune.'

Three of the bouquets were for Elizabeth, twenty-seven for Anna. Two, one for each of them, were from Alexander.

'Oh dear,' Anna said, surveying the veritable garden surrounding them, though a number of the bouquets had been borne off by housemaids, to be displayed elsewhere about the house. 'I do not even remember half these gentlemen, Lizzie. More than half. I surely did not even dance with half of them. How very kind they are.'

'Indeed,' Elizabeth said, fingering the petals of a cheerful daisy in one of her bouquets. 'Sir Geoffrey Codaire proposed marriage to me once. It was the day after I had accepted Desmond's offer. The notice had not yet appeared in the papers. He professed himself to be heartbroken, though I daresay he was not. And I was so in love with Desmond, I must confess I did not spare him another thought.'

'Is he the gentleman who danced the first waltz with you?' Anna asked, remembering Elizabeth's partner for that dance as a tall, solid, sandy-haired gentleman who had had eyes for no one but his partner.

'And the waltz after supper,' Elizabeth said. 'The one you started to dance with Sir Darnell Washburn and finished dancing with Avery. Sir Geoffrey lost his wife a year ago and has only recently left off his mourning. How tragic it was for him. She was trampled by a runaway horse and cart outside Hyde Park. She left him with three young children.'

'Oh,' Anna said.

But Elizabeth shook her head and smiled. 'Was it not a lovely, lovely ball, Anna? Goodness, I missed dancing only one set – at my age.'

'You looked lovely, Lizzie,' Anna told her. 'Yellow suits you. It makes you look like a ray of sunshine.'

Her friend laughed. 'It was kind of Mr Johns to

send me flowers too,' she said. 'He used to stay with us sometimes as a boy when his father hunted with Papa. I used to think him a horrid know-it-all, but he has mellowed. Or perhaps I have. But, Anna, all these admirers of yours – twenty-what? I have lost count.'

'Twenty-seven,' Anna said. 'It is the first time in my life anyone has given me flowers, and now twenty-seven people have all at once. It is a little overwhelming. It is a good thing there is nothing planned for the rest of the day and no one is coming here. I am already exhausted – or still exhausted.'

She was wrong about the rest of the day, however. They had luncheon and went to their rooms to change into frocks more suitable for afternoon wear even though they were going nowhere. But scarcely had they settled in Anna's sitting room, Elizabeth with her embroidery, Anna at the small escritoire to write letters, than John Davies came to announce that there were visitors downstairs, and he had shown them into the drawing room since there were two of them and they had not come together, and Mr Lifford had given it as his opinion that judging by the number of flowers that had come this morning, there were likely to be more visitors and they might become crowded in the visitors' salon especially since four of the bouquets were in there taking up most of the table space.

'Though they do look lovely,' he added, 'and

they smell a treat. But then, so do all the ones in the drawing room and these ones in here.'

'Thank you, John,' Anna said as she cleaned her pen and set it down and Elizabeth folded her embroidery and put it away. 'Whoever can they be, Lizzie?'

By the time they arrived in the drawing room, three more gentlemen had arrived, one of them with his mother, another with his sister. And that was just the beginning. They kept coming for all of two hours, the fashionable visiting hours, Elizabeth explained later, and stayed for half an hour apiece. Elizabeth poured the tea when the tray was brought in and Anna concentrated upon conversing with their guests. It was surprisingly easy, since everyone seemed to be in a hearty good mood and talked easily with one another. There was a great deal of laughter. She did not count the total number of visitors, but there were surely more than twenty in all, only four of whom were ladies.

Anna received five invitations to drive in the park later in the afternoon and accepted the one that came from Mr Fleming, since he asked first and his invitation included his brother – who had not accompanied him here – and Elizabeth. She also had three invitations to dance the opening set at Lady Hanna's ball four days hence, which they all assumed she would attend. She had one invitation to join a theater party the following week and another to join a party at Vauxhall, also next week.

She deflected all five of those invitations by declaring with a laugh that she had not yet had a chance to look through all her invitations and decide which she would accept and which dates were still open to her. Mrs Gray's lessons, though lighthearted and laughter filled, had been invaluable.

Written invitations really had been arriving all day, and the butler brought them into the drawing room on a silver salver after the last of the guests had left.

'Oh goodness, Lizzie,' Anna said as they sorted through them, 'how very kind everyone is. I really thought that after last night I might have put myself beyond the pale.'

Elizabeth was shaking her head at her. 'You really do not understand, Anna, do you?' she said. 'I will not say you are the wealthiest lady in England, but I am quite sure you are among the five or so wealthiest. And you are young and newly arrived upon the social stage. And . . . you are single.'

'But just a short while ago,' Anna said, 'I was an orphan and a teacher at an orphan school.'

Her answer struck them both as funny and they went off into whoops of laughter. Though Anna was not quite sure she was amused.

'We had better get ready to drive out with Mr Fleming and his brother,' Elizabeth said. 'Just do not expect it to be a quiet drive, Anna.'

Avery called at the Earl of Riverdale's rented house in the middle of the afternoon and found that he

271

had just returned home from escorting his mother to the library. He raised his eyebrows when Avery was admitted to the sitting room where the two of them had just settled for refreshments. He might well be surprised, Avery thought, for the two men, while not enemies, had never been friends either.

'Avery,' Mrs Westcott said, smiling warmly as she got to her feet. 'How delightful. Do come and sit down. I am just about to enjoy a cup of tea, but I expect you will have something stronger with Alex. You must have been very pleased with the ball last evening. It went very well, and Anastasia acquitted herself with admirable poise. As for what happened with Viscount Uxbury after supper, well, for my part I can only applaud her having spoken up in defense of poor Camille. I just wish I had heard her.'

'We can only hope, Mama,' the earl said, crossing to the sideboard, 'that the rest of the *ton* agrees with you. What will you have, Netherby?'

Avery sat and conversed for a while until Mrs Westcott had finished her tea. She got to her feet then and gathered up the three books piled beside her.

'I can see how it is,' she said, her eyes twinkling. 'You came for a specific purpose, did you not, Avery? You came to speak privately with Alex and are wondering how you can hint me away. And I have been wondering how I can get away without appearing ill-mannered. I have three new library books and cannot wait to dive into them.

No, no need to get up. You neither, Alex. I can hold three books in one hand and open the door with the other.'

Her son got to his feet nevertheless to open the door. He closed it quietly behind her and turned to look at Avery.

'To what do I owe this honor?' he asked.

'I need a second,' Avery said with a sigh, 'and thought it might be better to keep it in the family, so to speak.'

There was a beat of silence.

'A second,' Riverdale said, moving to the fire-place and leaning one elbow upon the mantel. 'As in a fight? A duel?'

'It is tiresome in the extreme,' Avery said, 'but I have been called out by Uxbury for causing him public humiliation and anguish – I believe that latter was the word Jasper Walling used this morning when he presented himself at Archer House on behalf of Uxbury to invite me to name my seconds. I believe he meant a singular second even though he used the plural.'

'The devil!' Riverdale said. 'Why Cousin Louise decided that it would be bad manners not to invite the man to the ball escapes my understanding. He was fortunate that either you or I did not throw him down the stairs and chuck him out the doors.'

'Quite so,' Avery agreed. 'But I need a second. Will you oblige?'

Riverdale frowned at him. 'What weapons will you choose?' he asked. 'The choice will be yours since you are the challenged rather than the challenger. I can remember that you were tolerably handy with a fencing foil in your senior year at school. I have heard it said that Uxbury is a crack shot with a pistol. How good are you?'

'Tolerable,' Avery said, withdrawing his snuffbox from a pocket and taking a pinch while Riverdale waited impatiently for him to continue. 'I would hate to put a bullet between his eyes, however, and cause a fuss. I would hate even more to shoot into the air and then have to stare down the barrel of his pistol. Swords draw blood, and blood is notoriously difficult to wash out of shirts, or so my valet informs me. Swords also make holes in shirts. No, no, my weapon of choice must be the body, unencumbered by any additional weapon that may cause holes or an excess of blood. Though nosebleeds can be messy, of course.'

'You will choose a fistfight?' Riverdale looked incredulous. 'Until someone is down and unconscious? It will be a slaughter, Netherby. You had better let me take your place. I was part of that scene too last evening and am actually related to both Camille and Anastasia. I am quite handy with my fives even though I do not get to Gentleman Jackson's boxing saloon as often as I could wish.'

'It is a second I am in search of,' Avery told him, 'not a first. If you are unwilling, I shall have to ask someone else, but that would be tiresome.'

'It will be a slaughter,' Riverdale said again.

'I hope not,' Avery said thoughtfully. 'I hope I

will have better control of myself than to cause him lasting bodily harm, though it will be tempting. I do not like the man.'

Riverdale laughed shortly, though he did not sound amused. 'At least you will still be alive at the end of it,' he said. 'I will see to that.'

'Will you?' Avery got to his feet. 'I am much obliged to you, Riverdale. I would rather the whole matter be kept private. One hates to be ostentatious about such things. Besides, one would not wish to draw more attention than necessary to the two ladies.'

'Camille and Anastasia?' the earl said. 'I shall try to persuade Walling to urge discretion upon Uxbury, though it may be difficult. Uxbury may well want an audience, especially when he knows you have chosen fists.'

'Bodies,' Avery said, correcting him gently. 'Fists are just one small weapon of the body and not always very effective – they shorten the hands. Do your best, Riverdale. I will not take any more of your time – Cousin Althea may be bored with her books already. You will keep me informed, I daresay.'

'I will,' Riverdale promised before accompanying Avery to the door.

This was all very tiresome, Avery thought as he moved off down the street and touched the brim of his hat to a lady who was walking with her maid in the opposite direction. He was very tempted to call upon Uxbury and settle the matter here and now. But Uxbury had chosen to be idiotic and issue a formal challenge, and proper gentlemanly protocol must now be followed.

Avery very much hoped, however, that the whole matter could be kept quiet. The thought that he might be seen as the champion of the honor of either Camille or Anna – or both – was shudderingly awful. It would ruin his reputation for effete indolence. But what was one to do when a fellow mortal chose to be an ass? One could not simply invite him to desist. Actually, one could, but it would be so much wasted breath.

Sometimes life could be quite bothersome.

Anna was standing in the window of the drawing room the following afternoon, gazing down at the street. Her family would be arriving soon with news and views – about the ball, about her triumphs and disasters, though she hoped the latter was singular rather than plural, about where she would go from here in her progress from being Anna Snow to becoming Lady Anastasia Westcott. It was hard not to be feeling a little despondent, though she knew she should be ecstatic with gratitude to the fates or whatever it was that had made all her dreams come true in such an abundant way. If only her sisters were here, sitting in the room behind her, or standing on either side of her, their arms linked through hers, everything would be different. But there would still be their mother, out there somewhere in the cold. And there would still be Harry, facing all the dangers and privations of war. And there would still be blanks in her history.

And who had ever said life could end up happily ever after the way fiction sometimes did? She gave her head a shake.

Elizabeth was still upstairs changing. The butler was to inform any other callers that she was not receiving today. There would be no repetition of yesterday, though there had been two more bouquets this morning, one of them clutched in the hand of a young gentleman who had stammered out a marriage proposal or at least the intention of a marriage proposal. He had actually asked to which gentleman he must apply for permission to ask for her hand. Anna had looked at Elizabeth, and Elizabeth had looked at Anna and suggested that the young man might wish to have a word with her brother, the Earl of Riverdale.

It would have been simpler and perhaps kinder for Anna to have said no, but how could she when he had not actually asked the question?

Her eyes focused upon the Duke of Netherby, who was walking along the street in the direction of the house. He was not escorting Aunt Louise today, then, but he was definitely coming here. After he had disappeared inside the door below, she waited for him to be announced.

He paused on the threshold of the drawing room and grasped the handle of his quizzing glass as he looked around, his expression somewhat pained.

'I am the first to arrive?' he said. 'How very lowering. It would almost suggest an eagerness to see you, Anna. And you are alone? No Cousin Elizabeth to chaperone you? No saucy maid to laugh at my wit?'

'Avery,' she murmured.

His eyes came to rest on her and for a brief moment his glass was trained upon her too.

'What is it?' he asked.

'Nothing.'

He dropped his glass and strolled farther into the room. 'There is a way of saying nothing,' he said, 'that suggests quite the opposite. All these flowers have come from admirers, I assume? And the ones in the hall and on the landing? I wondered for a moment as I came through the door whether I had moved outdoors rather than in. It was quite disorienting. What is it, my dear?'

The unexpected endearment brought tears welling to her eyes and she turned her head away. 'I had a letter at long last this morning from Mr Beresford,' she said. 'The solicitor who dealt with my father's business in Bath.'

'And?'

'He recalls receiving one letter from my grandfather more than twenty years ago,' she said, 'informing him of my mother's death and asking him to get word to my father. He does not still have that letter, and he cannot remember where it came from except that it was somewhere in the vicinity of Bristol. "Somewhere in the vicinity of" is very imprecise. It could be two miles away or twenty. It could be north, south, east, or west.'

'West would place it in the Bristol Channel,' he said.

'Perhaps they lived on an island,' she said crossly. 'But wherever it was, it was more than twenty years ago. They may both be dead and forgotten by now. There may have been a number of vicars at that particular church in that particular village since.'

'There have not been,' he told her. 'The church is St Stephen's. The village is Wensbury, twelve miles southwest of Bristol. The vicar is, and has been for almost fifty years, the Reverend Isaiah Snow. He lives in the vicarage beside the church with his wife of forty-seven years.'

She stared at him, as though through a long tunnel. 'How do you know?' Her voice came out almost as a whisper.

'I would like to be able to say that I have been on a long and dangerous odyssey throughout the length and breadth of England and Wales, slaying a few dragons along the way, on a quest to discover your maternal forebears,' he said. 'Alas, you would suspect I was lying. My secretary dug up the information. He claims it was not difficult. He pursued the search through the church, which found one lowly vicar for him just as though the man had never been lost. And indeed he had not been. It is difficult to get lost if one remains in the same place for fifty years.'

'They are alive?' She was still whispering. 'My grandparents?' She clasped her hands tightly to her mouth and smiled radiantly at him. 'Oh, thank you. Thank you, Avery.'

'I shall pass on your gratitude to Edwin Goddard,' he told her.

'Please do,' she said. 'But he would not have thought of making the search all on his own. Why did you ask him to do so?'

He took his snuffbox out of a pocket, gazed absently at it, and put it away again. 'You see, Anna,' he said. 'I increased his salary a short while ago, and then I had the alarming thought that perhaps I did not make enough of an effort to see that he earned it. I made an effort and thought of the Reverend Snow.'

'How absurd,' she said.

He looked up at her, his eyes keen. 'Remember, Anna,' he said, 'that they had you taken away after your mother died and apparently showed no further interest in you.'

The door opened behind him at that moment and Elizabeth hurried inside.

'I am so sorry,' she said. 'I stepped on the hem of my dress just as I was leaving my dressing room and tore it. I had to change into something else. And then there was all the bother – Oh, no matter. How do you do, Avery?'

'I am delighted,' he said, raising his glass to his eye, 'that you were forced to change into this particular dress, Elizabeth. You look ravishing.'

'Oh,' she said, laughing, 'and so do you, Avery, as always. I believe we are about to be invaded. I heard a carriage draw up outside as I was leaving my room.'

Within fifteen minutes everyone had arrived and disposed themselves about the drawing room, Alexander as usual standing before the hearth, Avery seated in a corner beyond the window, not participating in the general conversation.

The conversation itself had taken a predictable course. The ball had been triumphantly pronounced the greatest squeeze of the Season so far. Anastasia's debut had been a success. If there had been a hundred sets in the evening, Aunt Mildred declared, Anastasia would have had a partner for each one. Some ladies had been heard to remark upon the plainness of her appearance, Aunt Louise said, but a few of the most fashionable young ladies, most notably that diamond of the first water, Miss Edwards, had been heard to declare in a huddle together that they were tired of being so loaded down with jewels and of having to catch up trains and flounces whenever they wished to dance and of sitting for an hour or longer each evening while their maids curled and crimped their hair. How refreshing it would be, they had said, to appear in public as Lady Anastasia Westcott had – if only they dared.

Anastasia's Great Indiscretion – Aunt Matilda spoke of it as though the words must begin with capital letters – might well have been her undoing, and certainly there were those among the highest sticklers who had been shocked. But they appeared to be in the minority. Others applauded the way she had stood by her illegitimate half sister and dealt Viscount Uxbury a severe setdown.

'You have been launched upon society with great success, Anastasia,' Cousin Althea said with a warm smile. 'Now you may relax and enjoy the rest of the Season.'

Everyone was ecstatic over the number of bouquets that had been delivered yesterday and this morning. They were amazed and gratified to hear of the number of persons who had called yesterday afternoon and of the drive in the park with the Fleming brothers.

'I think, Anastasia,' the dowager countess said, smiling kindly at her granddaughter, 'we may expect more than a few very eligible offers for your hand before the end of the Season.'

'But there was already one this morning, Cousin Eugenia,' Elizabeth said. 'At least, it was not exactly an offer, was it, Anna, but a request to know to what gentleman he must apply for permission to make one. I directed him to you, Alex, though Anna is of age and does not need anyone's permission. She was looking somewhat aghast, however, and I came to her rescue.'

'Thank you, Lizzie,' he said dryly. 'Formsby, was it? He found me at Tattersall's. I informed him, as I informed another gentleman last evening and two more this morning, that I would discuss the matter with Anastasia's family and with her.'

'I had two gentlemen approach me at White's this morning,' Uncle Thomas said, 'as well as the uncle of another who is not a member. I told them the same thing.'

'Oh goodness gracious me.' Anna's grandmother clasped her hands to her bosom and beamed. 'This is even greater success than we anticipated. By the end of the Season, Anastasia – before the end – you will be able to make your choice from among a large number of suitors.'

'You must not rush into choosing, though, Anastasia,' Aunt Matilda advised. 'The matter of birth and breeding and fortune must all be weighed as must your own importance. You are the daughter – the only child – of the late Earl of Riverdale, my brother, and you are in possession of a vast fortune. There are no limits to what you can aspire to in a husband.'

Anna had been virtually silent, but she spoke now. 'I am one of my father's four children,' she said.

'Of course you are,' Aunt Matilda said, 'but you are the only one who counts in the eyes of the *ton*.'

'I am nothing but an object,' Anna said, her hands clasped tightly in her lap, 'as are my brother and sisters. They have become objects of no value whatsoever while I have become invaluable. Men – gentlemen of the *ton* – crowded about me at the ball two evenings ago and sent floral offerings yesterday morning and flocked to visit me yesterday afternoon. I was flooded with invitations to drive in the park, to dance the first set at some ball a few evenings hence, to attend the theater, to go to Vauxhall. Today several of them are making inquiries about marrying me. I daresay there will be more to come. And why? Because I am beautiful and accomplished? Because I am personable and charming and intelligent? Because I have character? Of course not. It is because I am a commodity, because I am rich. Very rich. One of the wealthiest single ladies in England, perhaps. Everyone wants to marry my money.'

'Anna!' Aunt Louise looked at her incredulously. 'The situation is not nearly so . . . vulgar. Of course members of our class choose eligible partners when they marry. Of course we marry within our own ranks. And of course it is desirable, though not always essential, to marry into money. Money is what sustains our way of life and the vast expense of running our estates and other establishments. But we do not consider just rank or fortune when we choose husbands and wives. We look too for someone we can respect, someone of whom we can grow fond, even someone we may love. I cannot say I loved Netherby when I married him, though I did like and respect him. And I grew fond of him, as he did of me, I believe, during our marriage. I mourned his passing with a very real grief. Yet I would not have married him if he had been either ineligible or impoverished. The absence of those things would not have been conducive to a happy life.'

'No one looks at you and sees an object, Anastasia,' Cousin Althea added. 'Far from it. Everyone sees a dignified and personable young lady, you may be sure. Remember that you will have choices – a rather dizzying number of them, it would seem. You will be free to choose someone who will appreciate you as well as your fortune. You may choose someone you can appreciate for his good character and kindly nature and any other positive attributes that are important to you. The marriage mart is not quite the impersonal thing you fear.'

'What you ought to do, Anastasia,' her grandmother said, 'is marry Alexander. And what you ought to do, Alexander, is swallow your pride and propose to her without waiting for everyone else to do so first.'

CHAPTER 16

There was a moment of silence. Anna was horrified and horribly mortified. Alexander, she saw in one brief glance, looked frozen in place.

'Cousin Eugenia,' his mother said reproachfully, 'it is hardly—'

'No, Mama,' Alexander said, holding up one hand. 'It is not that I have not thought of it for myself. I need the money, heaven knows, if I am ever to rescue Brambledean Court from further dilapidation and improve the deplorable living conditions of all those dependent upon me there. And it might be said that the entailed properties and the fortune ought to be reunited, as they were until Cousin Humphrey died. I have a regard for Anastasia and admire the way she grew up with dignity despite the circumstances in which her father left her. I admire too the way she has worked hard to adjust to her changed circumstances. If I were to marry her, I could save her from any further exposure to the marriage mart, which she is finding so repugnant. And I could certainly offer her respect, protection, affection, and a mother-in-law and sister-in-law who I know would welcome her.'

'Well, then,' Anna's grandmother said, 'there is—'

But he held up a hand again.

'I have thought about it,' he said. 'And indeed, now that the suggestion has been made openly like this, before the whole family, I am willing to make a formal offer if Anastasia can assure me that it is what she wishes. However, I admit that I would be marrying her primarily for the money, and that is repugnant to me. She deserves better of the man who is fortunate enough to win her hand. She deserves a man who wants her and does not care the snap of his fingers for her fortune.'

There was another brief silence, during which Anna was aware of Elizabeth drawing a handkerchief out of a pocket in her dress and pressing it to her eyes.

'Anastasia?' her grandmother said. 'You could not do better, and it is perfectly clear that Alexander is holding back only because he feels the difference in your fortunes and fears you will see him as no better than a fortune hunter. But he has the title—'

'No!' Elizabeth cried, lowering her handkerchief to her lap. 'It is not just that he fears his motives will be misconstrued. Alex has dreams, which he has been holding in check for years since Papa's death left him immersed in debt from which he has only recently freed himself. He dreams of love

287

and a quiet domestic life, and he ought not to have to sacrifice his dreams merely because the earldom has been thrust upon him. And Anna has spent most of her life at an orphanage, where there was no cruelty, apparently, but very little of what I think of as love of family either. Alex is right. She deserves love now. She deserves to be married because she is everything in the world to one particular gentleman. I love them both, Cousin Eugenia, but please, oh please, they must not be thrown together merely because it would be a convenient arrangement.'

'Lizzie.' Her mother had come to sit on the arm of her chair in order to rub a hand over her back.

Alexander was frowning. Everyone else was looking variously dismayed and embarrassed. Anna clutched her hands in her lap. They were freezing. So was she. The Duke of Netherby got to his feet and strolled across the room to stand before her chair.

'I have not compared your fortune and my own penny for penny, Anna,' he said. 'It would, I suspect, be an arduous task. Edwin Goddard might enjoy it if I set him to it. I would hazard a guess, however, that I am wealthier than you by a penny or two at least. I have far more than I can spend in a lifetime, even if I live extravagantly to the age of one hundred or one hundred and ten. I could have no possible use for your fortune, and I have no desire whatsoever to get my hands on it. If I were to marry you, it would be because

I would rather spend the rest of my life with you than not and because you had assured me that you would rather spend your life with me than not. You may consider the offer made since it would be a ghastly embarrassment to me and probably to everyone else if I were to drop to one knee before you now and declare undying devotion in the florid language that would doubtless be expected of me. You may be the Duchess of Netherby if you choose.'

Anna's eyes widened and remained fixed upon his – sleepy and keen both at once, as usual. He reached for his snuffbox but did not remove it from his pocket. And she felt a stabbing of such unexpected longing that the near pain of it engulfed her.

'Avery!' Aunt Louise cried.

'Oh!' Elizabeth said.

Everybody else said something too, it seemed, but Anna heard not a word.

'How—' she began.

'—absurd?' he said softly. 'If you will, my dear.'

'But what a very splendid idea, Avery,' Anna's grandmother said. 'I am only amazed it has not occurred to me before now. And you are not even related to Anastasia by blood, as Alexander is.'

'I had not thought you were the marrying sort, Avery,' Aunt Mildred said. 'Indeed, I had thought perhaps—'

'Millie!' Uncle Thomas said sharply, and she fell silent.

The Duke of Netherby ignored them all. He looked steadily into Anna's eyes. She wanted to ask him a million questions, though they could all be reduced to one.

Why?

'I want to go to Wensbury,' she heard herself say.

'And go you shall,' he said softly. 'I shall take you there. With an army of chaperones if you choose to go unwed. With me alone if you should marry me first.'

Oh. He was serious. He was serious.

But why?

And why was she tempted? Why had that ache of longing settled into a dull throbbing low in her abdomen and down between her thighs?

Wed. Unwed. Wed. Unwed. But they were not her only choices, were they? She could go alone to confront her grandparents. No one could stop her. She could go with Bertha for company and respectability and John for protection along with a coachman. Perhaps Elizabeth would go with her. They could go to Bath first, and Joel would accompany them the rest of the way – her own true and dear friend. She did not have to choose anyone.

'I would wish to go wed,' she said so softly she was not even sure the words had passed her lips.

'Then wed we will be,' he said.

But why? And now the question needed to be asked of herself as well as of him. What had she said? What had she done? She scarcely knew him. He was like someone from another universe. He hid himself behind heavy eyelids and artificiality, and perhaps there was nothing at all of any value behind it all.

Except that he had granted her a few glimpses beyond the mask. And he had waltzed with her – twice – and each time danced her into a brighter, happier world. He had kissed her once and aroused all the physical yearnings she had suppressed for so long that she had come almost to believe she would never be troubled by them again.

They were to be wed? He had asked and she had said yes? For a moment she doubted the reality of it, but only for a moment, for they were not alone in the room. And there was noise, first a murmur and then a great eruption of sound. Everyone spoke at once again.

'Avery! My dear boy!' his mother exclaimed.

'Anastasia! This is beyond my fondest hopes.' The dowager countess, her grandmother, clasped her hands to her bosom.

'Mama, allow me to hold the vinaigrette to your nose,' Aunt Matilda said.

'I was never more surprised in my life. Or so delighted.' The duchess, Cousin Louise, beamed from one to the other of them.

'How absolutely splendid! Cousin Avery and Anastasia,' Aunt Mildred said, casting a smile at Uncle Thomas.

'Allow me to congratulate you, Anastasia, Netherby. I wish you great happiness.' Cousin Alexander actually looked hugely relieved.

'Anna, Avery. Oh, I ought to have suspected. How blind I have been.' Elizabeth was laughing.

'You are fortunate indeed, Anastasia,' Aunt Matilda said, 'considering the fact that you have resisted more than half the advice we have offered in the past few weeks. You are to be the Duchess of Netherby! Allow me to fan your face, Mama.'

'Well, *this* will be a disappointment for a few dozen gentlemen and a few dozen ladies,' Uncle Thomas, Lord Molenor commented drily.

'We must gather here again tomorrow afternoon. We have a wedding to plan.' That was Aunt Louise, of course.

'Why Wensbury? Where on earth is it?' Aunt Mildred asked.

The Duke of Netherby had not looked away from Anna or she from him.

'I shall call here tomorrow morning, Anna,' he said, 'if you can fit me in between the reception of bouquets of flowers and marriage offers.'

Alexander cleared his throat. 'Tomorrow morning, Netherby?' he said.

'Ah, that appointment.' The duke fingered the handle of his quizzing glass. 'But it is early, Riverdale, far earlier than Anna would enjoy being called upon. I shall come after breakfast, Anna.'

'Perhaps you will be . . . unable,' Alexander said.

'But nothing will keep me from my affianced bride,' the duke said with a soulful sigh, and turned away from Anna at last. 'Every hour between now and then will be an endless eternity. I shall take my leave. I have business to attend to. I believe I must have. Edwin Goddard will know.'

And without even glancing at her again, he sauntered from the room, leaving Anna with the urge to laugh – or to weep. Or both.

The room erupted into sound again. Anna heard only Aunt Mildred.

'Where is Wensbury?' she asked. 'I have never heard of it.'

She deserves to be married because she is everything in the world to one particular gentleman.

Cousin Elizabeth's words rang in Avery's head as he walked down the street. Was it those words that had impelled him to make his offer? If so, what the devil did that say about him?

. . . because she is everything in the world to one particular gentleman.

Good God, he was a betrothed man.

It was unlike him to act impulsively. And what a time to break a long habit. He had been half expecting that she would take pity upon Riverdale and offer her fortune and her hand to serve his need, though to do him justice, Riverdale had made quite clear his reluctance to take advantage of her. But the family might at any moment have persuaded them that marriage to each other was the best option for both. And Avery had felt – what? Annoyance? Anxiety? Panic?

Panic?

And he had found himself listening to Elizabeth's plea against the marriage of Anna and her brother and then getting to his feet to reinforce it – by proposing to Anna himself.

What the devil? Could he not simply have invited her out for a walk, as he had done on a previous occasion?

She had said yes.

At least, she had not used that exact word. She had expressed the preference for being wed rather than unwed when she traveled to Wensbury to find her maternal grandparents. She had not actually said she wished to be wed *to him*, though, had she? But no, there was no hope to be grasped at there without being ridiculous about it. She had meant him.

He ought to have known he was in danger when he set Edwin Goddard the task of finding the Reverend Snow and his wife. He ought to have known it when Edwin greeted him on his return home soon after noon today with the letter that had been delivered earlier and he, Avery, had taken only the time to change his clothes before heading off to South Audley Street so that she would not be kept ignorant for one minute longer than necessary. He ought to have known it when, after escorting Uxbury off the premises a couple of evenings ago following the magnificent setdown she had dealt him, he had given in to the overwhelming and quite unmannerly urge to cut in on Washburn and waltz with her himself. He ought to have known it when she wept over Harry. He ought to have . . .

God damn it all to hell, he thought, coming to an abrupt halt on the pavement, he was in love with her.

He acknowledged with a curt nod a couple of acquaintances who seemed to think he had stopped to chat with them and showed signs of slowing down to oblige him. He continued on his way, and they presumably continued on theirs.

He tried to picture her as she had been that first day with her hideous Sunday best outfit and ugly shoes. And all he could see was the dignity with which she had explained her presence in his house and then sat in the rose salon, and the courage with which she had looked him over there even when she realized that he was scrutinizing her.

She deserves to be married because she is everything in the world to one particular gentleman.

God damn it and a million or so other profanities and blasphemies he would utter aloud if he were not on the public street where he might be overheard. *Everything in the world,* indeed. It was enough to make him want to vomit.

Though it was just as well if he *was* in love with her, since he was doomed to marry her. He needed to marry in the foreseeable future anyway. It might as well be sooner rather than later. He had imagined, though, that when he finally got around to making his choice, the chosen one would be an acknowledged beauty, someone like Miss Edwards.

He had danced with her once the evening before last and found himself wondering why he had so admired her just a few weeks ago. There was a certain softness to her face and figure that would almost certainly convert to plumpness and plainness within ten years, and he had wondered if she possessed enough character to make the inevitable changes of little importance.

Even then, with such uncharitable thoughts, he might have guessed the truth.

He had never been in love. He had never come close. He did not even know what the term meant. He was not off his food or off his sleep. He felt no urge to write a sonnet dedicated to her left eyebrow – or the right for that matter – and none whatsoever to sing a ballad of love lost below the window of her bedchamber in the dead of night. He did not feel lovelorn when he was out of her presence or lovestruck when he was in. He had not even suspected until a short while ago when it had popped into his head to offer to marry her himself and put the whole lot of them out of their misery.

No one had been miserable.

Yes, she had. She had made that impassioned little speech about feeling like an object, a commodity. She had described all the frenzy of male interest her appearance in society had aroused as though it were the worst possible insult that could happen to anyone. Most ladies would sacrifice a right arm for half the attention. To her it was a misery.

He had offered her marriage to put her out of her misery. He did not care about anyone else's.

At least she would know he was not marrying her for her money.

He climbed the steps to Archer House, rapped on the door, handed his hat and cane to his butler, and eyed the stairs, a frown between his brows. What he felt like doing was splitting a pile of bricks in two with the edge of his hand. But he had been taught long ago that he must never practice when he was feeling out of sorts. The arts he had learned were not an antidote to bad temper. What he *ought* to do was go up and have a word with Jessica. She would be less than delighted with his news, and it was not fair to expect his stepmother to break it to her.

He never did anything because he *ought* to do it.

Except this one thing, he thought with an inward sigh as he made his way up to the schoolroom.

Anna did not escape so easily from the drawing room. She sat there in near silence for the next hour or two – she had no idea how long – while everyone around her planned her wedding.

She must be married at St George's Church on Hanover Square. Everyone was agreed upon that, not just because it was within a stone's throw of Archer House, but because it was the church for fashionable weddings during the Season. Everyone must be invited, and everyone would attend, of course. Aunt Louise would borrow Avery's Mr Goddard again to draw up the list, which would not be difficult, since it would be essentially the same as the one for the ball two evenings ago – with the exception of Viscount Uxbury, of course. Mr Goddard would write the invitations too. He had a neat, precise hand. The wedding breakfast would be held at Archer House, as was only proper. The banns must be called on the coming Sunday so that the wedding would not have to be delayed longer than one month. Madame Lavalle and her assistants would be brought back to Westcott House to make Anastasia's wedding outfit and her bride clothes. Anna's grandmother would take her to her own jeweler's to see to it that she purchased jewelry suited to her current rank and future prospects.

'Though of course there will be the Netherby jewels for you to wear on state and other formal occasions, Anastasia,' she added.

'You will be supplanting me in the title, Anastasia,' Aunt Louise said, one hand over her heart, 'and relegating me to the position of dowager. I am delighted. I really feared Avery might never marry. One can only hope that he will now proceed to do his duty and start to populate his nursery within the year.'

Anna's mind seemed not to be working clearly. Everyone seemed to have forgotten her declared wish to go to Wensbury to see her grandparents for herself and find out just what had happened all those years ago. Of course, her mother's people would be deemed of no account by these aristocrats.

The duke had said he would take her there. He had given her the choice of going wed or unwed, and she had chosen to be wed first. Then he had simply taken his leave and gone away. How absolutely typical of him to leave her to the mercy of her well-meaning family. Her wedding was going to be at least a month in the future. Yet she had longed to get away from a life that was overwhelming her. All she had succeeded in doing was making things worse. Far worse.

The talk around her had progressed to betrothal announcements and betrothal parties.

Why on earth had she agreed to marry the Duke of Netherby? Was she in love with him? But what did that mean – being in love? And he was surely the last man with whom she might be infatuated.

At last everyone left, though Anna knew it was just a temporary reprieve. Elizabeth had gone downstairs to see her mother and brother on their way and was gone for a while.

'Did I hurt Alex's feelings?' Anna asked when she returned.

'No,' Elizabeth assured her. 'But he is afraid he has hurt yours. And he is afraid you accepted Avery's offer without due consideration because you were upset.'

Anna smiled ruefully.

'I hope I did not hurt you by what I said,' Elizabeth added.

'Oh, you most certainly did not,' Anna assured her. 'Neither did Alex. I do not know quite why I accepted Avery's offer, Lizzie – if you can call it that. I was taken totally by surprise. But – I do not believe I am sorry.'

'He will not be an easy husband,' Elizabeth said, 'but he will be a fascinating one, I suspect.'

'Yes,' Anna agreed. 'He will certainly be far more gorgeous than I. But in a number of bird and animal species the males are more showy than the females. Did you know that?'

They both laughed, but then Elizabeth bit her lower lip and Anna thought something was troubling her.

'What is it?' she asked.

'I could tell after Avery had made his offer and then left that something was bothering Alex,' Elizabeth said. 'He reminded Avery of an appointment tomorrow morning, if you will remember. And he did not participate in the general discussion afterward. I had it out of him just now when he walked a little way along the street with me after Mama was in the carriage. He begged me not to tell you, but how can I not? He asked only that I assure you tomorrow if Avery does not keep his appointment to call here that there is nothing personal in his absence, that he will surely come when he is able.'

Anna looked at her inquiringly.

Elizabeth bit her lip again before continuing. 'Oh, Anna, Viscount Uxbury has challenged Avery to a duel. It is to be fought tomorrow morning. Alex is to be his second, but he is worried. Avery could not refuse the challenge. Gentlemen cannot, you know, without losing face and even honor, though it is very foolish. But Alex is afraid it will be a slaughter. He has sworn to stop it before Avery is . . . hurt too badly, but he is very much afraid he will be in no fit state to call on you here in the morning.'

Anna felt as though all the blood had drained from her head. The air felt cold in her nostrils. There was a buzzing in her ears. 'A duel?' she said. 'A fight? To the death?'

'Oh no,' Elizabeth said. 'Alex will stop it before it comes to that.'

'How can he stop the course of a bullet?' Anna jumped up from her chair. 'How can he redirect a sword thrust? What are the weapons to be?'

'Alex did not say,' Elizabeth told her. 'He said only that he feared a slaughter.'

'I must go to Archer House,' Anna said, turning toward the door. 'It was I who angered Lord Uxbury. Avery must not die for something I said. I shall go and put a stop to it.'

'Oh, you cannot, Anna,' Elizabeth said, catching at her arm. 'You cannot interfere in gentlemen's business, especially an affair of honor. It would be horribly humiliating for Avery if you tried. He would be fearfully angry, and you would not change his mind. He is not the challenger. Oh, you must see how impossible it would be.'

Yes. Anna could. 'Where?' she asked. 'When?'

'Hyde Park,' Elizabeth said. 'I do not know just where, but I have heard that duels are usually fought among the trees on the east side of the park, where they are least likely to be observed and stopped. Duels are illegal, you know. They are usually fought at dawn, probably for the same reason. Alex will come here as soon as he may to relieve my mind. He promised that he will relieve it. We will hear by breakfast time.'

'The eastern side – this side – of Hyde Park, at dawn,' Anna muttered, frowning.

Elizabeth gazed at her. 'You are not thinking of going, are you?' she asked. 'It is absolutely not the thing, Anna. Women are not allowed . . . They are not allowed even to know of such meetings. There would be huge trouble for you if you tried to interfere. You would become a social pariah, and you would make Avery the laughingstock.'

Viscount Uxbury was a large man, Anna was thinking. He was tall and rather broad, and it seemed to her that the breadth of his chest and shoulders owed at least as much to muscle as it did to fat. He was twice the size of Avery, and she did not really believe, did she, that the duke had once put him down with a few fingertips to the chest. Anyway, that would not matter tomorrow. If swords were to be the weapons, the viscount's reach must be very much longer than Avery's, and he would have the advantage of height. If they were to be pistols, well . . .

Elizabeth sighed. 'What time will we be leaving?' she asked.

'We?' Anna's eyes focused upon her.

'We,' Elizabeth said. 'But just to watch, mind, Anna, if we are not caught before it even begins, as I daresay we will be. Not to interfere.'

'Not to interfere,' Anna agreed. 'As soon as darkness begins to turn to light? I shall tap on your door.'

Elizabeth nodded, and for some reason they both laughed. It was quite horrifying.

'I think,' Anna said, 'I had better ring for a fresh tray of tea.'

He was going to die, she thought, and all she could think to do about it was to drink tea?

CHAPTER 17

Avery and Alexander arrived at the appointed spot in Hyde Park when the sky was graying with early dawn. They were early, but they were not the first to arrive, by Jove.

'Walling agreed with me,' Riverdale said, clearly exasperated, 'that the quieter we kept this meeting, the better it would be for all concerned. It looks as though Uxbury disagreed and told every man he knows and they told everyone they know. This is intolerable.'

Avery was reminded of that first bout of boxing he had fought at school – if *fought* was the correct word. A crowd of men, buzzing with anticipation, was gathered about an empty clearing among the trees, their horses and curricles variously disposed in a rough circle behind them. If the Watch did not detect them and arrest the lot of them there was no real justice in the land. Avery suspected that the Watch, or whoever enforced law and order in Hyde Park, would develop a severe case of deafness and blindness – if it was out at all at this hour. The hum of excitement increased when the challenged hove into sight. Uxbury and Walling

304

had already arrived. So had a man dressed entirely in somber black, a largish black leather bag on the grass beside him. The sawbones, no doubt. How predictably ostentatious of Uxbury to engage the services of a physician for a fight that involved no weapon more lethal than the body. Or perhaps there was some wisdom in it.

Every face that turned his way to watch him approach bore the same expression. The lamb to the slaughter, they were all thinking. He curled his fingers about the handle of his quizzing glass and raised it to his eye, and almost everyone suddenly discovered something of more urgent interest to take their attention. Uxbury, striking a pose, was gazing at him across the circle of grass with haughty dignity. Avery examined the expression through his glass. He would wager it had been practiced before a mirror.

Walling strode into the center of the grass, looking somewhat embarrassed, and Riverdale went to confer with him there. Then each returned to his principal.

'Uxbury is willing to settle for an apology over anguish and embarrassment suffered,' Riverdale said.

'And will he make that apology before all these people?' Avery asked, dropping his quizzing glass on its ribbon and raising his eyebrows. 'Extraordinary! Let us hear it, then, by all means. Not that I recall suffering a great deal of either anguish or embarrassment, though it is possible I might have if I were the sensitive sort.'

'I understand you are not willing to tender an apology, then?' Riverdale asked.

Avery merely looked at him, and Riverdale turned.

'The Duke of Netherby,' he said in a voice that would carry across the empty space and doubtless to every gentleman gathered about it, 'is obliged for the offer of clemency. However, he cannot recall a single word he has spoken to Viscount Uxbury that he regrets.'

There was a swell of approval from the crowd and a few whistles. One unidentified gentleman called out, 'That's the spirit, Netherby. Go down swinging.'

He had spent thirteen or fourteen years avoiding just such a scene as this, Avery thought with an inward sigh as Riverdale helped him off with his coat and he divested himself of his neckcloth and cravat, his fobs and watch and quizzing glass, his waistcoat, and his shirt. But what was one to do when one had been challenged to a duel and the challenger had noised it abroad so that it would be surprising if there was a gentleman in London who was not here?

'I believe,' Riverdale said, 'it would be wiser to keep your shirt on, Netherby. Uxbury is keeping his.'

Avery ignored him. He sat down on the uncomfortably rough and uneven stump of a tree and hauled off one of his boots and the stocking beneath it.

'Good God,' Riverdale said, clearly aghast, 'you must keep your boots on.'

Avery hauled off the other.

'Good God, Netherby,' Riverdale said again as Avery got to his feet, clad only in his tight breeches – tight but flexible and comfortable. 'You must have a death wish.'

From the swell of sound about them, it seemed that everyone else agreed.

Avery rolled his shoulders and flexed his hands.

'Listen,' Riverdale said, speaking low and urgently. 'You asked me to act as your second, and it is my duty to offer you as much advice as I am capable of giving. Don't be a bloody martyr, Netherby. Use your arms and your fists to cover your face and your body. Use your feet to move out of harm's way – which would have been a great deal easier to do with your boots on. Uxbury has the advantage of reach and height and weight. Stay away from his fists as long as you can. Watch him. Use your eyes. If by some miracle you can get past his reach, use your fists on him. Put up a good show. And when you go down—' He paused a moment and cleared his throat. 'And if you go down, stay down. If you can somehow let a minute go by before it happens, all the better. You are not the challenger. He is. Most of the men here do not like what he forced Camille to do or how he talks about her. They are on your side. They will admire your courage in taking on an opponent twice your size, and in refusing to apologize. Defeat will be a kind of triumph.'

'I believe,' Avery said, 'Walling is waiting for you

to finish your monologue, Riverdale, so that he can get this meeting started.'

His second looked at him in some exasperation and fell silent.

'The fight will begin,' Walling announced. 'It will continue until one of the two gentlemen concedes defeat or until one is knocked down and is unable to rise.'

Uxbury strode onto the stage – one could not see that circle of scrubby grass as anything else when he did so – with purposeful strides and grim demeanor and clenched fists. He proceeded to take up a boxer's stance that would have done Gentleman Jackson proud. He danced a few steps on his booted feet. Avery strolled toward him and stopped a couple of feet away, his arms at his sides.

Uxbury leered at him and threw a straight right that, if it had landed, would have gone straight through Avery's nose and out the back of his head. Avery batted it away with the side of one forearm and then did the same when a left followed close upon the right.

'*Cover* yourself, Netherby,' someone from the crowd cried above the general swell of sound – it might have been Riverdale.

Uxbury danced a few more steps, leered again, and repeated the exact same attack – with the exact same result. He was a slow learner. It was amazing, Avery thought, what height there was to boots. Uxbury seemed a full two inches taller than usual, though probably it was he who was two inches shorter in his bare feet. The ground was uneven and a bit stony in places, very different from the attic floor, but he had encountered worse when working with his Chinese gentleman.

'You are just going to stand there like a fairy boy, are you?' Uxbury asked.

A few people tittered. A number cried, 'Shame!' though whether they meant Uxbury or the Duke of Netherby was not clear.

The next time, Uxbury followed the same two leading punches with his body and a flurry of ferocious blows. But he had signaled his intention with his eyes and his body, foolish man, and there was no method to the punches except the desire to end the fight almost before it had begun. It took just a little more effort of eye and reflex to deflect the flailing fists, though one of them actually glanced off his shoulder and turned him slightly sideways. Uxbury followed it up with another powerful blow intended to knock his victim into kingdom come. Avery stepped sideways, waited for fist and arm to whistle harmlessly by, twisted his body a little more, and caught Uxbury on the side of the head with the flat of his foot.

He went down like a sack of potatoes.

The crowd roared.

Uxbury blinked and looked dazed, then puzzled, then indignant, then wrathful. The man was as easy to read, Avery thought, as a book written in large, heavy print. He could not be much of a cardplayer. He scrambled to his feet, shook his head, staggered once, glared at Avery, then resumed his stance, while all the time in the background there were voices urging Avery to go for the kill while he had the chance.

'That was a dirty hit,' Uxbury said from between his teeth.

'*Did* you get dirt on your shirt?' Avery asked. 'But I daresay it will wash out.'

Uxbury had not learned a thing. He resumed the attack in much the same manner, though a little wilder this time, just as though weight and muscle and brute force made brain and agility and observation obsolete. Avery let him flail about for a time while he deflected every punch or moved out of its way. Uxbury's attack grew only more desperate. He paused after a couple of minutes, however, breathless, sweat pouring down his face, his shirt clinging wetly about his person. It was most impressive.

'The little prancing, dancing master,' he said through gritted teeth. 'Stand still like a man, Netherby.'

Avery spun about and caught him on the other side of the head with the flat of his other foot.

Uxbury bent to the side but stayed on his feet this time while the crowd roared again. His fists slipped a little lower.

'Man-milliner!' he said with contempt. 'Camille Westcott is not just a bastard, you know. She is a slut and a whore. So is Abigail Westcott. So is Lady Anast—'

When Avery launched himself this time, he planted both feet beneath Uxbury's chin and kicked out. His opponent went down heavily backward and stayed down.

There was a curious hush. Avery became only gradually aware of it. He was more aware of the fact that, unlike the other two blows, that last one had been struck in anger. It went against the discipline of his training, but he was not sorry. Sometimes anger was a justifiable human emotion.

He had not used his hands at all, he realized. It was probably as well he had not used *them* in anger.

Walling was hurrying toward Uxbury. So was the physician, clutching his black bag. Avery walked back to Riverdale and the neat pile of his clothes. It was only then that noise erupted to break the eerie silence. But no one spoke to Avery. No one even looked directly at him.

'Where *the devil*,' Riverdale asked as Avery sat on the tree stump and pulled on one of his stockings, 'did you learn to do that?'

'You see,' Avery said softly, 'I was a small lad, Riverdale, as you may remember. And a pretty one. And a prey to every school bully – and a boys' school abounds with the breed.'

'Wherever you learned it,' Riverdale said, hovering as Avery pulled on his boots, 'it was not at school.

311

Good God, I have never seen the like. Nor has anyone else here. I do understand now, though, why that aura of power and danger seems to hover constantly about you. I always thought there was no reason for it. But now I understand! Let me take you for breakfast at White's. It is still very early, but—'

Avery had finished pulling his shirt on over his head. 'I have some errands to run before I call upon Anna,' he said. 'But thank you for the offer and for standing with me this morning.' He held out his right hand and wondered if Riverdale would take it. But he did after looking at it for a moment, and they clasped hands briefly.

'It ought to have been me,' Riverdale said. 'Camille and Abigail are my cousins. So is Anastasia.'

'Ah,' Avery said, 'but she is my betrothed and they are her sisters. Besides, I was the one Uxbury chose to challenge.'

Riverdale helped him on with his coat. Some of the crowd had dispersed, but a good half still lingered, talking with one another and stealing surreptitious glances at Avery. Uxbury was still stretched out on the grass, the physician down on one knee beside him. It looked as though he was drawing blood. Walling, on the other side, was holding a bowl. Uxbury's head was moving slowly from side to side. He was going to survive, then.

Avery turned to walk away, and the Earl of Riverdale fell into step beside him.

Dear Joel,

How very devious you are becoming and how clever! I did not intend that you go to so much trouble on my behalf. I will not feel guilty, however, because there does seem to be a good chance that you may get work out of your maneuverings.

Did you cultivate the acquaintance of Mrs Dance merely because she is a friend of Mrs Kingsley, my sisters' grandmother, and then get yourself invited to one of her literature and art evenings? How would you have felt if Mrs Kingsley had not put in an appearance? I daresay it would have been an enjoyable evening anyway, though, and it did give you a wonderful opportunity to display the paintings you took with you. I am so glad Mrs Kingsley did appear, however, and looked with interest at the portrait you showed her of a young lady. How very sly of you to work in the comment about how rare a treat it is these days to find young persons in Bath to paint.

You must let me know if anything comes of all this. It is a disappointment that you have seen only Abigail, and even her only a time or two. I do worry about my sisters. I have thought of writing to them, but Cousin Elizabeth as well as my own good sense have advised against it just yet. They must be given time to adjust to the new facts of their lives, and I am the last person they need to be reminded of.

I do not even know where to begin with my own news. I have not written since the ball three evenings ago. It was a huge success. I felt like a princess in my ball gown (until I saw all the other ladies, who were far lovelier than I) and I was in any case treated like one. I believe even my grand-mother and my aunts were astounded. Not only did I dance every set, but I had at least a dozen prospective partners to choose among for each one.

And the next morning no fewer than twenty-seven bouquets of flowers were delivered here for me. I did not count how many gentlemen as well as a few ladies came to call during the afternoon. Several of them invited me to various entertainments. One of the gentlemen, with his brother, took Elizabeth and me for a drive in Hyde Park at what is known as the fashionable hour, and I now know why. Very little driving or riding or walking is accomplished, but a great deal of chatter and gossip is. Yesterday one young gentleman came to ask to whom he needs to apply before he can make an offer for my hand. And I heard during the afternoon that several other men have made similar inquiries of my male relatives.

Have I grown suddenly beautiful, charming, witty, and otherwise irresistible? Well, irresistible, yes. For I am rich. Very, very rich. Never wish great wealth upon yourself, Joel. And how very ungrateful that sounds. Ignore me.

Oh, Joel, Joel, Joel – I am betrothed. To the Duke of Netherby! I have no idea quite how it came about. He can surely have no real desire to marry me, or I to marry him for that matter. There is nothing whatsoever about me that might attract him and a great deal that might repel. He has no interest in my wealth – he has enough of his own, as he explained when I was complaining to my family about being a prey to every fortune hunter in the land and they were trying to marry me off to Cousin Alexander (he looked as uncomfortable and dismayed as I was feeling). The duke strolled up to me and told me I could be the Duchess of Netherby instead if I chose. It was surely the most extraordinary proposal in history. And, oh yes, I remember now. It all started when I said I wanted to go to Wensbury near Bristol where my mother's parents are still living. He found out that information for me and then he said he would take me there, either unwed with Elizabeth or Bertha or both to chaperone me, or wed just with him. And I chose to be wed. And so I am betrothed.

Can you tell that my head is in a hopeless jumble? What I ought to do is crumple up these sheets of paper and dash them to the floor and jump on them. But I have not told you all yet. He is to come this morning, presumably to discuss the wedding, which the rest of the family arranged down to the finest detail after he left. He did, you know – leave, that is. After he had made his offer and I had accepted, he just went away. One could search the world for the next century and not find anyone else half so strange. Read on if you are not already convinced!

Elizabeth told me last night that he had been challenged to a duel by Viscount Uxbury, that horrid nobleman who treated poor Camille so shabbily. I will not go into detail on how it came about, but the duel was set for dawn this morning in Hyde Park. Cousin Alexander was his second (it was through him that Elizabeth found out) and expected it to be a slaughter. I do not doubt everyone else who heard about it did too. Ladies may not interfere in any way in a duel. It is a gentleman's thing, all about honor and such nonsense. I could not make any sort of appeal to either one of them and of course I could not attend. But I did, and Elizabeth came with me.

Hyde Park is enormous, but fortunately we found the spot quite easily even though it was still almost dark when we got there, clad in dark cloaks and looking furtive, like Macbeth's witches. There was a huge crowd there, and even though they were not making a great deal of noise, there was quite enough to lead us in the right direction. Besides, there were horses stamping and snorting all around them. It was a miracle we were not seen. I believe there would have been dreadful consequences if we had been, though I have not pushed Elizabeth into describing just what they might have been. I might have found myself consigned to teaching in an orphanage schoolroom for the rest of my life! As it was, we got behind the trunk of a stout oak and I climbed up to lie along a branch. I have never done anything like it before in my life. I was terrified. I was probably eight feet off the ground and felt as though I were half a mile up.

I do not know how I am to describe what happened. The Duke of Netherby and Cousin Alexander were the last to arrive apart from a few stragglers. My heart was thumping against the branch, and it had nothing to do with how high I was. I was waiting for the pistols or the swords to be produced. And

Viscount Uxbury looked so very large and menacing. But there were no weapons. They had decided, it seemed, to fight it out with their fists, though that is not right either, since the duke did not use his fists at all. And, Joel, he stripped right down to his breeches – I blush to write the words. He even removed his boots and stockings, and then he looked so small, so inadequate to what was facing him, that there was not the faintest hope in my poor bosom. And yet he looked lithe and perfect too and incredibly beautiful. Oh dear. I wish I had not written that last sentence, but even if I erase it with half an ocean of ink you will be able to read what I wrote. Let it stand, then. He is terribly beautiful, Joel.

When the fight was announced and he walked out onto the grass to meet the viscount, I fully believed in what Alexander had predicted. And when the viscount threw the first two punches, I almost died. But I would not hide my face against the branch for I felt largely responsible, you see. I was nasty to Lord Uxbury at the ball and then Avery escorted him out – yet he was the one to be challenged. I suppose it is not the thing to challenge a woman to a duel.

Joel, his arms moved so fast I did not even really see them. But he pushed those deadly fists aside as if they were no more than gnats, and he kept doing it even when Lord Uxbury moved in for the kill with a whole series of punches, any one of which would surely have killed Avery if it had found its mark. But he moved his feet and his body and his arms with such agility that he deflected or avoided them all, and then he spun about and lifted one leg to an impossible angle and slapped his foot against the side of the viscount's head – although it was well above the level of his own – and the viscount went down with a crash. I still do not know quite how Avery did that, even though he did it again a little later with the other foot against the other side of the viscount's head.

Lord Uxbury, as well as everyone else, had clearly expected an early and easy victory. By then, though, he was clearly rattled. He had taunted Avery from the start, calling him ridiculous and silly names, but then, after he had been hit on the side of the head for the second time, he lost his temper and said some really nasty and shameful things, which I will not repeat, about Camille and Abigail and me too. I wish I were more adept with words to describe what happened then even before my name was fully out of Lord Uxbury's mouth. I have never seen anything like it in my life. I have never even heard of any such thing. He left the ground, Joel – Avery, I mean – and half turned in the air before planting his feet one at a time beneath the viscount's chin and kicking out and then landing on his feet. Viscount Uxbury was not on his feet by that time, however. He crashed backward and just lay there. He was still prone on the ground when Elizabeth and I left, but he was not dead, for which fact I was very grateful, much as I dislike and despise him.

Alexander came to the house later as he had promised Elizabeth he would to whisper privately to her – he did not realize that I knew about the duel and he certainly did not suspect that we were there – that Avery had won the fight and Lord Uxbury had been carried home, dazed and unable to stand on his own feet.

The Duke of Netherby is a terribly dangerous man, Joel. I have always suspected it but have been a bit puzzled about it. For he is on the small side, and he is indolent, and he dresses more flamboyantly than anyone else and has affectations, most notably his snuff-boxes and his quizzing glasses, which change with every outfit. But he is dangerous. And I am betrothed to him. I believe the banns are to be read this coming Sunday and the wedding is to be one month hence. I think I am a little frightened, which is absurd of me, I know. He would not hurt me. Indeed, he would not hurt anyone, I sense, unless severely provoked, as he was this morning. But when he is provoked . . .

Oh, I must finish. My letters are getting longer and longer. I often look back to that day when you and I were talking in the schoolroom and Bertha brought me the letter from Mr Brumford. If I had known then what I know now, would I have set fire to the letter and watched it burn? But he would have sent another, I daresay.

Thank you for all the other news in your letter. I do read everything you write over and over, you know. Every word is precious to me. If you cannot find a way to meet my sisters to find out how they are for me, do not worry about it. It is not your responsibility. But I do appreciate the fact that you are trying. I shall seal this and hand it to the butler without further delay, for he is supposed to come this morning – my betrothed, that is – and I do not know when that will be or how I shall look at him and not be afraid of the strangeness of him.

Is he from another world? And yet I am not really afraid. He is interesting – and what an inadequate word that is. I believe my life would seem dull if I were never to see him again.

Just as life seems a little dull without you.

Know that I think about you daily and remain, as I always will,

Your dearest friend,
Anna Snow
Otherwise known as Lady Anastasia
Westcott
Soon to be (oh goodness!)
the Duchess of Netherby

The letter was almost too fat to fold. But Anna did it somehow and sealed it, noted that Elizabeth's head was still bent over the letter she was writing at the table by the drawing room window, and pulled on the bell rope. John came in answer to the summons and Anna handed him the letter, asking that it be given to the butler to send out today.

'Oh, it's to Mr Cunningham, is it?' John said, looking at it. 'If you had not already sealed it, Miss Snow, I would have had you give him my regards. I always liked him as an art teacher. He knew just what help and encouragement to offer without ever telling us what to paint or how to do it. And he never said anything was rubbish. Neither did you. I was lucky in my teachers.'

'Thank you, John,' Anna said, noting that Elizabeth had lifted her head and was smiling with genuine amusement. 'I shall pass on your regards to Joel next time.'

'I do like your Bertha and your John,' Elizabeth said after he had left. 'They are quite refreshing.'

'I believe John is the despair of Mr Lifford,' Anna said.

'But he is such a very handsome lad,' Elizabeth said, a twinkle in her eye.

Anna seated herself in the armchair beside the fireplace. She did not pick up her book. What was the point? She knew she would not be able to read a word. How long would he be? Would he come at all?

How had he *done* that? He must have been six or seven feet in the air, and he had remained there while he kicked out with both feet, just as though the laws of nature did not apply to him. She would never have believed it if she had not seen it with her own eyes. And how had he been able to anticipate every blow that had rained down upon him and been able to defend himself against each one? Nobody could be that fast of either eye or arm – yet he was.

He did not have either a broad chest or bulging muscles. Yet everything about him, she had seen after he had stripped down, had been taut and perfect. Everything about him was in proportion to everything else. She had always thought him beautiful. This morning she had seen the full extent of that beauty and it had awed her even as she had been terrified for his safety.

She remembered suddenly his foolish claim to have felled Viscount Uxbury with three fingertips. He had not been speaking foolishly after all, she supposed. It had really happened.

He was a dangerous man indeed.

There was the sound of a carriage and horses from the street, and Elizabeth looked up from her letter.

'It is Avery,' she said, 'in a barouche. That is unusual for him. He goes almost everywhere on foot. Oh goodness, I feel almost afraid of him. Anna, are you quite sure you wish to *marry* him?'

'Yes,' Anna said, suddenly breathless. 'I am sure, Lizzie.'

The sound of the door knocker came from below.

CHAPTER 18

A very was later arriving at Westcott House than he had intended, but his errands had been delayed by the earliness of the hour. It seemed that people did not begin work at the crack of dawn or even soon after. However, here he was now, wondering, as he often did when he was about to see Anna, if a certain spell that appeared to have been cast over him would have been dispelled since the last time and he would see her as the perfectly ordinary young woman she surely was. Under the circumstances, it would be just as well if that was not about to happen.

John the Friendly Footman entertained him as they climbed the stairs by informing him that Miss Snow would be happy to see him as she had just finished writing a long letter to his erstwhile art teacher in Bath and was probably at loose ends – the footman's own words – as Lady Overfield had not yet finished hers. John thought, though, that Lady Overfield was writing more than one letter and that accounted for the fact that she was still at it. It did not matter, though, it seemed, as the post would not be picked up until one o'clock and she would surely be finished by then.

Avery thought about how servants in other houses effaced themselves into virtual invisibility and thereby deprived employers and guests of a great deal of wit and wisdom and good cheer.

'His Grace, the Duke of Netherby,' John announced, all prideful formality after he had tapped on the drawing room door and flung it open – and then he ruined the effect by grinning at Avery.

Anna was sitting by the fireplace, all prim and pretty in sprigged muslin. Elizabeth was seated at a table by the window, surrounded by paper and inkpot and blotter and quill pens. But she was getting to her feet and smiling.

'Avery,' she said as he bowed to her. 'Anna has been expecting you. I have just finished my letters and will take them down to set on the tray to go out with today's post. Then there are one or two things I need to do in my room.'

He turned to open the door for her, and she came very close to winking at him.

'I shall not be gone for too, too long,' she said. 'I take my responsibility as Anna's chaperone very seriously, you know.'

He closed the door behind her and went to stand before Anna's chair. She had not said anything yet beyond a murmured greeting. She was looking a little pale, perhaps a little tense, with her feet planted side by side on the floor, her hands clasped in her lap, her posture very correct even though that chair had surely been made to be lounged in. He had heard all about the plans for their wedding from his stepmother, and when he had called on Edwin Goddard this morning to see if there was anything in the post that needed his personal attention – fortunately there had not been – he had known without even asking that his secretary was just waiting for the word before springing into action. Between the two of them, with a little encouragement from other assorted Westcotts, the duchess and Goddard would doubtless produce a wedding to end all weddings. The duchess had even made a passing mention of St Paul's Cathedral, paving the way, perhaps, for a definite suggestion within the next day or two.

By now, of course, Goddard was no longer waiting for the word. He had been assigned another task.

Typically, although she was clearly not at ease, his betrothed was looking directly and steadily at him.

He leaned forward to set his hands on the arms of her chair and brought his mouth to hers. She was not an experienced kisser, and that was something of an understatement. Her lips remained closed and still, though there was nothing shrinking or reluctant about them. He parted his own lips, moved them lightly over hers, licking them until they parted, and curled his tongue behind them. She moved then. He sensed her hands unclenching and felt them light against his chest and then curling over his shoulders. He pressed his tongue past her teeth and into her mouth. She drew breath sharply – through her mouth – and gripped his shoulders. He drew the tip of his tongue along the roof of her mouth, and she sucked on it.

She could give lessons to courtesans, he thought as he withdrew his tongue and lifted his head. She smelled faintly of lavender water. He straightened up.

'Go and fetch your bonnet,' he said. 'Knock on Elizabeth's door and get her to bring hers too if she does not have other plans for the rest of the morning. If she does, we will have to take Bertha instead.'

'Where are we going?' she asked him. 'Will I need to change?'

'You will not need to change,' he assured her. 'I am going to take you to an insignificant church on an insignificant street. Neither has any architectural feature to be remarked upon, and as far as I know nothing of any great historical significance has ever happened there.'

She smiled slowly at him. 'Then why are we going there?' she asked.

'To be married,' he said.

She cocked her head to one side while the smile was replaced by a look of puzzlement. 'To be married,' she repeated. 'In an insignificant church on an insignificant street. Grandmama and my aunts will not like it. They have their hearts set upon St George's or even St Paul's, which is very grand indeed. I have seen it from the outside.'

He drew a folded paper from an inside pocket of his coat, opened it, and handed it to her. She looked down at it, read it, and frowned.

'What *is* it?' she asked.

'A special license,' he told her. 'It permits us to marry in a church of our own choosing by a clergyman of our choosing and on a day suited to us.'

She looked up at him, the frown still on her face, the license dangling from one hand. 'We are going to be married *now*?' she asked him. *'This morning?'*

'The thing is, you see, Anna,' he said, 'that when you said you wished to be wed, it was for the express purpose of making it possible to travel to the village of Wensbury without any lengthy delay and without having to take with you a whole arsenal of female companions to make my presence in the entourage respectable. A grand wedding would delay our departure by at least a month.'

'For the express purpose—?' Her frown had not gone away. 'But marriage is forever.'

'Oh, not really,' he assured her. 'Only until one of us dies.'

Her eyes widened. 'I do not want you to die,' she said.

'Perhaps you will go first,' he said, 'though I rather think I hope not. I would probably have grown accustomed to you by then and would miss you.'

For a moment she looked horrified, and then she laughed, a sound of genuine glee.

'Avery,' she said, 'you are quite impossible and quite outrageous. We cannot marry *today.*'

'Why not?' he asked her.

She stared at him for a few moments. 'I am not – dressed,' she said.

'I beg to inform you that you are,' he said. 'I would be blushing horribly if you were not.'

'I—' She appeared to be tongue-tied before laughing again. 'Avery!'

He took his snuffbox from his pocket, opened it with a flick of his thumb, examined the blend, closed the box, and put it away.

'A question,' he said. 'Do you want the *ton* wedding, Anna? It will be very splendid indeed. Everyone will be there, perhaps even Prinny himself – the Prince of Wales, that is, the Regent. We are both very grand persons, and our wedding will be the Event of the Season – that is *Event* with a capital E, I would have you understand. It might be a bit overwhelming, though it would, I suppose, be the ultimate dream of girls growing up in an orphanage.'

'No,' she said. 'You are not a prince. *That* would be the ultimate dream. And a glass coach.'

He regarded her with appreciation.

'Do you want the wedding, Anna?' he asked again. 'The one your relatives are busy planning?'

She shook her head and closed her eyes briefly. 'I grow sick at the very thought,' she said. 'I have grown so weary of . . . grandness, yet it will only grow worse.'

'Another question.' He gazed into her eyes when she opened them. 'Do you want to marry me?'

She gazed back for a moment, then shifted her gaze to the paper in her hand. She spread it carefully on her lap and looked down at it.

'Yes,' she said, returning her gaze to him at last. 'But do you want to marry me?'

'Go and fetch your bonnet,' he told her, and he took the license from her lap, replaced it in his pocket, and reached out a hand to help her to her feet.

'Very well,' she said.

She paused to frown at him a few moments later when he held the drawing room door for her. She opened her mouth to speak, drew breath, and then left the room without saying anything.

It was his wedding day, he thought.

But marriage is forever.

Forever. A lifetime. A long time.

He waited for panic to assail him. But he waited in vain. After a few moments he wandered downstairs to await the ladies. Perhaps John would have some interesting conversation for him.

Anna sat beside Elizabeth in the barouche, facing the horses, while Avery sat with his back to them. It was a sunny day, and even when the carriage was moving it was warm. None of them was talking. Elizabeth had looked startled and quite incredulous when Anna had knocked on the door of her bedchamber and asked if she was free to accompany her to her wedding. But it had not taken her long to understand, and she had smiled and then laughed instead of swooning from shock and horror as Anna had half expected.

'But how very predictable of Avery,' she had said. 'I do not know why we did not expect it, Anna.'

'He is mad,' Anna had said. 'Judging just by the events of today so far, Lizzie, and it is only half past ten – he is utterly mad. I had better go and get my bonnet.'

He had handed them both into the barouche a few minutes later, Anna first. Elizabeth had paused when her hand was in his and her foot on the bottom step.

'How very splendid of you, Avery,' she had said. 'Everyone will be incensed.'

'I do not know why they would be,' he had said, raising his eyebrows and looking somewhat bored. 'A marriage is the sole concern of two people, is it not? Anna and me in this case.'

'Ah,' she had said, 'but a wedding is the property of everyone but those two people, Avery. They will be incensed. Take my word on it.' She had laughed.

Now, though, she was holding Anna's hand and squeezing it, for the carriage, which was proceeding along a nondescript street – Anna had not even noticed its name as they turned onto it – was slowing as they approached a nondescript church.

And it was very clear that this was indeed the street and the church where their nuptials were to be solemnized. A gentleman was waiting outside, and he stepped smartly forward to open the door and set down the steps before the coachman could descend from the box.

'All is in readiness, Your Grace,' he said.

Avery was the first to alight. He helped Elizabeth down and then offered his hand to Anna.

'You make a ravishing bride,' he said, his eyes moving lazily over her as she descended.

He did not sound ironic, though she was wearing her plain straw bonnet with her sprigged muslin morning dress. But, oh dear, she really was a bride, was she not? She had not grasped the reality of it yet.

'Meet my trusty secretary, Edwin Goddard, ladies,' he said when she was down on the pavement. 'Lady Overfield, Edwin, and Lady Anastasia Westcott.'

The gentleman bowed to them both.

'Edwin has come to witness the nuptials with Cousin Elizabeth,' Avery explained. 'If I had left him at home, he would no doubt have been wasting his time drawing up a guest list for my stepmother, the duchess. She likes to borrow him when I am not at home to protest. Shall we step inside?'

Anna took his offered arm and entered the church with him. It was larger than it seemed from the outside, high ceilinged and long naved.

It was dark, the only light coming from a few candles and tall windows with pebbled glass that had probably not been cleaned for at least a century. It was cold, as churches always were, and had the distinctive smell of candle grease and old incense and prayer books and slight damp. A youngish man was striding toward them clad in clerical robes. He had fair hair and eyebrows that were so light they were virtually invisible until he drew close. He was smiling. His face was dusted with freckles.

'Ah, Mr Archer,' he said, holding out his right hand to shake Avery's. 'And . . . Miss Westcott?' He shook Anna's hand. 'You have the license, sir? I am all ready to officiate for this happy occasion.'

'And Mrs Overfield and Mr Goddard as witnesses,' Avery said, reaching into his pocket for the license.

The clergyman smiled and nodded at them before examining the document briefly. 'It seems to be in order,' he said cheerfully. 'Shall we begin? The nuptial service is very brief when stripped of all the trappings that many people like to add. But it is just as sacred and just as binding. And just as joyous for the bride and groom. Flowers and music and guests are not essential.'

He led the way down the nave. Anna could hear the men's bootheels ringing on the stones as they walked. Foolishly she found herself trying to work out how many days ago she had received that letter from Mr Brumford, how many days since she had first set eyes upon the Duke of Netherby, standing indolent and gorgeous and terrifying in the hall of Archer House. Was it only days? Or weeks? Or months? She no longer knew. She thought of Miss Ford and Joel, of the children in her schoolroom, of Harry and Camille and Abigail and their mother, of her grandmother and aunts, of Alexander and Jessica, of the grandparents who had turned her out after her mother died. One's life was said to pass before one's eyes when one was dying, was it not? No one had ever said that the same thing happened when one was about to get married.

The walk along the nave seemed both endless and all too short.

She saw Avery as he was now, dressed with conservative elegance. And she thought of him as he had been a few hours ago, wearing only tight breeches and demonstrating a seemingly inhuman swiftness of reflex and an unearthly defiance of gravity. She felt the panicked fear that she did not know anything about him except that he was dangerous. And that his real self, whatever that might be, was hidden deep within layer upon layer of artifice and she might never uncover it.

But they had come to a halt at the altar rail, and it was too late to panic. They stood and faced the clergyman, while Elizabeth took a seat in the front pew and Mr Goddard stood beside Avery.

'Dearly beloved,' the clergyman said to the four people gathered before him, and he was using the familiar voice of clergymen everywhere. If there had been five hundred people in the pews, every one of them would have heard him clearly.

Neither of the witnesses spoke up when invited to do so if they knew of any impediment to the marriage. No one dashed into the church at the last moment to yell *stop!* Anna promised to love, honor, and obey the man in whose hand her own was clasped. He made similar vows to her. 'With my body I thee worship' was one thing he told her, his blue eyes very intent upon hers from beneath half-lowered eyelids. Mr Goddard handed him a gold ring, and he slid it onto her finger, watching her face, not her hand, as he did so. It fit perfectly. How had he done that?

And then, before she had quite composed her mind to the realization that she was getting married, she *was* married. According to the clergyman, she was Mrs Avery Archer.

So many names. Anna Snow. Anastasia Westcott. *Lady* Anastasia Westcott. Mrs Archer. The Duchess of Netherby. *Was* she? She found herself alarmingly close to laughing as she had a sudden picture of the children at the orphanage when Miss Ford read to them the letter that would announce the marriage. Their Miss Snow was now Lady Anastasia Archer, Duchess of Netherby. She imagined widened eyes, gasps of awe, sighs of satisfaction. What frivolous and silly thoughts to be having at such a moment.

They were being taken into the small vestry,

where the register was awaiting them, opened to the correct page, an inkpot beside it, a freshly mended quill pen laid across a blotter. Anna signed her maiden name for the last time – she stopped herself only just in time from writing Anna Snow. Avery signed his name with bold, swift strokes – Avery Archer. Their signatures were duly witnessed. And that was that, it seemed.

They were man and wife.

The clergyman shook hands with each of them outside the vestry, wished bride and groom a long and fruitful life together, and disappeared back inside. Anna still did not know his name. Elizabeth was hugging her tightly, tears swimming in her eyes, a smile on her lips, while Mr Goddard was shaking hands with his employer. Then Elizabeth was hugging Avery, and Mr Goddard was bowing to Anna until she held out her right hand and he took it.

'I wish you all the happiness in the world, Your—' He glanced at the door of the vestry, which was slightly ajar. 'Mrs Archer.'

'The poor man,' Avery said when they were all halfway back up the nave, 'would perhaps have had an apoplexy if he had been told of all the handles that attach themselves to my name, and now to yours too, Anna. But the marriage is quite legal even when I have been stripped to the bare bones of my identity. You are my wife, my dear, and my duchess.'

The sun seemed blinding when they stepped

outside, and the air full of summer warmth. A woman was hurrying by on the other side of the street, a child holding her hand and jumping cracks in the pavement. A horse was clopping along the road away from them. Farther back a young boy was sweeping a steaming pile of manure out of the street. From the high window of a house behind him, a maid shook the dust from a rug and called down to the boy. All the ordinary activities of daily life were proceeding around them just as though the world had not changed in the last fifteen minutes or so. Sunlight gleamed on Anna's ring, and she realized she had not even worn gloves. How appalling.

'There is a bookshop close to here that I have been meaning forever to have a look at,' Elizabeth said. 'Mr Goddard, do you like bookshops? Would you care to accompany me there? We can return home in a hackney cab. I am sure you must be an expert at summoning them.'

'It would be my pleasure, my lady,' Mr Goddard said. 'With His Grace's permission, that is.'

'Edwin,' Avery said with a sigh, 'you may go to the devil for all I care. No, perhaps I ought not to be that rash. The devil may not be willing to give you back when I have need of you, having discovered for himself how invaluable you are. And I will have need of you, I daresay. Not today, however.'

Elizabeth smiled sunnily at them both and availed herself of Mr Goddard's arm. They walked away along the street at a brisk pace without looking back.

'You do not need a chaperone any longer, you see, Anna,' Avery said as she watched them go. 'Not when you are accompanied by your husband.'

She turned her head to look at him, and it was as though the reality of it all finally hit her full force. She gazed at the Duke of Netherby and felt all the strangeness of him and all the reality of the fact that *he was her husband*.

It was as though he had read her thoughts. 'Until death do us part,' he said softly, and offered his hand.

He seated himself beside her in the barouche this time and took her hand in his again. He was not wearing gloves either.

'Much as I would like to take you back to Archer House and close all the doors and windows to the outside world until tomorrow morning,' he said as the barouche moved forward, 'it cannot be done, alas.'

'Oh.' A sudden thought struck her. 'The whole family is coming again this afternoon to discuss our wedding in greater detail.'

'The whole family,' he said, 'has been assembling at Westcott House for the purpose of arranging your life for altogether too long, Anna. It is in danger of becoming an ingrained habit. It is time they resumed their own separate lives. But my guess is that Cousin Elizabeth will lose herself in the depths of that bookshop until she is sure it is far too late for her to be the one to break the news. Edwin will be happy. He and books are the best of friends.' He raised his voice to address the coachman. 'Westcott House, Hawkins.'

'They are all going to be terribly shocked,' Anna said.

'I just hope,' he said, 'that John will not break the news to them as he escorts them up to the drawing room. He seems of the opinion that he must make conversation with your guests. Do you think you might impress upon him the importance of behaving like a regular footman for this occasion only, Anna? He appears to be quite unimpressed by my awful consequence.'

'He is so very thrilled,' she said, 'to be a footman at a grand house in London and actually to be wearing livery. I will have a word with him. We certainly do not want him telling my grandmother and my aunts that we went out and got married this morning.'

She laughed, and he turned his head to regard her with lazy, smiling eyes.

'I will hope, my duchess,' he said softly, 'to hear more of that in the days to come.' He raised her hand to his lips and held it there, his eyes holding hers.

Anna bit her lip.

'As soon as we are able to convince everyone that there is nothing else to plan for a while,' he said, 'we will hint them on their way. I doubt Elizabeth will need any persuasion to return home with her mother and Riverdale. With the possible exception of Jessica, she is by far my favorite of your relatives, Anna, and she will know that three is definitely a crowd on a wedding night. And that is what tonight will be – our wedding night at Westcott House. Tomorrow we will leave for Wensbury.'

He settled their hands on the seat between them and laced their fingers.

. . . *our wedding night.*

CHAPTER 19

Avery stood at the drawing room window.
Behind him his stepmother complained
and Jessica sulked. Anna was sitting quietly
not far from the door, her hands clasped in her
lap, the right over the left, he had noticed. She
had changed into a light blue afternoon dress,
which could not be more severe if it tried – up to
the neck, down to the wrists and the ankles, not
a bow or frill in sight. Bertha had redone her
hair and had combed it back so ruthlessly from
her face that her eyes almost slanted. Anna had
mentioned over luncheon – of which she had
consumed virtually none – that she wished she
could just run and hide. He had been tempted to
grant her wish, but there was, alas, family to be
dealt with first.

His stepmother complained to Anna because
she had not been at home this morning when
Madame Lavalle arrived to discuss bride clothes.
She complained to Avery because he had been
gone from home all morning when there was so
much to discuss with regard to the wedding that
she scarcely knew where to start. Had he made

arrangements to have the banns read on Sunday? But where? She wished to discuss the desirability of choosing St Paul's Cathedral. She complained that Edwin Goddard had disappeared from his office this morning before she could discuss the guest list with him and had not reappeared before she came here. It was very unlike him, and to do it today of all days was the outside of enough. She complained to Anna that if she would insist upon looking so much like a governess, she must not be surprised if Avery changed his mind.

She was clearly in a waspish mood – perhaps because of Jessica.

His half sister had not been pleased by the announcement he had made to her yesterday afternoon. She had been disbelieving, horrified, furious in quick succession. She had been about to throw one of the raging tantrums for which she had been famous until the advent of her current governess. But when he had raised his quizzing glass to his eye and regarded her in silent distaste, she had dissolved into tears instead and asked him between gasps and sobs how he could be so disloyal to Abby and Harry and Camille that he would actually betroth himself to that drab, ugly woman.

'Have a care, Jess,' he had said very softly, lowering his glass but not offering his arms for her comfort.

'I am being unfair, am I not?' she had said, her sobs abandoned, her expression rueful, her face blotched red, her eyes bloodshot. 'It is Uncle

343

Humphrey I should hate. But what would be the point? He is dead.'

'I shall expect you to treat my duchess with the proper courtesy, Jess,' he had told her, 'if you do not want to be confined to the schoolroom until the age of eighty or until I marry you off to the first man who can be persuaded to take you off my hands.'

Her lips had quirked and she had given in to a hiccuping giggle.

'I shall,' she had promised. 'But I do wish you had chosen someone else, Avery – anyone else. You will be bored with her within a fortnight. But I suppose that will not matter to you, will it? Gentlemen are able to have *other interests* while ladies have only their embroidery and their tatting.'

'Sometimes, Jess,' he had said, raising his quizzing glass halfway to his eye again, 'I wonder about what your governess has been teaching you.'

He had sent word with his coachman earlier that Lady Jessica Archer was to accompany her mother to Westcott House this afternoon. And here she was, silent and sulking and punctiliously courteous.

Molenor and his wife were arriving, Avery could see, and right behind them came the old fossil of a carriage in which the Dowager Countess of Riverdale and her eldest daughter moved about town when they needed to. The four of them were shown into the drawing room together, and there was a flurry of greetings before the complaints resumed. Their eldest boy had just been rusticated from school for the rest of the term, Cousin Mildred reported, having been caught climbing through the window of his dormitory at four o'clock in the morning – climbing in, not out – his hair and clothes smelling quite unmistakably of a floral perfume. The news had come in a letter from the headmaster this morning, and Molenor had not even been to his club. He was, in fact, planning to set out for their home in the north of England early tomorrow morning.

'Just when there is so much to be done here,' she lamented, 'and just as though our servants and the vicar cannot keep a stern enough eye upon Boris until after the wedding.'

'I will be back in time for the wedding, Millie,' Molenor said, patting her hand.

'That is not the point, Tom,' she complained. 'There are all the things that will need doing between now and then.'

The dowager countess also scolded Anna for being from home this morning when Madame Lavalle arrived. The young footman had told her. Anastasia really must make herself available to all those whose task it was to get her ready for her wedding. A month might seem to be a long time, but it would fly by.

'It will definitely be the wedding of the Season,' she said. 'And the more I think about it, the more convinced I am that you are right, Louise, and only St Paul's Cathedral will do.'

Cousin Matilda wanted to know where Elizabeth

was and hoped Anastasia had not been entertaining Cousin Avery alone.

'She went to a bookstore that has taken her fancy,
Aunt,' Anna explained.

Riverdale was arriving with his mother, Avery
could see. Within another minute or two everyone
would be present and accounted for.

'I believe,' Lady Matilda was saying, 'I ought to
move in here for the next month to add proper
respectability to the approach of the wedding. If
you can spare me, that is, Mama.'

While Cousin Althea greeted everyone and
hugged Anna and asked cheerfully how she was
feeling on this first full day of her betrothal,
Riverdale looked hard at Avery as though he were
wondering if the events of the early morning had
really happened. Avery inclined his head and
fingered the snuffbox in his pocket. He was given
no opportunity to withdraw it, however. Cousin
Althea was hugging him and asking the same
question she had just asked Anna.

'Never mind the betrothal, Althea,' his stepmother said. 'It is the marriage preparations we
must concern ourselves with, and Avery is drag-
ging his feet. When I asked this morning, his
secretary informed me that Avery had not yet
approved the betrothal notice I had helped Mr
Goddard draw up last evening. And Avery was
nowhere to be found. Then the secretary disappeared from his office. The notice ought to have
been submitted today to appear in tomorrow's

papers. And we must decide where the banns are to be read so that arrangements can be made before Sunday. Then we must—'

'But you see,' Avery said, his eyes upon Anna, 'I was busy this morning with matters related to my wedding. So was Edwin Goddard. So was Anna. We must all be forgiven for being unavailable to those who expected us all to be at home. We were together, the three of us, and Cousin Elizabeth before she remembered the bookshop and hurried off there with Edwin. By then, though, neither was needed any longer. By then they had duly witnessed my marriage to Anna and were tactful enough to make themselves scarce.'

There were a few moments of total silence while Anna gazed back at him, seemingly composed – just as she had been in the rose salon at Archer House a few weeks or an aeon ago – but with her right hand tensed as it clasped the left, hiding her wedding ring.

Jessica was the first to find her tongue.

'You are married?' she cried, leaping to her feet. 'Well, I am glad. That grand wedding everyone was planning would have been so *stupid*.'

Cousin Matilda had already produced a vinaigrette and a fan from her reticule and had turned toward her mother, seated beside her. It was only a pity she had no more than two hands.

'What?' His stepmother was on her feet too, her hand on Jessica's arm. '*What?*'

'You are *married?*' That was Cousin Mildred.

'Now you can come home with me, Millie,' Molenor said, 'and help me deal with our scamp.'

'Oh, you could not wait,' Cousin Althea said, her hands clasped to her bosom, her eyes shining as she looked from Anna to Avery. 'How utterly romantic.'

'*Romantic?*' the dowager said. 'Put those smelling salts away, Matilda, or use them yourself. Anastasia, you can have no idea what this will do to your reputation. Have you learned nothing in the past weeks except how to waltz? But Avery ought to know, and it is just like him to flaunt the unwritten rules of society and snap his fingers at its good opinion. You will be very fortunate if you do not find yourselves ostracized by the *ton*.'

'Anastasia,' Riverdale said, 'may I offer my sincere congratulations and good wishes? And to you too, Netherby.'

'Oh goodness,' Avery's stepmother said. 'I am no longer the Duchess of Netherby, am I? Anastasia is. I am the dowager duchess.'

'It is just a name, Mama,' Jessica said crossly.

And then Anna spoke, in that same low, commanding voice she had used in the rose salon all that time ago. 'Yesterday,' she said, 'I was overwhelmed by the realization that I had become a commodity, the most highly prized item on the marriage mart. I wanted to escape, even if only for a short while to catch my breath and order my thoughts. I said, in the hearing of you all, that I wanted to go to Wensbury to see my grandparents,

348

my mother's parents, to find out if I could learn why they turned me out after my mother died, to somehow put that part of my history in its proper place. Avery offered to marry me and take me there. He knew that I wanted – that I *needed* to go soon. He knew that waiting for the grand wedding you have all been kind enough to envisage for us would be more than time wasted to me. It would be an ordeal that would overwhelm me even more. So he brought a special license here with him this morning and took me to a church whose name I do not know on a street I cannot name to be married by a clergyman whose identity I still do not know. Elizabeth and Mr Goddard witnessed our nuptials. I know some of you are disappointed, both in me and in the loss of the splendid wedding you were beginning to plan. But this is my wedding day, and it was the loveliest wedding I could possibly imagine, and I must beg your pardon while not regretting for a moment what I have done. We will be setting out on our journey tomorrow.'

She did not take her eyes off Avery while she spoke.

He must surely, he thought, have fallen in love with her that very first day. Which was a puzzling possibility, especially when he recalled those shoes and that dress and cloak and bonnet. But even then he had spotted the quiet, poised dignity of the woman within. Actually the whole thing was puzzling. That the way she had conducted herself on that occasion and since had aroused his respect, even his admiration, was surprising enough. But romantic love? He did not believe in it. He never had and never would.

Except that it really must be romantic love he was feeling for her. His eyes traveled over her and found themselves well pleased, though he could not understand why. He looked back into her eyes and smiled. Good God, she was his wife.

'Well,' his stepmother said, resuming her seat and drawing Jessica down beside her, 'I will not declare that I cannot believe it. I can believe it all too well. It is just what I might have expected of Avery. We will just have to make the best of the situation. We must plan a grand wedding reception and explain away the hurried, almost clandestine nature of the wedding with a slight embellishment of the truth. Anna's maternal grandparents are elderly and infirm. They wished to meet their long-lost granddaughter before they die, and Avery insisted that he marry Anastasia without delay and take her there. We were all in reluctant but total agreement. Everyone will be charmed. The new Duchess of Netherby will be the sensation of the hour again. We need to get busy.'

'Which, I feel constrained to inform you, you will not do here and now,' Avery said. 'This is my wedding day, and I feel the urge to be alone with my bride. I see that Elizabeth has just alit from a hackney cab outside the door. I do not doubt she has come to collect her things so that she can return home with Riverdale and Cousin Althea. Edwin Goddard is already in possession of a written notice of our marriage and will see to it that it appears in tomorrow's papers. I believe I speak for my duchess when I thank you all for your intended efforts on our behalf and release you from the urge to do more.'

'That includes a wedding reception, Avery?' Aunt Mildred asked. 'If I go with Tom tomorrow, I really will not wish to face the journey back here in a few weeks' time. Besides, Peter and Ivan will be coming home from school too in the not too distant future.'

'That includes a wedding reception,' Avery said, and he noticed Anna closing her eyes briefly in relief.

They were all on their feet then, and all talking at once, it seemed. Everyone wanted to hug the bride and shake the groom by the hand. And then everyone wanted to hug everyone else, and something uproariously funny must have happened when Avery was not looking, for there was a great deal of boisterous laughter mingled with congratulations and good wishes and scolds and warnings. Cousin Elizabeth, poking her head about the door in the midst of it all, remarked with twinkling eyes that she could see the cat had been let out of the bag, for which loose use of language she was frowned upon by Cousin Matilda, though it was doubtful she noticed, and disappeared upstairs with her mother to fetch some of her things and leave instructions for the rest to follow her later.

And then everyone was gone, even the butler and Footman John, from the hall in which Avery and Anna stood side by side.

'Well, my duchess,' he said.

'Well, my duke.' She smiled at him – and blushed.

'Does your bedchamber door have a lock on it?' he asked her. 'With a key?'

'Yes,' she said.

'And your dressing room door?'

She thought a moment. 'Yes.'

'Show me the way,' he said, offering his arm. 'Let us go and lock ourselves in.'

'It is only the middle of the afternoon,' she protested.

'And so it is,' he agreed. 'There is plenty of time before dinner, then.'

It was full daylight. Moreover, it was a bright, sunny day, and her bedchamber faced south. Even after he had drawn the curtains across the window the sunlight was not much muted. There were the daytime sounds of birdsong and a dog barking in the distance and the clopping hooves of a single horse coming through the open window. A voice from far down the street called a cheerful greeting, and another voice answered.

Her bridegroom, her husband, stood before her. He was just looking, making no move to touch her or to kiss her. She wondered if she should step into the dressing room to change into a nightgown. But he had locked the door.

'I believe, my duchess,' he said, 'you are perfection. But let me unwrap my gift package and see if I am right.'

As well as startling her, his words puzzled her. Perfection? She was not particularly pretty. She had no figure to speak of. She had refused to dress fashionably. She was neither vivacious nor the possessor of any other obvious charms. Her fortune was of no interest to him. Was it just that she was different from every other woman he had known? Was it just novelty? Would today's toy be discarded for tomorrow's when the novelty was gone?

He stepped closer, though not right against her, and reached his arms about her to unpin her dress down the back. His fingers were accustomed to the task, she realized. He did not even have to see what he was doing. When it was unpinned to her hips, he drew it off her shoulders, the backs of his fingers skimming her flesh – coolness against warmth. Her instinct was to raise her hands to hold the bodice in place, but she kept her arms at her sides, and he worked the sleeves downward, pulling eventually at the hems to draw them free of her wrists. He was in no hurry. But once her arms no longer held the dress in place, the whole garment slithered down over her shift and stockings to pool about her feet.

It was difficult to continue breathing evenly through her nose. And it took effort not to lower her eyes, even close them, so that she would not see him standing there, looking at her – not into her face but at her body and her remaining garments, his eyelids half drooped as they usually were, his eyes almost dreamy.

He went down on one knee to remove her slippers and then began to roll down her stockings one at a time and work them off her feet. He stood again and removed her stays and her shift until she was left with nothing behind which to hide her modesty. Not even any jewelry except her wedding ring. The sunlight made a mockery of the curtains and cast a pinkish glow over everything.

He gazed at her, every inch of her. His fingers had scarcely touched her while he undressed her, yet she was convinced that every brush of the backs of his fingers, every graze from a thumb, every rub of a knuckle had been deliberate. She felt touched all over. He was still dressed in the immaculate more-formal-than-usual clothes he had worn for their wedding, even down to the Hessian boots.

'I was quite right.' His eyes were keen now and looking into hers. 'You are perfection, my Anna.'

Even his words were deliberate. *My duchess. My Anna. Let me unwrap my gift package.* Claiming her as his own. *You are perfection.* Only the very best would do, his words implied. She was not in the habit of deprecating herself, but . . . perfection? And it was of her body he spoke. She did not believe he was much interested in her character at the moment.

'I have the figure of a boy,' she said.

Characteristically, he considered her words before answering. 'You cannot have seen many boys,' he said. 'You are woman, Anna, from the topmost hair on your head to your toenails.'

Her stomach lurched. *Woman,* he had said – not *a woman.* Somehow there was a difference.

He touched her then, with his fingertips, with the flats of his fingers, the backs of his fingers, the heels of his palms, his knuckles, his whole hand. Light, feathering touches. Over her shoulders and down her arms, over the backs of her hands. Downward from her shoulders, through the cleft between her breasts, around beneath them, over, through again, down her sides to her waist, over her hips to the tops of her legs. Up behind her, along her spine, around her shoulder blades. Caressing her, learning her, claiming her. Downward with just one hand this time over one breast, past her ribs, over the flat of her stomach and down until the back of his hand rested lightly on the mound of hair at the apex of her thighs.

She wondered if he knew what even such light touches were doing to her and thought that yes, of course he did. *Of course he did.* She suspected he knew everything there was to know about . . . What was the word? Dalliance? Making love? She could almost hear her heartbeat. She could certainly feel it. There was a strange ache and a heavy throbbing within, just behind where his hand was. It was harder to breathe evenly without panting. She wondered if she should be doing something. But no. He was orchestrating this, and somehow he had issued the unspoken command that she stand still and relax.

He was dangerous, dangerous, dangerous, she thought, this small, slight, golden man.

Her husband.

His eyes had moved above the level of her own and he took his hands off her. 'Tell me, Anna,' he said, 'was it Bertha's idea to put such great stress upon the roots of your hair this afternoon, or was it yours? And do not slander your maid. I have fond memories of my one encounter with her.' His eyes were on hers again.

'I . . . almost panicked when I retired to my dressing room after luncheon,' she admitted. 'I thought – *what have I done?* I wanted to hide. I wanted myself back. I—'

'Have you lost yourself, then?' he asked, his voice very soft. 'Have you given yourself away, Anna? To some savage, heartless brute? You wound me.'

'I wanted to be Anna Snow again,' she said.

'Did you?' he said. '*Do* you, my duchess?'

'Avery,' she said, 'I am very frightened.' Ah. She had not known she was going to say that. And it was not quite true. *Frightened* was entirely the wrong word.

'But you are in good hands,' he said, raising them to begin withdrawing her hairpins.

'Oh,' she said crossly, 'that is precisely the point.'

He drew the pins out slowly, bent to place them inside one of her slippers, and straightened up again to run his fingers through her hair and arrange it over her shoulders, some in front, some behind. It reached now only to the tops of her breasts. It waved slightly at the ends.

'But they *are* good hands,' he said, holding them up in the space between them, palms toward her. Slim hands, slender fingers, gold rings on four of them. Three of those fingertips had felled a man and left him gasping for survival. 'They will protect you all the rest of my life and never hurt you. They will hold you and bring you comfort when you need it. They will hold our children. They will caress you and bring you pleasure. Come. Lie down on the bed.'

Our children . . .

He drew the covers back to the foot of the bed and she lay down and looked up at him. His hair glowed golden in the pinkish light of the room. His eyes roamed over her as he loosened his neck-cloth and discarded it. He took his time undressing. It took him a while in particular to remove his formfitting coat and his boots, but he was in no hurry. Anna watched. She had seen his near-naked beauty this morning but from some distance. She saw now when he pulled his shirt off over his head that the muscles of his arms and chest and abdomen were taut and well honed even though they did not bulge. But he was not a man who relied upon brute strength, was he?

357

'Oh,' she said as he dropped the shirt, 'your bruise.'

She had not realized that any of Viscount Uxbury's punches had found its mark. It was below his right shoulder, where it met the arm, a bruise that looked red and raw and had not yet turned black or purple or all the colors of the rainbow. He looked down at it.

'A mere nothing,' he said. 'I ran into a door.'

'Oh, that is such a cliché,' she said. 'I expected better of you.'

There was a gleam of something like amusement in his eyes. 'The worst thing anyone can say of me, Anna,' he said, 'is that I lack originality. You cut me to the quick. However, you are quite right. Let me be more specific. A door ran into me.'

She surprised herself by laughing. 'You are so absurd,' she said.

He tipped his head to one side and looked down at her, that suggestion of amusement still in his eyes. But he did not say anything. He proceeded to remove his pantaloons and his drawers.

She was twenty-five years old and a total innocent. She knew what a man looked like only because on one visit to the bookshop in Bath she had leafed through a volume about ancient Greece and come across pictures of sculptures of various gods and heroes. She had been both shocked and fascinated and had thought how unfair it was that the male physique was so much more attractive than the female – though perhaps she had thought that only because she was looking through female eyes. She had put the book back on the shelf with a guilty glance around to see that she was not being observed, and had never looked again.

Avery was more beautiful than any of those gods and heroes, perhaps because he was real flesh and blood. He was perfection itself.

He set one knee on the bed beside her and braced his hands on either side of her as he swung across to straddle her. With his knees he pressed her own together and moved his hands over her again. He lifted her breasts in the cleft between his thumbs and forefingers and set the pads of his thumbs over her nipples. He rubbed them in light circles and pulsed lightly against them until she felt such a raw . . . *something* that she closed her eyes and lifted herself closer. His mouth came to her shoulder, across to the hollow between it and her neck, to her throat – open, hot, wet. And he was down on her then, the full length of his legs clamping hers tightly together while his hands moved beneath her and down to cup her bottom while he rubbed himself against the tops of her legs and she could feel him hard and long and alien.

He moved his mouth to the other side of her neck and along her shoulder as one of his hands came between them and his fingers worked their way between her tight thighs and down into folds and depths until one finger came right inside her to the knuckle and she stiffened with mingled shock and embarrassment and longing. His legs pressed more tightly against the outsides of hers. She could hear wetness as he moved his finger, drawing it out, sliding it in again.

'Beautiful, beautiful,' he said, his mouth against her temple.

He raised his head to look down at her as his hands hooked beneath her legs and drew them wide and wrapped them about his own as he came between. He moved his hands beneath her again to lift and hold her. She felt him hard and hot where his finger had been, and then he came into her with one firm thrust. His eyes watched her while shock, pain, and something beyond words or thought engulfed her. He held still and deep in her while her mind and body grappled with a new reality and the tension went gradually out of her.

'Ah, my poor Anna,' he murmured. 'So hot, so beautiful. There was no way *not* to hurt you, you see. But only this time. Not next time or ever again. It is my promise to you.'

She touched him. She set her hands on either side of his waist – hard, firm muscled, so unlike her own. And she moved them to his back, along the column of his spine, down to rest lightly over tight buttocks. He drew slowly out of her, muscles relaxing beneath her hands, and she did not want to let him go. And then the muscles tightened and he came in again, hard and firm and deep. He turned his head to rest beside hers on the pillow and took some of his weight onto his elbows and forearms, though his chest pressed against her breasts and his shoulders held hers to the bed. He moved into her and out of her with a firm, steady rhythm. There was sound – a wet suck and pull, a slight squeak of the bed, labored breathing, laughter from a distance down the street. There was sensation, weight pinning her to the bed, heat, the slight coolness of air coming through the window and finding its way through or past the curtains, the hardness of him inside her, smooth, wet, not quite painful. She did not want it to end. She wanted it to go on forever.

Forever lasted a long time and no time at all. The rhythm broke and he pressed hard into her until there was no deeper to come, and while he murmured something unintelligible against her ear, she felt a gush of liquid heat inside and knew that it was finished. His full weight relaxed down onto her then and she wrapped her arms about his waist and untwined her legs from about his to set her feet flat on the bed. After a few moments he sighed against her ear, withdrew from her, and rolled off her to recline beside her, his head propped on one hand.

'Wedded and bedded,' he said. 'Anna Snow no more or even Anastasia Westcott. My wife, instead. My duchess. Is it such a terrible fate, Anna?'

There was something very like wistfulness in his voice.

'No,' she said, and she smiled. 'My duke.'

He got off the bed then, picked up one of the keys he had dropped onto the dressing table, unlocked the dressing room door, and went inside. He came back a few moments later, a small towel in his hand. He locked the door again and got back into bed, drew the upper sheet and one blanket over them, and slid an arm beneath her shoulders to turn her onto her side facing him. He slipped the towel between her thighs, spread it, and held it gently against her before removing his hand and leaving the towel where it was. It felt soothing. He arranged the covers over them and drew her closer. Within moments he was asleep.

How could he possibly sleep? But she supposed it had not been nearly as momentous for him as it had been for her. She did not want to think of other women, but she did not doubt there had been many. He was thirty-one years old, and he did not seem like the sort of man who would deny himself anything he wanted. The thought did not trouble her, she realized. Not as it applied to the past, at least.

She had hardly slept last night. Indeed, she would have believed she had not slept at all if she had not kept waking from bizarre dreams. She had been up well before dawn. She had been in Hyde Park with Elizabeth before there was full daylight by which to see. She had lived through all the terror and strangeness of that duel. Then she had returned home and, instead of dropping back into bed, had had an early breakfast with

Elizabeth and then written a long letter to Joel. After that there had been her wedding and then the visit of her family and now the consummation of her marriage. Could all that possibly have happened within so short a time?

Exhaustion hit her rather like a soft mallet to the head. And also the knowledge that she was warm and comfortable, that her body was against his, that the soft sound of his breathing was both soothing and lulling, that she was . . . happy.

She slept.

CHAPTER 20

'It is good to have you home again, Lizzie,' Alexander said at dinner that evening. 'I have missed you. Mama has too.'

'It does feel good,' she admitted, 'though I enjoyed my weeks with Anna. I like her exceedingly well.'

Their mother was regarding Alexander with slightly troubled eyes. 'Do you mind dreadfully, Alex, that she has married Avery?' she asked. 'You more or less offered for her yourself yesterday, and I believe she might have been persuaded to accept if he had not been there.'

'No,' he said, picking up his glass of wine and leaning back in his chair. 'I do not mind, Mama. Netherby saved me from the temptation to persuade Anastasia to take the easy way out of both our problems.'

'But you are a little sad anyway?' she asked.

'Maybe a little,' he admitted after hesitating for a moment. 'But only for a despicable reason. I could have restored Brambledean to prosperity without having to cudgel my brains further over how it is to be done.'

364

'You do yourself an injustice,' she said. 'You would have been good to Anastasia too. I know you better than to believe you would have cared only for the money and not for the bride who brought it to you.'

'I am going to have to marry for money anyway,' he said. 'I have come to that conclusion. Brambledean cannot recover from years of neglect as Riddings Park did, just with some hard work and careful economies. But I have the title and dilapidated property to offer a rich wife in return.'

'Ah,' she said, reaching out to pat his free hand on the table. 'I did not expect ever to hear you bitter or cynical, Alex. It hurts my heart.'

'I do beg your pardon, Mama,' he said, setting down his glass in order to cover her hand with his own. 'I feel neither bitter nor cynical. I am merely being realistic. I owe prosperity to those who are dependent upon me at Brambledean. If I can offer it through marrying a wealthy bride, then so be it. A bride does not have to be distasteful merely because she is rich, and I would hope that I need not be distasteful to her merely because I have an earl's title. I will expect to hold her in affection and to work tirelessly to win hers.'

His mother sighed, drew her hand free, and returned her attention to her food.

'Do you resent what Avery has done, Alex?' Elizabeth asked. 'I know you have never liked him.'

He frowned in thought. 'I believe I have revised my opinion of him recently,' he said. 'I – There is more to him than he allows the world to see or chooses to allow the world to believe. Part of me is horrified for Anastasia even so. He cannot possibly value her as he ought or treat her with anything but careless indifference. She will surely regret her impulsive decision to marry him just because he offered to take her to see grandparents who would have nothing to do with her after her mother died. I fear she will soon be very unhappy.'

Elizabeth tipped her head to one side and looked curiously at him. 'But—?' she said.

'But I have the strange feeling,' he said, 'that I may be completely wrong. I have known Netherby since we were both boys at school. Yet I discovered aspects of him . . . recently that I did not even begin to suspect.' He glanced at their mother. 'It is possible, even probable, that I have never known him at all. And yes, I still resent him for that, Lizzie, and could never, I think, call him friend. How can one be a friend to someone who has chosen to make himself unknowable? Yet if I ever needed . . . help, I believe I would not hesitate to turn to him. Beyond my fear for Anastasia lies a certain suspicion that she will be happy after all and that perhaps he will be too. Though one cannot quite imagine Netherby *happy*, can one?'

'Oh, I can,' their mother said. 'His eyes some-times give him away, Alex, if one looks closely enough. He has a certain way of looking at Anastasia . . . Well, I do believe he is in love with her. And she is in love with him, of course. What woman would not be if he turned his attention on her and informed her in that strange way of his that she could be his duchess if she chose and then whisked her off the very next day with a special license and two witnesses to marry her? Lizzie, was it a very romantic wedding?'

'I believe it was, Mama,' Elizabeth said, her eyes twinkling. 'I think it was perhaps the most romantic wedding I have ever attended. Cousin Louise would have had an apoplexy, not to mention Cousin Matilda – Anna wore her plain straw bonnet and forgot her gloves.'

She laughed, and her mother clasped her hands to her bosom and beamed with delight. Alexander leaned back in his chair and smiled fondly from one to the other of them.

Anna had thought she was traveling in great comfort when she came to London in the chaise Mr Brumford had hired, with her small bag containing most of her worldly possessions and Miss Knox for companionship. What a difference a few weeks had made. She traveled back west in a carriage so opulent that even the lamentable state of English roads could not seriously discon-cert the springs or make the seats seem less than plushly comfortable. This time there was so much baggage that a separate conveyance was coming along behind, together with a valet and a maid.

For companionship she had Avery, who asked her about her education and told her about his own, who conversed with her about books and art and music and politics and the war. He told her about Morland Abbey, his home in the country, hers too now, a house with character surrounded by a vast landscaped park complete with follies, a wilderness walk, a lake, shaded alleys, and rolling lawns dotted with ancient trees. He was sometimes serious, sometimes outrageously funny in his own peculiar way. He talked a great deal, and he listened just as much, his head usually turned toward her, his eyes regarding her in their characteristic lazy but attentive way.

Often they did not talk at all but watched the landscape passing by beyond the windows. Occasionally they nodded off to sleep, his head wedged into the corner beside him, hers burrowed between his shoulder and the back of the seat. Sometimes he held her hand and laced their fingers. If they had been silent too long, he would tickle her palm with his thumbnail and smile lazily when she turned her head.

They traveled at a far more leisurely pace than she had on that other journey. Whenever they stopped to change the horses, he always stayed out in the yard to look over the replacements, often with a pained expression because this journey had been planned in too much of a hurry to allow time to send his own horses forward to the various staging points. Then he would join Anna for refreshments or a full meal, always in a private parlor, even when it seemed the inn at which they stopped was full to overflowing. They were treated with a deference often bordering upon obsequiousness that amazed Anna, though she realized that Avery was so accustomed to it he did not even notice. His coat of arms was, of course, emblazoned on both doors of their carriage, and his coachman and footman and two outriders were dressed in a distinctive livery. There could be no missing their passage west. Even if he had been alone, though, and without all the trappings, Anna suspected that everyone would still have known at a single glance that he was no ordinary gentleman but a distinguished member of the Quality.

They stayed two nights on the road in the very best of accommodations with the very best service. They were presented with a seeming banquet each evening, walked for a couple of miles afterward since the days of travel allowed no chance for exercise, and then went to bed, where they made love, slept deeply, and made love again in the early dawn.

Anna fell more deeply in love. But no, that was not quite accurate, since she had probably been in as deeply as it was possible to get even before they left London. On the journey she began to *love* him as she got to know him more – his intellect, his knowledge and opinions, his obvious love of his home, his brand of humor, his way of making love. Though there was no single way about that. Every time was different from the time before and the time after.

They were in what some people referred to as the honeymoon stage of their marriage, of course, and she had too much good sense to expect it to last indefinitely. But, forced into each other's company as they were for the first two and a half days of their marriage, a certain ease had developed between them. They could sit in silence without embarrassment. They could doze in each other's company. More important, something of a friendship was surely being built, and that perhaps would carry into the future so that they could be comfortable together even when the passion died – as surely it would.

An ease of manner in each other's company and a friendship would be enough in the years ahead. And – oh, please, please – children. He had actually referred to them on the day of their wedding. And he must, of course, want sons, an heir. No, she told herself firmly when once or twice doubt teased at the edges of her mind, she had not made a poor decision. She was happy now. In the future she would be content to be content. She smiled at the thought.

'A penny for them, my duchess,' Avery said. They were somewhere south of Bristol, not far from the end of their journey. It always amused her to be called that – or aroused her if he said it in bed.

'Oh,' she said, 'I was thinking that I could be contented with being contented.'

He looked pained. 'You cannot, surely, be serious,'

he said. 'Contentment, Anna? Bah! Utter bland-ness. You were not made for any such thing. You must demand blissful happiness or grapple with deep misery. But never *contentment*. You must not sell yourself short. I will not allow it.'

'You intend to be a tyrant, then?' she asked him.

'Did you expect anything less?' he asked her. 'I shall insist that you be happy, Anna, whether you wish to be or not. I will not brook disobedience.'

She laughed, and he turned his head. 'That is your cue to say, *Yes, Your Grace*, in the meekest of accents,' he added.

'Ah,' she said, 'but I never learned my part. No one gave me the script.'

'I shall teach you,' he said, turning his head away to look out at the countryside.

And he was only half joking, she thought, puzzled. Perhaps he did not understand that this was only a honeymoon period. Perhaps he thought his feelings would last. But what *were* his feelings? Was his passion for her only physical? Why had he married her of all women? He was thirty-one years old. He was an aristocrat, rich, powerful, influential, beautiful. Within the past ten years he might have married anyone he chose. No one, surely, would have refused him.

Why her?

But only half her attention was on the mystery that was her husband. The rest was upon the slight sickness she was feeling in her stomach. They had stopped for luncheon a short while ago. The other carriage had remained there along with their baggage and all the servants except the coachman. They would return there for the night. But soon they would come to Wensbury, where she had spent a couple of years of her infancy, where her mother was presumably buried, where her grandparents still lived at the vicarage beside the church, where her grandfather was still vicar.

Was this all a huge mistake? Since they had not wanted her, would it have been better to leave well enough alone and forget about them? But now that the blank emptiness of years had been wiped away, how could she be content not to know everything there was to know? She had to see them, even if they turned her away again. She had to see what she so dimly and inadequately remembered – the room with the window seat, the graveyard below, the lych-gate. Yes, she had had to come.

And then, long before she was prepared for it, they arrived in what looked to be a small, sleepy, picturesque village. Wensbury. There was almost no one outside – except a young boy who was bowling a hoop along the street until he spotted the carriage. He stopped then, yelled something in the direction of the thatched, whitewashed cottage beside him, and gawked at them, his mouth at half-mast, while a young woman came to the door, wiping her hands on her apron. A small dog a little farther along the street took exception to their invasion of its territory and barked ferociously, waking with a start the elderly man who had been sleeping on a bench outside his cottage, the dog at his feet, and setting him to staring after them, his hands clutched about the handle of the cane planted between his legs. Two women gossiping across a garden hedge stopped, probably midsentence, to stare in open amazement.

Anna doubted Avery had noticed any of it.

'It is a pretty church,' he said, looking across the village green. 'Many country churches are. I wonder if there is a bell in that tower. I would wager there is.' Then he turned to look at her and, seeing her expression, said, 'Anna, Anna, no one is going to eat you. I will not allow it.' He took her hand in a firm grasp.

'If they do not wish to see me,' she said, 'we will just leave, Avery. At least I have come.'

'It sounds to me,' he said, 'as though you are about to say you will be content.'

'Yes,' she admitted.

He squeezed her hand to the point of pain as the carriage turned sharply about the green.

And then they were drawing up outside what must be the vicarage beside the church, and an elderly gentleman with white, bushy hair and eyebrows and no hat was stepping out through the . . . oh, through the lych-gate from the churchyard and turning their way, an amiable smile of welcome on his face. As Avery descended from the carriage and turned to hand Anna down, the vicarage door opened and an elderly lady, tiny and birdlike, gray hair more than half hidden beneath a lacy cap, stood there looking out with placid curiosity. Not many grand carriages passed through Wensbury, Anna guessed, and even fewer stopped outside the church.

'Good morning, sir, ma'am,' the gentleman said. 'May I be of assistance to you?'

'The Reverend Isaiah Snow?' Avery asked.

'I have that pleasure, sir,' the gentleman said as the lady came along the garden path toward the gate. 'And vicar of the church here for the past fifty years. Some of my younger parishioners believe I must be almost as old as the church. And this is my good wife. How may we be of service to you? Is it the lych-gate that caused you to stop? It is a fine example of its type, and has always been kept in good repair. Or the church, perhaps? It dates back to Norman times.'

'Is that a bell tower?' Avery asked, his quizzing glass in his hand.

'It is indeed,' the Reverend Snow said. 'And there are four faithful bell ringers in the village who duly waken all sleepyheads on a Sunday and ring them to morning service.'

'Isaiah,' his wife said, 'perhaps the lady would care to step into the house for a glass of lemonade while you show the gentleman the church. You have started him on his favorite subject, sir, and will not get away from him within the hour, I predict.'

'Allow me to introduce myself,' Avery said, while

Anna's hand turned cold in his warm clasp. 'Avery Archer, Duke of Netherby.'

'Ah,' the vicar said, 'I knew when I saw the crest on the door of the carriage that you must be somebody of importance, sir. We are honored that you have seen fit to stop here.'

'And may I present my wife, the duchess,' Avery continued, 'formerly Lady Anastasia Westcott, though she has been known through most of her life as Anna Snow.'

The lady's hands crept up to cover her cheeks and her face grew as pale as her name. She swayed, and it seemed to Anna that she would surely fall. But she clutched at the fence before it could happen.

'*Anna?*' she said, her voice little more than a whisper. 'Little Anna? But you died twenty years ago. Of typhoid.'

'My dear God,' the vicar said, and it did not sound like a blasphemy. 'Oh my dear God, he lied to us, Alma, and we believed him. But look and see and tell me if I am right. Could this not be our Anna standing before us here?'

His wife merely moaned and clung to the fence.

'Gramma?' Anna said. She did not know where the name came from – it just came. 'Oh, Gramma, I did not die.'

CHAPTER 21

Avery always felt more relaxed in the country than he did in London. It was as if he took off an armor he unconsciously donned for society and allowed himself to be the person he had always wanted to be. He had never blamed his parents for the child he had been. He had never even really blamed the boys and masters at school for spotting the weak one among them and pouncing upon him to make sport of him. Everyone had his own path to follow in life. And they all – the negative forces in his life, and the positive too – had had a hand in directing him to his own path. He would have things no different. He rather liked his life. He liked himself. But he liked his country life best of all.

He had undertaken this journey for Anna's sake. But he had found himself relaxing as soon as London was behind them, despite the fact that traveling long distances usually made him restless and irritable. He had found himself not wanting the journey to end, for he had feared there might be disappointment awaiting his wife and perhaps real pain. He could not do anything to shield her from whatever was to be, however. He could only be there with her. She needed to do this.

Those who knew only his public self might have expected him to feel nothing but disdain for the small, pretty village where her grandparents lived, and for the humble vicarage beside the old Norman church, and for the elderly, slightly stooped, amiable vicar and his small gray-haired wife with her overlarge cap, whose one servant worked in the mornings only – except Sunday, which was a day of rest for all workers.

'Except the vicar,' that gentleman observed with a chuckle.

As it happened there had been no disappointment lying in wait for Anna, though there was plenty of pain to go around. The truth had been instantly apparent to Avery even before they all stepped inside the vicarage and disposed themselves about a cozy square sitting room generously decorated with crocheted doilies and china figurines and pottery jugs. Only the details of the story needed to be filled in.

To the Snows, Riverdale had only ever been known as Mr Humphrey Westcott. He had said nothing of his courtesy title or of the fact that he was heir to an earldom. They were amazed – and perhaps unimpressed – to learn that their daughter had been Viscountess Yardley, not simply Mrs Westcott. They were quite sure she had never known it herself. Avery exchanged a glance with Anna and knew that she was remembering their wedding a few days ago – Miss Anastasia Westcott to Mr Avery Archer.

'Alice went to Bath to be a governess,' the vicar explained. 'She met and married Westcott there before we even knew of him. All was rosy for a while. They had rooms there, and then Anna was born – Anastasia they christened her, but Alice always called her Anna and so did we. Then her husband started disappearing for weeks at a time, and she got sick with what turned out to be consumption, and the rent was in arrears and the landlord was after her for it because Westcott was never at home, and there was not enough money for food. Finally she begged a ride with some people she knew and came back here, bringing little Anna with her, and he made no more than a token protest. He came here once and blustered a bit – we never warmed to him, Alma and I – but he did not stay. He never sent her any money and only one or two letters, which always came through a solicitor in Bath. Never any gifts for the child. After Alice died, we talked it over, my wife and I, and decided the decent thing to do was let him know, though we did not expect it would matter much to him. It mattered to us. Our daughter, our only child, was gone, and little Anna was wandering all over the house, looking lost and asking where Mama had gone and when she was coming back.'

He stopped to blow his nose loudly into a large handkerchief.

'But he came,' he continued, 'and he insisted upon taking Anna away with him even though we begged him to leave her here. She was all we had left, and Alma had been more mother than grandmother to her while Alice was ill. He took her anyway, and he never wrote. It was thirteen months before he finally did – just a brief note regretting to inform us that his daughter, Anastasia, had died of typhoid fever. He did not reply to the letter I wrote in reply.'

'He took me to Bath,' Anna told them, 'and left me at an orphanage there as Anna Snow. He never came back, but he did support me all through my childhood and right up to his recent death. He had already remarried before my mother died. They had three children, my half brother and half sisters. The marriage was bigamous, of course, and the children illegitimate, a fact that has caused endless anguish since the truth came out after his death. His title and entailed properties have passed to my second cousin and his fortune to me. I suppose he feared to leave me here with you lest somehow you discover and expose the truth.'

'If we had not written after Alice died, Isaiah,' his wife said, 'perhaps he would have forgotten all about us and left us alone. Perhaps Anna would have grown up here where she was loved. Oh, what a dreadful wickedness. I grieved for you, Anna, dead so soon after Alice, until I took to my bed and would have stayed there if I had not suddenly realized that if I died too I would leave your grampa with a burden too heavy for any mortal shoulders to bear. But in my heart I have grieved ever since. You were such a . . . lovely little child. And you grew up all alone in an orphanage? So close to here? Only in Bath? Ah, my heart aches.'

Anna was sitting on a crochet-covered stool beside her chair, holding her hand. 'But at least,' she said, 'I am not dead. And at least I now know that you did not turn me away because you did not want me.'

Her grandmother moaned.

'Sir.' Avery turned to the old gentleman, who was blowing his nose again. 'If it is not too much trouble, I would like to have a closer look at that lych-gate and the church. I am sure my wife will enjoy a comfortable coze with her grandmother.'

The vicar got so quickly to his feet that it seemed to Avery he was relieved. There was only so much sentiment a man could take.

'And you are a duke,' he said, shaking his head with incredulity, 'and Anna a duchess. Your marriage must be of recent date?'

'Three days ago, sir,' Avery said. 'We married quietly by special license rather than wait for the banns. Anna wanted to come here as soon as my secretary discovered where you were, and I wanted to make it possible for her to do so without unnecessary delay.'

'You are an angel,' Mrs Snow said. 'You even look a bit like one. Does he not, Isaiah?'

'It is the hair, ma'am,' Avery said, deliberately grimacing. 'The bane of my existence.'

'Never say so,' she said. 'It is your halo. Come into the kitchen, Anna, and I will brew us some tea. You must tell me everything about your life and more than everything. Oh, please do not let anyone pinch me. I am still afraid I am going to wake up any moment. You are so pretty. Is she not, Isaiah? Just as your mother was before her illness. Come.'

And she got to her feet and drew Anna to hers as the vicar led Avery outside.

And the thing was, Avery thought over the following hour or so, that he was not merely being polite, showing a feigned interest in what was clearly the vicar's pride and joy. He enjoyed examining the structure of the lych-gate and poking around in the dark, dank little church and climbing the tightly winding stone steps to the platform in the tower from where the bells he could see above his head were rung on Sundays and for weddings and funerals – though only one of them was tolled on those last occasions, the vicar explained. Avery enjoyed listening to the history of the church, which the Reverend Snow clearly enjoyed telling in great detail. And he allowed himself to be led slowly about the churchyard while the vicar pointed out a number of the headstones, which bore the names of families who had lived in the area for centuries. He was shown the grave of Anna's mother: *Here Lies Alice Westcott, Beloved Only*

Daughter of the Reverend and Mrs Snow, Devoted Mother of Anastasia, Sorely Missed. And the dates, showing that she had been twenty-three years old at the time of her death. Younger than Anna was now.

Avery turned his head toward the vicarage and could see that Anna and her grandmother were at an upstairs window looking out. He raised a hand, and Anna raised hers in return. He would bring her out here afterward. Though perhaps her grandparents would want to do that.

A short while later Avery sent his carriage back to the inn where he had taken rooms for the night and the rest of his entourage was already ensconced. He sent word that they were to remain there until further notice, including his valet and Anna's maid, though each was to pack a bag of essentials and send the two bags – no more – back to the vicarage.

When two elderly people had looked at him with anxious, pleading eyes, and one young lady had gazed at him with eager trust in his answer, he had agreed they would stay for a few days. Those who knew the Duke of Netherby would have been filled with amazement bordering upon incredulity. But the duke himself was fast discovering that wherever his wife was or wished to be was where he chose to be too, even if it happened to be a vicarage surely no larger than the entrance hall at Morland.

The realization was somewhat alarming. It was

also novelty enough to be explored. Perhaps being in love was what his soul had long yearned for.

Or perhaps he was merely mad.

They stayed for eight days. Anna weeded flower beds with her grandmother and cut off faded flowers and gathered bouquets for the house. She sat with her grandmother in the sitting room, talking endlessly, dusting all the little knickknacks and the surfaces under them, learning how to crochet, one form of needlework in which she had never before felt much interest. They spent time in the kitchen during the afternoons, baking cakes and tarts, mixing big jugs of lemonade, and brewing tea. They went visiting a few neighbors and wandered the churchyard together. On one hot afternoon they sat for a while on a stone bench inside the lych-gate and laughed over how Anna had been both fascinated and frightened by it as an infant.

She spent time with her grandfather too, but it was usually when all four of them were together. Avery spent most of the time with him. Even when Grampa was shut up in his study composing Sunday's sermon, Avery sat in there with him, reading. The two men seemed really to enjoy each other's company, to the wonder of Anna. Sometimes she looked at her husband and remembered him as she had first seen him. It was hard to believe he was the same man. He dressed similarly, except that his quizzing glass, his snuffbox, and most of his jewelry were lying neglected in a china bowl in the small bedchamber they shared. And his neckcloth was tied with a simple knot, she noticed, and his boots lost some of their sheen, and he seemed unconcerned about it. His manner too was more relaxed, less languidly affected. He treated both her grandparents with warm respect and no hint of condescension. He conversed openly and sensibly, with none of the verbal affectations that had half irritated, half amused her in London.

Her grandmother could not be shifted in her opinion that he was an angel.

'And he worships the ground you tread upon, Anna,' she said. 'The good Lord has looked after you, my love, without any assistance from your gramma and grampa. That will keep me humble. However, I shall have a bone to pick with him over it when I come face-to-face with him in heaven. I assume that is where I am going. Indeed, I will not take no for an answer.'

She laughed heartily, and Anna was struck, as she was over and over again during those eight days, with a wave of . . . not memory exactly. She remembered precious little of the years she had spent here. But there were sometimes snatches and whiffs of familiarity, nothing definite enough to be captured by the mind, but real enough to prod at the heart and linger there. The only real memories were the lych-gate – though why that she did not know – and the window seat in what she learned had been her mother's room, with its view down over the churchyard and the church. But there were Gramma's laugh, the doilies, the big round china teapot with its faded painting of an idyllic rural scene and the small, triangular chip in its lid, Grampa's way of always seeming to get the many small buttons of his waistcoats into the wrong buttonholes, and his quiet, affable smile. There was a feeling in church on Sunday too that she had once gazed upon her grandfather in his role as vicar and wondered if he was God. And the feeling – or was it a memory? – that she had asked Gramma once in the middle of the service and been shushed with a hand over her mouth and a whispered assurance that indeed he was not.

Her grandmother laughed heartily when Anna asked her about it after the service, as they were walking home, each of them with an arm linked through Avery's.

'Indeed it did happen,' she said. 'At the time I felt I could have died with embarrassment, for you chose the very quietest, most solemn moment in which to pipe up in your little voice, which must have carried right up into the bell tower. But I have held it as a fond memory since.'

'You thought perhaps your grandpapa was God, Anna?' Avery asked. 'But how very foolish of you. God is far sterner, is he not?'

Gramma moved her arm sharply and caught him in the ribs with her elbow as she laughed.

It was an idyllic week in too many ways to

count. Anna and Avery went for walks in the countryside, along lanes and cart tracks wherever they led, her arm drawn through his or sometimes hand in hand, their fingers laced, or sometimes, when there was absolutely no one in sight, with their arms about each other's waist. Occasionally he stopped to kiss her and revert to his old manner.

'Anna,' he said once with a noticeable shudder, 'you are acquiring the rosy complexion of a country wench. You actually look *healthy*. I am not sure I dare take you back to London. Perhaps rosier lips would be a slight improvement.' And, after kissing her thoroughly and regarding her with the old, lazy eyes, 'Yes, that definitely helps. I shall have to keep on doing it.'

'Absurd,' she said, smiling at him.

'Quite so.'

He made love to her each night, slowly and quietly, for the house was not very large. It was wonderful beyond words.

On the evening before they left, after several days of hesitating, her grandparents agreed that they would come to Morland Abbey for a few weeks during the summer – Avery had mentioned a month or two or ten. Anna's grandfather had been threatening to retire for at least the past five years, her grandmother reported, and there was a perfectly delightful young man of their acquaintance, a curate at a church in Bristol, who would be only too eager to step into a living of his own.

It would not take much effort to persuade him to come as a locum tenens for a few weeks.

'Perhaps, Isaiah,' she added, 'you will see when we return that the parish has not collapsed without you.'

'Perhaps, Alma,' he said, smiling fondly at her, 'that is what I am afraid of.'

He would send his own carriage, Avery told them, and would brook no protest, and sufficient servants to ensure their safety and comfort during the journey. He would make all the arrangements for horses and refreshments and accommodations. All they would need do was come.

'It will mean the world to Anna,' he told them. 'And it will give me great delight. There are some remnants of the old abbey remaining, including the cloister. They will interest you, sir.'

There were tears shed the following morning before Avery handed Anna into the plainer of his two carriages, which had returned from the inn where the rest of their entourage awaited them. But there were smiles too. They would all see one another again soon.

'So different from the last time I was torn from them,' she said, sitting back in her seat as the carriage made its way out of the village.

'Do you remember?' he asked, taking her hand.

'Not with my head,' she said. 'But with my heart, yes. I can remember crying and crying. I can remember my father's voice, gruff and impatient, telling me to be a big girl. I believe I was very fortunate not to have to grow up with him as Harry and Camille and Abigail did.'

'That is one way of looking at it,' he said. 'Yes, indeed, my Anna, you were fortunate to grow up in an orphanage.'

She turned her head to smile at him. 'It was not so very bad,' she said. 'It shaped me into the person I am now, and boastful as it may sound, I like myself as I am.'

'Hmm.' He looked rather arrested for a moment. 'Yes, I do too. I even like that bonnet, though every finer feeling ought to revolt at the very sight of it.'

It was the straw bonnet she had worn to her wedding – and every day since.

'And so we return to London,' she said. 'I can face it now.'

'London can wait a day or two longer,' he said. 'We are going to Bath.'

'Bath?' She raised her eyebrows.

'I want to see that orphanage of yours,' he said. 'And I want to meet that . . . friend of yours.'

'Joel?'

'Joel, yes,' he agreed. 'And we will pay our respects to Mrs Kingsley and Camille and Abigail.'

She stared at him, her heart thumping uncomfortably. 'But will they receive us?' she asked him. 'Will they receive *me*?'

He handed her a large linen handkerchief and she realized that two tears were rolling down her cheeks.

'The Duke of Netherby is received everywhere,' he said quite in his old manner. 'He is a man of enormous consequence. The Duchess of Netherby will be received with him. Besides, Anna, there is the family connection, and Mrs Kingsley at least will be curious to meet you.'

'She is the former countess's mother,' she reminded him.

'Yes,' he agreed, taking the handkerchief from her hand and drying her cheeks and eyes with it.

Mrs Kingsley owned a house on the Royal Crescent, the most prestigious address in Bath, curving in graceful, classical lines at the top of a hill with a panoramic view down over the town and the countryside beyond. Kingsley had been a wealthy man – hence the marriage between his daughter and the late Earl of Riverdale. Avery sent his card up with the butler early in the afternoon of the day following his arrival with Anna, and they were shown up to the drawing room a few minutes later and announced with formal dignity.

Avery had met Mrs Kingsley once or twice before. She was a tall, white-haired, formidable lady. She came toward them across the room, greeted Avery cordially while shaking his hand, and then turned to look steadily at Anna.

'Duchess,' she said in chilly acknowledgment of his introduction. 'It would be unjust to blame the sins of the father upon the child. You are welcome to my home.'

'Thank you, ma'am,' Anna said, and Avery, turning to look at her, was not surprised to see her calm and dignified, her hands clasped before her. He would wager, though, that if he could see through her gloves he would find that her knuckles were white. She had toyed with both her breakfast and her luncheon after eating heartily for the past week.

Camille and Abigail were both present, and both were on their feet. Neither made any move toward the door, however. Camille was looking thinner and paler, Avery thought, while Abigail looked merely pale. He bowed to them and strolled closer.

'When passing through Bath,' he said, possessing himself of the handle of his quizzing glass, 'one feels the desire to call upon one's cousins by marriage.'

'Not even that, Avery,' Camille remarked.

'Ah,' he said, 'but your father and my stepmother were brother and sister. That surely makes us cousins of sorts. And never tell Jessica there is no connection between you. Not only would she weep an ocean; she would also throw a horrid tantrum and strain my nerves to the breaking point. How are you, Camille? And you, Abigail?'

'Well,' Camille said curtly.

'Yes, well,' Abigail said. 'And much obliged to you for calling on us, Avery. I trust you left Aunt Louise and Jessica in good health?'

'I did,' he said, 'but in high dudgeon too over the fact that Anna and I chose to marry quietly and secretly rather than be subjected to all the delights of a Wedding with a capital W. Will you greet my wife? She will be very unhappy if you will not, and then I will be unhappy too. It is a dead bore to be unhappy.'

Abigail looked at her and greeted her with a little curtsy. Camille looked gravely at her as they all seated themselves.

'I had a letter from Jessica a few days ago,' Abigail said, 'though the announcement in the London papers had already been brought to Grandmama's attention. I wish you happiness, Your Gr—' She stopped briefly and frowned. 'I wish you well, Anastasia. I wrote back to Jessica to suggest that perhaps it is time to let go of bitterness. I ought to take my own advice.'

'Thank you, Abigail,' Anna said. 'We have just spent a week in the village of Wensbury with my maternal grandparents, whom Avery discovered for me. They thought I was dead. My father wrote to them not long after he brought me to the orphanage here to inform them that I had died of typhoid.'

'Oh,' Abigail said.

Camille frowned at the hands clasped in her lap.

'Mr Kingsley was very set upon marrying Viola to the Earl of Riverdale's heir,' Mrs Kingsley remarked. 'His head was quite turned at the prospect of having a future countess for a daughter. And she was willing. He was a handsome young man. I was opposed from the start. I did not like him. I considered him selfish, and I saw that his charm concealed a lack of character. I kept my peace for years after my misgivings were brushed aside, but no longer. He was a wicked man.'

'I am pleased,' Camille said stiffly without looking up, 'that you have rediscovered your grandparents and they you.'

'Thank you, Camille,' Anna said. 'Have you heard from Harry? Is he safe?'

Harry had arrived safely in Portugal after being one of the few passengers on the ship not to be seasick and had apparently sent a brief, very enthusiastic letter to his sisters – as he had done to Avery. He was looking forward to his first battle and the chance to have a go at Napoleon Bonaparte's armies.

They stayed for half an hour while the ladies made stilted, polite conversation. They said their farewells with thanks and good wishes on both sides. And Avery, thankful it was over, took Anna's hand through his arm and started downhill with her in the direction of the abbey and the Pump Room and the main part of the town, on foot as they had come because the hill straight up was too steep for a carriage.

'Tell me, Anna,' he asked, 'was it an error in judgment on my part to bring you here?'

For a moment she rested the side of her bonnet against his shoulder.

'No,' she said, 'for they did receive me and they were civil and I could see for myself that they are in good hands with their grandmother. And perhaps now they will hate me less, though the fact that I have married you has surely not endeared me to them. Is it true that time heals all wounds, Avery?'

'I really have no idea,' he said with all honesty. 'But for argument's sake I will state quite dogmatically that yes, of course time heals all ills.'

'Thank you.' She smiled ruefully at him.

CHAPTER 22

'I t was civil of them to call.' Camille was the
first to break the silence.

'I thought so,' her grandmother agreed. 'It
is what I would expect of Netherby, of course.
It must have taken considerable courage, though,
for his duchess to accompany him. I was surprised
to find her so modestly attired, though it is clear
she has the finest of dressmakers. I could detect
no trace of vulgarity in her, and her manners are
excellent.'

'I still do not understand why Avery married
her,' Abigail said. 'He has a reputation for having
an eye for only the most acclaimed of beauties.'

'That, I believe, Abby,' Camille said, 'is the very
point. Did you see the way he looked at her?'

Abigail sighed. 'I thought perhaps Cousin
Alexander would marry her,' she said, 'in order to
reunite the title and fortune. But Avery married
her instead. He would not have done it just out of
pity, would he, and certainly not out of avarice.'

'Certainly not,' Camille said. 'Oh, we have been
around and around these arguments in the few
days since Grandmama read the announcement

until I am mortally sick of the subject. I believe he married her for love, Abby, astonishing as it seems.'

'Poor Jess,' Abigail said. 'She does so resent Anna on our behalf, though she is perfectly well aware that nothing in this whole dreary situation is our half sister's fault. And now Anna is her sister-in-law as well as her cousin.'

'She must learn to adjust,' Camille said, getting restlessly to her feet and crossing to the window, from which she looked across to sloping parkland and the view below, 'just as you advised her to do, Abby. I wonder if she – the duchess, I mean – will take Avery to see the orphanage. Do you think they will find out if she does?'

'That I have been there?' her grandmother asked. 'That I have agreed to fund a large book-case for the classroom and books to fill it? It is the sort of thing a number of citizens of Bath do out of a spirit of charity. I see no reason why the Duchess of Netherby would be informed or why she would find it remarkable if she were.'

'That *I* have been there, Grandmama,' Camille said, turning from the window.

'*You?*' Her grandmother was all astonishment. 'You have been to the orphanage, Camille? When, pray? To my knowledge you have left the house only twice since you came here, both times to take a walk with Abigail, and both times with a heavy veil over your bonnet to cover your face just as though you were in some sort of disgrace and were afraid of being recognized.'

'The first time we walked past,' Camille told her. 'The second time I went inside and asked to speak to the manager. Abby would not come with me. She walked up and down the street until I came out.'

'I did not have your courage, Cam,' Abigail said.

'And?' their grandmother asked, frowning.

'Miss Ford, the matron, was gracious enough to show me some of the rooms,' Camille said, 'after I had explained who I was. She still misses . . . Anna Snow. So does everyone else, apparently. She was quiet and unassuming, but – how exactly did Miss Ford phrase it? – her real value to them all loomed far larger when it was no longer there. The replacement teacher has not worked out well. She has threatened several times to leave, and I understood that Miss Ford hopes she will before she is dismissed.'

'Cam,' Abigail said, her face unhappy, 'I still think you—'

But Camille held up one hand to stop her. 'I have offered to take the teacher's place if there should be a vacancy, Grandmama,' she said, 'even if only for a short while until someone better qualified and more experienced can be found.'

'What?' Her grandmother's hand crept up to the pearls at her neck. 'Camille? There is really no need of this.'

'There is,' Camille said. 'I must somehow put myself in her place – Anna Snow's, that is – even if only for a short while and even though I can never know what it feels like to be a child there. I must stop hating her. Perhaps I can do it if I take her place.'

Abigail spread her hands over her face.

'It would seem to me,' Mrs Kingsley said, 'that hating – or loving – are a matter of willpower, Camille. You do not need to put yourself through this humiliation.'

'Willpower does not appear to work,' her granddaughter said. 'It works on the mind but not on the heart.'

'Well,' her grandmother said briskly, 'perhaps the schoolteacher will not leave her post and perhaps the matron will not have the courage to sack her or will have someone else in mind before she does. And perhaps one day you will come to the Pump Room with me for the morning promenade and meet some gentleman to take your mind off Viscount Uxbury. Abigail has accompanied me twice and has drawn interest both times. Not many people here will refine too much upon your change of status. You are, after all, my granddaughters and I am held in the highest esteem in Bath society.'

'We will see,' Camille said, returning to her chair. 'But it *was* civil of them to come. And to ask about Harry.'

'Harry is her brother, Cam,' Abigail said, dabbing at her eyes with her handkerchief before putting it away. 'And we are her sisters.'

★ ★ ★

Miss Ford did not mention Camille's visit to the orphanage. She did, however, mention the fact that Mrs Kingsley, a prominent citizen of Bath, had shown a welcome interest in the home recently and was to fund the purchase of a large bookcase for the schoolroom and books of all kinds to fill it. The matron mentioned it only because the Duke and Duchess of Netherby made the identical offer. Anna did not believe she had made the connection between Mrs Kingsley and herself. It had long been Anna's dream when she taught there of having books for all the children to read regardless of age or interest or reading ability. However, when she had sent a large draft of money to the home soon after inheriting her fortune, she had not specified on what it ought to be spent, and Miss Ford, with the approval of the board, had purchased some much-needed new beds and other furniture for the dormitories and new windows for the dining room.

The kitchen was old, from the ovens to the fireplace to the larder to the worktables and the uneven floor, and the laundry equipment was even older. Everything had been repaired and fixed so many times, the cook explained to the duke after she had recovered a little from her speechless awe, that by now there were repairs and patches upon repairs and patches. It would delight him and his duchess, Avery assured her and Miss Ford, to renew everything if they could stand the inconvenience of having workmen belowstairs for as many days as it would take for the work to be done.

He looked as he had during their stay at the vicarage. All his chains and rings and fobs had been left at the Royal York Hotel, where they were staying, along with his quizzing glass and snuffbox. His neckcloth was neatly tied but without any of its accustomed artistry. His eyes were wide-open, his manner that of a refined, kindly gentleman. It amused Anna how he could change at will. It touched her too that he had not come here with an air of affected boredom or condescension. When Winifred Hamlin plucked up her courage to step up to him and inform him that she had prayed for Miss Snow when she left for London and her prayers had been answered, he looked at her with a smile that crinkled his eyes at the corners.

'Without your prayers, then,' he said, 'I might never have met your Miss Snow and married her and made her my duchess. My life would have been all the poorer for the lack. I will remember that I have you to thank for my happiness, young lady.'

'Oh, not me,' Winifred assured him, pointing piously upward.

It happened in the schoolroom, where Miss Ford had summoned all the children, school for the day having been dismissed. And they had all come pouring in, even the toddlers in the care of some of the older girls, and gazed in wonder and awe at their Miss Snow, who was now as close to being a princess as it was possible to get without actually being one. Most of them were still in high spirits after a visit from Bertha Reed earlier in the day.

Anna introduced her husband, and he bowed and smiled while the children applauded and cheered.

'Miss Snow,' Olga Norton said, waving her hand high in the air when the noise died down a bit. 'Miss Nunce told us you were wrong to teach us to dream because dreams don't come true for nine hundred and ninety-nine out of a thousand people, especially people like us. She said you were a bad influence.'

There was a swell of aggrieved assent.

Oh dear. Miss Nunce, Anna recalled, was the new teacher.

'Olga!' Miss Ford sounded acutely embarrassed.

'Well, you know,' Anna said, 'Miss Nunce is quite correct. Very few dreams come true in exactly the way we dream them. But dreams can come true in unexpected ways that bring just as much happiness. If you dream of being the captain of a great sailing ship, you may not achieve your dream. But you may realize that a life on the seas is what you want and become a sailor and see the world and be the happiest person you can possibly be. And if you dream of marrying a prince – or a duke – you may not achieve that dream, for there are not very many princes and dukes available.'

She paused to let the delighted laughter die down, during which several of the children pointed at Avery and screeched with glee. 'But you may find a man who will love you and provide for you and win your devotion, and you may marry him and be happy for the rest of your life. The same may be true in reverse for the boys. Dreams are very important, for they can give us many hours of pleasure, and they can help inspire us and point us in the direction we need to go in life. But what is the most important fact about ourselves that we must always, always remember? Who can tell me?'

Several hands stretched high.

'Tommy?'

'That we are just as important as anyone else, miss,' Tommy said. 'Just as important as him.' He pointed cheekily at Avery. 'But not more important than anyone else.'

'Exactly so,' she said, beaming at him. 'But I do not mean to contradict what Miss Nunce has taught you. I believe she does not want any of you to be disappointed if the grandest of your dreams never come true. She does not want to see you hurt. She wants you to see that there are success and fulfillment and happiness to be found in all sorts of surprising places. Life often moves us in unexpected directions. But goodness me, most of you have already spent much of the day in the schoolroom here learning your lessons. I will not keep you longer. I will allow

Miss Ford to dismiss you. But I think of you all every day, you know. I was happy here. It is a happy place.'

The children cheered again but showed no reluctance to be set free. Anna bit her lip, on the verge of tears. She loved them all so dearly. It was not a sentimental or a pitying love, though. They all had a path in life to forge and follow, and really they had as much chance of a good life as most children who grew up in a home with their parents. Even those children's lives were not without challenges.

'I am not at all sure I spoke the truth about Miss Nunce,' she said to Avery as they made their way back to the hotel, still on foot. 'If she kills those children's dreams, she will take away from them something that is infinitely precious. What would they be, what would any of us be, without dreams?'

'You must not distress yourself,' he said. 'The woman sounds like a killjoy to me and ought not to be allowed within two miles of a schoolroom. She opposed the idea of books for the children, did she not? But she does not have the power to kill dreams, Anna. Dreams are as natural and as essential to us as breathing. Those children will dream on. The boys will want to be another Lord Nelson, though presumably without his death. The girls will want to marry a prince or be another Joan of Arc without the martyrdom.'

'Do even dukes dream?' she asked him.

'I was not a duke as a child,' he said, 'merely a marquess.'

'And do marquesses dream?'

'Of course,' he said.

'What?' she asked. 'What did you dream of? What *do* you dream of?'

He was silent for so long that she thought he was not going to answer her. They were almost up to the doors of the hotel before he spoke.

'Someone to love,' he said softly when it was just too late for her to make any reply.

Anna's friend Joel Cunningham joined them for dinner that evening in a private dining room at the Royal York. He came striding into the room, three minutes early, dressed unexceptionably but unimaginatively for evening. He was tall – though not particularly so – and broad of girth though not by any means fat. He had a round, open countenance, very short, dark hair and dark eyes. He had good teeth – he was smiling.

Avery hated him on sight. His hand itched to grasp his quizzing glass, but he resisted.

'Anna.' Both his hands were outstretched toward her. Avery might have been part of the furniture. 'Just look at you. You look . . . elegant.'

'Joel.' She was looking at him with a smile to match his own and both hands outstretched to his grasp. 'I am so glad you could come. And that is a new coat. It is very smart.'

They joined hands and both bent their elbows

as though they were about to embrace. Perhaps they did not, Avery thought, because he was *not* part of the furniture. Anna turned her still-beaming face toward him while still grasping the man's hands.

'Avery,' she said, 'this is my dear friend Joel Cunningham.'

'I rather thought it was,' Avery said on a sigh, and despite himself his fingers curled about the handle of his glass. 'How do you do?'

'Avery, my husband,' Anna said, 'the Duke of Netherby.'

Cunningham released her hands and turned to make his bow, and Avery was interested to note that the man looked at him with the same sort of critical appraisal and veiled hostility as *he* had just looked at Cunningham. Like two dogs coveting the same bone? What an alarmingly lowering thought.

'Delighted,' Cunningham said.

Anna was looking from one to the other of them, and Avery could see that she had sized up the situation quite accurately and was amused.

It was not an auspicious start to the evening, but Avery certainly did not like the image of himself as a jealous husband – it was enough to give him the shudders. And Cunningham swallowed whatever hostility he might have brought with him or conceived at his first sight of the man his friend had married. They settled into a three-way conversation that was really rather pleasant, and the food was certainly superior.

Cunningham was an intelligent, well-read man. He was making what Avery understood to be an increasingly lucrative income as a portrait painter, though he dreamed of making a name for himself as a landscape artist, and he had a vague dream too of becoming a writer. 'Though people with some talent in the visual arts are not always similarly talented with words,' he said.

'Are those who sit for your portraits still mostly older people?' Anna asked him. 'I know you always longed to paint younger persons.'

He thought about it. 'Yes, I enjoy painting youth and beauty,' he said, 'but older people tend to have more character to be captured on canvas. They present a more interesting challenge. It is only recently that I have realized that. Perhaps it is a sign that my own character is maturing.'

He had not made much if any progress in keeping an eye on the Misses Westcott, he reported to Anna. Cunningham had seen who he assumed to be the younger sister enter the Pump Room with her grandmother on a couple of occasions, but he had not set eyes at all upon the elder.

'I did meet Mrs Kingsley with the younger Miss Westcott at one of Mrs Dance's literature evenings,' he said, 'and she was complimentary about the miniatures I had taken with me. She made mention of *two* granddaughters she had living with her and was clearly thinking about the possibilities. I wrote to you about this, Anna, did I not? But I have not heard from her since, and I have not knocked upon her door, easel in hand. Sometimes these things take time and patience and a little maneuvering.'

Anna smiled in understanding. 'Avery and I called there today,' she said. 'They are in good hands with Mrs Kingsley, Joel, and I never intended you to do more than locate them for me and assure me, if you could, that they were settled here.'

Cunningham also volunteered his time to teach art at the orphanage a few afternoons a week. Avery asked him how well he worked with the new teacher, and he grimaced.

'She is a nincompoop,' he said. 'But a dangerous nincompoop, for she seems highly respectable, the sort of person who must know all about teaching and the needs of growing children. She knows worse than nothing. She resents the fact that I teach art and keeps alluding to the fact that she is an accomplished watercolorist and has won acclaim from all sorts of dusty people. She has taken to listening in on my lessons and occasionally openly contradicting me. In the Gospel according to Miss Nunce, good art has nothing whatsoever to do with talent or the imagination or – heaven forbid – an artist's individual vision, and everything to do with correctly learned and meticulously applied craftsmanship. When one of my boys painted a sky full of light and color and life and glory, she refused to have it displayed in the schoolroom because the sky was not a uniform blue and there was no yellow ball in the top right-hand corner with yellow rays of equal length coming from it. I thanked her, in front of the children, with awful courtesy – you would have loved it, Anna – for making it possible for me to take the painting to display in my studio.'

Oh,' Anna said, her elbow on the table, her chin in her hand, 'if I could just have been a fly on the wall.'

'She is trying to make it impossible for me to stay,' Joel said. 'But I am too stubborn to go, and I care for the children too much to oblige her. I hope I am making it impossible for *her* to stay. You ought to see how I allow the children to stuff all the art supplies into the cupboard, Anna. You would have scolded me for a week. Miss Nunce merely looks grim and martyred and complains to Miss Ford.'

Anna laughed and Avery began to like the man.

'You are a fortunate man, Netherby,' Cunningham told him not long before he took his leave. 'I made Anna a marriage proposal a couple of years or so ago, but she refused me. Has she told you? She informed me that I was just lonely after leaving the orphanage. She told me I would live to regret it if she said yes. She was undoubtedly right – she often is. I envy you, but she remains my friend.'

He was sending a distinct message, Avery realized. He was in Anna's life to stay, but since she had married Avery, there would be no resentment, no jealousy. There would be no reason for continued hostility.

'I envy me too,' Avery said while Anna looked between them again, as she had earlier, aware of the undercurrents. 'My wife has been very fortunate to grow up with someone who will remain a lifelong friend. Not many people can make the same claim. I hope we will meet again.'

He meant it too – almost. But he did not for a moment believe that Anna was no more to Cunningham than a friend. He rather suspected that Anna did not even realize the true nature of the man's feelings for her.

Soon after that they all shook hands and Cunningham set off home.

'Oh, Avery,' Anna said, turning to him when they were alone, 'it feels so strange to be back here with everything the same yet altogether different.'

'You are sad?' he asked.

'No.' She frowned in thought. 'Not sad. How could I be? Just—' She laughed softly. 'Just sad.'

He cupped her face in his hands and kissed her. 'We will leave here tomorrow,' he said. 'But we will return. We can never go back, my duchess, but we can always revisit the past.'

'Yes.' Her eyes were swimming with tears. 'Oh, what a strange and emotional couple of weeks these have been. But I am ready to leave.'

A couple of weeks ago they had not even been married. He could not imagine himself now without Anna – a slightly alarming thought.

'Come to bed,' he said. 'Let me make love to you.'

'Yes,' she said, leaning into him.

But she still looked sad.

CHAPTER 23

Falling in love had been easy. In fact, it had not even been that. It had just happened. Avery had neither planned nor expected nor particularly wanted it. He had fallen in love anyway. Deciding to marry and make an offer had also been easy. It had been done without forethought, entirely on the spur of the moment, largely because – he winced slightly at the thought – it had seemed altogether possible she might be persuaded and persuade herself into marrying Riverdale. Getting married had been easy. There had been no trouble or delay in acquiring the license or in finding a clergyman willing and able to marry them that very morning – or in persuading Anna to go with him.

The following two weeks had been blissful. Yes, that was a suitable word and not at all exaggerated. He had relaxed into the wonder of his marriage – and yes, even that word *wonder* was appropriate. He had allowed himself to enjoy companionship, friendship, and sex with his wife. He had fallen half in love with her grandparents and their way of life. He had felt a bit like a child in a playhouse during that week at the vicarage, with not a care in the world and without self-consciousness. He had even enjoyed Bath. Camille and Abigail were very obviously still suffering, but they were in safe hands and they would work things out. He was confident of that. They had not taken their half sister to their bosoms, but they had made an effort to be civil. He had marveled at the orphanage, which had not been the grim institution he had half expected, but which had nevertheless been his wife's very spartan home for twenty-one years. She was loved there, and she was deeply fond of everyone, staff and children alike. He had even rather enjoyed the evening they had spent with Cunningham, whom he had been prepared to dislike and despise. But the man was intelligent, interesting, and honorable. It was clear he had feelings for Anna, but he had chosen, apparently a few years ago, to be her friend if he could be nothing more.

Yes, everything had been easy and idyllic until their return to London. Almost happily-ever-after idyllic. But in London, Avery discovered that he did not know how to be married. Not an idea. Not a clue. And so, true to himself, he withdrew into his shell, like a tortoise, until he felt reasonably comfortable.

Even reasonable comfort was not easy, though. There had always been a distance – a self-imposed one – between him and the majority of his acquaintances. Most people, he knew, stood somewhat in awe of him. Now, suddenly, the distance was enormous. He had married one of the greatest heiresses ever to set foot upon the marriage mart almost before everyone else had had a chance to catch a glimpse of her – there had not even been a notice of their betrothal in the morning papers, only of their marriage. And then he had disappeared with her for two weeks in the very midst of the Season. Now he was back.

Among the men, of course, there was something of far greater import than his marriage – except perhaps among those who had hoped to marry the fortune themselves. There was that damned duel, which Avery had vainly hoped would be forgotten about by the time he returned. Instead, the incident had reached mythic proportions in the collective mind, and men stared at him – and looked hastily away when he and his quizzing glass caught them at it – with fascination and fear. Uxbury was said to be still in his bed, though doubtless the lump on the back of his head had shrunk from the size of a cricket ball to that of an ant's egg – if ants had eggs – and the bruises on his chin had probably faded to pale mustard from black and purple.

Avery made his appearance in the House of Lords a number of times, having neglected his duties there lately. He visited his clubs, accompanied his wife to a number of social events, and very correctly kept his distance from her until it was time to escort her home. He took her driving in Hyde Park a couple of times at the fashion-able hour and walked with her once down by the Serpentine, weaving their way among other people. Most evenings he dined at home with her and his stepmother and Jessica, who was now deemed adult enough to join them. He slept in Anna's bed and made love to her at least once each night. They ate breakfast together and looked through their invitations together after Edwin Goddard had sorted them.

There was absolutely nothing wrong with his marriage. It was no different from any other *ton* marriage as far as he could tell. And that – devil take it! – was the trouble. He had no idea how to make it better, how to recapture the glow and euphoria of those two weeks. It had been what people referred to as a honeymoon, he supposed. Honeymoons, by their very nature, could not be expected to last.

Perhaps things would be different – better – when the parliamentary session was at an end and with it the Season and they could go home to Morland Abbey for the summer. Her grandparents would be coming for a few weeks. But he was well aware that the future could never be relied upon to be an improvement upon the present. The future did not exist. Only the present did.

The present was . . . disappointing. He had known happiness for a couple of weeks. Yes. He tested the thought in his mind. Yes, he had been happy. He was not enjoying being back to normal.

And of course, even normal was no longer normal. For there was his wife and there was his marriage and he did not know quite what to do with either one. He was not accustomed to feeling inadequate, out of control of his own destiny.

He spent long hours upstairs in his attic room – he suspected Anna did not even know he was at home – but though he worked himself mercilessly until he was bathed in sweat, and sat in meditative pose until he almost turned into a sphinx, he could find no peace. He could not find that place beneath and behind his whirling thoughts into which to sink and find rest. And always, always, in the attic, out of it, in bed, everywhere, he could not escape the echo of a slow, peaceful voice telling him in its pronounced Chinese accent: *You are whole, my boy, right through to the hollow center. Love lives at the center of wholeness and pervades it all. When you find love, you will be at peace.*

But, so annoyingly typical of his master, he had never been willing to explain such remarks. Deep and lasting truths could be learned only from experience, he had always explained. It had been pointless for Avery to argue that he did love – his dead mother, his father, his little half sister, oh, numerous people. The Chinese gentleman had only smiled and nodded.

Avery was unhappy.

Archer House on Hanover Square, so intimid-ating the first time she stepped inside it, was now

Anna's home. All her belongings had been moved during her absence. John and a few of the other servants had been brought over too.

'Your duke made a special request for me,' John explained to Anna with a beaming smile. 'That must mean I am doing my job well, don't you think? The butler over at the other house would have me believe I ought not to speak to people unless I was spoken to, but it seemed rude and unfriendly to me. I like this new livery better than the other one – no offense to you, Miss Snow. Actually I am happy just to be wearing livery. I might easily have ended up at a bootmaker's like poor Oliver Jamieson.'

'I think, John,' Anna explained, 'his apprenticeship has been a dream come true for Oliver.'

'Well,' he said cheerfully while Avery's butler came into the hall and looked taken aback to see the new footman chatting with the duchess, 'it takes all sorts, doesn't it, Miss Snow? Which is just as well, I suppose. It would be a bit odd if everyone in the world was a footman.'

Besides the fact that she was married and in a different house, life resumed much as it had been before Anna left London. Her grandmother and the two aunts who were still in London were as concerned about her as ever. There was potentially great damage to be repaired, it seemed. Just when she had been presented to society with great success and some acclaim, she had committed the huge social error of not pressing onward but of marrying in indecent haste and then disappearing for two whole weeks. It would be amazing indeed if the highest sticklers at the very least did not frown upon her, even shun her. It would be amazing if she was not struck off the guest lists of some of the more prestigious events of the Season and if her vouchers for Almack's were not revoked. Only her new title and Avery's enormous consequence might save her. But a great deal of work was needed.

There were conferences at Archer House and at the dowager countess's house. Aunt Mildred and Uncle Thomas were no longer in London, of course, and the second cousins did not involve themselves this time. A round of visits was planned with Anna's grandmother or Aunt Louise to accompany her. She was advised over which parties and which balls it would be most to her advantage to attend.

Avery accompanied her to some of the evening entertainments. He informed her with a sigh one morning when they were looking through the invitations the post had brought that she did not have to attend anything if she preferred not to but could let the *ton* go hang, but it did not sound like very helpful advice to Anna. She had made the decision soon after her arrival in London to stay and learn the role of Lady Anna Westcott, and it was no longer possible to go back on that, for she was now the Duchess of Netherby, and it was necessary to perform the duties expected of a duchess. It was all very well for Avery to consign the *ton* to the hangman, but he had always been an aristocrat. His eccentricities were accepted because he was indisputably the duke. Any eccentricity in her would be dubbed gaucherie or vulgarity.

She was conscious of a certain dissatisfaction with her life as it proceeded and tried to deny it. The honeymoon could not have lasted, after all, and this was the real part of her marriage. But she missed the days of long conversations upon everything under the sun and the walks with joined hands and laced fingers and the laughter and kisses. There was nothing wrong with their marriage except that their busy lives kept them apart through most of each day, and even when they were together they seemed to be with other people most of the time. It was the way of life in the *ton,* she came to realize. Her marriage was no worse than any other – which was a horribly negative way of reassuring herself. She wanted better.

Perhaps everything would be better during the summer when they went to live in their country home. Or perhaps not. Perhaps she must simply get used to the new reality.

Finally she rebelled.

She was at her grandmother's house while the rest of her Season was being planned in some detail. Aunt Matilda had raised the point that though Anastasia had been presented to the queen, she had not been presented as a married lady – as a *duchess*. Grandmama and Aunt Louise looked identically shocked and agreed with her. The presentation must be made.

'No!' Anna was as surprised as they by the firmness with which she had spoken the single word. But she continued after crossing the room to sit on the stool by her grandmother's chair. 'This must stop. I believe I have become an obsession with you all. You were kind enough to put your own lives to one side in order to prepare me for the life that ought to be mine as my father's daughter. You did that, and I appreciate your efforts more than I can say, for I would have been all at sea without your help and influence.'

'We do not need your thanks, Anastasia,' her grandmother said. 'We have done only what had to be done for one of our own, and we will continue as long as is needed.'

'Grandmama,' Anna said, taking her hand, 'I understand how much you must still be grieving for the loss of my father despite what he did, and for Camille and Harry and Abigail and their mother. I know that you have seen it as your duty to take me into the family and prepare me for my rightful place. I think you have done it out of love as well as duty. And that is all I want from you and from my aunts and my cousins. It is what I have craved all my life. I need your love. And all I need is to be able to love you. You cannot imagine

418

what it is like to have nobody of my own and then to have a whole family devoted to taking me in and helping me make my way forward. Please. Be done now. I have been introduced to society, and I have a husband with whom to make my own way forward. Just love me.'

'Anastasia!' Aunt Matilda exclaimed. 'Of course we love you. I have even begun to think of you as the daughter I never had. Here, there is no need to shed tears. Let me hold my vinaigrette beneath your nose.'

Her grandmother was merely patting her hand.

'You do not want to meet the queen again as the Duchess of Netherby, Anastasia?' Aunt Louise asked. 'Or go to Almack's on Wednesday or attend the balls and concerts we have marked out for you?'

'I do not wish to be a hermit,' Anna said. 'But I want to decide for myself or with Avery where and how I will spend my days and evenings. When I visit Grandmama and Aunt Matilda or Cousin Althea and Elizabeth, I want to do so because I love them and want to spend time with them. I want you to be my family, not my secretaries and teachers. Oh, please, I do not want to hurt any of you. I love you.'

'There.' Her grandmother leaned over her and hugged her. 'Oh, do put that vinaigrette away, Matilda. Neither of us needs it. It will be as you say, Anastasia. And indeed, it seems that despite all our fears of impending disaster, you are still the sensation of the Season. You and Avery both. Do you love him, child?'

'Oh, I do, Grandmama,' Anna said.

And she did. But, oh, sometimes she was unhappy.

Avery's stepmother was dining with her mother and sister and had taken Jessica with her. He and Anna dined alone together for the first time since their return to London. It seemed like a rare treat, and he relaxed into it, especially when she told him she was not going to attend the concert her relatives had thought important for her.

'Will you be going out?' she asked him with what he hoped was a note of wistfulness.

He had intended going with her even though the main performer was to be a soprano whose voice did not agree with his ears.

'No,' he said. 'I will be remaining home with my wife. Sometimes one feels constrained to behave like a staid married man.'

'I think,' she said as their soup was placed before them, 'Aunt Louise went back to Grandmama's tonight because of what happened this afternoon. I believe I may have hurt them. I do hope I have not.'

He looked at her in inquiry.

'I told them,' she said, 'that I do not want them to manage my life any longer. I know I am not quite the polished lady they would like me to be, and I know there may be people who frown upon me for all sorts of reasons. I know that at any moment the whole of the *ton* may turn its back upon me—'

'Anna,' he said, 'you are the Duchess of Netherby. You are my duchess.'

'Well, yes.' She chose to smile. 'And I know that you would have merely to raise your quizzing glass and everyone would rush to receive me again. But I am tired of leaning upon other people, Avery, of feeling inadequate and incomplete. I begged them simply to love me and allow me to love them. I do love them, you know.'

'Ah.' He sat back in his chair, his soup forgotten. 'And what would you beg of me?'

'Oh,' she said, 'that you would pass the salt, please.'

They conversed upon inconsequential topics through most of the rest of the meal while Avery wondered what his wife's new spirit of independence would mean to him, to *them*, if anything. But the conversation changed course again after their dessert plates had been removed and replaced with fruit and cheese and he had given the signal for the servants to leave.

'Avery,' she said abruptly, 'I need to make plans for Westcott House and Hinsford Manor and my fortune.'

'Do you?' He looked lazily at her before continuing to peel his apple.

'Mr Brumford told me – oh, a long time ago,' she said, 'that I did not need to worry my head over any of it, and I took him at his word because my head was so full of other things there was no room for more. But both houses are empty. I thought perhaps Cousin Alexander should live at Westcott House when he is in London. He is, after all, the earl. Do you think he would? And I *wish* Camille and Abigail and their mother would return to Hinsford. It was their main home. Is there any way I can persuade them, do you suppose? And all my money and investments – I *cannot* like being the sole possessor of it all. Oh.' She looked suddenly arrested and gazed at him. 'Is it all *yours* now? Do you own me *and* my fortune because you are my husband?'

'You pain me, my love,' he said. 'I own you in exactly the way you own me. We are married to each other – until death do us part, which might sound alarming if we were ever to regret the fact. I made very sure with my solicitor that what was yours before our marriage remains yours – to do with as you wish. Riverdale may be persuaded to lease Westcott House when he is in town, though I am willing to wager he will not accept it as a favor. You are quite at liberty to try to persuade him, of course. My guess is you will not persuade Cousin Viola or your half sisters to return to Hinsford, but again you are free to try. What do you wish to do with your fortune, apart from watch it grow?'

'I want to divide it into four parts,' she said, 'as ought to have been done by my father in a new will before he died. Can it be done now? Even without the permission of my brother and sisters?'

'I will place all these questions before Edwin Goddard,' he said, cutting his apple into four and helping himself to a slice of cheese. 'He will know some answers and have some sage advice, I do not doubt. And I shall summon my solicitor. He will attend to all legal matters according to your wishes and what is legally possible.'

Her own apple was sitting untouched in the middle of her plate, and he reached over to peel it for her.

'No,' she said. But she was not talking about the apple. 'No, that would not be fair to Mr Goddard. He works hard enough as it is. And it would not be fair to dismiss Mr Brumford just because he is prosy and a little pompous. I shall entrust any instructions to him. And I will employ my own secretary. I know someone—'

'—from the orphanage,' he said.

'Yes.'

They both watched as he peeled her apple in one strip and then cut it in four and cored it.

'Thank you,' she said.

He sat back in his chair and bit into one piece of his own apple. 'Are you angry about something?' he asked her.

'No.' She sighed. 'No, Avery. But I have been drifting with the tide, it seems, ever since I opened Mr Brumford's letter in the schoolroom and decided to come here. I have let life happen to me. Oh, I have exercised control in small, unimportant ways, like the design of my new clothes, but . . .' She shrugged.

'Did you drift into marrying me?' he asked, and then wished he had not. He did not particularly want to hear her answer.

She had been arranging the four pieces of her apple in a neat row across her plate. She looked up at him then.

'I think I married you,' she said, 'because I wanted to.'

Well, that was a huge relief. 'I am flattered,' he said. 'Honored. Your apple is starting to turn brown.'

His relief was short-lived. Her hands disappeared into her lap and she continued to stare at him. 'Avery,' she asked softly, 'where did you learn to do that?'

Strangely, he knew exactly what she was talking about, though he hoped he was wrong. *'That?'*

'Fighting a far larger man the way you did and defeating him without allowing him to lay a hand upon you – apart from the fact that a door ran into you soon after,' she said. 'Leaping into the air higher than your own height and still having the power to render him unconscious with the soles of your bare feet.'

He gazed back at her for a few moments, his body absolutely still. That damned Riverdale had told her, he thought for a moment. But no. 'Where were you?' he asked.

'Up in a tree,' she said. 'Elizabeth was hidden behind it.'

'A few dozen men would have been severely displeased if they had caught you,' he said. 'Including Riverdale. And Uxbury. Me.'

'Where did you learn it?' she asked again.

He set an elbow on the table, passed a hand over his eyes, and leaned back in his chair. 'The short answer to your question,' he said, 'is from an elderly Chinese gentleman. But the short answer will not do, will it? You are my wife, and I am fast realizing that my life has been turned upside down and inside out as a result of those brief nuptials of ours and has become a terrifying unknown.'

'Terrifying?' Her eyes widened.

He closed his eyes and took several slow, deep breaths. 'I married the wrong woman,' he murmured, his eyes still closed, 'or else the only right woman. You will not remain on the surface of my life, will you, Anna Archer? You will not be content to bring me comfort and delight, though there has not been much of either, has there, since we returned to London. Is it because this question has needed asking and answering? Is it because you will not be content until you have seen to the very core of me? And perhaps because I will not be content until I have allowed you there?'

He opened his eyes and looked at her. Her own were still wide. Her face had lost color. He smiled ruefully at her. 'There should be someone to warn a man what he is facing when he marries.'

He tossed his napkin onto the table, got to his feet, and reached out a hand for hers. 'Come,' he said.

She frowned for a moment, eyed his hand with obvious unease, and then placed her own in it.

CHAPTER 24

He took her upstairs, past the drawing room floor, past the bedchambers on the next floor, and on up to the attics. He turned left and into a large room. He had been holding her hand tightly, but let it go after shutting the door and strode about the room to light all the many candles that were placed about it, in wall sconces, on the floor, on the windowsill. He lit them despite the fact that the evening sunlight was still slanting in a bright band through the window.

The room was bare apart from two wooden benches along one side of it and lots of cushions – and all the candles. The floor was of polished wood. There was no carpet. There was something about it all that Anna would not have been able to explain in words if she tried. It was alien, strange, yet she felt instantly and thoroughly at home there and at peace. There was the faint scent of incense.

'Wait there,' he said without looking back at her, and he disappeared through a door across from the benches. Anna was still standing just inside the door when he came out again a few minutes later, wearing loose white trousers and a loose white jacket that wrapped across the front and was belted at the waist. He was barefoot. He strode toward her, his hand outstretched for hers.

'Come,' he said, and led her to the wooden bench closer to the window. When she had sat down, he moved a cushion and sat on it facing her, his legs crossed, his hands on his knees. 'No one comes in here except me. I even clean it myself.'

Yes, she could sense that about the room. It felt a bit like a sanctuary or a hermitage despite its size. 'And now me?'

'You are my wife,' he said, and for a moment there was a look in his eyes that was almost bleak, almost fearful, almost pleading. But it was gone before she could quite grasp it. It was a look of vulnerability, she thought. He was afraid.

'Avery,' she said, her voice almost a whisper, as though they were in church, in a sacred place, 'I do not know you at all, do I?'

'I have made myself unknowable,' he said. 'It is a comfortable way to live.'

'But why?' she asked.

He sighed. 'I will tell you a story,' he said, 'about a little boy everyone thought ought to have been a girl because he was small and delicate and pretty – and timid.'

It was of himself he spoke – in the third person, setting himself even now at a distance from his own story.

'His mother adored him and coddled him,' he said. 'She devoted almost all her time to him and admitted only her old nurse into the inner circle. She taught him his lessons because she refused to allow a tutor near him and could find no governess who suited her exacting standards. She kept him from his father as much as possible – not a difficult thing to do, as it happened, because his father looked upon him with a sort of puzzled disfavor. And then, when he was nine years old, the child's mother sickened and died. The nurse stayed on to care for him, but after another couple of years his father decided it was time to toughen him up and sent him off to school.'

'Poor boy,' she said, keeping up the illusion that he spoke of someone else. 'I wish I had had him in my schoolroom.'

'You were five years old at the time,' he said. 'All new pupils in a boys' school are vulnerable to bullying. It is not even frowned upon. It is considered part of a boy's education. School is meant to toughen him, to bring out the brute in him so that he will be able to survive and thrive in a man's world. Bullying is something boys take from above and give below. It is a system that works beautifully well. Our society is founded upon it. The strong rise to the top and rule our world. The weaker find a useful place in the middle. The weakest are destroyed, but they were useless anyway. The child of my story was the very weakest. He was a timid, puny, pretty, frightened little boy.'

Anna leaned slightly forward and began to reach out one hand toward him, but she returned it to her lap to clasp the other. His story was only partly told.

'I refused to be destroyed,' he said. 'I discovered a stubbornness in myself even while everything I tried – boxing, fencing, rowing, running – resulted only in failure and ridicule. I tried harder – and harder. And I survived. Perhaps I would have clawed my way up into the lower part of that middle group by the time I left boyhood behind. I was the heir to a wealthy dukedom, after all, and that would command some respect. But then something happened. A life changer. When I was walking back to school alone one day during my second to last year, I saw an elderly Chinese gentleman in a bleak and barren empty space between two buildings. He was dressed as I am now, even down to the bare feet.'

She raised her eyebrows while he paused and smiled, a distant look in his eyes.

'I stood and watched him for . . . oh, perhaps half an hour,' he said. 'He must have known I was there, but he gave no sign, and I was unaware of anyone or anything except him. I cannot really describe it to you, Anna. I can only show you. Shall I?'

'Yes.' She slid along the bench to set one shoulder against the wall beside the window, and hugged her elbows with her hands while he got to his feet and went to stand in the middle of the floor. He pressed his palms together prayer-fashion and closed his eyes. She watched him breathe slowly for perhaps a whole minute, and she knew that he was somehow going away from her and into himself. He moved his neck in slow circles, first in one direction, then in the other.

She was afraid, Anna realized, though that was not quite the right word. It was more awe that she felt. She was in the presence of the unknown, of something strange and exotic, and it was embodied in the man she had married less than a month ago. It occurred to her that he was perhaps forever beyond her understanding. Yet she yearned toward him with a love that was almost physical pain.

And he moved – in ways so totally beyond anything she had ever experienced that all she could do was watch and hug her elbows.

He used the whole of the floor area. But the movements were slow, exaggerated, stylized. At first she thought they were simple moves, imposing no great demands upon his body. But then she could see that they made great demands indeed, for no body could be naturally as supple, as graceful, as precise in its movements without a great deal of practice and pain. She could see the stretch of arms and legs and body, the impossible arch of spine, the unwavering balance. His feet never once left the floor at the same time, but he could twist his body, extend the sole of each foot in turn toward the ceiling, his legs a straight line with only a small bend in the knee of the lower one. But in truth she did not observe verbally. It would have been impossible to capture in words the grace, the control, the power, the athleticism, the strength, the sheer beauty of what she watched for endless minutes.

It was lovelier, more moving than any dance she had ever watched, including the waltz. But it was not a dance. The movements were far too slow, and they were performed to a melody that was all his own – or to a silence that sang with an unbearable sweetness.

It was not a performance she watched. He was unaware of her presence.

And then he stopped as he had begun, and after a few moments he came back across the room toward her, moved his cushion, and sat cross-legged before her again, his knees touching the floor.

'Avery,' she said. She could say no more.

'I asked if he would teach me,' he told her, 'and he did. But when he understood the depth of my desire and need and commitment, he taught me infinitely more than what you have just seen. He taught me that my body could be all in all to me, but only if my mind was under my own power and control, and only if I laid claim to the soul – he called it my real self – at the core of me. He taught me to impose my will upon my body, to make it do whatever I directed it to do. He taught me to make it into a weapon, a potentially deadly weapon, though I only demonstrated those abilities upon inanimate objects – and one tree. But he taught me, to go hand in hand with that physical power, self-control. For any deadly weapon does not have to be used – ever. It is very much best for everyone if it never is. Nothing is ever gained from violence but the brutalization of those who perpetrate it and those who are provoked into seeking revenge against it.'

'You could have killed him if you had wished, could you not?' she asked him, hugging her elbows more tightly.

'Uxbury?' he said. 'I was not even tempted, Anna. I merely wanted to put an end to the idiocy as quickly as possible and get away from there. The thing is, you see, that when you know you have power, you do not need to demonstrate it. When you know you have a weapon that is proof against most aggression, you do not need to use it. And you do not have to boast of it or even talk of it. It is a secret I have always kept strictly to myself. I am not sure why. Perhaps at first I feared ridicule or being thought weird. And when people started to treat me differently, I accepted that as good enough, and the secret of how much my life had changed seemed like a precious thing that might only be sullied if I spoke of it.'

'The bullying stopped?' she asked.

'Strangely it did,' he said, 'though no one knew of the existence of that Chinese gentleman or of the long hours I spent with him. I fought no one except during the regular boxing and fencing sessions, at which I never excelled. I said nothing to anyone. And yet . . . the bullying stopped. People fear me or at least stand in considerable awe of me, but they do not know why – or did not before that lamentably public duel. When you believe in yourself, Anna, when you are in command of yourself, when nothing derogatory anyone says of you or to you has the power to arouse your anger or any desire to retaliate, people seem to sense it and respect you.'

'But what has been the cost to you of your secret life?' she asked him.

He gazed at her for several moments before answering. 'Everything in life comes at a cost,' he said. 'One has to weigh what one gains against what one gives up. I have gained immeasurably more than I have lost, Anna. Freedom from bullying was the most minor benefit of my transformation.'

'But no one knows you,' she said. 'You have deliberately shaped your adult life so that you are unknown and unknowable.'

'I was unknown before,' he said. 'I was not that timid, puny little boy any more than I am now the invincible warrior. Not inside myself. Inside myself I am still me, as I have always been. I do my living in here, Anna.' He patted one lightly clenched fist against his breastbone. 'But I am not a hermit.'

She gazed at him, still hugging herself.

He leaned to one side and grasped another

cushion, which he set down in front of him. 'Come,' he said, reaching up a hand for hers.

'Oh, I cannot sit like that,' she protested.

'With those skirts? No,' he agreed. 'I shall have an outfit like my own made for you to wear here in this room, Anna, if you wish. I have let you in, you see, to this room where no one comes except me. The room is a sort of symbol. What I have really let you into is my life, myself as I am, and at the moment, Anna, I am that little boy again. For I cannot control you or the way you will deal with what I have told you and shown you, and I would not if I could, but I am terrified. Yes, sit thus. I like looking across at you rather than up – or down.'

She was sitting on the cushion, hugging her knees, which were drawn up in front of her. Her feet were touching one of his ankles. He looked at them and then raised them one at a time to remove her slippers and her silk stockings before tucking her feet beneath his crossed ones.

'Shoes keep one at a remove from reality,' he said, looking up into her eyes. He smiled and leaned across his folded legs and hers to kiss her. 'I am still terrified. I have been since we returned to London and I was faced with the reality that I am a married man and have absolutely no idea how to proceed. I am in deep and out of my depth. And I have not been doing well. The wonder of those two weeks after our wedding has vanished and I fear it has gone forever. I want it back. How do we get it back, Anna? Have you felt its loss too?'

Was this the all-powerful, self-contained, always-confident aristocrat who had so awed her when she first encountered him? She blinked back tears.

'Yes,' she said. 'You once told me, Avery, that your dearest dream was to have someone to love.'

His eyes gazed back into hers, wide-open, very blue in the fading evening sunlight and the flickering light of the candles. 'Yes,' he said.

'Can I be that someone?' she asked him.

His eyes dropped from hers. He set his palms against her ankles and moved them up to her arms clasped about her knees and along them to her shoulders. He raised his eyes to hers again and got to his feet. He gathered up an armful of cushions and tossed them down in a heap beside her, beneath the windowsill. He knelt beside her, turned her, and laid her down on the cushions. He unclothed her with swift, skilled hands and then untied the sash at his waist to shed his jacket and then the loose trousers. The sun was gone suddenly, but candlelight remained, and it seemed to Anna again that this large, mainly empty space was the warmest, coziest, happiest room she had ever been in.

Her hands moved over him as he kneeled between her thighs. He was a perfectly formed, utterly beautiful, and all-powerful, attractive, potent male.

'Anna,' he murmured as his hands and his mouth went to work on her. 'My duchess.'

'My love.'

Dreamy blue eyes gazed down into hers for a moment. 'My love?'

'My love,' she repeated. 'Of course. Did you not know? Oh, Avery, did you not know?'

He smiled then, a look of sweetness so intense that it took her breath away. And he entered her and lowered himself onto her and turned his golden head to rest against her own.

They made love, and there were no words. Not even thoughts. Only a sweetness and a rightness and a gathering need and a pain so pleasurable that when it crested they could only cry out together and descend into a nothingness that was somehow everything.

Ah, there were no words. No thoughts. Only love.

They lay among the cushions, spent, relaxed, still joined, their arms about each other. Candlelight wavered, forming moving patterns on the walls and ceiling, and the world seemed very far away.

'I wish we could stay here forever,' she said.

He sighed and withdrew from her and sat up. He reached out for the white trousers and pulled them on and sat cross-legged beside her again, the trousers riding low on his hips.

'But this is just a room, Anna,' he said, turning his head to look down at her. 'You and I, we go beyond the room and beyond time.' He touched a hand first to his own heart and then to hers. 'We have only to be aware of it. It is very easy to lose that awareness – when one gets caught up in the busy life of fashionable London during the Season, for example. I learn and relearn my awareness. And I will teach you if you wish.'

'I do,' she said. 'What I really want, though, is the white outfit.'

He laughed at the unexpectedness of her words, and he was transformed into a warm, relaxed man. Her husband.

'But we will be leaving here soon,' she said, looking around the room, 'and going to Morland Abbey.'

'You will love it, Anna,' he told her, his face lighting up. 'You will adore it. I promise. And I have a room there just like this.'

She smiled up at him, at his eagerness, his unexpected boyishness, the person he must have been from the start, made whole and happy.

His smile faded, though it lingered in his eyes.

'When I left school,' he said, 'and said a reluctant farewell to my master – actually it was goodbye. He died in his sleep just one month later. When I went to take my leave of him, he told me I was whole except for one thing. There was still a hollow at the center of my being, he told me, and only love could fill it. But he would not explain. He never would. It was all about finding out for oneself with him. He could be very annoying. He would not tell me if it was love of humanity or love of nature or love of family or romantic love. All he would say was that I would know it when I found it and it would make me whole and finally at peace with myself. I have found it, Anna. It is romantic love.'

She touched his knee, which was pressing lightly against her stomach.

'I fell in love with you,' he said, 'and married you. And suddenly I was filled to the brim and to the innermost depths with love. Love of you and love of everyone and everything. But then I doubted and I stumbled. I doubted the power of love and happiness to last. I doubted your feelings; I doubted my worthiness to be loved. And then and at last it occurred to me that I had to bring you here, that I had to bring you fully and completely into myself and trust that you would not simply laugh or – worse – not understand at all. Oh, you cannot know how vulnerable I am still feeling, Anna, mouthing such absurdities. But if I do not say them now I never will and I may have lost the missing part of myself forever.'

'But you are always mouthing absurdities,' she said.

He looked down into her eyes and laughed again. He leaned sideways over her and scooped her up and deposited her, naked, on his lap. And he closed his arms tightly about her, as hers closed about him, and they clung to each other for endless minutes.

'Yes,' he said eventually, 'to return to your question. You can be and may be and already are, Anna. My someone to love. My everything.'

They smiled at each other before their mouths met.